Cold City

Cathy McSporran

FREIGHT
BOOKS

First published September 2014

Freight Books
49-53 Virginia Street
Glasgow, G1 1TS
www.freightbooks.co.uk

A CIP catalogue reference for this book is available from the British Library.

ISBN 978-1-908754-79-0
eISBN 978-1-908754-80-6
Typeset by Freight in Plantin
Printed and bound by Bell and Bain, Glasgow

the publisher acknowledges investment from
Creative Scotland toward the publication of this book

To Willy, for all his help and encouragement,
and to Lesley, for the wolves.

What men shall be left alive, when the great Winter is past?
What powers shall be left on Earth, when Surt's fire is quenched?
What sun shall rise in our fair heaven, when the Wolf has this devoured?

...

The Poetic Edda

Prologue

Remember me when I am gone away,
Gone far away into the silent land;
When you can no more hold me by the hand,
Nor I half turn to go, yet turning stay.
...
Christina Rossetti

Two years ago my Dad died. He'd been ill for years, almost a decade, but Jamie was still in bits about it. Mum was even worse, which took me by surprise. I was the one who stayed calm. I dealt with all the practicalities. I seemed to be coping well.

Then, three weeks after his funeral, I saw my Dad walking along Argyle Street. It was a Saturday, so the place was mobbed, but it was him all right. He had his back to me, but I recognised that thick untidy fair hair, just like Jamie's and mine, only faded with grey. He glanced to one side and I saw his profile. He was walking easily, gracefully, like his old self. He looked as he might have if the disease hadn't caught up with him. But it was him; I'd have known him anywhere.

As soon as I recognised him, I felt something tear inside me. It was quite a gentle sensation, as if a membrane had been ruptured but was still holding. I watched Dad head for a tall building at the end of the pedestrian precinct, a tower of clean blond sandstone. There is, of course, no sandstone tower on Argyle Street.

I thought, matter-of-factly, I'm looking into a different world.

Then a huge man loomed up and bumped into me. By the time he was out of the way my Dad and the new building were both gone.

Calmly, I caught the underground to my GP's surgery. Then I sat in the packed waiting room and cried, until the doctor saw me. She was kind; we talked about stress and grief and coping. She gave me a sick line and a prescription. I went home, and didn't leave my flat for the next fortnight.

It didn't happen again. I thought I didn't have to worry any more.

But that's not true.

Ever since Lewis left, I've been feeling cold. Not chilly, not draughty: *cold*. Like the door's blown open in an Arctic wind. No one else ever feels it.

Lately, it's begun to happen when I'm falling asleep. I jerk awake – I can't let myself sink into that kind of cold, I won't survive! That's been going on for months.

But it's only now – sitting at my desk, the fax burbling behind me – that I understand how bad this is. Someone is clattering up a ladder before me, Christmas garlands waft down to the floor. Someone else is saying 'a day late, it's bad luck!' I can't remember who these people are.

I am looking out of the window, which only moments ago was streaming with rain. Now it's piled high with snow. The top pane is clear but I can see that the blizzard is still coming down. It's a whiteout.

The membrane inside me rips open, like burnt but still-living skin, from top to bottom. And I know that something, now, is going to come through.

Part One
Slipping

....

Axe-time, sword-time, shields are sundered,
Wind-time, wolf-time, ere the world falls.

...

The Poetic Edda

Chapter 1

I'm wringing wet by the time I get to Bowie's. The rain is bouncing off the pavements, and of course I left my umbrella behind with my coat. I always change before I come to Bowie's, but tonight I haven't. My long skirt is plastered against my skin. My office shoes are waterlogged. I should be freezing, but I'm not. I push through the heavy doors.

The lobby has changed from black to white and gold. The walls have been panelled with ivory and swathed with white netting. The nets have scooped up dozens of fake gold rings, glass tiaras, paper flowers and hearts. On the wall is a screen showing two men in tuxedos; then there's a top-to-toe ripple, and it's the same couple naked but for top hats over their cocks. The pink bust of Mozart has vanished from its podium, and been replaced by a shiny plastic wedding cake topped with two miniature grooms. The lobby is stuffy, and smells of dope and cigarettes. Downstairs the music pounds.

It's too bright. I stand there blinking, until something dunts into my back. I try to step out of the way, and tread on a foot. Even so a voice murmurs 'Sorry,' and two bodies ease past me. The two young guys in cropped jackets glance over their shoulders, one with a polite half smile for the soaking freak who just trod on him, before turning quickly away to the cash desk.

I hear voices and laughter, the discreet beeping of the till. I'm not listening to any of it. The white netting loops and drapes across the creamy background, and I can't figure it out at all. A voice is saying, 'Hi? Hello?' and I'm thinking, fishing nets? Then it comes to me: 'Brides' veils,' I say.

'Sorry?'

I look round. The two young guys are gone, and the guy at the desk is staring at me. I point at the walls. 'They're brides' veils.'

'That's right. Is it just yourself?'

'What?'

'Are you by yourself?' His voice is loud and careful.

'Oh, yes, sorry.' I'm wasting his time. 'Yes, just the one please.'

'You know it's mostly guys tonight?'

'Yes, I know.'

He shrugs: he thinks I'm an idiot. I step up meekly to the desk and hand over my bankcard. He watches me warily the whole time, but when the payment goes through he nods. 'That's you now, Ms…' He glances down at the card and smiles. 'Pherson? You Jamie Pherson's sister?'

I nod. My stomach suddenly knots. 'He is in tonight, isn't he?'

'Aye, he's down there.' The smile broadening, he nods towards the basement steps. 'Tell him Jake says hi, yeah?'

'Sure.' I head for the stairs, towards the pulsing beat. I know the way, placing my feet on the running lights sunk into the floor. Stepping carefully on each strip of electric blue, and trailing my hand down the already sticky chrome banister, I head down into the silvery flashing light. A horde of guys is heading up, dark shuffling bodies and blue-white faces. The faces turn to me, floating moons, cool and curious. One says 'Hi!' so I suppose I must know him. No doubt he'll tell the others, 'Jamie's big sister. Real fag-hag. No life of her own…' I keep walking down.

Once, when I'd lost my phone and was retracing the previous night's steps, I saw Bowie's in the daytime. It was a small, shabby basement. The light was nicotine yellow. The walls were painted black. It smelled of stale sweat, stale alcohol and stale puke. The walls were close and the ceiling was low. I left quickly.

But now, of course, it's vast. The dancefloor is a heaving mass swept by spotlights. Beyond the floor there are no walls, just a fading into darkness. As I step round the corner the beat resolves itself into a tune. It's a fusion mix of 'Get Me to the Church On Time'; over the superfast salsa a Cockney voice squawks 'Get me to the church! Get me to the church!'. It's silly, and the dancers are laughing, though you can't hear them. White teeth shine. I can see now why the light is silver: the giant screen is showing black and white. Cary Grant, in a grey morning suit, is marrying Clark Gable in a black tux. They kiss before the altar; the guests cheer and throw confetti. Clark and Cary melt, seamlessly, into Kevin Costner in silver-grey buckskins (wasn't that movie in colour?) snogging Christian Slater in a flowered headdress. Then a young Brad Pitt and George Clooney beneath the desert sun. Then Kermit the Frog in a veil, kissing The Great Gonzo. The laughter is audible now.

I step down onto the dancefloor.

Mistake. A forest of bobbing heads all around me. Some of them have something white and triangular on their heads. Bodies bumping and crushing, elbows in my ribs and heavy boots on my toes. Smooth male faces glancing down, always down, and looking away. There's no air. I start to push through them, towards the quiet zone. I can't get them to move. Suddenly I imagine them panicking, running from a fire, trampling me down. I start barging, shoving against sweaty arms and muscled backs. A DM connects with my shin, perhaps on purpose, and for a moment I'm going to fall. But I don't. I get to the edge of the floor and up the three steps into the quiet zone.

As soon as I pass under the ceiling mufflers I can hear my breathing. I'm gasping like I've been running uphill. The alcove is lined with couches like big pouty lips; the light is brighter here, so you can almost see the stains on the red velvet. A couple are already sitting on one of the couches, or rather one's on the couch and the other one's sitting on his partner; they're both fully dressed but there's a fair bit of rubbing and moaning going on. Normally I'd take the hint and fuck off, but tonight I just sit as far away from them as possible. I'm not going out there again.

I scan the crowd in front of me. It's useless – any one of those spiky-haired heads could be Jamie. The music changes to something much different, New Primal I think, a slower beat but much heavier. The screen shifts to colour, to writhing flesh tones. It's New Primal all right, and it's *that* video. I watch them, the young Indian singer pressed between the ebony Zulu man and the albino woman. The woman turns to the camera, stretching up to show pallid nipples and white underarm hair. Her pink eyes look blank, traumatised. I recall I used to like this video. But now the three of them look like a knot of snakes. In time with the beat, an ache starts to pulse behind my eyes.

The couple on the other couch disentangle themselves and head off, hand-in-hand, shooting me disapproving looks. But I'm going to sit here for a while. My soaking skirt is lukewarm, not uncomfortable so long as I don't move. I can close my eyes.

But now there's someone waving and climbing out of the dancefloor towards me. Someone who seems to be dressed in black liquid. Someone crowned in a white triangle. I blink rapidly a few times, but I don't recognise Carl until he flings himself down beside me. 'How're you doing, hen?'

I nod, wondering bemusedly what's different about him. Dark eyes. Healthy tan from Christmas in Florida. Lantern jaw that's never going to look boyish no matter what he does. Wet-look black vest that I always tell him looks tacky, to which he smugly retorts that he's never had any complaints. Glossy black hair, topped by a cardboard triangle trailing white ribbons.

'Carl,' I say, 'what the fuck have you got on your head?'

'Oh, this?' He pulls it off and gives it to me. 'They're giving them out. It's a wedding thingmy. What d'you call them?'

'Tiara?' Sure enough, there's a pattern of pearls stencilled on the cardboard, and the ribbons are fine white netting.

'That's the one. Here, try it.' He leans over to put it on my head, steadying himself with a hand on my knee, then recoiling in surprise. 'Christ, Suze, you're soaking!'

'It's raining out there. No.' I bat the cardboard tiara aside. 'I don't want it.'

I spoke sharply, but he doesn't seem to notice. 'Suit yourself.' The music has changed again, to Iggy Pop. The screen's showing a very young Ewan McGregor running up Princes Street in Edinburgh. Carl laughs, but he's ignoring the screen and looking at the dancefloor. 'Look at him go,' he says.

There's Jamie, jumping up and down in the crush, grinning like a fool. He's wearing jeans and a plain T-shirt. He's surrounded by guys in designer gear and skimpy vests and makeup, and they can't look at anyone but him. One of them is putting a wedding tiara on his head; he knocks it away, he hates any kind of drag. Another guy's tapping him on the shoulder, pointing up at Ewan McGregor and back at Jamie; we can't hear him but it's obviously, 'You look just like him!' That's not going to get the poor bastard anywhere; Jamie's been combing men out of his fashionable buzz cut ever since he came out, and he hears the Ewan McGregor line every other night of the week. Carl laughs again. I say, 'I don't know where he gets the energy.'

'He's fizzed to the tits,' Carl says, but he's still smiling. He lifts an arm and waves, pointing downwards at me. Jamie spots me and starts pushing through the mass, smiling and waving. I watch him, my baby brother, and suddenly I'm about to cry. I wait, but by the time Jamie's bounding up the steps, the feeling has passed.

'Suzey!' I'm wrapped in a sweaty hug. I cling on to him a little too long. Usually, he would notice, but when he pulls away I see that his pupils are tiny dots. He slides onto the couch, so he's sandwiched between me and

Carl. 'Suzey-Sue! I didn't know you were coming tonight!'

'I just thought I'd come by,' I say.

'S'great, that's great…' He looks down at where his denim thigh presses against my skirt, and looks almost comically puzzled. 'You're all wet.'

There's that crying feeling again. 'I got caught in the rain, Jamie. I walked home from work.'

'How come?'

Carl chimes in, 'Did you have a bad day?'

'I walked out,' I say. I don't think they catch it, and Jamie is busy anyway, rummaging through his pockets. 'Here,' he's saying, 'I know what'll cheer you up. Ah, shit…' He leans away from me, presses his face into Carl's neck and says in a stage whisper, 'Got any more sherbet?'

'You've had it all, you greedy fuck.' Carl is stroking his short brown hair. Jamie settles back against his hand. 'Sorry, it's away,' he says to me. He puts an arm around me and pulls me against him. He is very warm. We all sit like that, just for a moment.

But Jamie's restless. He sees the cardboard tiara lying beside me, and snatches it up. 'Isn't it great, Suzey?'

'What is?'

'I can get married. We can get married. You knew that didn't you, Suze?'

'She was there when Stonewall rang,' says Carl. 'God, you're out of it, aren't you?' Carl's eyes are almost black, so it's only now I notice that his pupils are almost as tiny as Jamie's.

Jamie's nodding. 'Oh yeah, so she was. So we can get married. Yeah? We don't have to go to California or Wales or anywhere fuckin' weird. We can walk into the Registry Office and say, "We want to get married."'

'Walk into the marriage suites,' Carl corrects, with satisfaction. He's a traditionalist. 'The decent place in Park Circus. They're reopening it. Increased demand.'

'Oh yeah. The proper marriage place. Not some pokey wee office. And none of this civil partnership crap. We can say, "Get us married right fuckin' now." And they'll need to do it.'

'Katie would be spitting teeth,' I say. I don't know why I said it. It really was mean. There's a moment's silence, but then Carl laughs. 'Can I tell her?'

'Can I tell her mum?' says Jamie. They both howl with laughter. I try to join in. Then Jamie twists around suddenly and plops the cardboard tiara on

Carl's head. 'What do you think?'

'It's not my colour,' Carl says. But he's looking right into Jamie's eyes, suddenly very serious.

'I mean it.' Jamie is serious now too. 'What about it?'

'You know what I think,' Carl says. I realise this is an old conversation, one that's been running a while, and I never had a clue it existed. I realise I should be a long way away at this moment.

'I think the same,' Jamie says. Slowly and carefully, he takes his partner's hand. 'Will you marry me?'

'Yes,' Carl says. 'I will.'

Within minutes the whole room knows. Gay clubs have all the privacy of a beehive. Someone on the dancefloor spots the jubilation in the quiet zone, the news is blurted out, and next thing we know the DJ's made an announcement.

In the chaos that breaks out, I am glad. Jamie and Carl are surrounded by the congratulation and envy they deserve. I'm happy for them, I tell myself, I truly am; Carl will take care of Jamie now, better than I can, or than I ever have. He doesn't need me now. Amidst all the hugging and kissing and crying I could cry a little too, but I don't.

The DJ puts on 'Going to the Chapel of Love'. With a happy yell, the whole place rushes to the dancefloor. And suddenly, it's too much for me. It's too loud, too airless.Carl and Jamie are on the dancefloor, right in the middle, wrapped around each other. I watch for a moment. I want to go to them and say, 'I'm sick, please, take me home with you, let me stay, don't leave me alone…' But of course I can't. I can't even catch Jamie's eye, and that's only right and proper.

So I head for the stairs. I'll just slip away, I think. I begin placing my feet on the lights on the floor, blocking them out, one by one.

As I let myself in I hear a murmur of voices. There's someone in my flat.

I stand, clutching the key in the lock, and for a moment I feel

– *something trying to get through something cold something* –

dizzy. But that's the draught, I tell myself, the draught from the close behind me. And the voices are from the TV. I let the door slam and wander into the kitchen-living room.

It's chilly, and it stinks of rubbish. I switch on the central heating, think briefly about emptying the bin, and then flop onto the couch. I kick off my wet shoes and that's all the movement I seem able to make. Rainwater is actually running from my hair, seeping from my clothes into the tan linen upholstery. I should do something about it, but then who cares? It's not my couch. I stare at the TV instead.

It's *Newsweek* – people in dark suits quarrelling across a black glass table. Matthew McLean is shouting down the rest: '… a sacrament between a *man* and a *woman*, Sonia. It's right there in black and white. You can't pick and choose which Bible texts you…' Those weird pale eyes of his look washed out under the studio lights. Sonia McCall is looking at him with distaste, but he still rattles on.

My eye is caught by a scratch at the top of the screen. Fuck it, the TV isn't mine either. Nor are the brown-and-white walls. The whole ugly place was rented as a stopgap after Lewis and I split up. Six months later and I'm still here.

Not for much longer, though. I press the mute button and the people on the screen jabber and point silently. No, not for much longer, because without a salary I won't be paying the rent. And then what? Mum? She won't like that. Jamie and Carl? Just married and big sister's crashing in the spare room? Don't think so.

I sit and listen to the rain spattering against the window. My heart is hammering. My stomach knots. Outside, a woman's voice shrieks in protest. I can't make out what she says.

The clock says 11:13. I decide: I am going to get some sleep. I stand up and start peeling off my sopping clothes – I should hang them up, but I just chuck them away from me, so they go splat on the kitchen lino. I shuffle through to the bedroom, look in the drawers, then look in the overflowing wash basket and pull out a huge pair of pyjamas. I pull them on, and, because I'm not paying attention, catch an accidental glimpse of myself in the full-length mirror.

I don't look good. It's another six months till I'm thirty, but I already look middle-aged. My hair hangs in long wet straggles. My face is pasty, pulled into a tight-lipped frown, although I don't feel like I'm frowning. My body is hunched; my hands are clasped together, arthritically.

To hell with it. I sit on the edge of the bed, pull the big white chemist's bag out of the bedside drawer and tip my little pharmacopoeia onto the duvet. I locate the pack of yellow sleeping pills and pop out two. It says only one, but what the fuck. The antidepressant pack rattles accusingly – did I forget it again this morning? I add it to the pile and knock the whole lot back. I think of going to get some water, but instead I crawl between the sweaty sheets and switch out the light. The glowing bedside numbers say 11:30.

I lie there, and my heart is still hammering so hard I can hear it. Strips of streetlight lie across the bed. I can hear the rain too. But it's only rain, it's not snow. It's all right. I can sleep.

At 11:34 I switch on the light, get up and blow-dry my hair. Without any conditioner it crackles, and starts to smell scorched. I switch off the noisy dryer; my next-door neighbour is thumping on the wall. I go back to bed and switch off the light.

At 11:44 I get up and go to the kitchen. I take a carton of milk from the fridge, sniff it, and take a drink. I leave the carton on the worktop and go back to bed. Take another pill, just a relaxant, not one of the biggies.

At 11:57 I roll onto my back, and start taking slow, deliberate breaths. The counsellor told me this is how to relax. Breathe in… Breathe out. My heartbeat doesn't change.

I will sleep. I haven't slept right through for weeks. But tonight's the night. It must be – I'm shattered.

Maybe this is it. Drifting. Yes. Sleep. At last…

– *cold it's cold it's* –

Falling. It's dark. I'm freezing. Not chilly, not goose bumps. Freezing. Arctic. I won't survive.

I start awake. I used to sit bolt upright when I woke like this, but I'm too tired now. My hand claws for the lamp.

It's 12:30.

I can't survive the cold. But, I realise now, I can't survive like this either. Miserable tears begin to trickle down my face. My heart is something trapped in my chest, trying to get out. It will burst.

Fumbling in the dark, into the paper bag, I find a blister pack, almost empty. Find a fresh one. Big pills, good. Press out a handful. Cram them in, swallow.

Turn my back on the clock. Curl up tight. Tears run over the bridge of my nose, join with others. Pillow soaked.

Oh please, sweet Jesus, let me sleep, just for once. I don't care any more. Please, God. Just sleep.

And then... The heart begins to slow. Quietening. Oh, thank you. I'm sinking into the mattress.

Oh God, thank you.

Oh God, thank...

'Oh shit, Suzey!'

Light. Hurts. Cheek on damp pillow.

Loud voice too close. 'Carl! Carl, oh fuck, get in here!'

Open eyes, just a bit. Jamie, white face looming over me. Shut up, Jamie.

Another voice: quieter, thank God. Calm. It's Carl. 'Go and call an ambulance.'

'Oh Christ, she's—'

'She's not, she's breathing. Go and call 999.'

Carl's face now, beside Jamie's; Carl's voice. 'Suzey? It's okay. You're okay. Stay awake with me, okay?'

Jamie, far away, yelling something. Carl says 'Back in a minute' and then he's gone.

Good. Close eyes. Back to sleep. Back to...

'HELLO! HELLO! What's her first name, son? SUSAN! CAN YE HEAR ME? SUSAN!'

A man's voice so loud it hurts. 'Leave me be,' I say.

'WHEN DID YE TAKE THEM? SUSAN! HOW LONG'S IT BEEN SINCE YE TOOK THEM?'

I'm awake now. Moving bodies. Clattering metal. Whisking of nylon on nylon. Open my eyes a bit further. Eye-watering green. Huge bearded face. 'WHEN DID YE TAKE THEM, SUSAN? DO YE KNOW?'

I should know this... But it's gone. 'Don't know...'

'Give her it anyway. Stand back there, son. Two – three – ' Before I can protest, I'm lifted, swung, dumped onto something padded. I'm wheeling rapidly through my flat. Something's in my mouth, hard plastic between my teeth, and cold liquid squirts down my throat.

I swallow, and immediately I'm throwing up. I can't control it. The rest of my body could be dead and my stomach would still be cramping. There's a plastic tub under my mouth – I see bright yellow stuff, smell it, and I'm retching again.

We trundle out into the close. I've never felt so terrible. 'Jamie,' I'm howling, 'Jamie!'

'I'm here.' But I'm hoisted in the air, and he's whisked away. Some detached part of me is impressed; these paramedic guys, they're speedy all right. We're down the stairs, past opening doors and staring neighbours, then out to rain and wind, then bumping into light and warmth again. A slam, and revving engines, and we're off.

Sirens shriek overhead. Someone takes the plastic tub away, and I get a mouthful of clean air. But then the man's voice says 'Check airways' and gloved fingers are thrust into my mouth. I start to puke again. 'Jamie,' I wail.

'I'm here.' He's sitting opposite. His face is grey. 'You're going to be okay.'

'Make them leave me alone, Jamie.'

'It's okay, it's okay.'

'It's not fucking okay.' The bearded face is looming towards me again, and I scream, 'Fuck off!'

'She's conscious.' The ambulance stops jouncing and the doors are flung open. Good, they're letting me off. But outside hands are reaching and I'm out into the chilly wind

– it's dark and I'm cold and it's soft and something—

and then into warmth and bright light. I'm on a trolley. I'm bowling along, fluorescent lights flashing past. Then I stop – curtains are swishing around me.

Faces peer down. One of them is Beardie. 'Ten ccs. Think we got most of it out.'

'Fucking turned my stomach out,' I say. Laughter. Beardie leaves. Middle-aged female face close to mine. 'Okay, Susan, we—'

Still dark. Still cold. On my back. Streetlight slanting across the bed. Movement beside me.

'Oh shit, Suzey!' Jamie. Light. Hurts. I'm in my own bed. Pillow sticky but dry.

'Susan? Still with us? Keep your eyes open, pet. Susan, can you look at me?'

Obediently I look.

– cold dark cold –

'Somebody help!' Jamie is shouting. Arms under my knees and my shoulders, carrying me. I'm being bounced around, I can't move.

I can see the walls of my close. It's very cold. Jamie's voice is raw and hoarse.

'*Can somebody fucking help me!*'

'Look into this light? Can you look? Susan?'

I try hard to look. This time I feel it happen. A sinking, not painful. I hear someone say 'She's going' as the chill seeps in.

I'm outside. Warm arms still wrap around me. In the distance, a siren is wailing. I am eased down into absolute cold.

I'm lying in snow. Icy needles prick my face – tiny flakes are landing there. I'm lying in a deep bed of powdery snow. It hurts. The cold hurts.

Then I'm hoisted just above the snow, and supported on someone's knees. Arms pull me against a warm body. My face presses against something nylon: a coat.

Jamie's face hangs over mine. He has long hair, somehow. It straggles over his face, like mine does. He is crying. 'Suzey, oh God, Suzey, please, wake up!'

I realise he has carried me down the stairs. All alone. Where's Carl? Gone for the ambulance? The siren is still very distant.

Sobs shake his body and mine. There are streaks of ice, like snail's trails, down his cheeks. His tears have frozen. 'Stay with me, Suzey. Don't leave me. Please don't leave me.'

'I'm sorry, Jamie,' I say. I spoke loudly, but he has to put his ear to my mouth. 'I'm sorry...'

And then I'm falling. A cry from Jamie, and he's gone.

Darkness. Cold that numbs and turns you to nothing.

There is still sound. The howling of wolves. A shrieking wind.

And a voice. Raj Chaudhury's voice, saying, 'The end of the world. Ragnarok. The end of the world.'

And then, nothing.

Chapter 2

The ice-cream van is coming up the drive. We can hear it through the pine trees. It can probably be heard all the way to the village, jingling 'Waltzing Matilda' like the loudest music box in the world, terrifying the sheep in the fields that surround the hospital.

As usual, it causes a stir in the common room. It's the most exciting thing that happens all day, apart from visiting hour, and visiting hour can be something of a mixed blessing. But no one ever comes away in tears from an encounter with a Bounty, not unless they're here for an eating disorder. People are rummaging in pockets and looping handbags over their arms, heading for the door with something like enthusiasm. The dressed people are, anyway. Us dressing gowns watch enviously, those of us not goggling at *Neighbours* or staring at the walls.

I half turn in my chair so I can look out of the window. The glass is white and opaque. I wipe it with my hand – the condensation is cold, so I use my terrycloth sleeve instead. Through the clear space I see the ice-cream van bounce over the speed bump into the car park. A crowd has already formed in the doorway. As the van comes to a stop and the jingle is choked off, the crowd surges forward like refugees going for the food-truck, then remembers itself and forms a straggling queue. A woman in a pink dressing gown emerges from the hospital doorway and trots briskly towards the front of the line. A nurse leaves the queue, waving at her pal to keep her place; she catches the woman's arm and steers her back inside.

'Nice try,' I mumble. I sympathise, and not just because I want some chocolate. I know it's cold out there – I can see feet stamping, arms wrapped around chests – but the winter sun is bright and the frost is sparkling. It's the outside world. I turn to the only person left in the room who's fully dressed. 'Rachel,' I say, 'I want my clothes.'

Nurse Bailley keeps her eyes on the telly. She's always in the common room after lunchtime; she's a daytime TV addict. 'When Doctor says you can have them, Suzey,' she says.

I watch her. She is small and slight, pale in her white uniform. Last week I saw her face down a huge angry bruiser of a woman, who was screaming about God-knows-what; Rachel didn't move a muscle. I know she's not going to give way to me, but still I say, 'When's *that* going to be?'

'I don't know.'

I turn away and stare out of the window. I feel like I've been sitting here in my nightie my whole fucking life. I don't say or do anything, but suddenly Rachel's talking to me again. 'Who's your doctor, Suzey?'

'Old Bovver Boots.' She looks blank; I sigh. 'Dr Martin.'

'When are you seeing her next?'

'Today.' I turn to look at the telly, where identical blonde teenagers are shopping for vests. 'Not till three.'

'Why don't you go along and wait outside? She might see you early.'

I snort: I've waited in that corridor before. 'Only if the guy before me's died.'

Rachel's looking at me earnestly. 'Nobody dies in here, Suzey.'

Oh, for God's sake. I stand up. 'I'll go and wait.'

Dr Martin always sits with her back to the window. When you're in the chair before her desk, you have to squint to look at her. Not that she makes much eye contact anyway. She's a broad woman, fifty-ish, with grey bobbed hair that swings in front of her face when she leans over to write. She writes a lot, especially when you're talking. She spent all my first session flicking through a prescription drugs handbook, before finally writing a script and sticking it in my file. She says very little.

I settle down in front of her, smoothing my nightshirt over my knees and trying to tuck my bare ankles behind the folds of my bathrobe (Dr Martin's office is draughty). Right, I think, this time I'm really going to tell her how I feel. At the moment she's flicking through the pages of my file; before I can speak she says, 'How are you getting along on the Prozac?'

I'm not feeling one bit different. 'All right, I suppose…' She nods and writes. Is that it? 'I don't feel any better,' I say.

'It's only been a week.' Scribble, scribble. 'Are you sleeping any better?'

'Yes.' At least there's that – after my nightly horse tablet I don't know a thing until lights on at half six. 'Yes, a lot better.'

'Any waking?'

'No. It's great, it's really great to sleep again…'

She's flicking through the file. 'Good. We'll look at taking you off the sleeping pill then.'

I don't believe I'm hearing this. 'But then I won't sleep any more.'

'The sleeping pill isn't designed as a long-term option. As the Prozac starts to work you'll feel a sedative effect—'

I'm getting panicky. 'But I'm not feeling it. I'm not feeling anything!'

She looks at me for a moment. 'All right. We'll keep the sleeping pills in place for a while longer. Now…' she flips back through the notes again. 'Can you tell me about the day you took the overdose? You were at work for part of the day, weren't you?'

'That's right. I… I left early.'

'Why is that?'

'I don't know. I just wanted to get out.'

Long silence. 'Do you like your job?'

'It's okay. It's a job. You know.' I laugh. 'It's inside. No heavy lifting…'

I am horrified, because tears have started to leak from my eyes. I grab a tissue from the box on the desk and dab them away. After another, even longer silence, Dr Martin says, 'You said you went to visit someone that day?' She rustles through her notes. 'Your brother?'

I shake my head. 'His boyfriend. He works in the same building as me. But he wasn't in.'

'So what did you do?'

'It's not really important.'

'Please tell me anyway.'

So I do.

Earth Sciences is on the top floor of the University.

There is a lift, a rackety metal cage; you can see out on every side, and through the floor down into the drop. Lately, I've been taking the stairs.

I'm gasping by the time I reach Carl's office. He isn't there. I stand for a moment, not knowing what to do.

After a while I think to try the departmental office. This room is empty too, and the computer's switched off; the secretary must have gone for lunch. I stop for a moment to get my breathing under control, and look around.

I like this room. It catches the sun, which is still bright at the moment, in spite of the rain pattering against the windows. The windows themselves are small, but if you get up close you can see half of Glasgow spread out below: the red and blond sandstone, the grey concrete office blocks, the dull glint of the river.

The room is pleasingly cluttered. One wall is covered with photos of the department's pride and joy: the Wild Wolf programme. From floor to ceiling, it's a sepia mass of glossy pictures: a pack running free in Glen Nevis, a mother suckling her cubs in Lochnagar, a lone wolf in the rain on the banks of Loch Ness. In the centre is a poster of the project's most famous image, the one that made all the papers; a close-up of the Glencoe Monument with a grey wolf's face peering around it. Two of the other walls are a jumble of maps and charts and Greenpeace brochures, stretching all the way around the office.

But the right-hand wall is different. I actually jump, as if someone previously unseen is standing there. There is a large painting there, new, and unlike anything else on the wall.

Most of the canvas is black. In the centre is a bright circle, yellow-white. The sun, I realise: a winter sun. This sun is surrounded by black cloud. Here and there are hints of pale grey sky, but you know the cloud is closing in on them fast.

I walk over to the painting. With every step it becomes more diffuse. When I am right in front of it, the sun has turned to swirls of ivory, and the cloud is a mass of tiny black dots. Pointillism – that's the word, I think. The canvas is set in a narrow frame of pale smooth wood. A word is stencilled on the frame: *Ragnarok*.

I step back from the painting and the sun and the cloud begin to reform. I go to the very centre of the room, close my eyes for a moment and look again.

I see it now. The black cloud has formed into the head of a wolf. The wolf's jaws hold the sun, like a ball. It is about to bite down.

I jump when the office door creaks open and a man comes in. I know everyone in this department, but I've never seen this man before in my life.

He's tall and skinny, the type who can never get trousers long enough to cover his ankles. He is Indian or Pakistani. About forty. Black hair, shot through with white. His skin is quite pale, though that might just be the grey rainy light. His face is angular and unsmiling. I'm reminded of an eagle. 'Can I help you?' he says.

An English accent, quite pukka. Finally my brain kicks into gear – a visiting lecturer. I heard the girls talking about him. Some of them think he's sexy. 'I'm just looking at the picture,' I say.

'Ah.' He smiles, a crooked little smile. 'What do you think of it?'

I look at the painting, at the mouth, about to close. 'It's horrible.'

'Oh. Do you really think so?'

Something, finally, is getting through to me. 'Who – I mean…' Oh shit. 'You didn't paint it, did you?'

'Actually I did. And thank you.'

'What?'

'It is horrible. You're right. It's meant to be horrible. It's the end of the world.' He smiles again, more broadly. 'Raj Chaudhury.'

'Sorry?'

'That's me.' He's holding out his hand. 'I'm Raj Chaudhury.'

'Oh! Oh. Suzey Pherson.' We shake. 'I work downstairs.'

I'm still staring at the painting; I can't help it. 'Ragnarok. Is that…'

'It's an ancient myth. The Vikings believed that the world would end with a great winter – the gods would die, and a great wolf would swallow up the sun. Then all life would end.'

Any minute now, it could move. Any minute. I hear him say softly, 'Suzey, are you all right?'

I look up at him, and realise I'm still gripping his hand. Then there's a movement in the corner of my eye. It's moving. It's biting down.

'I have to go,' I say. I pull away and bolt for the door. He says something, but I can't stop. I scramble out into the corridor. I don't look back.

Dr Martin is scribbling like a fury. What the hell did I tell her that for? I can't read upside down, but I can just imagine: *paranoid, hallucinating, thinks a giant wolf's going to munch up the world like a chew toy*. I'm going to be here till I'm drawing my pension. 'It was just a painting,' I say lamely.

Dr Martin looks up as if she's surprised I'm still here. 'Would you like your clothes back?'

'What? Oh, yes. That would be great.'

I half expect her to say, 'Well you can't have them!' but instead she nods. 'I'll tell the nurses to get them tomorrow. Now.' She glances at her watch. 'I'm seeing you again in two days, aren't I?'

In another minute I'm out in the corridor again. I hold Dr Martin's door open for a plump girl in a green velour bathrobe, who mutters 'Here goes nothing' and pulls the door shut behind her. I stand there, looking up and down the white-and-blue corridor, wondering how the hell I'm ever going to say what I really mean to that woman.

There's nothing else to do, so I wander back to the common room, where it's nearly time for *Jeremy Kyle*.

I meet the plump girl later, in the drugs queue. 'You getting your clothes back soon?' she asks.

'Tomorrow.'

'You're lucky.' She pulls her bathrobe tighter around her as we shuffle forward a little further. We were slow off the mark this evening – even the geriatrics are ahead of us. The girl is winding a strand of bottle-red hair around her finger. 'I'm Shaz, by the way,' she says.

'Hi.' At visiting time I overheard Shaz's designer-clad parents addressing her as 'Sian', but I don't comment. 'I'm Suzey.'

We move a little closer together. She must be five years younger than me, but in a ward full of menopausal women and pensioners it's good to find someone else still in their twenties. Shaz may have an ulterior motive, though, because she asks, 'Was that your boyfriend visiting you today?'

'No, my brother.'

'He's a total honey, isn't he?' I shrug and wait, and sure enough she asks, 'Has he got a girlfriend?'

'No. A boyfriend.'

'Fuck.' A tut from the queue in front of us. Shaz raises her voice and lowers her accent. 'Ah'll just need tae rip off all ma clothes and jump him then, won't Ah?'

'He really is gay, Shaz.'

'Naebody's that gay.'

I think she's overestimating her charms. Shaz is more than a little plump, and I think perhaps she knows it. So I smile and say, 'He'll never know what's hit him.'

She laughs. 'Comes to see ye a lot, doesn't he?'

'He's been here every day.' My eyes are starting to prickle, so I add hurriedly, 'Must be you he's after, though. He'll want to get into your dressing gown.'

'Aye. It's the velour. Drives 'em wild.'

By this time I'm at the front. The sour-faced night sister is standing in front of me, ready to throw herself on the medication trolley should some drug-crazed pensioner make a lunge for it. A pleasant-looking student nurse is leafing through the clipboard of notes – she smiles and holds out a tiny paper cup, which rattles. 'Susan Pherson? There you go.'

I'm about to knock the whole lot back when I realise something's missing. A capsule, two small green tablets… where's the big yellow one?'What about my sleeping pill?'

The student rustles through the clipboard. 'Doctor's taken you off the sleeping pill, Susan.'

'No.' My heart's starting to thump. 'She was thinking about it, but she didn't do it.'

The sister takes the clipboard from the student. 'Dr Martin's stopped the sleeping pills, Susan.'

'She changed her mind.'

'We've got to go by what's on the notes—'

If I just explain, they'll understand, they have to understand. 'Yes,' I say, 'but she changed her mind. She did, I heard her.'

'We'll check with her tomorrow.' They don't believe me, of course they don't. 'Just take those ones just now—'

'But they're not enough.' My voice has risen to a wail. I can hear it, but I don't care. 'I need the sleeping pill. I won't sleep without it.'

'It's only for the one night—'

'Why don't you phone Dr Martin?'

'Don't be silly.'

'Why not? It's only ten o'clock.'

'We can't do that, Susan.' The student is smiling, holding out the cup. 'Just take these other ones.'

I go to take the cup, but I'm so shaky I knock it out of her hand. 'You can't just leave me like this. You *can't*.' I look to Shaz, who tries to smile supportively, although her eyes are wide. I turn back to the nurses – surely if I'm reasonable… 'Please. You don't know what it's like. It's like freezing to death.'

The sister has taken my arm. She is very strong. She is leading me away. 'You're all right, Susan.'

'No, wait, I'm just telling you—'

There's another nurse beside me now – someone smiling and large. 'You're fine. Just lie down.'

We're at my bed. My stuff – cards and chocolate – is arranged on top of the locker. They're making me sit down. I tell them, 'It's like dying. It feels like dying.'

'You're not dying, Susan.' Curtains swish around me. I'm lying on my stomach. The large nurse is trying to get my nightie up. 'We're just going to give you a wee jag, okay? It'll help you sleep.'

I pause. There's a draught around my backside. 'Is it the same stuff?'

'Aye, it's the same.' The needle sinks into my buttock; I yelp, more from indignity than pain. 'There now, you're all right…'

The lights go out, and I'm sinking.

The nurse was lying. Whatever she gave me, it wasn't the same stuff as my sleeping pill. I shriek at her – 'You liar!' – but I make no sound.

I am falling. There is no light. I can't make a sound but I can hear. The wind is whistling. There's another sound – a child's voice, shrieking. Somewhere there is a siren.

And then the cold comes.

I'm dying. They've given me too much, and I'm dying.

Cold. The cold is painful. It's stabbing me in the ribs. It's chopping at my fingers and toes. It's shaking me.

If it hurts this much, I must be alive. As soon as I realise that, the light starts to come back. It's flesh pink.

My eyes are closed, but the light is shining right through. When I open them, finally, they sting and water, the light is so bright. An absolute, glaring white.

When I breathe out, mist puffs in front of me. The white light is not dying away. It could make you blind.

I know what this light means. When I closed my eyes, it was a mild, rainy winter's night. But now, long before my tears clear, I know it is daytime, and that I am looking out on a landscape of deep and heavy snow.

Chapter 3

I duck my head against the cold and the glare and find I'm wearing my good wool coat, although the wind goes through me as if I were still in my bathrobe. Just below my knees I recognise the tops of my red high-heeled boots. The tops are all I can see because I am standing up to my calves in snow.

I can hear children screeching somewhere up ahead. But I am not ready to look up yet. Instead, I bend and scoop up a freezing handful of snow. It doesn't clump in my hand; it's a fine dry powder, and it trickles away through my fingers. It doesn't chill my bare skin; it stabs. Wiping my hand on my coat, I find it already dusted with ice. Hastily I turn out my pockets, scattering tissues, and find my thin leather gloves. Gratefully I pull them on.

I have to look up now.

I'm looking out over a cityscape rounded and blurred by a thick snowfall. The sky is white and low. I can still hear the children, but I can't see another person anywhere.

Before me is a road which rises sharply to a blind summit. Concrete pillars run down the middle and support an arching roof, which might have been meant to give shelter, although the drifts are just as thick under there. The road is seamed on either side by a low wall topped with a railing. Beyond the railings, the world ends.

I'm reminded of something – there used to be a fashion for picture postcards of Glasgow, so heavily filtered and coloured you couldn't tell what the view was meant to be. I recall staring at one silver-tinted image for a good five seconds before the shape of the Necropolis hill leapt into focus. That's what happens now. Suddenly, I know I'm standing looking out over Bell's footbridge, over the river to the South Side. I turn around and look up; sure enough, the hotel towers over me, its mirror walls reflecting the pewter sky. Reassured, I turn back to the view of the South, and realise that everything is gone.

The twisty bridge is gone, but it's not just that. The Science Centre, the

Needle, the silver Armadillo, the conference centre. The rounded bulk of the Hydro. All gone, leaving just gaping spaces in the skyline, like missing teeth, and the empty ground smoothed over with white.

No – it's a trick of the light, or of the snow. I look away. Suddenly I think my hair must be soaked right through, because my scalp is freezing. But I'm not wet at all – there's no moisture here, and I realise now it's not the light that's making my eyes stream. They're struggling not to dry out. I'm pulling dry air into my lungs, and they are starting to ache.

I can't stay here.

A single track of floundering footprints descends from the summit of the bridge and stops at my feet. I lift a foot – skidding a little as I balance on one leg – and twist around to lower it into the nearest print. It fits. My face is freezing; I pause to pull up my hood as far forward as it will go, and pull my collar tight so I'm looking out through a tiny window. Then, high-stepping like a stork, I start to place my feet into the tracks and make my way out onto the bridge.

An icy wind sideswipes me and I skid. The spike-heeled boots have no grip; I bought them for pubbing and clubbing, not walking on ice. I teeter whenever I lift a foot. I try wading for a couple of steps, and immediately cold begins to trickle through the side zips. I go back to picking 'em up and putting 'em down – I start humming to get into a rhythm. *In his master's steps he trod, where the snow lay printed...* I must sound like a fucking maniac. I keep my tunnel vision pointed at my feet.

Riverside Road is only five minutes away. I'm not carrying a bag, but – thank God – I can feel the oblong shape of my phone in my inside pocket. I manage to fumble the mobile out without undoing any coat buttons, switch it on with my thumb, and wriggle one finger out of the thin glove to touch *Mum – Home* on the screen. Then I notice the absence of vertical bars, and the capital letters below where they should be: *NO SIGNAL*. The stupid piece of crap is dead in my hand.

Well, doesn't matter. Mum will be in, of course she will. Relief makes me warmer.

There is a screech, then a stream of childish swearing mixed with laughter. I am abruptly aware that the children's voices seem to be coming from my right-hand side. This is impossible, of course, because I am now halfway across the Clyde. It must be some trick of acoustics, and I don't want to lift my head to the cold just to track down these damned kids. Until I realise that the cursing voice – now sobbing between obscenities – is getting closer. Is now right underneath me.

I wade to the railing – more freezing water seeps through to my ankles, but I hardly notice. I see that the river has been covered over. It's been surfaced with snow for as far as I can see, past the white-topped cranes and on to the heavy horizon. It is blotched here and there with dirty yellow. I look down; there is a wide yellow space below me, where small figures slide and scream.

Of course, I am looking straight down on a clearing made in the snow cover. Off-white walls surround the wide arena. For a moment I think there is something disproportionate about the children playing there – they are too bulky, like apes. But then I realise they are just bundled up against the cold, so heavily that if they fall they will hardly feel it. Fluorescent anoraks are pulled tight over jumpers and fleeces, scarves are wrapped around oversized hats and ski masks. The boy – age and sex is indeterminable under the parka, but the still-sobbing voice is young and male – comes sliding out from under the bridge and cannons into two of his pals, bringing them down. The others jeer and throw snowballs, which they have to pack very tight.

I am looking at the grubby marbled surface they are sliding on. For a while I've been thinking of some artificial flooring: didn't the council do that one year, with part of the river, just like that film with the dancefloor over the pool? But I can't get away from it any more.

The river is frozen over.

I should find their parents, I think, the ice could crack at any moment. But I can see it won't. It is thick and solid. The temperate Clyde, which has only ever frosted along its shallowest banks, is sealed over with ice.

I realise I am shivering badly. My gloved hands are gripping the railings as if they too have frozen solid. I wonder for a second if the leather has frozen onto the metal, if I'll be able to pull away… Of course I can, but my hands are clumsy paws in the thin leather, almost numb.

I have to move.

Wading now, I push on towards the riverbank. My boots are full of slush, and my feet are soon as awkward as my hands. I cling to the railing like an old woman. I don't care; I must get inside, I must get to my Mum's.

The tracks join with a footpath on the bank; to my relief, someone has cleared a narrow trench down the middle. I stop for a moment to look back. The skyline is iced like a Christmas cake, but mercifully familiar: the mirrored hotel and the waterfront flats, and beyond that the black towers of Glasgow University. As I watch, white flecks begin to swirl before my eyes, and for a moment the view is a snow globe, pretty and harmless.

But the flecks are getting thicker. I have to get going. I turn, and the empty space that should be the Media Park is right before me. It's a wasteland. Then a thick flurry whirls before me, like the prelude to a migraine, and I can't tell what I'm seeing any more.

I realise I am whimpering. I make myself stop. I turn left and begin shuffling along the trench.

There is a broad dark figure heading towards me. Another one of the ape people, an adult. A man, I think, but in the Scott-of-the-Antarctic jacket it's hard to tell. We're on a slow but sure collision course in the narrow pathway. When the figure's a few yards away I try to step sideways out of the way; my feet skid, and I'm down in the thick soft snow.

A great padded mitten grabs my hand and hauls me up. I'm hazily aware of massive boots, waterproof trousers and a parka – I'm half expecting the face to be Inuit. But the guy's eyebrows are blonde, and his cheeks are red and chapped. 'Y'allright, hen?' he says.

I mumble something and disengage my hand. The man is staring in amazement at my thin coat and ridiculous boots. I turn and shuffle away, the adrenaline from the fall pushing me on, trying to keep my feet as flat as I can. Behind me the guy shouts, 'You get home, hen, okay?' but I don't look back.

By the time I turn into Riverside Road I'm walking through a blizzard. The row of neat terraced houses usually cuts off the wind-chill from the river, but I can feel no difference now. Generally, I dawdle up this street – but not today. I can actually feel the snot in my nose setting hard. My throat is parched.

Another Eskimo figure, a woman this time, is waddling by on the other side of the road. She stops to stare – her gloved hand lifts to point at me. Her high urgent voice is familiar, she's a neighbour, but I don't stop. We can discuss my crappy dress sense another time; I'm nearly there.

At last, I come to the end of the terrace, number 48. The front windows are dark. I dig my hands deep into my pockets; no keys.

I hear myself sob, but then realise that the windows are dark because the curtains are drawn. Vaguely, I wonder why she's pulled the curtains in the middle of the day, but at the same time I'm hurrying round the back. The back door sticks; I shove, quite ready to break it down if needs be, but it gives way and I stumble into the kitchen.

It's warm. The gas oven is going. I slam the door and rush to huddle against the oven door. It's not till then that I look around and realise how wrong all this is.

My mother's kitchen – my kitchen and Jamie's once, and long before that my father's too – is as I remember it from childhood. The same dingy wallpaper printed with kettles and pots. Gone is the fresh turquoise-and-terracotta paintwork I helped her apply just last year. Gone is the breakfast bar – the old wooden table is back in place. I have tracked melting snow onto the old lemon-tinted lino, which is now nicotine-yellow.

It's as it was when we were teenagers – but even shabbier, even older. And it's dark. The windows have been covered with thick red cloth, stuck all around with masking tape. Why the hell has she put up blackout curtains?

What's going on here?

At that moment the door is shoved clumsily open from the bottom, as if a pet is pushing its way through. A tiny girl – not even two years old – falls into the kitchen. I think she must be plump, but then I realise, yet again, that it's just clothes – a thick woolly jumper, and a second pair of leggings tight as a sausage skin over the first. The kid has fine dark curls – there's something familiar about them.

The child sees me, and squeals. She launches herself at me; I kneel down just in time to catch her. She is a warm, solid armful. She is shrieking, 'Anny too! Anny too!'

'Hello,' I say faintly. She's trying to plant wet kisses on my cheek; I hold her back so I can look at her. I find I'm looking into familiar eyes: wide and grey-blue – Jamie's eyes, my eyes. I have never seen this kid before in my life.

'Anny too! Mumma, anny too!' Now she's squirming away from me, rushing to the kitchen door. There's a woman standing there, in a long skirt and a shapeless fleece. Loose black curls fall to her shoulders. The woman's hands are over her mouth. Her face is like whey. 'Oh my God,' she's saying. 'Oh my God.'

It's Katie. I stand up to face her. The last time I saw Katie was my final afternoon at work. The last time I saw her in this kitchen was the day she slapped my brother's face, called him a filthy pervert and rushed out in tears. She swore then she'd never be back. Now here she is. 'What the hell are you doing here?' I say.

She makes a sound like a scream against her hands. The child is jumping up at her, pointing at me and still yelling 'Mumma, anny too!' but Katie doesn't seem to know she's there. I say, 'Is this your kid?'

Then an old woman appears behind her. I blink; it's my mother. The last time I saw her she'd just been to the salon to get her regular hair tint, the chestnut-brown that makes her look ten years younger. But now her hair is white. My mother had her eyes sorted five years ago, but now she's looking at me through her old glasses. She is wearing thick cord trousers and a fleece like Katie's. As she looks at me her face is going grey.

'Mum,' I say, looking from her to Katie to the kid and back, 'what's going on?'

And that's when the screaming starts.

Apparently, I have been dead for two weeks.

I'm installed in the living room, in front of the gas fire, which is on full. My wet coat and boots have been spirited away and now I'm wearing two fleeces, thick cords and two pairs of socks. I'm wrapped in my old blue flowered quilt, which I thought had been thrown away.

I'm still cold. The air nips my face.

Low voices carry from the kitchen: Mum's, still sobbing a little, and the doctor's, slow and calm. There's the occasional shriek from the child – who tried to get into the living room with me but was hauled away – cut off by a sharp word from Katie. I can't hear what they're saying. But then I've heard it already.

'We cremated you last week,' Katie said to me, while my mother was crying down the phone to Dr Spencer. I laughed, but Katie wasn't smiling. 'We thought it was you.' Then Mum came back in, and clung to me again, and cried and cried.

I sat there, numb, as if I was never going to thaw. I actually felt relieved when Dr Spencer showed up, although I haven't been pleased to see the old bastard since he refused me the pill when I was sixteen. You had to hand it to him, though: within ten minutes of my mother telling him her dead daughter was sitting in her living room, he was knocking on the door, and the shocked look was gone from his dour face within seconds. 'It's yourself,' he said.

'So it would seem.'

'Where have you been for a fortnight?'

'In the mental hospital. Out in Lanarkshire.'

He nodded, and turned to Mum and Katie, who were hovering in the doorway as if afraid to cross the threshold. 'There must have been a mix-up,' he said, 'in Accident and Emergency.'

Mum said, 'But we identified her…' but Dr Spencer was already leading her away into the kitchen, murmuring about your eyes playing tricks when you're under stress, and no doubt rummaging in his bag for something nice and strong. I was left alone in this room.

It's different too. Last year, my Mum bought a leather Chesterfield-type suite, but the chair I'm sitting on is upholstered with worn, dark green fabric. The walls are ivory sponged with dark orange, at least as far as I can tell by the yellow overhead light. The windows have been covered with thick velvet, which is taped all around; draught excluders, made from old tights stuffed with more old tights, have been wedged along the bottom. There is not a chink of daylight to let in a draught, but the cold breathes in anyway, passing through the thick velvet as if it were handkerchief cotton. I pull the quilt up to my chin.

The mantelpiece is lined with framed pictures of pink babies and meringue wedding frocks. Mum's never gone in for that kind of portrait gallery, but here they all are. One of them, a wedding one, is bothering me slightly, but I'm not curious enough to leave my quilt-cocoon and investigate.

I pull out my phone and thumb it on. *NO SIGNAL.* The wind screams outside.

Footsteps scramble past the window, as if they're running to escape the wind. I hear the back door bang. There's more murmuring in the kitchen, and babbling from the kid, then the door bursts open. Another Arctic explorer – he pushes back the hood, and it's Jamie.

His hair is long. I saw him earlier today, at visiting time, and he'd had it cut close. But now it's straggling around his face, the same length as mine. And I can remember long hair framing his face, the tears freezing on his cheeks as I lay in the snow.

He's already kneeling beside me, his head on my shoulder, holding me so tight it hurts. 'Suzey. Suzey.'

'I don't know what's happened, Jamie,' I say.

'I don't care,' he says. 'I don't care.'

We sit like that for quite a while.

'The ambulance couldn't get through,' he says, at last. I push his head off my shoulder so I can see him. He doesn't look like he's talking to me. 'They said it was because the ambulance couldn't get through. But I didn't leave in time. I stayed on…'

His face is pale. Light brown hair trails around it. I can't take my eyes off it. 'How did you do that to your hair?'

There's a scratching at the door. The little girl bursts through, looking like she's just escaped and she's making the most of it. She's yelling, 'Da da da da da da!' She launches herself at Jamie, who catches her expertly and heaves her onto his lap. At the same time he's saying to me, 'What's that about my hair?'

I'm watching as he hoists her to his shoulder, fending her off absently as she grabs at his nose. 'Jamie,' I say, 'who's this kid?'

He looks afraid of me. 'What?'

'I don't know. I don't know who she is.' I start to cry, helplessly. 'Jamie. I really don't know. Who is she?'

He's nodding, gripping my hand. 'It's all right. It must be… amnesia or something. I'll get the doctor. No,' he says, as the child starts climbing towards me, 'leave Auntie Sue alone just now—'

The kid shrieks in protest. 'Dadda!'

Anny too… Auntie Sue. I stand up abruptly and grab the wedding picture from the mantelpiece. A big puffy dress almost fills the frame. Katie's head, crowned with flowers, sticks out the top. She is smiling. Beside her, standing carefully away from her skirts, is Jamie. With long hair. In a kilt. Holding her hand. Jamie.

I start to laugh. Jamie's reaching out to me. I hold out the photo. 'Katie?' I ask. '*Katie?*' It's a great joke. Any minute now he'll be laughing too.

But he doesn't. He's trying to take the picture away from me. His face is deadly serious, but it's still framed by that silly long hair. I laugh and laugh and laugh.

The door opens. The doctor's coming in. He's opening his bag.

Chapter 4

The dining room is full of afternoon light like chilly gold. No tears or quarrelling; I'm surrounded by low, almost musical voices. All in all, it's a beautiful day, and I'm thinking, my God, you two really need to lighten up. 'It's okay, really,' I say, again. 'It's fine.'

Carl, at least, attempts a smile. 'So he was like totally straight?'

'Straight. Married. To *Katie*, no less.' I laugh. People at the next table glance at me. The nurse leaning in the corner looks over. No laughing at visiting time! I laugh again. 'Talk about your worst nightmare.'

The main room is full today. Each of the tables has a little group huddled round it. By the window is Shaz, orange hair blazing in the sun, listening solemnly to her posh parents. She catches my eye; I smile and wave, but she looks away, with only the briefest of glances at Jamie. I can hardly blame her – my brother is looking at me like I've only got six months to live. 'God Almighty,' he says. 'What was that stuff?'

'I don't know. A sleeping potion? Temazepam? Hey, they're giving me free jellies!'

'They don't inject Temazepam any more.'

'Aye, well, you'd know.'

He doesn't smile. 'I'll ask the nurse about it.'

'She'll not give you any, Jamie.'

Still not a flicker. And this from the guy who's been off his face on something every other weekend for the past five years. 'God, Jamie, it's all right. I got a jag in the bum and had a wee dream, that's all.'

'It's not a wee dream if it seems that real.'

'It is if it's a wee trippy dream. And I feel fine now.' That's true. I feel better today than I have in months. Lighter. 'I'm really starting to feel better now.'

Carl's nodding. 'Antidepressants're starting to kick in,' he says, with a sidelong glance at Jamie. Translation: *Side-effects. Weird, but they'll wear off soon.* I let it pass; whatever keeps them happy. And Jamie is looking slightly relieved.

'The doctor didn't seem to think it was anything to worry about?' he asks.

'She didn't seem worried at all.' Dr Martin wouldn't look worried if I turned into the Human Fly on top of her desk, but I'm not about to tell him that. 'It's just drugs. Weird drugs. That's all.'

The electronic bell – the type that always makes you think you should be running off to double Maths – starts to ring. Some of the visitors are on their feet and have their coats on by the time the ringing stops; some stiffen their shoulders and stay seated. Jamie is one of the latter – in fact, he reaches across the table and takes my hand. Carl, who's now putting on his scarf, looks at him in faint surprise. I squeeze Jamie's hand. He looks as if he's about to say something, but I've spotted something sticking out of his coat pocket; the corner of a pastel-pink envelope. 'Is that for me? Gimme!'

'Oh, yeah.' He pulls out the Hallmark envelope and passes it across. 'It was dropped by the flat when we were out, I don't know who it's—'

'It's from Lewis.' The envelope says *To Suzey*, although if I didn't know the writing so well I would never have guessed. I laugh. 'I always said he should have been a doctor. His writing's worse than my shrink's.'

I'm still laughing, but Jamie is dithering over me like I've collapsed into tears. 'Want us to take it back?' he says. 'I'll tell him to fuck off if you want.'

'That wouldn't be helpful,' says Carl.

Jamie ignores him. 'Seriously, Suze. Be my pleasure.'

'My hero. No, it's okay.' I hug them one after the other. Jamie goes for a second bear hug and won't let go. My lovely brother; I've worried him. I probably shouldn't have told him any of that stuff, but today it just seemed too funny to keep to myself. 'Go on,' I say, 'it's past chucking-out time. Better run, or they'll lock you in with the other loonies.'

'Are you going to be okay?' His voice is muffled.

'Aye, I'll be fine. I'm off to see my dealer now anyway.' He stiffens again. 'I mean the doctor? Who gives me the nice drugs? It's a joke, Jamie?'

Finally, a smile. And then they're gone. I watch Jamie reach for Carl's hand as they leave the room; for a moment I want to call him back. But visiting time's over. The room is quiet now. I sit down and tear open the pink envelope.

There's no writing on the front of the card, just a cartoon cat in a hospital bed, a giant thermometer sticking out of its mouth. Inside, the printed message says *Get Well Soon*. Under that, in black biro, is scribbled *from Lewis*.

I laugh a little. A man of few words. I wish I'd opened the card while Jamie and Carl were still here, then I could have said it. I say it anyway: 'A man of few words'. It echoes in the empty room.

I put the card back in the envelope. Now it's time for my appointment.

Dr Martin is writing up her previous patient's notes. She says 'Good afternoon' into the other patient's file. I flop down into the chair; well, I guess I'll just start without her. 'Good afternoon to you too,' I say. 'Yes, I'm still feeling better, thank you so much for asking.'

She glances up. 'How did you sleep last night?'

'Oh, not bad. No one rammed a needle in my arse, anyway.'

She stabs a full stop into the file, snaps it shut and opens up another: mine, presumably. She reads for a moment. 'Any more vivid dreams?'

I burst out laughing. 'Did you really have to look that up in my notes just there? D'you have that many patients who travel to Narnia in their fucking sleep? Do you just think, oh, there goes another one? Better tick that one off on Susan's list of psycho symptoms?'

She's writing again. 'How do you feel today, Susan?'

I nearly fall off my chair. 'I'm sorry. I could've sworn you said "How do you feel". But you'd never say that, would you? I must be hallucinating again, mustn't I?' I squint at the page – I'm getting better at reading upside down – and burst out laughing again. 'Does that say manic?'

She glances up again. 'How *do* you feel, Susan?'

I point at her. 'Do you know what you are?' She doesn't respond, so I carry on. 'You are a person of few words. A person of few words. I think I've found you a new friend. Isn't that nice?' I'm still gripping the pink envelope; my thumb's made a smudge out of *Suzey*. I pull out the card and skite it across the desk. 'Here. Want it for the file?'

She looks at it, looks at me. I don't wait for her to say anything, what's the point? 'That's from Lewis. Remember Lewis? I'm sure I told you about him. Or maybe that was a vivid dream as well. No? He's the one who said we'd either get married or murder each other. We couldn't understand couples who split up and then said "Let's be friends." One of us would have to emigrate. We always said so.'

Dr Martin is looking steadily at me now. I'm still pointing, at the card now. 'Get Well Soon,' I say. My head is starting to hurt. 'From Lewis. This is after five years, you understand. That's all he's got to say to me. Get Well Soon from Lewis. Beautiful, isn't it?'

Suzey, wake up

Someone's calling me outside. But Dr Martin doesn't want me to answer, or even turn my head, because she's thrown something at me. Or maybe she just got up and stuck it in my forehead while I wasn't looking. What is it, a pen? I can feel it sinking in, painful. Cold.

Suze, can you hear me

I gape at Dr Martin. A chair screeches on the floor, and she's gone. There's nothing but light.

The light has dimmed to a dull yellow. I'm lying on my back. My face is cold, but the rest of my body is sweaty; I'm wrapped in fabric, tight as a parcel. Oh God, I think, they've got me in a straitjacket.

'Suzey, are you getting up?'

My mother's face is hanging over me. She looks tired, annoyed, and old. Her hair is white. She says, 'Are you going in to work today or not?'

I'm in my old single bed at my mother's house, wearing two layers of pyjamas. The bedcovers – a sheet, blanket and two duvets – are tucked in tight.

I struggle to sit up. My old flowered curtains are drawn. There's blackout behind them but it must have come loose, because there's line of white light at the far side. Bright light. Snow light.

'Suzey,' my mother's saying, 'do you hear me?'

Once again I burst out laughing. 'And we're back,' I say.

Chapter 5

I am disappointed by my office. It's no different at all. Really, I'd have thought I could do better than that.

The drug must be wearing off, at last.

I'm a little confused about the time frame, but I think it's been one week since I came back from the dead. Today is my first day back at work. Earlier this morning, I intended to skive off – what's the point of having the trippiest dream of your life if all you do in it is go to work? I was planning on doing nothing but sitting around the house and congratulating myself on my creative imagination. This was mostly because of the little girl.

Apparently, my mother watches her during the day, so she came tumbling through the back door while I was eating cornflakes in watery milk. Jamie floundered in after her, clumsy in what were presumably snowshoes, but looked like tennis rackets. Katie was right behind him. The sight of them together was still pretty bizarre to me, but the kid was pulling at my hand for attention, so without thinking I scooped her up onto my knee.

I'm apprehensive around small children, usually – they stare at you too hard, and I'm always afraid I'll drop them – but this one seemed different. She knelt up on my lap, straddling my leg; with any other kid I'd be afraid it looked like some sort of child molestation and make her turn round, but I wasn't uncomfortable at all. Of course, I remembered, she *was* different. She was a perfect composite of Jamie and Katie; or rather, her hair was from Katie's side, but in every other way she was ours. Our family's colouring, our eyes, our Dad's eyes, in perfect miniature, beaming back at me.

She could have been mine. And really, she *was* mine. Didn't I invent her? 'Hiya, beautiful,' I said. 'You're just gorgeous, aren't you?'

She giggled, and then gave me a slobbery kiss on the lips. I resisted the temptation to wipe my mouth, it might have upset her. I could hear the other three adults laughing around the table. We were a family; and here was the next generation to prove it. Stroking back the fine dark curls I said absently, 'What's her name?'

Silence. I looked up. Katie was staring at the table, Jamie looked worried, and my mother looked as if she didn't know whether to shout at me or cry. I felt chilly suddenly. This was a dream – they were meant to laugh with me. Or at least turn into giant squirrels or something. This just wasn't right. 'I… I don't remember,' I found myself saying. 'It's amnesia? The doctor said…'

After a moment Jamie said, 'Her name's Claire.'

'Claiwey!' yelled the kid, shoving at me. Pissed off because she wasn't the centre of attention any more. I smiled down at her, but then Katie said sharply, 'I think you'd better stay at home today, Suzey, don't you?'

I was about to agree, until I saw a single tear creep down my mother's face. She looked like she didn't even know it was there. I'd never seen her look like that in all my life. 'No,' I said, 'I'm going in to work.'

So that's where I went.

I pause in the middle of unzipping my parka, and look around. The Registry is not much different at all. It's noisier; the silent laser printers are gone, and old dot-matrix machines are rattling out streams of paper. The room seems dingy, like it hasn't been painted in a while, but that might just be the snow piling up against the windows. The windows bother me, for some reason, so I look away, and find that my colleagues are all staring at me.

They're not much different; paler, maybe, with more lines on their faces and grey in their hair. Their heavy clothes look like they came from a jumble sale, but these people dress like that anyway. Everyone seems more or less the same, except for Sara, the office trainee. I realise she's not there. Nor is her desk.

I look around for Katie, who walked here with me, but she's disappeared. Jamie came part of the way with us. Apparently he works in an office a few streets away. He doesn't work in the Terrence Higgins place here, but then I suppose he wouldn't. When he seemed to be following us to the University, I'd thought he must work beside me and Katie, and I laughed about how twee that would be. But I wish he was here now.

Hugh Munroe is in front of me. 'Susan,' he's saying, 'welcome back. We were glad to hear that the, um, rumours of your death were greatly exaggerated.'

'What?'

'Sorry.' His laugh is nervous. 'You know, Mark Twain – "Rumours of my death have been greatly exaggerated"?'

'I've never read any Mark Twain.'

'Oh, well, it doesn't—'

'How could I know that? I've never heard it before.'

'It doesn't matter, Susan—'

'Excuse me.' I hurry out of the room. The parka is so huge I can hardly move; the air is cold, but I still wrench down the zip and let the coat drop to the floor. I'm making for the stairs. I'm thinking, nonsensically, Carl. I'll go and see Carl.

I'm at the door to Carl's office. I don't know what to do. On the way up here I met two people who told me rumours of my death had been greatly exaggerated (in future I'm avoiding the English Lit department) but that's not what's bothering me. The door is locked, but that's not it either. What's worrying me is the name on the door: *Dr Albert Hughes*.

I've wandered twice round the department, checking all the doors. No sign of Carl at all.

There is no way I would write Carl out of my dream world. Is there?

He must be around somewhere. Perhaps Earth Sciences has been expanded into another building? Yes, that must be it. The secretary will tell me where he is. I hurry along to the departmental office.

The office is drab and colourless, and empty of people. One corner has been partitioned off by a bank of filing cabinets and the secretary's neat workstation has been replaced by an oversized desk topped with a yellowish computer screen. The printer is even more geriatric than the ones downstairs. Worst of all, the colour posters have been replaced by yards of printout, clustered around two maps of the British Isles. The only colour left in this room is in the thick bands traced around the coastlines. In the first map the tracing is red – in the second it's blue.

The white snow light throws the window arch into sharp relief. There's something about this window, too… I wander over and look out. From here, you can see most of the university. Clearly the sandblasting schemes haven't happened here – the place looks more Gormenghast than ever, black under its icing of snow. Beyond the clock tower I can see the motorway, usually a river of cars at this time of day, now a crawling line behind a snowplough. Frigid air breathes over me as if I were outside; the window, like the ones in the Registry, has never been double-glazed.

'Can I help you?'

'Christ!' I jump about a foot in the air. Dazzled by the light, I peer into the corner. Someone is sitting at a desk in the corner walled off by cabinets. While I'm frantically reviewing my actions over the past few minutes (any arse-scratching/farting/nose-picking? No, thank God) the someone is standing and coming towards me. 'Sorry,' he's saying.

It's Raj Chaudhury. He's wearing a brown suit. He's thinner, and his smile looks slightly carnivorous. 'Sorry,' he says again. 'It's Suzey, isn't it? Suzey... McPherson? You were declared dead?'

'It's Pherson.' I'm still cross about being startled. 'And yes, rumours of my death *have* been greatly exaggerated. I was just... missing.'

I wait for the curious stare, but he just nods. 'I'm glad to hear it.'

An awkward silence stretches out. 'I'm looking for Dr Trainor,' I say.

'Who?'

'Carl Trainor? He works here.' Oh God, not the blank look again. 'He's maybe in another building? Or off campus or something?'

'I don't think so...' I must look close to tears, because he adds hastily, 'But I'll check.' He goes to the secretary's PC and taps at the keys. I perch on a wooden chair behind him, so I can watch the monitor. I'm expecting to see the university system's bright red screen but instead, after a sequence of painful grinding noises, up pops a version of Windows I haven't seen since I was twelve. Raj doesn't seem to find anything amiss, he just clicks on an icon marked *STAFF* and says, 'What's the full name?'

As I spell it he types the name into a text box, waits for the computer to catch up then hits *SEARCH*. 'It'll take a little while,' he says. And by God, he's not kidding. After a full minute I notice a blue band creeping one millimetre at a time across the bottom of the screen. I let my eyes wander around the room, across the printouts and the maps, to Raj's cramped little space behind the filing cabinets. I'm pleased to see that the Wild Wolf photograph is hanging above his desk. 'I love that photo,' I say.

He looks surprised again, but this time pleased as well. 'I'm glad to hear it. I thought I was the only one.'

I remember hundreds of people admiring that picture. I say, carefully, 'Wouldn't it get much better light over there somewhere?' I wave a hand towards the place I last saw the photo, now covered by the blue-rimmed map.

He smiles, rather bitterly. 'Yes, it would. But of course that would mean the department standing by its principles rather than pandering to lunatic beliefs. I am *allowed* to keep the picture so long as I hide it if the press come round.'

I have no idea what he's talking about, but I'm not risking embarrassing myself again. While the computer chugs away, I stare at the wall in Raj's little space. Close to the wolf photo, mostly hidden by a filing cabinet, there's the pale wooden side of a picture frame. 'So you've got the Ragnarok one hidden away too?' I say.

'*What?*'

Shit. 'The, um – the painting—' I push my chair back so I can point it out, but mostly so I can retreat from the stare he's giving me. Now I can see some of the painting itself, solid black lines of various heights. It's a charcoal drawing of the University, nothing like the giant wolf's-head cloud. 'Oh,' I say. 'Sorry. I'm thinking of something else—'

'How do you know about that?'

'About what?'

'My painting. *Ragnarok.* The great wolf devouring the sun. That's what you've seen?'

Maybe he's put it in an art gallery or something? 'Yes, maybe I've…'

'That painting has never been out of my flat,' Raj says. 'No one has seen it.'

'It must have been a different one. Maybe it's a popular subject—'

'I assure you it isn't.'

There's a beep from the computer. The screen says *C(ARL) TRAINOR: NOT FOUND*. Raj's hand lands on my arm. 'Suzey,' he says, 'how can you have seen my painting?'

I pull away, standing so quickly I hear the chair tip over behind me. 'Get off me. Do you think I fucking broke into your house or something?'

'No, I don't—'

'Just leave me alone!' Heading for the door, I stumble over the chair and bang my shin, hard. It hurts. Dreams aren't meant to hurt.

'Suzey!' He's coming after me.

I want to wake up now. I fling open the door and step out into the corridor, slamming the door behind me.

'I want to wake up now,' I say. 'Wake up, wake up, wake up—' I'm leaning over the banister. The drop is trying to pull me in.

The door opens behind me. Raj says, 'You should come back inside.'

I think about going back to work at the Registry, and turn around instead. Raj leaves the door open and takes care to sit a few yards away, as if I were a skittish cat. I feel colossally stupid. I should go home… home to my family who think I'm the walking dead.

To my mortification, I'm starting to cry. 'Sorry,' I croak.

'It's all right.' It doesn't seem to be all right, though – he's up and turning his back to me. But no, he's clicking on an ancient kettle, pouring, setting a mug down in front of me. I take a sip of the hot sweet tea, perfect for shock and distress. I start to cry even harder. 'I feel so bad,' I wail. I sound like Clairey, but I don't care. 'If this is a dream, why does it feel so *bad*?'

'If what is a dream?'

'This.' He's looking at me questioningly, so I tell him everything – about the hospital, the snow, Jamie. Like the tears, it seems it all has to come out.

When I'm done there's a pause, filled only by the tick of the cooling kettle. I'm trying to mop up my face with a soggy tissue. Then Raj says, carefully, 'So you come from another world?'

I burst into (rather snottery) laughter. He looks so serious. Why does everyone have to humour me? 'You sound just like my shrink. And my brother, and my mother. Why can't you just say "Christ you're a loony" and be done with it?'

'And nothing's different there?' He's not listening. 'There's been no Change?'

'You mean this?' I wave a hand at the snow piled on the window ledge. 'No.'

'And no flooding. No warming. Nothing like that?'

'Well, there's been floods. A couple of years ago Paisley Road was blocked off at the—'

'But no encroachment. No flooding of coastal towns?'

'That's *happened*? Where?'

'Coastal areas. Largs. Places like that. The streets fill up in the high season.' He's waving a hand impatiently. 'The flooding's extensive.'

Still reeling from the image of Largs as the Venice of the North, I don't catch what he says next. 'Sorry, what?'

'The Gulf Stream.' He's looking at the two maps of Britain on the wall. 'Is it still intact?'

I'm having a memory of a geography class, staring at the back of Alison

McGuire's neck in catatonic boredom, cringing at the teacher's wild-eyed enthusiasm, catching only the odd phrase. 'The Gulf Stream… What keeps our country warm… The "hot tap" of the British Isles.' Now I look up at the two versions of Britain: one outlined in warm red, the other in cold blue.

It's a before-and-after picture.

We are as far north as Canada or Siberia, and now our hot tap has been turned off. 'What happened?' I whisper.

'I can direct you to entire conferences on the subject.'

'So you don't know?'

'I have my theories.'

'Like what?' I'm going for a light tone of voice, but I'm still looking at the snow beyond the window, and the word comes out sounding savage. 'Ragnarok?'

He smiles, shaking his head. 'Ragnarok is eternal darkness. This would be Fimbulwinter. The time of terrible winter.'

I laugh. 'Aren't you meant to be all rational and scientific about this sort of stuff?'

'Aren't you meant to be dead?'

Touché. 'I'm not dead, though, am I. I'm just *ill*. I'm just *deluded*.'

He's looking careful again. 'I don't want to contradict anything you've been told. I'm not a doctor.'

'You're doing a lot better than my doctor.' He's talking to me, for a start. 'So what do you think? Am I a loony or what?'

He regards me for a moment. 'Yes,' he says at last. 'You are a deeply disturbed young woman, Suzey.'

There's another long pause. And then we both burst out laughing. I pick up a handful of paperclips and throw them at him. 'You evil bastard.'

'Sorry.'

'Sorry's not good enough. Put the kettle on and I'll maybe forgive you.'

Good as gold, he heads off for the kettle. I stretch out on my seat, getting comfy, absurdly reassured to have met someone even more insane than I am.

Chapter 6

I ask to go home early; Jamie's office runs a bus to the South Side to get the workers home, and I could do with a lift. Everyone agrees, smiling brightly, although I was away from my desk half the morning talking to Raj. They didn't even ask where I was. 'You get off home,' Hugh says. 'Take care of yourself.'

In other words, fuck off and be weird somewhere else. Well, I daresay the novelty of working with Lady Lazarus will wear off eventually. And of course, I remind myself, I'm dreaming: what's the point in being offended by a dream? So I pile on the heavy clothes and make my escape.

It's barely four o'clock, but it's already dark. The steps outside the uni aren't lit at all, so I cling to the banister as I hurry down, and then cross the footbridge over the frozen burn at a brisk trot. By the time I emerge onto the comparatively well-lit street (only every second streetlamp is working), the snow has stopped, but the Arctic wind immediately swoops me up again; I have to cower in a doorway while I wrap my scarf around my nose and mouth. The walk to the street where Jamie works should only take five minutes, but after ten I'm only halfway there.

I don't like this. It's much too real. The cold is much too real; it hurts, it stings, I can hardly breathe. The wind roars and shoves like a bully, sending me thumping into a wall. A little cry escapes me, but the huddled figures scurrying past pay no attention; in these conditions you don't lift your face to the wind for anything less than a dying scream. Every street feels a mile long.

I'm near a familiar shop: Ali's. I duck inside. I want a newspaper anyway. The shop is much the same as I recall: shelves of beans, biscuits, shoe polish, nails, bleach, and everything else you can think of. The only difference is that the counter has been moved to the back; I remember it being right by the door, but that's obviously too cold. Even at the back, Ali is wearing a thick fleece, a scarf and fingerless gloves, and is rubbing his hands together vigorously. He nods to me. 'All right?'

I unwind enough facial wrapping to answer him. 'Hi, have you got a *Herald*?'

He shakes his head. 'Only the *Standard*.' He points to a tabloid on the counter. I've never heard of it. I turn it towards me, and the headline almost jumps off the page: *SAVAGED*. And, in smaller letters,

Second Wolf Cult Killing.

'Second?' I say, without thinking.

He nods. 'Aye. Another one. Terrible, isn't it?'

I scan the article. *Body of an unknown young woman… mutilated… unidentifiable… experts confirm victim was torn apart by wolves.*

'I didn't think wolves really did stuff like that,' I say.

'No' just the wolves by themselves but, was it?'

Skin painted with strange symbols… runes… occult… human sacrifice. Christ, that's sick. How could I possibly dream up this stuff…?

But I give myself a shake: no self-analysis while the guy's waiting for his money. I dig out some coins and pick up the paper. Clumsy in my huge mittens, I catch it by the turned-up corner, so that the first page flutters open. I glance at page two, see a photo, and groan. Him, of all people…

Matthew McLean. Evangelist and all-round queer basher. His bluff, no-nonsense face is gazing seriously into the camera. The caption below reads, *Reverend McLean condemns 'work of Satan'*. 'God almighty,' I say. 'Don't tell me *he's* here as well.'

'Mr McLean? Aye, he's in all the papers these days.' I've always known Ali as a dyed-in-the-wool liberal. But now his voice is indulgent, almost warm. 'He's got his own column in the *Standard* now, have you seen it?'

'A column?' Sure enough, under the photo it says *Comment: page 15*. I flick through the pages until I find the same picture, under the banner *VOICE IN THE WILDERNESS*. It's more than a column, this 'wilderness' voice has almost half a page to itself. It says:

Sacrificed to Satan
Another Life Lost to Odin

...

Our city grieves for another young life lost: thrown to the wolves.

There can be no doubt that this young woman met a terrible death at the hands of Odinists, cultists devoted to the worship of the so-called god Odin.

Odin was the 'god' of the Vikings, worshipped in bloodthirsty rituals of perverted sex and mass human sacrifice, often involving children.

Odin's followers believed they would gain magical powers by carrying out these murders. They still believe it today.

Make no mistake - the priests and wizards of Odin are among us again.

Decent people of all faiths have always rejected Odinism. Only the wicked are attracted to this cult – among them Hitler and his Nazi thugs. The Fascists were encouraged to worship Odin, using Odin's symbols, the wolf and the raven.

Yet now Odinists claim they have the 'right to worship' this devil 'god'. And many foolish people would like us to turn a blind eye in the name of tolerance.

But the people of Scotland are wiser than this. We know that such cruelty is not the work of a 'god', but of Satan.

Odin is, therefore, none other than the Devil himself.

So I say to you, be vigilant and guard your children. The cult of Odin is very real. And it will kill again.

Be sober, be watchful: your adversary the Devil, as a roaring lion, walketh about, seeking whom he may devour.

(1 Peter 5:8)

This is *journalism?* 'But that's rubbish,' I say. 'Magic powers from Odin? Does anyone actually believe this stuff?'

Ali shrugs. 'Those people believe it,' he says. 'The Odinists.'

'We don't know that.'

He nods firmly. 'They do. Sick bastards. They believe it.'

Suddenly I don't want to walk home alone, and not just because of the cold. 'Well,' I say reluctantly, 'I'd better be off.'

'Safe home.'

I head off back into the cold, moving quicker this time.

Jamie's not in his office, even though the rest of the bus passengers are. 'You've just missed him,' the receptionist says. She's giving me the wide-eyed stare I've come to recognise. Without thinking, I dip into my pocket for my mobile: *NO SIGNAL.* I remember that Jamie – like most people here – doesn't bother to carry a phone any more. The receptionist's eyes are wider than ever. I put the useless mobile back in my pocket and hurry outside again.

Breathing in the warm wool of my scarf, I look up and down the street; sure enough, there's the back of a familiar parka receding downhill. I expose my face and yell, but I haven't a hope against the wind. There's nothing for it but to set off after him.

The going's not too bad here: the snow's been shovelled into a two-foot bank of brown slush to my right, so the pavement is pretty clear. I could walk quite quickly if I didn't have to lean into the wind like a stupid mime. As it is I can just keep up with Jamie – he's used to this I suppose. When I have to pull down the scarf to breathe (and I'm trying not to) I call him again, but he still doesn't turn.

Where the hell is he going, anyway? We're now heading down Gibson Street, which isn't on the way home. He slides down the last few feet, dodges a slush bank and hurries across the road. I follow gingerly, trying to grip the icy path with my toes (through my boots and three pairs of socks). By the time I cross Gibson Street he's turning left onto the bottom of University Avenue, and by the time I've struggled up there he's heading for Kelvin Way, through the park.

God, he's not off for a fumble in the park, is he? But then I remember Katie, the meringue wedding dress, Clairey. He's straight. Besides, I can't imagine anyone being desperate enough to fumble out here. It'd snap off.

The park is unlit, as usual, but I can see a faint glow from the drifts of white. There don't seem to be as many trees as usual. The wind sweeps white powder across the open spaces like a desert storm. I pull down my scarf, drag in a lungful of the bitter cold and scream, 'Jamie!' Still he doesn't turn around – that hood must be bloody soundproofed. And now the snot in my nose is freezing. Thanks very much, Jamie.

He's turning off to the right now. Up ahead, looking lopsided with only one wing lit up, is Kelvingrove Art Gallery and Museum. I follow, although I'm now thinking seriously about going for that bus. He can't be going to the museum, it shuts at five. And right now I want to be inside somewhere – anywhere with heating. Jamie is walking up the middle of the road, along the narrow cleared track. Ignoring the possibility of cars, I follow him.

By the time Jamie is climbing the steps to the main door, I can see lights on inside. The glass door swings out and two bundled-up figures emerge. I wonder briefly if Jamie is here to meet them, but he passes them without a glance and they set off in the opposite direction. Jamie catches the glass door before it shuts and disappears inside. Half running – even if I fall on my arse it can't hurt as much as this freezing gale – I follow.

I catch a whiff of stale piss even before the door has swung shut behind me. Of course, I don't care, at least it's warm. I pause for a moment to pull down my scarf and push back my hood. The light is dimmer than I recall it, yellower. The museum looks dingy. Then I realise why – it hasn't been renovated. The shiny twenty-first century hallway is gone. We're back with the dusty Victorian sepia.

The stuffed animals, those nightmares of Edwardian taxidermy, are back in pride of place. The marble tiles are dull, stained with brown watery footprints. I cross to the middle of the great hallway, and look up. The upstairs galleries are in darkness; I'm sure I see a movement, but it may just be shadow. Jamie has disappeared.

Canteen sounds – plates rattling, steam hissing – are echoing around the great hallway. I turn towards the sound of footsteps and see a man in a dull green Council overcoat emerge from a door to the right. He is middle-aged and frowning. He sees me and looks suspicious, but this must be his usual expression, because he just nods and looks away. Then two men, one forty-ish, one younger, appear from the left. They are wearing heavy coats, tightening scarves and hoods as they pass. They ignore the other man and me. Cold buffets me as they go out. Council Coat watches them go, *tshhh*–ing angrily between his teeth. He catches my eye and shakes his head. Whatever's pissing him off, he wants to talk about it. I smile and hurry off to the right, towards the Natural History section, towards the café.

The ancient exhibits are back, all the model dinosaurs and glass-eyed stuffed animals. The canteen sounds are getting louder: the old café is back where I remember it. I'm wondering what on earth would induce Jamie to come here. Dad used to drag us here sometimes on Sundays, and neither of us ever liked it.

Outside the café, I stop at the foot of the grand staircase leading up to the art galleries. Its sweeping effect is rather spoiled by the metal barriers along the first step. No art appreciation permitted tonight, it seems.

Inside the café, the small round tables are chipped and bashed. Two youngish women in blue sweatshirts are moving between them. The less-than-fresh smell is getting stronger. It seems to be coming from a man sitting near the door, mumbling into a mug of weak tea. I look around the room – everyone seated is shabby, filthy, the differences of age and sex and colour erased. Someone I can't see is crying loudly.

Now one of the sweatshirted women is approaching me. She is very young, and wearing the super-bright smile of someone who's gone right through overworked and exhausted and out the other side. 'Hi!' she says, 'Would you like to come in?'

'Er, no—'

'Are you sure? Would you not like a wee cuppy tea?'

'No, I'm just looking for somebody.'

'Oh, aye?' Then someone starts bellowing on the other side of the room. The girl makes a mock-tragic face as if an infant is crying over a dropped toy. 'Oh dear. Best get on, eh?'

I hurry off and leave her to it. I make my way back through the dinosaur room and out, this time, at the foot of a side staircase. There's a barrier here too, but it's been moved forward at one side. No one's around. I don't want to go out in the cold yet, but I don't want to go back to the smells and bellowing either. I step past the barrier and start to climb the stairs.

The first-floor gallery lights are still out. The overhead light makes striped shadows on the floor. I move in close to the wall, trying to move softly in my heavy boots, and follow the corridor until I come to a pair of glass doors. They are closed but not locked. From inside the darkened room I can hear small animal sounds: unmistakeable. I start to move away.

'RIGHT!'

I am halfway down the stairs, and jump so hard I nearly fall down the rest of them. Yellow light glares out through the glass doors.

'YE DIRTY FUCKIN' BASTARTS!'

With near-miraculous speed another door opens and two figures are out and hurrying away. Then on the other side of the balcony, three more slip downstairs. Then ten yards up the corridor, more glass doors swing back and four more men emerge. The first one's a Bowie's regular. He rushes past me, taking the stairs three at a time. Then two more come out – and the first one's Jamie.

He sees me and stops dead. The man behind him, a younger guy in a red quilted coat, puts his hand on Jamie's shoulder to push him aside. The brightly lit doors beside me are flung open, and out comes Council Coat, roaring about 'GETTING THE FUCKIN' POLIS ON YE!'

I grab Jamie's arm, smile my brightest smile and trill, 'It's okay! They're with me!' Before the man can answer I grab hold of a red-quilted sleeve and start dragging both of them away. 'C'mon, yous two, downstairs now! Let's go and get a cuppy tea!'

All three of us clatter downstairs, with a shout of 'DIRTY WEE BASTARTS!' echoing after us. I'm giggling by the time I reach the bottom, but they aren't. We all go straight outside with our coats still undone. The sudden cold and dark shock me into silence. The guy in the red jacket pulls away from my hand and bolts as if I were the polis. Jamie sets off in the other direction; I stop to do up my coat, but he grabs me, hard enough to hurt, and pulls me away.

I remember this place as a wine bar. It's changed to (or, presumably, stayed as) a spit-and-sawdust pub. Actually I like it this way. There's an old-fashioned snug, with wooden booths, and you can get a whisky-and-water for less than a month's salary. I'm making a start on my second one as Jamie squeezes into the corner booth opposite me. He looks as if he's just thrown up, but he still knocks his whisky back in one.

But still, I can't help grinning. It's Jamie; he's back. . 'I should've known,'

I say. 'You. Mr Heterosexual. Didn't think so, somehow.'

He's watching me warily. 'I'm not getting the lecture, then?'

'What lecture?'

He laughs shortly. 'The think-of-your-wife-and-child one, for a start.'

'I never said that.' God, am I really like that in this world?

'Maybe not. But you should've.'

'Look.' I lean in, whispering. 'You're gay. You can't help that. You're not going to change that.'

'I love her,' he says very quietly.

'Clairey?'

'I love *Katie*.' Does he mean it? He looks like he does. 'And Claire. I love them. You'll not say anything?'

'Course not.' We're quiet for a long time. I'm still trying to make sense of it. Katie. But maybe kids do change things. 'Aye well,' I sigh, 'I suppose what she doesn't know willnae hurt her.'

He doesn't say anything. But there's something, a flicker…

'Jamie? You're being careful, aren't you?'

I meant is he being discreet, not trying to get off with his wife's brother or anything, but he keeps staring down into his empty glass, and I start to think it's much worse. 'Jamie,' I say at last, 'you're using condoms, aren't you?'

'When I can get them.'

'Jesus Christ, Jamie!'

'I keep her safe,' he says fiercely. 'I'm not stupid…'

'What about *you* being safe?' He doesn't answer. I take his hand. It's still cold. 'Jamie. Promise me. You won't take risks with those guys. You know what I mean.'

'I don't,' he says softly. 'I don't fuck every one of them, y'know. Or I only do it when I've a condom.'

I think he really believes that. I try to believe it too. 'I couldn't stand it without you,' I say. 'I couldn't bear to lose you.'

He takes my hand. We sit like that for quite a while.

Part Two
City of Wolves

....

In Scotland, you can't believe how strong the
homosexuals are. It's just unbelievable... (Scotland)
could go right back to the darkness very easily.

...

Pat Robertson
700 Club, Christian Broadcasting Network
May 18 1999

Chapter 7

A fugue state.

That's what I've been going into, apparently. No one's told me so, and Dr Martin is as close-mouthed as ever, but the nurses and the med students suffer from the common delusion that mental illness damages the hearing; they talk about my case right in front of me. They shuffle through acres of clipboard paper, reading out phrases: dissociative disorder... derealisation... identity disorder. Partial amnesia.

And fugue state.

I don't mind. The word has a pleasant sound. Fugue. Fyoooooogue. I tell Dr Martin so, and she just looks at me like I'm a lab rat. So I ask her directly: 'What does fugue state mean anyway?'

She is surprised into a straight answer. 'Blackouts. Periods of functional amnesia. But that isn't necessarily what's happening to you.'

'Then what is happening to me?'

She doesn't answer, of course. Because she has no idea. How could she? This morning I'm here in the mild winter sunshine. Yesterday I was wading home through heavy snow. I laugh to think just how little idea she has.

Then suddenly she says, 'A consultant will be visiting us over the next few weeks. Mister Lisbon.' That's how she says it: *Mister* Lisbon, with an undertone of reverence. 'Has anyone mentioned it to you?'

They have. The med students practically fall to their knees at the mention of him. 'The *Top Man* for the district,' they told me: you could hear the capital letters.

'When's he coming?' I ask.

'We don't know.' Dr Martin sounds faintly pained. 'He favours surprise visits.'

They said that too. Turns up out of the blue: you never know the minute. 'Does he want to talk to me?'

'I suspect you're the reason he's coming, Suzey.'

'That's very flattering. I'll practice my curtsey.'

She doesn't smile. 'Do I have your permission to discuss your case with him?'

'Do you need my permission?'

'Of course.'

'All right.' I shrug. 'I'll try to be here.'

'You'll be here, Suzey.'

I laugh at her confidence. 'You have no idea. I could be miles away.'

She looks at me for a long moment. Then she starts to write again. 'I'm increasing your medication, Suzey. We'll get you feeling more settled.'

I'm still laughing about this when I'm out in the corridor.

That night a new pill appears in my white paper cup. I sneak a look at the bottle. *Clozaril.*

The nurses say they don't know what it's for.

I don't mind. I just close my eyes and sleep…

And wake up standing in deep snow.

I'm just outside the university, although it must be a lot later than five o'clock. More like seven or eight. Perhaps I've been working late, or seeing Raj. My immediate past is wide open. I laugh, and slide all the way down the hill like a kid.

Better get home, though.

I decide to make my way via the Clydeside. River Street actually leads away from the river; not the quickest way, but it's snowploughed twice a day so it's easier underfoot. And almost all of the streetlights work. I find the small pass through the range of ploughed snow on the kerbside, and step through gingerly onto the almost-black road.

Now I'm exposed to the cold that comes off the river. Strange how something frozen solid can breathe out cold like this. My nose and cheeks begin to ache instantly. I stop to rewrap my scarf securely over my mouth and nose – a moment's touch of ice on my bare face, then it's covered again. The smell of wool is suffocating, but I figure I can do my breathing later. Unfortunately I can't cover my eyes, so I lower my head and push through the cold as if I were fighting against a gale, although the night is still.

After a minute my lungs are starting to hitch, so I tug the scarf slightly away from my face and drag in the air as fast as possible, hoping to heat it up by the time it reaches my mouth. I succeed, partially. Then I carry on, clumping along the icy tarmac and thinking warm grateful thoughts about the thick gripping soles of my boots. In another few minutes I have to do the coming-up-for-air thing again; then I retie my scarf.

All this of course I do without raising my eyes. After a few minutes, a pale shape comes into my line of vision, trotting towards me, no more than ten yards away.

I stop dead. It stops too, and looks at me. There is no way this is a dog. The legs are too long. Its eyes are pale, the shade indeterminate in the cold light, but not a dog's warm chocolate brown. I've seen wolves before, loping around their enclosure in the zoo. They were well cared for, but they still looked thin. There was raw meat on the ground but still they circled, moving easily in a pack, eyes bright and tongues lolling. Their fur was short and sleek.

But the wolf in front of me is shaggy as a bear, dark grey about its head and flanks, white all down its lanky legs. It's carrying something, some light-coloured fabric—

It's holding a baby in its mouth.

I hear myself make a whimpering noise. There is warmth spreading between my legs, and some distant part of me is wishing I'd gone for a pee before I left the uni.

The baby is wrapped tightly in a blanket; the wolf has hold of it by the leg. There is nothing behind me but a mound of snow and a blank wall. The wolf is still looking at me. It shakes its head just a little, to get a better grip, and its jaws make a gnashing sound. There is a horrible cry, *Maaa-maaa*! Now I hear myself scream, high-pitched and girly, not my voice at all.

The wolf leaps backwards on all fours, like a lamb. The baby clatters to the ground, the blanket falls across its twisted legs. The wolf turns and canters away, pausing to glance back at me once before turning towards the river and disappearing through the bank of snow.

I don't want to look at what's on the ground in front of me. I concentrate on getting out my mobile, fumbling to switch it on – still *NO SIGNAL*, but that's all right, I'll run. I'll turn and run, I'll get help… Then there's another *Maaa-maaa*! I look at the baby. Yellow curls, rosebud smiling lips. Eyes closed. Flowery frock with one sleeve torn off, so the join between the arm and shoulder is visible. I step forward, grasp the plastic arm and lift; there's an obliging *Maaa-maaa*! and a click as the blue eyes roll open.

'Oh, thank fuck. Fuck's sake…' My voice trails off into laughter. I look up the road after the wolf. 'You stupid fucker. What did you want a doll for, for God's sake? Christmas present?'

Still holding the doll, I go to where the wolf disappeared into the snow bank. There's a dip in the snow, and beyond that a broken place in the wall. I climb over and look out over the river. After a moment I can make out a grey shape moving across the ice. The wolf stops and looks back at me, resentfully, or so it seems. 'What the fuck did you think you were doing?' I call after it. 'You're meant to be in the fucking Highlands!' It ducks its head and carries on, disappearing into the darkness on the north side of the river.

I'm still warm and squishy. I've pissed myself. Very fucking heroic, Suzey. When I get home I'll have to go straight upstairs before anyone sees me. My legs are still shaking.

It takes a long time to walk home.

Fortunately, when I fall through the door, there's no one in the kitchen but Clairey. She sees the doll I'm still clutching and her eyes widen with childish greed. 'Dowwy!'

'Dolly,' I agree, shoving the doll into her grasping little hands and fleeing upstairs. I hear Mum call hello, but I don't stop. I make it to the bathroom and lock the door before I hear Katie's shriek from downstairs. She must have found the teeth marks in her daughter's new toy. But I ignore her, strip off my bottom layer of clothes, throw them into the bath and wrap a threadbare towel around my middle. Only then, with voices calling my name and footsteps on the stairs, do I let myself sit down hard on the floor and start shaking.

Next morning I wake up with a jump. Something was chasing me in my dream, but I've already forgotten what.

I look up and find I'm still in my own single bed, surrounded by my old posters and familiar wallpaper. The tip of my nose is freezing. I squint at my alarm clock; it's half ten on a Saturday morning, and I'm looking forward to another wonderful day of washing in cold water and staring out at the snow. Only one thing for it: I'm going back to sleep.

No luck. My face is freezing, my bladder is full and my stomach's empty. I reach out from under the covers, drag my tracksuit trousers under the duvet and struggle into them. My fleece and dressing gown are too far away, so it's up into that bracing air to pile on as many clothes as I can find and make a run for the bathroom. I hop and skip across the floor tiles, baring as little flesh as possible to do my business – it's like pulling down your pants on an ice-rink – before finally hurrying downstairs into the warmth of the kitchen.

I can hear Katie's voice in the living room. Doesn't she ever go home? While I'm buttering the toast there's the usual Eric Morecambe scrabbling about at the bottom of the curtains, and Clairey emerges, holding the doll by its punctured leg. When she's sure I'm watching she cradles it in her arms and starts rocking it rather violently, crooning, '*Baby* baby, *baby* baby, *baby* baby…'

'Hiya wee mummy,' I say.

She giggles happily. 'Baby!'

'Is that your baby?'

'Ma baby!'

'She's a lovely baby.' Right, that's my conversation exhausted. 'Come and we'll go into the living room and show Mummy and Granny?'

'Yeah!' Off she goes. I follow, looking down at her dark silky head, once again feeling absurdly pleased with myself, as if I've gotten a wild animal to trust me. She barges into the room ahead of me and rushes across to my mother, who is sitting by the fireside with, not to put too fine a point on it, a face like fizz. Clairey must see this, because she veers off towards Katie. Bad move: as soon as Katie sees her, she grabs hold of the doll and starts tugging. 'No! Leave it! Dirty!'

Clairey shrieks as the doll is pulled away from her. Then there's that three-second silence while she sucks gallons of air into her lungs, and then the screaming starts. My God, you could record it and use it as a fire bell.

My mother speaks over the howling to me. 'Oh, *there* you are.'

I know this voice: it means she thought of something to say to me hours ago, while I was 'still in my lazy bed', and wasn't clairvoyant enough to hear her in my dreams. 'Forgot the toast,' I call, and go back into the kitchen to wait till the kettle's boiled.

When I finally return, we're at the stage of heart-rending sobs and reaching pathetically towards the high shelf where the doll has been deposited. A tear-stained face is turned to me beseechingly – '*Bay-beee!*' I look at Katie but she's staring at the fire again. 'I'll wash the damn doll for you, if you like,' I say, as pleasantly as I can manage.

Katie gets up, takes the doll and thrusts it at Claire. 'Here!' In the sudden silence, I realise I've walked into an Atmosphere. My mother is glaring at me. 'I don't suppose *you've* seen your brother?'

'No, I've not. Why?'

'*Why?* Why do you think?'

Oh, my God. I lift Claire onto my lap, to cover a moment's silence. 'How should I know?'

''Cause he's buggered off. Again.' I keep very quiet. 'Since first thing this morning. Not a word since.'

'He'll not have gone far,' says Katie, apologetically.

'That's nothing to do with it. This is getting beyond a joke.'

'He works hard. He's allowed to meet up with his pals at the weekend.'

There didn't seem to be anything weighted about that statement. I relax a little. Besides, she's probably right, he wouldn't go off cottaging in the morning, would he?

'Don't keep making excuses for him,' Mum's saying. 'This isn't nineteen-canteen. He's to take the burden off you once in a while.'

She looks to me as if for confirmation. I get the sudden impression that this conversation happens regularly; and what's more, it's usually three-sided. 'Well, he does work hard,' I mumble.

They both look at me in surprise. What the hell do I usually say to them? Whose side do I take? 'But it's still not right though.'

I've always assumed Katie was one of the old school of Glaswegian females, who expect their menfolk to come and go like cats. But now there are tears in her eyes, and I haven't been so shocked since I saw their wedding picture. 'I just wish I knew where he went,' she whispers.

I get very busy straightening Clairey's clothes. After a while Mum says, 'He'll need to pull his socks up, that's all.'

'I'll have a word with him,' I say.

A surprise again, but this time from Katie: a smile. 'Thanks. He'll take it coming from you.'

'I'm his big sister,' I say. 'He'll not dare do anything else.'

We all laugh a little. Then Katie, smiling and a bit embarrassed, mutters something about the kettle and goes out. I start re-buttoning Claire's cardigan, although it doesn't need it. Mum's eyes are drilling into my head, but I'm not going to look up. How much does she know?

'Oh God!' Katie's voice makes us all jump. She's still out in the hall. I think she's found a condom in his coat pocket. Then I remember Jamie's not here, so his coat can't be either. When Katie comes back in, she's pointing to the newspaper in her hand. 'Look!'

She holds it out to me. Clairey slides off my lap, apprehends the paper for a second before it's whipped away. 'Doggy!'

It's the *Standard*. I take it reluctantly, feeling the oily newsprint rubbing off on my fingers. On the front page is a picture of a snarling wolf, with bright red blood Photoshopped all over its teeth. And – oh, hell…

WOLF SNATCHES BABY. Glasgow woman: 'I heard cry from the jaws of death'.

'What?' Mum's already looking over my shoulder, but I still read aloud. 'Reports flooded in last night of a wolf seen prowling the streets, carrying a baby. Three women saw the horrific sight while crossing Bells Bridge. A huge wolf with a helpless baby dangling from its jaws.

"'I heard her cry out," sobbed Kelly McGuire, 23. "It will stay with me as long as l live."'

After this I skim. *A tiny pink dress… no missing tots reported as yet… police asking for… please call…* Finally I get to the hotline number. 'Is the phone working?' I say to Mum. 'See us it over, then…'

An hour later and the morning has become a lot more interesting. There are two police cars outside. The neighbours have given up curtain twitching and are standing in their open doorways to gawp, apparently oblivious to the cold. Four huge policemen, with crackling radios and uniform snow jackets, are in our living room. Three of them are happily ensconced on the couch drinking tea, their unsubtle hints about the 'cold day' having been taken. The other one is picking up the doll: 'This the victim?'

'Don't tell me,' I say. 'I shouldn't have moved the body?'

'S'all right.' He's waggling a finger through the largest toothmark. 'We'll get the guy on his dental records.'

Well, we are all in a very jolly mood. Mum and Katie are smiling. Even Clairey, who happily exchanged the doll for a shot of the polisman's radio, is giggling, playing peek-a-boo and flirting outrageously with these four strange men. I think, that's our girl.

Then the door bangs open and Jamie is there, white in the face. The polis go quiet and look at him, like terriers who think someone's going to run. 'It's okay, everyone's fine,' says Katie, and then we're all explaining and reassuring. A few minutes later he's in a chair with Claire on his lap, saying, 'The polis cars. I don't know what I thought,' and everything's fine. But the party's over: the polis are draining their mugs and heading for the door. We cluster in the hallway to wave bye-bye, chittering in the cold.

There are other people outside, waiting to come in. One of the cops calls over his shoulder: 'Press is here.'

Finally they're gone too. Most of them looked like their mums didn't know they were out anyway – apparently this story doesn't merit the senior journos. They perked up when they heard how I 'faced down' the wolf, though. They wanted pictures, so I stood in the living room holding up the 'baby' and sticking my fingers through the holes in its plastic leg, while the cameras snapped away. 'This going to be on the front page?' I asked.

Maybe, they all said. Not likely, I thought. But the guy from the *Herald* was smirking at the guy from the *Standard*. So it might get a good few columns in the *Herald*, if only to piss off the *Standard*, which was apparently the only rag to lead on the baby-eating wolf thing. Anyway, at last they've all gone, leaving us all looking at each other in the sudden silence.

Katie goes into the kitchen, and we can all hear the water gushing into the kettle. Works every time: within seconds, Jamie's off for a piss. When I hear the bathroom door closing, I head upstairs. I can hear Claire trying to follow me, but mum's luring her back with sweeties. I wait in my room. When Jamie emerges I call softly, 'Can I have a word?'

He follows me into the room, glancing from me to the stairs and back again. He's guessing that the womenfolk have manipulated him – he's a little annoyed, but he's smiling. For some reason this pisses me off. 'I need to speak to you,' I begin, closing the door behind him.

When he hears my tone the smile vanishes. He sits down hard on the edge of the bed. 'What?'

'It's all right, it's nothing to do with that.' I'm not speaking loudly, but he's looking wildly at the door as if he expects someone to be pressed up against it with a glass. 'It's okay,' I say. 'I had the polis sweep for bugs while they were here.'

Jamie smiles again, but cautiously. 'So what is it?'

'It's about your wife.' I sound angrier than I intended.

'What about her?'

'She wants to spend a bit of time with you, that's what. Where the hell were you?'

His face has gone very cold. 'I thought you said you were okay about this.'

'What, so you *were* out trolling? First thing on a Saturday?' I laugh a little. 'You horny wee so-and-so!'

'So this is the talk after all?'

'No, it's *a* talk, that's all—'

'So I should be thinking of my wife and child, shouldn't I?'

'Well, yes. Katie's upset.'

'Oh, yeah, that's right. I'll just change my whole fucking nature overnight, shall I?'

'That's not what I'm saying—'

'Isn't it?'

'No.' What the fuck is he yelling at me for? 'Don't pull that gay martyr shit on me—'

'Shh!'

I lower my voice. 'If you're going to have a wife then treat her like one. I don't want her crying in my living room every other day because her husband won't—'

'Crying?'

'Yes, crying.'

He sits forward, rubbing his forehead with his thumbs the way he and I both do when we've a headache coming on. 'Aye, well. I'll talk to her.'

'She just wants you around a bit more. She's stuck with a kid all the time, it's not fair.'

'I know.'

The thumbs are still rubbing away. After a moment I say, 'Is there no way you can just… I mean, it's not right. Wouldn't it be better if you started telling folk about it?'

He gives me a look of astonishment. 'No. It wouldn't.'

'Look, you told me something once. While you were coming out—'

'While I was what?'

Of course. He's not out here. Focus, Suzey. 'Just don't interrupt, okay? What I wanted to say is that it's better to be hated for what you are, than loved for what you're not.'

A long pause. Then he says, 'That's the stupidest fucking thing I ever heard, Suzey.'

'Well you said it.'

'No, I didn't.'

'Och, anyway. You know what I mean. Will you think about it?'

'I don't need to think about it.' He's smiling now. 'I'm not getting loved for what I'm not. I love my wife and I love my daughter.' He glances at the door. 'Being bisexual's got nothing to do with it.'

Bisexual? I give up. If he wants to be King of Denial, that's up to him. I suppose there are worse ways to live. 'Okay,' I say, 'let's get downstairs before they think I've killed you.'

He stays sitting down, not meeting my eyes. Eventually he says, 'I can't help it. I really can't.'

'Yeah, I know.'

That seems to cover everything. After a moment he gets up and gives me a hug. I squeeze him tight, and for a moment it's just him and me against the world, like it's always been. Then we hear footsteps on the stairs, and he lets go and opens the door. Katie is just stepping onto the top landing. She smiles nervously and indicates she's going into the bathroom, which she would never do if she actually was going in there. Jamie stops her and puts his arms around her, murmuring something and drawing her close. They stand there like that for a minute. It's weird, too weird. I squeeze past them and go downstairs.

At the bottom I meet Clairey, who's clambering determinedly upwards. I'm tempted to let her past, but I suppose I'd better let those two have their private moment. 'Come we'll go and see Granny?'

She shakes her head. 'Mumma!'

'Leave Mummy just now.'

'Mumma. Mumma. *Mumma!*'

She's trying to push past me. In desperation I say, 'Want to come and play outside?'

She stops. 'Side?'

'Side,' I confirm. 'Go on, away and put your wellies on.'

It takes a lot of running and giggling, but I finally get her suited up and outside. Before I close the door I look back longingly into the nice warm kitchen; I'm freezing my arse off so those two can have their tender moment together, and they'd better bloody appreciate it.

Clairey is pulling at my trouser leg. 'Anny Too!'

I turn around: the garden is a pure white page of undisturbed snow. I'd intended a quick run around the house, then back in as soon as possible, but what the hell. 'Watch this,' I tell Clairey. I turn and lie down gingerly on my back, sweeping my arms and legs out as far as they'll go. 'Snow angels!'

I do it twice then try to show her how, but she keeps flinging herself on top of me and giggling. Then she wades off into the deeper snow, her little jester hat bobbing – she looks like a tiny Viking.

Then she disappears. Even the hat is gone. I flounder after her – good grief, where has she… But there she is, deep in a drift, wheeling her arms around to push off the snow, looking up at me and laughing.

As I haul her out she struggles out of her topmost fleece, letting it fall as she runs back towards the door. She doesn't go in, though, she flings herself full length into the snow between my two angels. As she scrambles out again she whips off her hat and throws it down, all the time looking me in eye and giggling. Ah – a challenge. I pick up the hat and chase her in and out of the snow angels, growling like a grizzly bear.

By now the light's starting to fade so I get a candle out of the kitchen and set it up in the snow; I roll up a dozen profiterole-sized snowballs and build a circular tower around the candle. 'Watch this,' I tell her, trying to hold her back so she doesn't kick the whole thing over. 'Snow lantern.'

Then I light the candle (on the fourth match – she keeps blowing them out) and sit back. The tower glows in the twilight, pale and gold. In the chinks between the snowballs we can see the little flame wobbling. Claire makes a cooing sound like a pigeon. 'Pretty?' I ask.

'Pitty!'

'That's a snow lantern.'

'No lantah!'

'Close enough.' While she's distracted, I try to put the hat back on her. She brushes it off impatiently and I give up after a couple of goes. She doesn't seem bothered by the cold anyway. I watch her for a moment, the pale clear skin an adult would kill for, set off by dark hair and lashes, her eyes bright and fearless in the firelight. She looks into the shadows beyond the lantern and laughs. And why shouldn't she? This is her world.

'Come on, snow-baby,' I say. 'Let's get you inside before you freeze.'

She twists out of my grip and scuttles off, still giggling. Fortunately the back door now opens a crack, and Katie calls, 'Clairey?'

'Mumma, Mumma!' Off she goes, and I trail gratefully behind. She pushes through the crack of the door, yelling, 'Mumma, no lantah! Dadda! No lantah!'

'Snow lantern,' I translate, following her in. Katie and Jamie are standing together; his arm is on her shoulder as she bends to pick up Clairey. He meets my eye and smiles. Katie straightens up as I close the door, and she smiles too; she is so beautiful it makes me stop and stare. She says to the wriggling bundle in her arms, 'Were you playing out with Aunty Sue?'

'Yeah!'

'That was awful nice of Aunty Sue, wasn't it?' She leans into Jamie; he puts his free arm under hers, so that they're both holding Clairey. If these three got any more adorable they could be on a Christmas card. Clairey is pulling at Jamie's fleece and pointing to the door. 'Lantah! Dadda!'

'Yes, it's lovely, isn't it?'

She's getting more insistent. 'No lantah, Dadda! Side!'

'No, it's getting a bit late now, pet—'

Claire's bottom lip is starting to tremble. 'Side, Dadda! Siiiide!'

Jamie sighs, and starts looking around for his boots. I give him Clairey's hat. 'All yours, Daddy.' Then I retreat, gratefully, into the living room.

Chapter 8

The University Refectory is a high-roofed, draughty old hall. It is, according to the University handbook, steeped in history. At the moment it just looks steeped in dust. The long windows are boarded up against the snow, except for the upper arches; white daylight illuminates only the ceiling, leaving the rest of the room yellow in the artificial light. The cheap tables seat four at most, but here and there have been dragged together to seat eight, ten, sixteen. A few students are grouped around them, feet up on the chairs opposite to keep their ankles out of the floor-level draught. A long counter stands at the back; through the door behind it comes steam, echoes of pots and pans, laughter.

I get a table near the counter, where it's warm. The table's wobbly, and half my watery coffee ends up in the saucer; I tip it back in hastily, not because I want to drink the foul stuff, but because I've got both hands clutched around the cup for warmth. I take away one hand long enough to pick up the tiny, solid-looking scone I've just bought, and have a bite: heavy, and tastes of rhubarb. It's going to sit in my stomach like lead.

I'm going to damn well sit here and eat it, though. It's my tea break; they've sent me to take it early, and I'm not hurrying back. The office isn't busy at this time of year, but everyone's been bitching at each other all morning. Despite my efforts to be nice to Katie, she's been a torn-faced cow since I got in. They can damn well kill each other without me for a while.

The door screeches horribly and in walks Raj Chaudhury. I wave; he smiles, collects a cup of watery tea, and heads towards me. The floorboards creak and squeal. The students look up, although the floor made just as much noise when they came in. He points at the seat beside me. 'May I join you?'

'Please.' He sits down as I cut the scone in two and offer him half. 'I wanted a chocolate biscuit, but they haven't got any.'

'Chocolate is harder to get hold of these days.'

I groan. 'This really is hell. Some scone, then?'

'Maybe not.' He watches me take another rhubarby nibble. 'How are you today? Apart from risking serious indigestion?'

'Okay. Have you seen the paper?'

'No.' He watches me fish out the *Standard*. 'I'm sorry, I thought you meant a *newspaper*.'

'You're not a fan, then?'

'A delightful work of fiction.' He flattens his palm against the headline, then lifts his hand to show me the inky smuts. 'A newspaper that gets you dirty just reading it. The irony is often noted. But not often enough, in my opinion.'

'How often would that be?'

'Every day, I suppose.'

'So they should just put *We are dirty bastards* under the title?'

'Those would be the first honest words they've ever printed.'

I love this guy. He's posh *and* crazy. 'Look at this,' I say, pointing out the small, unobtrusive article on page 8: *Wolf Baby 'Only a Doll'*.

The text gives only the bare facts, and there's no picture, but Raj catches on fast – my fake-casual voice isn't very convincing. He skims through the article and says, 'A "local woman"? Is that you?'

'Yup.'

He reads the article. 'Wolves are timid creatures,' he says at last. 'It was probably more afraid than you were.'

I wouldn't put money on that. But I just say, 'I thought they were all up in the Highlands somewhere. God knows what the thing was doing round here.'

'They're scavengers. At least in winter. They live on scraps and rubbish.'

'And folk with occult symbols written all over them.'

He grimaces. 'I take it you mean the so-called Odinists.'

'That's the ones.' I wait till he takes a mouthful of tea and add innocently, 'Though I always thought that had something to do with masturbation.'

He chokes. 'That's Onanism. Not Odinism…' He sees me grinning. 'Do you often make fun of your colleagues like this?'

He's smiling, though. The skin around his eyes crinkles up when he smiles. I say, 'Most of my colleagues aren't nearly enough fun.'

'I'm happy I amuse you.'

We smile at each other for a moment before it starts to feel awkward. My gaze lands on a familiar picture in the paper. '*He* must be disappointed,' I say.

'Who?'

'Him.' I show him the photo of Matthew McLean. 'Baby-eating wolves would be right up his street. Did you read his thing on the horrors of paganism? According to him it's an Odinist tradition to throw human sacrifices to packs of wolves.'

'Ridiculous,' says Raj.

'Isn't it.'

'They hanged their sacrifices from trees, they didn't give them to wolves.'

It's my turn to choke. He looks smug. I scowl at him. 'Not funny.'

But I still don't want to go back to the office.

I have to in the end, though.

When I walk in the whole Registry goes quiet. No one looks up as I go to my seat. Ellen, the woman who sits opposite me, glances at me and smiles wanly.

I'm about to say something when someone appears behind me. Katie. 'You've to go and see Hugh, Suzey,' she says. She won't look me in the eye.

Hugh Munroe is standing in the doorway of his office. He nods at me. I turn to Katie: she starts to say something then changes her mind. So I head over to Hugh's office, threading my way through people who won't look up at me.

Hugh closes the door and retreats behind his desk. There's already someone in the chair beside his: a middle-aged woman who looks familiar. She gives me a reserved smile. 'Please sit down, Suzey.'

I sit. Hugh clears his throat. 'Suzey, do you know Hannah Bradbury? From Personnel?'

'What's going on, Hugh?' I say, although by now I think I've guessed. I grip my hands together in my lap so they won't get shaky.

'Suzey. We know you've been ill lately. We sympathise. But I'm sorry to have to tell you that we have to let you go.'

'But...' This is all a dream, I shouldn't care. But my eyes are starting to prickle. 'I've been ill,' I say. 'It's not my fault.'

'No, of course not—' Hugh begins, but Hannah cuts in. 'We do sympathise, Suzey, but your work hasn't been up to standard.'

'Since when?' I stare at Hugh, who has the decency to look abashed.

'Since you came back,' he says, 'from your time, uh...'

'Being dead?'

'Since you were away.'

'You never said anything.'

Hannah breaks in again, quite gently. 'You're having these health problems, Suzey. This work is demanding and we don't think you should be under that kind of pressure.'

'So you're putting me on sick leave, then?'

'The work needs to get done, Suzey,' says Hugh. 'I'm sorry.'

I take a deep breath. 'If there's a problem with my work you should have said something. You didn't. There's meant to be a verbal warning then a written warning. Isn't there?' I look at Hannah.

She shakes her head. 'I'm sorry.'

'Look. Now that I know there's a problem, I can do something about it. You should have said.'

'We're sorry, Suzey.'

I look from one to the other. They're not going to budge. My eyes are starting to fill up now, but these bastards aren't going to see me cry. I get up, steadying myself against the back of the chair. 'You've not heard the end of this,' I say, although it comes out squeaky and pitiful. So I take another deep breath, and walk out. Behind me Hannah calls out, 'We hope you feel better soon—' before I slam the door behind me.

I go to my desk without looking left or right. I can tell that some people are looking at me now, but I don't meet their eyes. I pack all my stuff together, the comb and biscuits in the desk drawer, the pictures stuck to my tiny space on the wall. It seems to take ages. I'm trying to cram everything into my handbag, but it keeps falling out. After a while someone puts a plastic bag in front of me; I don't look up to see who it was, but I throw all the junk into it anyway.

Then it's time. I've worked with these people for five years, I should say something, but I've got to get out. 'Bye,' I say. Several voices reply, a hand reaches out. If I take it I really will burst into tears. 'Cheerio,' I whisper, and leave. On the way I see Hugh and Hannah standing in the doorway with Katie. I don't acknowledge them as I let the door swing shut behind me.

It doesn't close all the way. Katie's right behind me. 'I'm sorry, Suzey,' she says. 'Please don't—'

'Did you know about this?'

'I knew it might happen, but I wasn't sure—'

'You weren't *sure*?'

'I mean, I didn't think it would all come to a head so quickly.'

'Unbelievable.' I start struggling into my outdoor clothes. 'Fucking unbelievable. Well, I'm not letting them away with this. I'll go to the union. I'll go to the law, they can't just sack me cause my face doesn't fit any more.'

But I can tell from the look of disgusting pity on her face that they can do just that. 'Hell with it,' I say, and head for the door.

'Don't run off.' Katie tries to catch at my arm.

'I'm not going to vandalise anything. You don't have to march me off the premises.'

'That's not it. I just want to see you get home okay.'

'Why? So no one gets sued if I jump off a bridge?'

'Please, Suzey,' she says. She's crossed her arms across her chest; she's standing out in the chilly hallway without even a jacket on. 'Just go back in,' I say. 'I'm fine.'

I leave before she can answer.

As I stomp away from the main gates I come to a decision: fuck the lot of them. Fire me? Just saved me the bother of walking out. It was a shitty job anyway. Time for something better. I'll show them.

I was heading for home, but I abruptly change direction. Strike while the iron's hot, I think. Off to the job centre.

The job centre is packed.

I've to stand in the queue, which loops back on itself around the noticeboards so that no one has to stand outside in the cold. Even so there's a blast of freezing air every time the door opens. Everyone in the queue keeps their outdoor clothes half on. Snow stamped from boots makes slushy brown puddles on the floor. At the end of the queue, the noticeboards block the view of the counter; people stand on tiptoe every so often to see how fast the counter staff are working. Or maybe just to gaze in envy at the employed people, in their blessed job-ful state.

As I wait, I read the cards posted on the boards. There aren't many of them, and they all want some expertise I haven't got – plumbing, electronics, childcare. No admin or clerical. Maybe there'll be some later on, I say to myself, ignoring the churning in my stomach.

We get to another noticeboard. Nothing.

The guy in front of me is looking over a piece of paper. His CV, I realise. I don't have one… But cheer up, girl, you can get one. That one looks well laid-out, you can copy it. I read over the guy's shoulder. My eye is drawn to *Education*.

The guy's got a degree. A good one, a 2:1 Honours from Glasgow Uni. And he's still queuing up in a job centre, standing beside me, with my barely-completed HND. And *he's* having bother finding a job.

I leave my place in the queue and rush out into the hallway. A sign points to *Toilets* – I make a run for the ladies'. It's cold and grubby, and the smell of piss competes with the stink of industrial-strength toilet cleaner. But it's empty.

My head hurts. I lean over the sink and rest my forehead against the cold mirror. Enough. This isn't fun any more.

Time to wake up.

I shut my eyes and dunt my forehead gently against the glass. Make the headache worse, that's it. Trauma, that'll trigger it. Dunt that head again. And yes, breathe in those fumes, everything helps.

Wake up. Wake up.

The toilet-cleaner smell is chokingly strong. It makes me queasy. The room is a fridge, chilly white tiles and cracked sinks. Yes.

Time to go back. *Wake up…*

I open my eyes. There's just gloom.

I close my eyes again, screwing them tight shut, and count to ten. Slowly, I open them again.

Still gloom fading into light. I lift my head. I know what I'm going to see: there's no closing out that smell. But I look anyway, into my own reflected face, with its gaping mouth and pallid skin. The mirror has left a red mark on my forehead.

I'm still in the ladies' in the packed job centre. Still here.

I start to cry. I want to go home. I don't want to be here. It's not real.

But I can see and smell this squalid little room so clearly, there is *no way* it doesn't exist.

I still feel fired. And I cannot believe for one minute that this feeling isn't real.

This is it. I'm stuck here.

I start to cry properly. After a while the door creaks open and a woman looks in at me, mumbles an apology and withdraws again.

I lean against the sink, and cry and cry.

Chapter 9

I've discovered another reason my niece is wonderful: my mother can't have full-blown conniptions in her presence. She bounces Claire on her knee and hisses to me over the top of her head, 'What do you mean, *sacked?* What did you do?'

'Nothing.'

'They can't just sack you for nothing. Didn't you tell them you were ill?'

'Of course I did. They said my work hadn't been up to scratch since I got back.'

'That's all that skiving off you've been doing. Always all over the place talking to God-knows-who. Well, you'll just have to say you'll try harder.'

'I've already said that.'

'You can't just sit here and do nothing, you know. My pension won't cover it. You'll have to pull your socks up, Suzey.'

'Oh, for Christ's sake—'

'Don't speak to me like that.'

'They kicked me out after a few days. They didn't give me any warning. They sacked me 'cause I'm *weird*, all right?'

Her lips tighten: she doesn't believe me. Claire has stopped messing around with the beads around Mum's neck and is watching us, owl-eyed, her thumb firmly corked in her mouth. Mum says, 'I think you should phone them.'

'What the hell do you want me to say?'

'Just say what's happened.'

'They *know* what's—' We both jump as an electronic bell rings. Claire says excitedly, 'Teffylone!'

I pick it up, glad for the break in conversation. 'Hello?'

A young female voice, friendly and businesslike says, 'Hello, is that Susan Pherson?'

'Yes.'

'This is Shelley Fisher. I'm calling on behalf of Anita Black?'

'Who?'

'Anita Black,' she says, a note of surprise in her voice. 'From the *Glasgow Standard*?'

Mum's frantically mouthing 'Is it them?' I wave her away. 'We've already got a subscription, thanks.'

There's a moment's silence, then a laugh. Obviously I'm just having a wee joke. 'So, anyway, Anita would like to do an interview with you. Would you be able to come in today?'

'An interview?' I'm getting further behind every minute. 'What for?'

'Because of you with that wolf?' She's speaking slowly and clearly now. 'The wolf you chased away? Anita would love to talk to you about it.'

'Hang on.' I put my hand over the mouthpiece, even though I know it never properly muffles the sound. I whisper to Mum, 'Anita Black? Heard of her?'

Mum's nodding vigorously. I speak into the phone again. 'Well. I'm not sure about this. I mean…' I pause and laugh awkwardly. 'Would I get paid or anything?'

'Of course.'

'Oh… How much?'

'The usual fee.' She names a figure. It's as much as I make in a month. When I can speak again I say, 'Well, okay then. Yes, I'll do it.'

'Great. Two o'clock today?'

'Yes. Fine.'

'At the *Standard* Building? You know it?'

'I'll find it.'

'See you then.'

'Okay. Bye.' I hang up. Mum says immediately, 'What? What?'

I sit back, feeling my shoulders relax. The blessed state of solvency; temporary, but good enough for today. 'I'm going to be in the paper,' I say.

'Again? What for?'

'The wolf thing.'

'What else could you tell them about that?'

'Don't know. Don't care. D'you want to hear what they're paying me?'

I tell her. Her eyes go as big as Clairey's.

Later, when Mum and Clairey are upstairs doing something related to toilet training (I don't want to know), I call the university switchboard. It rings and rings. Just when I'm starting to think they've got some sort of software that blocks calls from ex-employees, they answer. And for once, they put me straight through, and he answers on the second ring. 'Earth Sciences.'

'Raj,' I say, 'you're going to hate me.'

'Suzey. Why?'

'I'm going to be in the *Standard*. But what can you expect from an unemployed waster like me?'

'Pardon?'

So I tell him. Afterward he says, 'I'm sorry.'

'About the job, or the *Standard*?'

'Both, actually.'

'Aye, well. Pride goes out the window when you're skint.'

'I know. I'm sorry.'

There's a pause. At last he says, 'Although the interview could work to your advantage, of course.'

'Oh?'

He lowers his voice. 'Tell the reporter the university fired you while you were still in shock. After meeting the wolf. Bad publicity for them.'

'You think they might offer me my job back?'

'It's possible.'

I sigh happily. 'I was hoping you'd say that.'

'You'd already thought of it?'

'Yes. But I wanted a second opinion. Plus it's a bit sneaky, isn't it?'

He sounds amused. 'So you wanted the affirmation of another sneaky person?'

'Yup. You've encouraged me now. I can say it was peer pressure. Really, though, wouldn't I get done for libel or something?'

'Just tell the reporter what happened. Look brave and tragic. People will fill in the blanks themselves.'

I laugh. 'D'you think I can do brave and tragic?'

'Suzey,' he says, 'you've come back from the dead. What can't you do?'

'I suppose. Look, are we okay to have this conversation on the university line? No one can listen in or anything?'

'You're right. Next time we'll meet in the park by the duck pond.

Exchange identical briefcases.'

'You're mental. And I should know.'

When we're finished laughing, there's a pause. 'Well,' I say at last, 'I'll let you get on.'

'Yes.' He hesitates for a moment, but then just says, 'Goodbye, then. Let me know how you get on.'

Chapter 10

The lobby of the *Standard* building is smart and shiny. I let the heavy door whisper shut, and already the cold outside is just a memory. The walls are a tasteful cream, decorated with large framed photographs: black-and-white shots of politicians, colourful pictures of children, landscapes, grinning celebrities and waving royals. Against the far wall is a long reception desk. Above it hangs a huge heraldic sign: the *Glasgow Standard* logo traced in gold and purple. Wrapped around are the smaller gilded words of a motto: *TELL THE TRUTH AND SHAME THE DEVIL.* I cross the lobby, already overheated and clumsy in my outdoor layers, my wet boots squelching on the polished floor.

A heavily made-up receptionist is studying a printout, and does not appear to see me. Like hell – I've worked in places like this, and I know fine she's just deprioritised me because my clothes don't look expensive. 'Excuse me,' I say loudly. 'I've an appointment with Anita Black.'

She looks at me like she doubts it, but checks her list anyway. 'Name?'

'Susan Pherson.' Even upside down, I can see my name on the printout; I lean over the desk and point to it, probably because I know how annoying that is. 'Just there, see?'

I get a killer stare with a big smile under it. 'Office 114. Tenth floor. Lift's just round to your left.'

I take off my parka in the lift, but I'm still struggling to pull my fleece over my head when the doors ping open on level 10. A slim, smartly dressed young woman is waiting there; she smiles at me. 'Hi, is it Suzey?'

'Yes.' I step out of the lift before the doors close, still trying to extricate myself from my fleece. 'Anita?'

She smiles as if I've made a joke. 'No, I'm Shelley, her PA. I'll take you to Anita now.'

She pauses to help me out of my fleece, and then steers me along the thickly carpeted corridor, taps respectfully on a door and ushers me inside.

It's a big corner office, with wall-to-wall windows. As if the snow glare from outside isn't enough, the carpets and walls are white to match. The large, uncluttered desk is of pale pine, the chairs upholstered in pale leather. And a white being is coming towards me.

'Suzey? Hi! Anita!'

I blink rapidly till my eyes adjust. The woman extending her hand is tall and slim, with dark blonde hair. She must be thirty-something, and is immaculately dressed in a linen shirt and slacks the colour of vanilla ice cream. Her eyes are large and dark, set off by the coral of her lipstick and the silk scarf around her neck. I'm acutely aware of my bulky clothes, my tousled hair and my red, un-made-up face. 'Hi,' I mumble, taking her hand.

Her grip is strong and surprisingly bony, but her smile is sympathetic; she waves towards a set of low chairs around a small coffee table, and turns tactfully away while I rake my fingers through my hair. 'Coffee?' she says.

I agree readily, having already spotted the filter coffee machine in the corner. Soon she's handing me a white cup of something dark and wonderful; I can't help closing my eyes as I inhale its delicious scent. '*Real* coffee.'

'Nothing like it, is there,' she agrees. She settles into the chair opposite, and we both sip in silence. For a moment I consider asking if she'll give me half the fee in coffee grounds… But no, let's be serious.

She smiles. 'I'm glad you're here, Suzey. I've been wanting to meet you since I heard about you and that wolf.' She leans back, comfortable in her super-expensive outfit. 'I mean, weren't you terrified?'

'Yes, I was.' I'm leaving out the part about wetting myself. 'I thought it was a real baby.'

'So what did you do?'

I shrug. 'I just stood there looking at it.'

'And what did it do?'

'It looked back.' Afraid I sound like some monosyllabic teenager, I add, 'It was strange. Then it dropped the doll and I realised it wasn't actually a baby.'

'Then what?'

'It turned around and went off. It went down onto the river. I think I shouted something after it. I wasn't… you know.'

'You shouted after it?'

'Well, yes.' Now she's going to ask me what I said, and I can't remember.

'So you made eye contact with it. You faced it down, and then you shouted, and off it went?'

'No, I don't think so. I think it was running off anyway…'

She's nodding, and writing in a notebook on her lap. 'Do you think that's why it didn't attack you?'

'Sorry?'

'Do you think it didn't attack you because you faced it down? Drove it off?'

'I don't know. Isn't that what you're supposed to do? I mean, they don't really *want* to attack people, do they?'

She looks up at me. 'Wolves have killed two people in the last three months, Suzey. Didn't you think about that?'

'No, I didn't. I didn't think about it at all.'

'I'd have been terrified. You're very brave, Suzey.'

'No. I'm really not.'

'You are. You've had even more than that to deal with lately, haven't you?'

'Oh. Yes.'

'And your family too?' I nod but say nothing, so she adds, 'They thought they'd lost you, didn't they? For quite a while?'

'Two weeks.' I haven't given this enough thought. They went through all that…

Her voice is very gentle. 'What happened, Suzey?'

'They thought I was dead. They were called in to identify someone and they thought it was me. The body must've been damaged or something.' The lies sound feeble. 'I came back a fortnight later, and I walked in through the door…' I go through it all: the screaming, Clairey, all of that, omitting to mention that I had no idea who the little girl actually was. 'But it was just a mistake,' I finish. 'Just a terrible mix-up.'

'Where were you all that time?'

'In the hospital. You know, the one near Livingston?'

'I know it. But they say you weren't there, Suzey.' She still looks sympathetic – but very, very alert.

'What?' I say.

'The hospital. They say you weren't there. They've never heard of you.'

'That's not true.' My face starts to feel hot. God, why didn't I see this coming? 'Of course I was there. I was there for two weeks. Where else would I be?'

'That's what I'm asking.' She smiles a little, to take the sting out of it. 'Were you at a friend's house? A boyfriend's? Did you meet someone, Suzey?'

I look her in the eye, and realise she's checked – everyone I might have been with, everywhere I might have gone. 'I was somewhere else. I don't know how I got here. I just opened my eyes and there was only white light. Another world. And now everything's different.'

Anita is nodding kindly, but her expression is hungry. 'But that's silly,' I say loudly, waving a hand to dismiss the confused ramblings of a psychiatric patient. 'I was in the hospital… I don't know why they'd say I wasn't. Perhaps it's something to do with patient confidentiality…' No, shut up, I tell myself. Ignorance is my best defence here. 'It's just a mix-up. I suppose.'

'A mix-up.'

'Yes.'

'Like you being declared dead.'

'Of course. What else could it be?'

A slow smile, lacking her previous warmth, spreads across her face. 'You're a fascinating person, Suzey.'

'Thanks. So are you.'

She laughs, and the moment's passed. We carry on with the interview, Anita checks my birthdate, family, details, blah blah blah, inconsequential blether over another two cups of that heavenly coffee. 'So what are your plans for the future?' she says at last.

God, the whole point of this, and I nearly forgot. 'I'm not sure. I've just lost my job, you see.'

'Oh?'

'Yes. The university asked me to leave.'

'They fired you?'

'Yes.'

'What for?'

'Well, it's a bit awkward for them.' I take a deep breath. 'I tend to weird people out. You know, with coming back from the dead and all.' That's certainly true. I go for a self-deprecating smile. 'Can't blame them, I suppose.'

Actually I blame them quite considerably, but I don't say so. Anita is scribbling away at her notepad. 'Do you weird a lot of people out?'

'Just about everyone. Except—' I'm about to say except Raj, but bite the words back. 'Except my family. You know.' I watch her writing. 'Don't I weird you out?'

She smiles into her notepad. 'It takes an awful lot to weird me out, Miss Pherson.'

Then she's on her feet, hand outstretched. Clearly the interview is over. 'Thanks again for coming in, Suzey. If you go down to the fourth floor, the photographer should be ready for you.'

'You want another picture of me?'

'Of course.'

'Oh, but...' My hand goes to my shiny face, my deranged hair. 'I'm not really, you know...'

She smiles, rather pityingly, I think. 'Shelley will lend you a hairbrush. And some makeup, if you want it. Goodbye, Suzey.'

A moment later she's closing the door behind me. Shelley the secretary is behind her desk. I dither, wondering which would be more humiliating – looking like a bag lady in the paper, or begging this glamorous girl for a comb and some lipstick. I decide I can't look into a camera in this state, so I have to ask Shelley. She clearly doesn't like it, but when I tell her Anita said so she hands over the goods without a word.

Shelley's skin is darker than mine; her makeup bag is full of reds and browns and plum tones. I settle for some powder, eye shadow and a tiny smear of lipstick. Then I head off for my photo, still looking distinctly unglamorous. God almighty, this had better be worth it.

Chapter 11

The next day, I'm up a lot earlier. Even so, I have to compete with my mother in the race to grab the *Standard* from the doormat. 'Is it in?' she demands as I scoop up the paper a moment before her. 'Can you see it?'

'Put the kettle on first,' I say severely. We make tea in record time, trying not to peek. It's like Christmas morning. Eventually we get settled on the couch, and paw through the inky pages until my picture is staring out at us.

It's not the me I'm used to seeing in the bathroom mirror – amazing what photo software can do. My eyes are large, outlined by slightly smudged makeup; there's no redness in my cheeks, and my lips are just a shade darker than my whitened skin. I look pale and remote, almost ethereal. I quite like the look, but Mum says, 'You might've smiled for the camera.'

'I did. For most of the pictures.' But we're already onto our next surprise: the headline. *BACK FROM THE DEAD: MIRACULOUS RETURN OF WOLF-WHISPERER SUZEY.*

'What on earth does that mean?' Mum demands, but I'm already reading on.

Suzey Pherson, the Glasgow girl who faced down a savage wolf, has returned from the dead.

Suzey (29) was last week praised for driving off a huge male wolf which she believed to be holding a baby in its jaws. 'There was only one thing to do,' Suzey said yesterday. 'I looked it in the eye and shouted right in its face.'

The wolf turned tail and fled.

Thankfully, the tot was only a doll. 'I was so relieved,' Suzey said. 'I have a little niece. For all I knew it could have been her.'

'That's absolute garbage,' I say, but Mum shushes me.

Praise for Suzey's courage flooded in yesterday. Dr David Cunningham, of Edinburgh Zoo, said, 'She did the right thing. Wolves are cowards – chances are they'll run if you stand up to them. But it was still very brave.'

But that's just half the story.

Suzey has returned from the dead.

In an exclusive Standard interview, Suzey revealed that she was believed dead for two weeks.

'There was a mix-up,' she explains. 'The hospital got the wrong person.

'My family thought I was dead for over a fortnight. I just can't imagine the pain they were in.'

So where was Suzey all this time? 'I don't know,' she confesses. 'It was like another world. There was white light everywhere. Then I was back home.'

Authorities are baffled as to Suzey's whereabouts for those two weeks. No witnesses have come forward. In current temperatures, it's unlikely she could have survived sleeping rough.

Suzey herself is stumped. 'I can't explain it. I just know it was a miracle.'

Sadly, the future is not rosy for this remarkable girl. 'I just lost my job at St Mungo's University,' she explains. 'I suppose they were just weirded out. Anyone would be.'

But she is still in good spirits. 'I'm back home with my family. And that's all that matters.'

I push the paper away from me. Praise for my courage is still conspicuously failing to flood in. 'What a load of absolute *crap*,' I say.

'You didn't tell me any of this.'

'Because it's lies, Mum. I never said any of it.'

The phone rings, making us both jump. I grab it. 'Hello?'

A soft, deep voice is singing. 'Who's afraid of the big bad wolf, the big bad wolf, the—'

'That's not very funny.'

'Tra-la la la la—'

'Raj!'

'Sorry.'

'You've seen it then.' I try to ignore Mum, who's miming 'Who's Raj?' at me. 'What were you doing reading the *Standard*, Mr Brainy?'

'I told you, I enjoy Scottish fiction as much as anyone.'

'D'you reckon Personnel will have seen it?'

'I should think so. I've just sent them a copy.'

'You're an absolute star, Raj.'

'Of course I am.' There's a pause and in the background I can hear a door opening, the chatter of voices. Raj says, 'My students are here. I have to go.'

'Me too. I have to go and tell my mother who you are.' I glare at Mum. 'Before she actually explodes with curiosity.'

'Goodbye then.'

'Bye, Raj.'

Chapter 12

Dear Sister and Fellow Scot,

Come unto Him, all ye that labour, and He will give you rest.
Matthew 11:28
...

I am happy to invite you to the Spirit Fire conference and assembly this February.

Spirit Fire will draw together good Christians from all over the globe. For three days, we will praise God and thank Him for His great goodness. Together we will pray for His righteousness to rule the world once more, sweeping away the false gospel that is bringing our country to its knees: a creed that hides behind the name of 'tolerance', actually a web of politically-correct lies, permissiveness and perversion.

We will call upon sinners to come to Him, before these, the Last Days, should finally draw to a close and His Kingdom comes. Therefore we will baptize those who have lived in Godlessness and wickedness, so that they may be whiter than snow and fit to meet their Maker. 'The Shepherd rejoices in the Lost Lamb that is found.'

Our programme of events will include:
- 'Come out from among them, and be ye separate' *(II Cor. 6:17)*. Living a Christ-ful life in a Christ-less world
- Restoring the family in Scotland
- The power of prayer
- Healing of broken sexuality

- 'Suffer the little children to come to Me' *(Mark 10:14)*.
  Protecting children in a time of wickedness

Spirit Fire will be held in the Glencoe Lodge, from February 12 – 16.
I very much hope you will be able to join us. You are welcome to bring a friend or family member.

May you live in Christ, and He in you.

With best wishes,
Kerry McLean

On behalf of Matthew McLean

....

'Dear Brother and Fellow Scot,

'Thank you for your letter and your invitation, which I accept wholeheartedly. How wonderful to hear that the scourge of tolerance and religious freedom may some day be banished from our shores.

'Re. bringing someone else: as a non-Christian, I naturally despise my entire family and so will be unable to bring a family member. However, one of my two live-in lovers may be able to attend. My male lover, as a God-fearing person, rightly shuns men like you, who openly flout God's law by cutting off their forelocks and wearing more than one type of fabric at a time.

'My lesbian lover, however, will be delighted to come along. As a practicing medium and Wiccan, she accepts the validity of all religions, and so will happily submit to being patronised and reviled by fuckwitted bigots who—'

'Now you're just being childish, Suzey,' Mum says.

I stop reading, but Jamie's still laughing – Katie hasn't arrived yet, you can tell. He catches my eye and rolls his eyes at Mum. 'Read out the rest of it, Suze,' he says.

'That's all I've done.'

'Good.' Mum's gone tight-lipped. 'You're not going to send it, are you?'

I sigh. 'Probably not.' I tear it out of my notebook, and crumple it up together with McLean's letter. I've had a few dotty letters over the past couple of days, most of them kindly, badly spelled and written on cheap Basildon Bond. But McLean's letter is on heavy parchment notepaper; it's a good solid weight to throw, and I hit the waste-paper basket first time. 'That's the nicest notepaper I've ever chucked out.'

'You're not planning on going then?' Mum says.

'Course I'm not. The man's off his head.'

Mum shrugs. 'It's meant to be a really nice place to stay, that's all.'

'What is?'

'The Glencoe Lodge. It's his hotel.'

'Is it actually *in* Glencoe?'

'I think so.'

'I'm definitely not going then.'

'I thought you liked Glencoe.'

'I do. In summertime, with normal people. Not people like *him*.'

She sighs. 'Please yourself. You always do.'

Before I can think of a suitable retort, we hear the back door opening, then Clairey shouting, 'Ganna!'

'Granny's in here, pet,' Mum shouts.

'Ganna, Ganna!' For a small person she's got a big voice. She bursts in, half out of her coat, clutching her woolly hat in a small mittened paw. Katie is behind her, trying to wrestle her out of her heavy layers, but Clairey escapes, running in delighted confusion between the three of us. 'Ganna! Dadda! Anny Too!'

I swing her up onto my knee. 'Hi, Clairey-bear.'

'Anny Too!' She stands up on my knee, face close to mine, and starts bouncing up and down. By the time I've persuaded her to stop doing that, and to get her coat and boots and gloves off, Katie is comfortably settled beside me on the couch, a copy of the *Standard* on her knee. We've declared a truce, she and I, although to be honest I'd rather she was sitting on the other side of the room.

Jamie goes to put the kettle on; I shake my half-full mug at him. Clairey rushes through to watch him, still all systems go, but she'll probably settle down for a sleep soon. All in all, we're set for another riveting Saturday of sitting here doing absolutely nothing. If anyone else is bored by our scintillating weekends, they've never shown it. I see a flash of colour in Katie's newspaper and ask, for the sake of doing something, 'What's that?'

'Did you not hear about it?' She turns the paper towards me. 'Isn't it terrible?'

The picture takes up most of the front page. It's a young boy; he really is the most beautiful boy I've ever seen. His skin is golden. His fair curls make a halo. There is a shine to him – this may have been added by the *Standard*'s Photoshop software, but I don't think it was much of an exaggeration. He is *Peter Balfour (12)*. He was *discovered by a man walking to work* yesterday, in Moss Park. The headline says simply: *RAPED AND MURDERED*.

I've got the gist of it already, so I look away. Katie, however, is reading aloud in suitably horrified tones. I squirm away from her.

She drones on: '"Early hours of this morning, wearing only a T-shirt"…'

'Do we need to hear all this?' I snap.

'I'm listening,' retorts my mother.

'Can't you just read it yourself?'

'Just hush.'

Jamie comes through with the tea, Clairey bouncing at his heels. I'd hoped her presence would get the subject changed, but Katie's turning to the next page. There are more pictures: a grim-looking suit before the police logo; a stunned middle-aged couple pallid in the flashbulbs; a park in the snow.

Katie reads aloud: '"Moss Park, a notorious gay hang-out"…'

'Is it?' I say, and come within an *instant* of looking at Jamie. I look at the page instead, and scan it quickly. *Gay scene… cottaging… cover of darkness… male partners.*

Katie flips to the next page, savagely. 'They should be fucking shot.'

'Who?'

She looks up in surprise. 'Them.' Her hand stabs angrily at the paper. 'Fuckin' animals.'

'Katie,' Jamie says, glancing at Clairey.

Katie waves her hand dismissively. 'She's not listening. Just look at that poor wee boy. Hanging's too good for them.'

I should leave this, but... 'Just who are we talking about here?'

Jamie cuts in. 'We're talking about paedophiles, Suzey.' He's giving me a shut-up look.

'Paedophiles. Fuckin' monsters more like.'

My mum, who usually won't have swearing in the house, much less in front of Clairey, is nodding solemnly. 'Do they know who it is yet?'

Katie checks a different column. 'A man in a red parka jacket and dark trousers was seen acting suspiciously.'

'What's "acting suspiciously"?' I want to know.

'He was "loitering in the area in spite of sub-zero temperatures".'

'They've just said it was a cottaging park – now they think "loitering" is suspicious?'

'Read it your bloody self then.' Katie slaps the paper onto my lap. She scoops up Clairey, apparently just so she can clutch her child theatrically to her breast. Any minute now it's going to be 'when you're a mother yourself you'll understand'. I pick up my mug and stomp off into the kitchen. It's dark and it's cold. For a moment I think about Peter Balfour walking home in the dark, small and alone, and a hand reaching out... Then I snap on the lights.

In a minute Jamie joins me. 'You okay?'

'Course I am. I didn't even know the kid.' I pour what's left of my lukewarm tea down the sink and switch on the kettle. When it's roaring good and loud, I murmur, 'It's going to be hard on you for a while, isn't it?'

'I'll keep my head down.' He is matter of fact and grim, a soldier anticipating action. 'They'll get someone for it soon.'

'The right someone?'

'Probably not.'

'You just stay well out of it then.'

The kettle is whistling; I pour the water into my mug. 'We'd better get back to the weep-in,' I say, nodding towards the living room.

'You're a hard-hearted cow,' he says, smiling.

'Don't tell me – I can't understand because I'm not a father?'

'Behave.' He ruffles my hair as if I were Clairey. 'And don't worry. I'll be good.'

Chapter 13

The phone rings on Monday morning. I'm up and tottering around, but far from wide awake: I'm not a morning person. Mum's not here, she's gone with Clairey to the shops. It's a bright, clear day, but almost painfully cold, so I don't suppose they'll be long. In Mum's absence, however, I'm defiantly wearing my dressing gown; she gets pissed off seeing me wear it in the morning. Unemployed people don't get to wear dressing gowns past half eight, after which we have to switch to hair shirts, presumably. So when I pick up the phone I'm not exactly alert. 'Hello?'

'Can I speak to Susan Pherson, please?'

I wake up a little more. 'Speaking.'

'Ah, hello, Susan. It's Hannah Bradbury here, from the university personnel office.'

Now I'm wide awake. 'Yes, hello.'

'Susan, a position has opened up here, and I wonder if you might consider it.'

'Is it my old job?'

'I'm afraid not. Registry Services have been streamlined now, so that position no longer exists.'

Streamlined. Of course. 'How many other folk got sacked?'

'There have been some voluntary redundancies. Susan, the job we have in mind for you is the role of Document Assistant. You'll be keying and preparing electronic documents for the university as a whole.'

'You mean a typist?'

'Of electronic documents, yes. You'd also be formatting and proofing documents.'

'So I'd be typing with the spellchecker on?'

'If you're not interested, Susan…'

'All right, all right. I'm interested. Who would I be working for?'

'For the university as a whole.'

I have a surreal image of the university building leaning over my shoulder while I type. 'I mean who would I report to? Where would I be based?'

'You would report to the Head of Admin Services. And we would lend you a machine so you could work from home.'

'From home.'

'Yes. Many of our staff are taking that option these days. It's much easier for them not to travel every day in this weather, as I'm sure you understand.'

And that means you don't have to heat an office for them, or insure them against accidents. It means you'll get lots of mums who can't get childcare; they'll work from home, do lots of hours, and not complain because they can't get anything else. And, in this rather specialised case, you get Suzey the Walking Dead to stay well out of normal folks' sight. Oh, yes, I understand all right. 'How much does it pay?' I ask.

She tells me the hourly rate. 'That's not enough,' I say.

'That's all I'm authorised to offer.'

'It's less than my old job. And with no holidays or sick time.'

'That's what the job pays, Susan.'

I say nothing for a long time, hoping she'll fill in the silence. She doesn't. 'All right,' I say at last. 'I'll take it.'

'Good.' She is bright and breezy again. 'If you could come by within the next few days to sign the forms and pick up the laptop.'

'I'll come today,' I say.

The computer is the size, and weight, of a hod of bricks. When I set it down, the cheap refectory table creaks alarmingly. 'Look at this thing,' I say. 'It's meant to be a laptop. If I put it on my lap I'd break both legs.'

Raj peers at it. 'Primitive.'

'I'll say.' I collapse into my chair with a sigh. 'Ach, at least it means I've got a job.'

He pours from the teapot, and hands me a cup of brownish hot milky water. 'I'm sorry you didn't get your old job back.'

'Aye, well. It's the same all over, isn't it.'

'In this university, certainly.'

'Are they making more cuts?'

'Probably.'

'Is your job safe?'

'I'm not sure. But then no one is.'

I swirl my tea around the cup for a moment. 'What would you do if…'

'I'd go back down south, where my family is.'

It occurs to me that he knows my personal life better than I know his. 'Where are you from? Originally?'

He looks pained. 'My family came from near New Delhi three generations ago—'

'I meant where in England, you twit.'

'Ah.' He raises his eyebrows. 'Don't you want to talk about my glorious Indian heritage?'

'Do you?'

'As a matter of fact, no.'

'Don't then.'

He's quiet for a moment, then says, 'My father's father was a Hindu who married a Christian. My father was an agnostic Indian who married a Methodist Englishwoman. I have more heritage than I know what to do with.' He sets down his cup. 'To answer your question: Islington.'

'Well, I hope you don't have to go back there,' I say. 'I mean because of the job.'

'I know what you mean.' He smiles. His eyes are dark hazel, shading through to honey. 'Anyway, since we're discussing traditions, would you like to come to Fire and Ice this weekend?'

'Come to what?'

'Fire and Ice. The festival in Kelvingrove Park. Fireworks, stalls, hyperactive children. The usual.'

I've never heard of it. 'How long's that been going?'

'Three years now.'

'Not really a tradition, then.'

'Of course it is. Just a very new one.'

I laugh. 'I suppose they've got to start somewhere.'

'So would you like to come?'

'I'd love to.'

There is no snowfall on Saturday; the cold is bright and crystalline. I'm hardly going to get lost en route to Kelvingrove Park but Raj still insists on coming to collect me, even though it's miles out of his way.

I was apprehensive about it. My mother is prejudiced: prejudiced, that is, against any man I choose to go out with. Dad was pretty far gone by the time I had any real boyfriends, so Mum had to take on the fatherly role of growling at any strange males who came to the house. And of course tonight, just before Raj was due to arrive, Jamie appeared for a 'surprise' visit on some ridiculous pretext which completely failed to disguise how much his nose was bothering him. I told him off for it, but I didn't really mind; he stopped doing things like that when he moved in with Carl, and it's surprising what you miss. Raj, however, is a big hit. Respectful without grovelling, he shook hands with Jamie, offered to help Mum make the tea, and casually mentioned his brainy university job so Mum would be assured of his prospects. All the while reassuring them I'd be escorted – and protected, presumably, from murderers, rapists, Odinists and ravening wolves – every moment I was outside the house.

It takes ages to get away. But at last we're heading down the path, with Mum waving from the window and Jamie smirking knowingly after us. 'Sorry about that,' I tell Raj.

'Don't worry. They were just looking after you.'

'I'd rather they didn't, to be honest.'

The park is already busy when we get there. Last time I saw Kelvingrove, it was darkened tundra – now all the streetlamps are on, and there's a fiery glow in the distance. Within the main gate, fairy lights have been looped from tree to tree overhead, so we walk in under strings of glowing plastic icicles. The paths have been cleared and gritted, lined on both sides with banks of grubby orange slush.

Raj and I walk to the top of the slope, our feet crunching on the grit. I breathe in fairground smells: oily machinery, frying onions, candyfloss. Kids run past, waving bright green glow tubes. At the top I stop to look at the park and have to laugh. It's like Blackpool on ice. The stone soldier on the Boer War memorial has a burning torch strapped to his head. Tinny loudspeakers belt out *Dancing Queen*. Covered stalls line the path, which is thronged with happed-up humanity. I catch a smell I haven't picked up before, like hot fruit mixed with dental anaesthetic. 'Do you smell what I smell?'

Raj sniffs. 'Mulled wine?'

'Lemme at it.' We dive down into the crowd. It's less chilly surrounded by so many warm bodies, and many have boldly undone top buttons, although we are all still puffing like dragons in the freezing air. Kids are doing lightsaber effects with glow tubes, fluorescent blurs in red, green and blue. We wind our way past stalls of wooden carvings, cheap plastic toys, suspicious-looking hot dogs and warm Bovril. When I get left behind, held up by a large mother telling off her kids, Raj reaches back and takes my hand.

Before I can think about this, we are at the hot drinks stall, so he has to let go. Soon we're each gripping a polystyrene cup of mulled wine. 'I love this stuff,' I say, swigging a hot, bitter mouthful. 'Very warming, don't you think?'

'Magma in a cup,' agrees Raj, taking a sip and wincing only slightly. We're strolling close together, side by side in the crowd; our knuckles bump together a couple of times before he takes my hand again. I leave it there.

'Look at this.' Raj is steering me downhill to the river, where it's quieter and less child-infested. The lights here are white, and shining through what looks like a row of glass pillars. We get closer, Raj drawing me through the crowds of tall people. I find I'm looking at a giant crystal ornament – Cinderella's coach, five feet high. An ice sculpture: opaque white wheels, pumpkin-shaped body of clear ice. Cold radiates off it. The sculptor is still at work, on his hands and knees, scraping lightly at the head of the single ice horse.

We stroll slowly from sculpture to sculpture: a crystal swan; a ballet dancer; a fairytale archway of spun glass; a six-foot goddess, or Blessed Virgin, with a sapphire heart. We coo and exclaim with the rest of the crowd. The sculptors, smoothing and tending their creations, smile indulgently.

After a while, the food smells draw us back uphill again. Agnetha urges us to *Take a Chance on Me*. Raj and I buy hot doughnuts, straight from the fryer and smothered in sugar, and we wander further into the park. The Kelvingrove fountain, vandalised and dry for so long, has found a new lease of life, not in water, but fire. It is strung about with more fairy lights, yellow ones shaped like flames. Some of them have failed already, but more than enough are still working to pick out the fountain's blue-and-gold Zodiac mosaics. The crowning statue, the Lady of the Lake, shares her plinth with another fiery torch, larger than the Boer soldier's, as tall as the bronze Excalibur in her hand. The flames wash around her long skirts; she looks like a martyred saint. I walk on, towing Raj behind me.

We come to the edge of the crowd and find crash barriers, with no lights beyond. I can make out a small hillock in the empty space where the old playground used to be. After a moment's squinting, I see that it's an unlit bonfire, about twenty feet high. I move forward for a better look, and catch the eye of a security guard beyond the crash barrier. He smiles, but it's clear I'm not going any further. I drain the last of the mulled wine and turn to Raj. 'Do you know when they're going to light—'

There's a squeal of feedback from the loudspeakers, and *Super Trouper* comes to an abrupt halt. Everyone turns and looks back the way we came in; small children are hoisted onto parents' shoulders, and there's a drunken cheer from a group of blokes beside us. In the distance is a blaring sound like car-horns, which resolves itself into the blast of trumpets. Under it is a deep thunder. As I stand on my tiptoes, trying in vain to look over the heads around me, I realise it's drumming. 'What's going on?' I yell, tugging Raj's sleeve like a five year old. 'I can't see.'

'It's coming this way. Don't worry.' Raj glances surreptitiously behind us. The security man has been joined by three others; they're holding one of the crash barriers, waiting for their cue to push it aside. Others are moving the crowd back from the main pathway. People are trying casually to move in front of us. No chance. I grab Raj's arm and we slide to the very edge of the road.

I can see the drummers coming now: twenty or so women, each with a different drum. They step in time and swing from side to side in unison, like a marching band. The sound is primeval, it goes straight to the feet – everyone is moving with the rhythm, kids hopping up and down, the drunk guys beside us waving their arms in the air. I step on the spot a little, still holding Raj's arm, taking the opportunity to bump gently against him from time to time. He takes his arm back, and wraps it round my shoulders. I put my arms around his waist, or rather, around his coat; somewhere under the duvet-thickness padding, there's warmth.

The drummers are almost past us now. Behind them comes a white and glittering float. Soon we can see it clearly: a Santa's grotto of white paper icicles, sparkly frost and frozen green stalagmites. In the centre stands a huge throne fit for a Snow Queen, moulded from plastic snow and topped with jagged crystal. The figure in the throne is nothing like Santa: a tall, skinny Nosferatu-like creature, dressed in stark purple and white. Not a real person, thank God: it's just a dummy, with blue skin, a white beard and dark, hollow eyes. Its hair has been twirled up into two devil horns and its blue papier-mâché hands, complete with foot-long silver fingernails, grip the arms of the throne. As the figure is wheeled past, children hide their faces in their mother's coats; I don't blame them. 'What the hell's that?'

'Jack Frost.' Raj smiles down at me, his face flushed from the wine. 'Old Man Winter.'

'Of course it is.' I start to giggle. My face is probably flushed too. 'What are you on about?'

'Old Man Winter. We burn him on the big fire, and that makes the winter go away.' He's using a mock-serious, singsong voice. It's the funniest thing I've ever heard. While I'm giggling helplessly into his shoulder, the float comes to a halt beside us. The float is actually a cart, pulled by four people whose heavy coats are draped with red batik-print scarves. The two men at the back each carry a long bronze horn; that explains the trumpets, I guess. At the front are a small man with a ginger goatee, and a woman with round glasses and a desperately earnest expression. She's with a theatre company, I think; I remember her in a production of *Hamlet* where the set consisted entirely of boxes (it was a lot more effective than you'd think). The two of them clamber onto the float, heavy boots thudding on the wooden flooring. They reach behind the throne, and pull out a long cloak of plush purple, trimmed with white fake fur, and covered in pieces of paper.

They pull the heavy fabric around Jack Frost's skinny shoulders, and I see that the papers are newspaper cuttings with big shock-quotes headlines. *WINTER STORMS WORST EVER... PENSIONERS FREEZE... BLIZZARDS SHUT DOWN MOTORWAY.* There are dozens of them, stapled onto the dark fabric. The crowd cheers as the ginger man reaches behind the throne again, and produces a large papier-mâché torch topped with papier-mâché flames. He pauses for a moment, while children are being manoeuvred to the front row; then his voice, deep and fruity and bigger than he is, rings out: 'What do we do with Old Man Winter?'

His three companions cry, 'Send him on!'

Ginger waves the fake flame over our heads. Hands grab for it, but he's too quick. 'Who's sick of winter? Who's sick of the cold?'

Voices shout 'me, me!' and it's not just the kids. He waves the torch at them again. 'Who's had enough of slipping when you walk? Who's had enough of the phones being down? Who's fed up of corned beef in a tin?'

'Me, me!' We're all shouting it now, Raj and I included. Our man cups a hand around his ear, pantomiming deafness. 'What? Nobody?'

'Me! Me! Me!' We laugh, but we get louder. Some folk are punching the air like it's a rock concert.

The man nods theatrically. 'Ahhh. So what'll we do with him?' he asks, gesturing at the king in his newspaper cloak. 'Shall we… leave him alone?'

'No, no!'

The other three shout, 'Send him on!' but our yells drown them out.

The man on the float puts his hands to his face in deep thought. 'Shall we… elect him to the Scottish Parliament?'

Laughter mingles with more cries of 'Send him on!'

'Shall we…' He leans over towards the kids around the base of the float. 'Send him for a week at Disneyland?'

Outraged childish squeals of 'Nooo!' drown out everything else.

'I know. Shall we… chuck him on a bonfire?'

We roar in approval. The threesome starts to chant, 'Old Man Winter! Send him on! Old Man Winter! Send him on!' The ginger man proffers his papier-mâché torch to the front row. 'Who wants to set fire to the bastard?'

A dozen little hands reach for the torch. Ginger-beard points to someone, and a little girl in a pink snowsuit is hoisted onto the float. Stage-struck, she has to let the man guide her hand; the paper flames are touched into the Ice King's torso. At the same moment there is a flare as three sparklers, previously hidden in the icy crown, fizz into life. The little girl starts to howl in fright, and is handed down from the float to her waiting mother.

The people on the float hoist the throne into the air, carrying it like a sedan chair. They're still chanting, and we pick up the mantra – 'Old Man Winter! Send him on! Old Man Winter! Send him on!' – except the drunk guys, who are shouting 'Old Man Winter! Get tae fuck!'

The security guards pull back the barriers; one of them does a hand-twirling bow as the throne is borne past. From behind us, painfully close to my ear, comes a long nasal blast from the trumpets. The drumming recommences as the Ice King, lolling from side to side like a hopeless drunk, is carried to the bonfire.

The bearers begin their slow, awkward climb to the top; wooden steps have been built into the pyre just for this, but it still looks like tricky going. At last they place the throne triumphantly at the summit, adjust His Majesty's robe and crown, then back away down the steps, kowtowing as they go.

Once they get to the bottom, though, they go into the scuttling run of someone retreating from a lit firework. The drumming changes again, to a slow drumroll. Someone starts to count down loudly – 'Ten! Nine!' – and everyone joins in. 'Seven! Six!' I'm doing it as well, although I have no idea what I'm counting down to. Now we've started to clap. 'Four! Three! TWO! ONE!'

We all start whooping like it's Hogmanay. A moment later there's a series of cap-gun bangs, which make a lot of people shriek even though we were expecting something like it, and suddenly there are lots of little fires nestling amidst the stacked timbers. They grow and join up quickly; I can smell petroleum. Sparks swarm upwards, and some of them settle on the throne's paper icicles. The icicles catch, so do the stalagmites behind them, so does Old Man Winter himself. A moment later the throne is sheathed in flame, and the blackened figure on it is curling forward, collapsing in on itself.

As it does, something shoots up from the Ice King's crown and explodes into white stars over our heads. At this cue, more rockets go sizzling skywards and burst into blue and red sparks. I can just see where they're coming from – a dark hut a hundred yards beyond the fire – but it looks for all the world as if the ice crown has launched itself into the sky. More fireworks follow, squealing and bursting like gunshots, scattering yellow sparks.

I lean back against Raj, pulling his arm around my waist. I love fireworks; I love to hear a crowd watching fireworks, actually going *ooooooh* and *aaaaaah* as if they've never seen anything like it. Somewhere on ground level, on the other side of the crowd, I see a golden light and hear the accompanying crackling sound: a Catherine wheel. In front of us a short dull post erupts into silver rain. I pretend to be startled a couple of times, and Raj's arm tightens around me.

At last there's a series of sky bursts, chrysanthemums of every colour, one right after the other. Then comes a huge explosion of sparks with a noise like a cannon: unquestionably the finale. Applause, whistling and cheering breaks out. No one emerges to take a curtain call, however. There's only the King, now all but disintegrated on his skeletal throne. Being so close to the fire is getting uncomfortable, and we begin to turn away.

Raj and I walk back towards the gates, cold air in our faces, the heat of the fire still on our backs. I link arms and smile up at him. 'So all that sends the winter away, does it?'

'Spring is on the way now,' he says.

'Wouldn't it be on the way anyway?'

'Better safe than sorry.'

I giggle, and hug his arm against me. 'Old Man Winter. Bet you've painted a picture of him. Getting barbecued, of course.'

'Funny you should say that.'

'Where's that one on display? Your office? The university crèche?'

'No, it's in my flat.'

We fall silent. I'll wait for him to speak. Play it cool, Suzey... Oh, what the hell. 'Better go and have a look at it then, hadn't we?'

He lives on a tenement street a mile away, close to a tiny park. The lights are all working, so we cross the park itself. Only one part is in darkness: a group of trees around a pond. A nickname comes to me: the Drowning Pond. It brings back memories of newspaper items: a child lost falling through the ice, a man lost trying to save her; a dog falling through, drowning with the owner who went in after it. It makes me shiver; Raj puts an arm around me.

He lives on the third floor, in a one-bedroom flat that's as much an artist's studio as a home. Canvases and sketchbooks lean against the living-room wall; a wooden easel is stashed behind the couch. He must have to rearrange the entire room if he's going to paint, unless he's just tidied up because he was hoping I'd come back with him. I smile over at him, and he smiles back. 'Coffee?'

'Yes, please.'

While he's in the kitchen I inspect the paintings. It wasn't just a case of come-and-see-my-etchings when he invited me here – the whole flat really is an art gallery. Every wall carries five or six pictures. I'd assumed all his art would be as monochrome as the two pictures I've seen, but almost all of these are in colour. They seem purely abstract until you've looked for a while, then landscapes and figures stand out. There's a tree with golden leaves, and black roots snaking across the ground; a figure in crimson, holding an apple; a rainbow made purely of ice colours – chilly blues and greens, arctic white. The rainbow is cracked in several places. There's also what looks like a waterfall of warm turquoise, surrounded by snow; a female figure, with hair about my colour, bends over the water. There's a word on the picture frame: *Winterburna*.

Raj walks in, carrying two mugs. I ask over my shoulder, 'What's "Winterburna"?'

'A winter stream. A stream that only flows in winter. Milk?'

'Sorry?'

'Do you take milk?'

'Oh. Yes, please.'

He goes out again. I should probably offer to help, but my attention's been caught by a large picture hanging over the gas fireplace. It's a swirl of gorgeous colour: spring green merging with emerald, russet melting into gold. A band of white encloses the colours like an eggshell. I do the stepping-back-and-forth thing, and slowly I begin to see them: two figures, hand in hand, with forest green all around them. One figure is tall, shoulders broader than hips, the other smaller, shoulders narrower, the slight curve of a breast visible as she stands turned a little to one side. A man and a woman, crowned in golden flame. The man has a halo of white-yellow curls; the woman's tawny hair falls to her waist. Within the outline of gold and green their shapes and their faces are blank. But you can tell they are gazing raptly at the green all around them.

I'm aware of Raj hovering behind me. I look over my shoulder and ask, 'Who are the—' I'm about to say "Hitler Youth", but his face is serious, so I substitute, 'these two?'

'Lif and Lifthrasir.' He's gazing at the picture, speaking half to himself. 'The two survivors of Ragnarok. The new Adam and Eve.' At last he smiles. 'Sentimental, I suppose.'

'Oh, yeah. Six billion folk in the world and only two survive. It's a real fairytale.'

'You're a very cynical person, Suzey.' He's still smiling. 'See if you like these any better.'

He talks me through the small square pictures: a fleshy mass of arms and legs ('the time of wickedness, when mothers will seduce their sons and brothers bed with sisters'), a red mass of severed arms and legs ('the time of warfare, when fathers will slaughter sons and brothers will be drenched in one another's blood') and a pale-grey ship apparently covered in scales ('the ship made from dead men's fingernails'). By the end I'm giggling uncontrollably. Still looking at the fingernail picture he says, 'Do you think I'm so funny, Suzey?'

I'm not fooled. I'm standing behind him, but I can hear the smile in his voice. I wrap one arm around his waist and the other around his shoulder and hug him to me. I rest my forehead on his shoulder; the top of my head scarcely reaches the nape of his neck. I whisper into his hair: 'You *are* funny. I wish you'd forget about the end of the world, just for once.'

'Do you, now?' He lifts his arm across my shoulders so I'm drawn around to face him. 'And what should I be thinking about instead?'

'I can think of a couple of things.'

'And so can I.' His breath is warm on my cheek. 'You can drink the coffee I made you, for one thing.'

'Oh.' Shit, I'm making an arse of myself. 'Oh, okay—'

That's when he kisses me.

Chapter 14

Sex is different here. Most of it takes place under blankets, in semi-darkness. Well-lit, movie-type sex – all bare limbs, beads of sweat, flimsy white sheets – doesn't happen in arctic climates with inadequate central heating. There's a lot more burrowing and nuzzling under covers. A lot more giggling. A lot more clinging together for warmth.

It's been a long time since I've had anything like this. I didn't realise how much I've missed it.

We keep most of our clothes on. There is an art to this. There should be a whole Kama Sutra of clothed sex. How much has to come off? How many shirt buttons have to be undone, before a hand can slide through to bare skin? Can we manage by just pushing everything aside, and sliding into place fully dressed? I catch a glimpse of this in the mirror – we look ravenous, as if we just couldn't wait.

We try different rooms – the living room is warmer, more freedom. But we always end up back under the blankets, whispering and laughing and crying out in the darkness, where the world begins and ends in the wide, covered bed.

'The Pole Star. See? Follow the farthest stars of the Dipper.'

'Where?'

'Up there.'

'No, is it really?'

'Cheeky girl.' He prods me in the ribs, or rather through the three layers of clothing around them. 'Directly above us. Look.'

I squint upwards. The sky has a generous freckling of stars, but I still can't make out any patterns. 'No, I can't see it.'

He sighs. 'I know. It's the light pollution. Keep looking, your eyes'll adjust.'

I keep looking, leaning back into him. I take his hands and pull them around my waist, giggling as he obligingly meshes his fingers together:

'You're my human seatbelt. And my back warmer, all in one.'

'All part of the service.'

I tip my head back onto his shoulder, keeping one hand on the guardrail in front of me – Raj's apartment block has a flat roof, but it's still slippy underfoot. Raj places one heavily gloved hand on top of mine; then, daringly, he peels off his top-glove and slides his fingers under my quilted mitten, so there's only a thin layer of wool between my wrist and his fingertips. You wouldn't believe how sexy it feels. 'Hey, doesn't this count as unsafe sex?'

'You wish. Can you see it yet?'

I open my mouth to say something obvious – but then, yes, I *do* see something. I point upwards, tracing a faint blur of lighter sky. 'Is that it? The Milky Way?'

'That's it. Bifrost. The rainbow bridge to Asgard. The home of the gods.'

It looks like a streak of polish against glass, nothing god-like about it. Raj, however, is off again: 'At Ragnarok the gods cross the bridge to fight the dark forces. The end comes, and the bridge breaks.'

'The gods are overweight?'

'No. Behave.' But he leans forward to nuzzle against my nose. Eskimo kisses: a real kiss might make us stick together. But it's enough – skin against skin, warm breath. I look out over the lights of the city; there aren't that many of them, really, but I find myself wishing them away, just for a moment, if that would make him happy…

This is getting scary. I've just met him. It's not real… I have a moment's vertigo, grab at the railing. He catches me, both hands around my waist, solid and secure. 'Are you okay?'

'Aye, fine.' The moment's passed. 'Can we go inside now?' I have to add the most un-erotic line ever. 'I've got to call my mum.'

We finally go to sleep exhausted, curled around one another in our nest of blankets.

I'm very tired. But as soon as I fall asleep I'm awake again.

I'm sitting upright. My clothes are thin and light. My neck isn't wrapped up, but the air is warm against my skin, almost stuffy.

I can hear distant voices, the heavy clatter of the drugs trolley. Close by, the quiet murmur of the TV. I am sitting quite comfortably, sunk into upholstery, my hands gripping something soft.

I'm back in the hospital.

I sit for a moment, heart thumping, trying to adjust. The common room is in restful semi-darkness. Slowly I look around. I'm sitting in one of the armchairs, facing the TV. Behind me are two of the geriatric dressing gowns, who never speak and never move if they can help it. In the next chair is a man in a suit. I've never seen him before.

I'm trying to examine him out of the corner of my eye, then I think, fuck it. Being mad has to give me some licence. I turn to look at him directly. He's not paying attention to me anyway, he's watching TV. He's in his fifties; he has an Einstein hairdo, white and sticking up all over. His suit looks nice, expensive. He doesn't look at me but says absently, 'Don't mind me, I'm just watching this.'

I look at the TV. The screen is orange and red; a terracotta desert and a pink sky. A silvery metal bug, flying a tiny Stars-and-Stripes flag, hobbles determinedly across the sand. I wonder why it bothers – surely one part of Mars is much like another? The thing isn't stopping, though. The horizon is jagged with chocolate-coloured hills; perhaps it's making for them.

'Look at that,' he says. 'A different world. Imagine it.'

I laugh. He seems genuine, but I'm getting wise to it now. Acting casual, appearing to be interested in the subject's delusions – it's the shrink's equivalent of a chat-up line. And it is a *very* nice suit.

'Mister Lisbon,' I say, 'I presume.'

He turns to me. His eyes are a dark, rich green, like pine needles. 'How do you know I'm not another patient?'

'Your pyjamas are a bit fancy, aren't they?'

He actually laughs. 'And you're Susan Pherson. They told me you were clever.'

Too clever to fall for *that*. 'Dr Martin says you're an expert on my kind of problem. But she hasn't actually told me what my kind of problem is. So, what exactly are you an expert on?'

He shrugs. 'What my colleagues tend to call dissociative disorders.'

'And what do you tend to call them?'

'Generally I call them dissociative disorders. But not in every case.'

'Not in my case?'

'No, not in your case.'

'Then what?'

He's watching the screen again. It's gone black and silver; an astronaut is bouncing around the surface of the Moon. 'It's a very particular form of fugue state. Do you know what fugue means?'

'Blackouts.'

'No. It means *rapid travel*. And that's what you do. You travel to different worlds, don't you?'

I nod. I lean towards him, conspiratorially. 'Do you know what we all hate in here?'

'What's that?'

'Folk pretending to believe us when they really think we're talking shite.'

He smiles, still looking at the TV. 'I don't think you're talking shite.'

'Oh, please.'

'I don't.' He looks straight at me, serious now. He really is good at this. 'So do you? Travel to different worlds?'

'It's in my file. Look it up.'

'I already did.' After a moment he says, 'Are you familiar with the idea of alternate realities?'

'No, I've been living in a fucking cave my whole life. Of course I'm familiar with it.'

'Do you believe it?'

'I don't know.'

'Do you believe that different realities can intersect?'

'I don't *know*.'

He's looking at me. 'Can I tell you about something that happened to me?'

I laugh shortly. 'That's a new one.'

'Can I tell you?'

'Yes.'

He turns back to the screen, but he doesn't seem focused on it. 'My wife,' he says, 'died four years ago. She was in a car accident. I believed I was coping well.' He pauses. 'A month after the funeral, I saw her in the garden. Our back garden.

'I shut my eyes and turned away. The next day I started a course of medication. One I'd always prescribed for hallucination disorders. An antipsychotic, similar to the one you take. I took the medication for several months. It didn't work.'

He is whispering now. I whisper too: 'Did you see her again?'

'Frequently. Mostly in the garden. But also in the street outside, or in the hospital. Always with her back turned.'

'Did you tell anyone?'

'Not at first. I tried different drugs, stronger ones. But after six months I was seeing her every two or three days. I'd stopped working. I was afraid to leave the house. Then I told a colleague, an old friend of mine.'

'What did he say?'

'He told me to speak to her. See what happened.'

'And did you?'

'Yes.' Longer pause. 'I saw her in the garden, so I went outside. I said her name, and she turned around and looked at me. She looked surprised.'

The silence stretches. He laughs shortly. 'Then I tripped over a loose flagstone. I'd always meant to fix the damn thing. By the time I looked up again, she was gone.' He turns back to the TV. 'I never saw her again.'

He's lying, I tell myself. Don't fall for it. But instead, I say, 'I can't control it. Going to the other place. This place, it's… it's not all bad. Not at all, but…'

'But?'

'There's something wrong there. Really wrong. But I can't stop myself going.'

'If you can't stop it, you'll have to go along with it.'

'Is that the best you can do?'

'Dr Martin will keep trying new treatments. Something will work in the end. But you know very well you can't just make this go away. Go along with it and see what happens. What else can you do?'

He's on his feet, holding out his hand. 'I'll check on you, Suzey. Good luck.'

I shake his hand, and then he's gone. The night nurse appears at the door. She looks irritable, not at all impressed that the great Mister Lisbon has just walked past her. 'Bedtime, Suzey,' she says.

I wake up spooned against Raj's back. It sounds like there's a blizzard outside; but it's nice and cosy in our cocoon of quilts and blankets, just like I'd never left.

So it was probably just a dream, then. Relieved, I settle down next to him to sleep. Yes, just a dream.

Part Three
The Harline Centre

....

Bolt and bar the shutter,
For the foul winds blow:
Our minds are at their best this night,
And I seem to know
That everything outside us is
Mad as the mist and snow.

...

WB Yeats

Chapter 15

It's our anniversary. Two weeks today.

I pounce on Raj as he tries to escape the flat. 'It's our anniversary, did you know?'

'Is it?'

'Two weeks since our first shag.'

'That's very romantic.'

'Isn't it. Want to celebrate?'

'I really do have to go.' But he lets his case fall to the floor. 'Are you trying to make me miss my train?'

'Get a later one.' I've already unzipped his coat. 'Blame it on the snow.'

'That's what everyone says.'

Now it's the buttons on his jacket. 'Okay, blame it on your insatiable girlfriend.'

'That would be very wrong of me.' He's using his serious voice, deep and drawling. 'Very…' The coat drops to the floor, 'very…' The jacket follows, '*very…*' Shirt buttons pop, 'wrong…'

He misses the next three trains. But I have to let him go eventually.

I make my way home via Kelvingrove Park. The sun is out; the park is blue-white and sparkling. The pines are Christmassy, and the holly bushes still have some red berries. I walk along the cleared path, looking down the smooth white slope at the frozen river. A man on skis whizzes past, white breath trailing behind him.

On my other side are steeper slopes. I can see the long shallow runway where kids have been sledging, now covered with a sheet of fresh snow. On impulse I clamber up to the top of the slide, until I'm looking down the runway. It looks like a ski jump. Before I lose my nerve, I dig out a black glan I can see poking through the top layer of powdery snow; then I take off my backpack, settle my bum onto the bin bag, and push out onto the hill.

The gradient grabs me, and I'm hurtling down. Rattling over bumps and dips, gaining speed, the world whirling around me. My own scream trails behind me like a banner. Then there's a cliff coming up, white-grey, and I'm going too fast, oh no, too fast—

I fly headlong into the bank of swept snow at the foot of the hill. There's an unpleasant moment when my eyes, nose and mouth are choked with snow, then I climb, spitting and laughing, out onto the path. A woman and a small boy are walking past; he points excitedly, she just stares and smiles. I smile back, and go clambering up the hill again, with the bin bag.

Just look at me. It's only been two weeks, and I'm already like something out of *It's a Wonderful Life*. What a sap. Jamie's going to laugh at me.

I'm still going to have another go, though.

It's evening by the time I get home. A strong wind has gotten up, and I'm glad to fall through the back door into the warm kitchen.

The wind is howling so loud I don't hear the yelling till the door is closed: an old woman's hoarse voice, bellowing, a second voice, high and protesting – my mother's.

I hurry out of the kitchen and burst through the living-room door.

Three faces turn towards me. Jamie is sitting in the chair by the fire, his face half hidden in his hands. My mother is standing to one side of him. Standing over Jamie is a white-haired woman I don't know. All three have stopped in place; they look like a freeze-frame from a soap opera. I laugh in spite of myself. 'What's going on? Who's this?'

The woman looks at me sideways, like a bird. 'Do you think this is funny, lady?'

I know her now. Irene, Katie's mother, though I remember her with expensively dyed auburn hair… A moment's dizziness, which I shake off determinedly. 'Mum, what's she doing here?'

'I'll tell you what I'm fucking doing here, shall I?' Her scarlet, pop-eyed face has turned all the way round to me. It's usually smooth and rather pretty, although the last time I saw it, it was rather like this. 'I'm here to tell this fucking perverted bastard he's not part of my family any more. He's to fucking keep away from us.'

Mum is hissing to me, 'I've been trying to get hold of you all day.'

Part of her family? But then of course he is. She's his wife's mother.

I look at Jamie, whose head is in his hands. 'Jamie, what's going on?'

'I'll fucking tell you,' says Irene. 'He's a bloody pervert and he's been caught at it. My daughter's at home now crying her eyes out.'

I'm watching in amazement. I've seen this scene before. Irene fancies herself, I suspect, as an enraged mother tigress; the day Katie rushed out of our kitchen in tears, Irene was round a few hours later. We didn't let her in, so she had to do this whole foul-mouthed routine from the other side of the living-room window. She was still out there, honking like a foghorn, when the police arrived. We all laughed about it, I remember. But no one's laughing now. 'All right,' I tell her, 'you've said your bit, you can go home now.'

I might have been talking to myself. 'You're not a part of my family any more. Stay away from us! Do you hear me! You *disgusting wee bastard*—'

She's leaning over Jamie's bowed head as if she's about to start clawing at his scalp. I manoeuvre in between the two of them, trying not to brush against her in case she goes for me. 'You leave him alone.'

For a moment I think her eyes are going to pop right out of their sockets. 'You're just going to let him get away with this.' Her voice is rising to a breathless shriek. 'Fucking *child molester* and you don't fucking *care!* Fucking pervert *bastard!*'

Her voice screeches out into a mute shaking. Good, maybe she's about to pass out right here on the hearthrug. I ask my Mum again, 'What's happened?'

'He got *arrested*—' She takes a deep breath, and goes on in her Sunday-best voice. 'Your brother was arrested. He's been accused of having sex with a young boy.'

A *boy?* 'Jamie, how old was he?' I ask.

'Nineteen,' he whispers.

I burst out laughing. '*Nineteen?* Christ, had he still his nappies on?' But Jamie and Mum are staring at me. After a moment Jamie says, 'I thought he was over twenty-one. I really did.'

Twenty-one? Oh, shit. Oh *shit*…

But Irene's off again. 'Fucking child molester. Don't you come near her again, do you hear me? Thank fuck she wasnae a boy. But you come near her and I'll fucking kill you—'

Jamie's on his feet, and I realise she's not talking about Katie. 'She's my daughter—'

'Not any more she's not. You keep away from us.'

Mum's trying to catch hold of Irene's arm. 'He'd *never* hurt Claire, he'd *never—*'

But Irene retreats to the door. 'You just stay away from us,' she says, and then she's gone.

'She's full of shite,' I say to Jamie. 'She can't stop you seeing Claire.'

'I'm being done for *child molesting*,' he shouts into my face.

And now my mother's screaming too. She's swatting at his head with the palms of her hands. 'How could you be so *stupid*, you *stupid*, *stupid*—'

'Mum, leave him alone. The guy was nineteen. He's not done anything wrong.'

'This is his *wife*. This is his *child*.' She collapses onto the sofa. 'I don't know what to do. I don't know what I'll—'

I go and put the kettle on.

'All right,' I say, one round of tea-and-gin later. Disgusting, but at least we've all stopped shaking. 'Never mind what the old cow said. Tomorrow we'll get a lawyer. It'll get sorted out.' Mum draws breath but I talk over her. 'There are people you can see for this. We'll find someone Jamie can see. These things happen more than people think.'

'Really?' They don't believe me, but they want to.

'Really,' I nod, trying to maintain my confidence.

Jamie says he's going to bed soon after.

I find him sitting on the single bed, looking dazedly around his old bedroom. I remember Mum redecorated it after Jamie had been with Carl a full year and obviously wasn't about to come home, but this is the old wallpaper, dingy yellow, spotted with blu-tack. One poster has survived: a black-and-white of Marilyn Monroe, smiling and holding down her skirt. Under Marilyn's feet are a stack of boxes, a tennis racket and an old hoover. Jamie is staring at them as if he doesn't know what they are. 'Try and get some sleep,' I tell him.

He nods. He's wearing striped nylon pyjamas, like Dad used to have – they might even be Dad's. No sweatshirt or socks. He must be freezing, but still he makes no move to get into bed.

'I'm perishing,' I say. 'Can I come in with you?'

He nods again, and this time gets under the pile of coats and thin duvets. I switch off the light and get in. It's a squash; I haven't shared a single bed with him in years. I remember when he was small enough to sleep in the curl of my stomach. I used to go and get him out of his cot, when Mum and Dad were fighting. I used to whisper bedtime stories into his fine baby hair. Now my toes are level with his shins and my nose is pressed against the back of his head, and we're as close as sardines. I put my free arm around him, and he takes my hand. My other arm is trapped against the mattress; I'm going to have pins and needles soon, but for now it's just good to be warm. 'We haven't done this since you came out,' I mutter.

He is silent, although I know he's not asleep, and I realise what I've said. 'Never mind,' I tell him. 'Forget I said that.'

After a moment he says, 'You said something like that before. Me coming out.'

'Just forget it.'

'I've never come out, I couldn't just *come out*—'

'Not here, no.'

'Then where?'

I don't know how to say it. What if he tells me to call the doctor, go back to the hospital? 'I've come from… somewhere else, Jamie. A different world.'

There's a long pause. Then he says, 'And I've come out there?'

'That's right.'

Another pause. I wait. At last he says, 'How did I do it?'

'You were young. You'd only just turned twenty.' I fall into the same murmuring tone I used to use for the bedtime stories. 'You'd started going out on the scene, but you were still engaged to Katie. You told me you loved her, but you'd stopped having sex with her because she was stressed out planning the wedding. Everyone kept saying you were in total denial, but you never listened.

'Then a whole bunch of us went through to the Pride Day in Edinburgh. It was the biggest ever. Archie Garry led it. We took over the whole city, they even flew the rainbow flag over the Castle.'

He laughs softly. 'Aye, right.'

'No, they did. A bunch of neds tried to pull it down, but the polis chased them off. And in the evening we all went to Step We Gaily, in the concert hall—'

'"Step We Gaily"?'

'The Pride ceilidh. Yes, I know. Anyway, we were doing the Dashing White Sergeant and you started saying, "I'm gay. I've got to tell her. I'm gay." And you went to see her next day and you told her.'

'What happened?'

'You just saw what happened. Katie ran out, Irene was round ten minutes later having a total conniption: *Oh, how could you, you're a pervert, blah-de-blah..*' But we left her out in the garden that time, I think. She never got past the door.

'And is Katie all right now?'

'God yes, she's fine. She's got a boyfriend. She asks about you sometimes but she's perfectly happy—'

'She's not a single mother, though, is she?'

'Shush, you'll wake Mum.' It's better if she doesn't know about the bed sharing. She never liked it, always made a fuss about it when we got older. But Dad didn't mind. 'That's your brother,' he'd say to me. 'You look after him, that's your wee brother.' I think about him now, and my arm tightens around Jamie. We lie in silence for a while, listening to the tiny creaks of a settling house, and the arctic howl of the wind.

'You awake?' Jamie whispers.

'Yeah.'

'What about everyone else then?'

'After Katie, it was fine. You were worried about Mum but she said she'd known for years. Davie was a bit off with you at first, but he came round okay.'

'What about Clive?'

'Clive?'

'Yeah, did he take it badly?'

'Clive *Miller*?'

'Yes. Was he… Oh, what, are you trying to tell me *Clive* is—'

'Clive came out when he was fifteen, Jamie.'

'He's got a girlfriend.' Jamie's starting to laugh. 'He's got a photo of this beautiful Swedish girl—'

'Don't tell me – lives in Sweden, no one's ever met her?'

'He plays rugby.'

'I know he does. He's living with the scrum half.'

'You're making this up.'

'I'm not. Honestly, Jamie, he spends his free time making animated porn movies. He showed a Disney one at you and Carl's flatwarming: Mickey Mouse fisting Goofy. I thought you were going to die laughing.'

By this time we're both giggling into the pillow like kids after lights out. My arm's gone to sleep but I'm not about to move, because for the first time in hours I'm warm enough. Besides, Jamie is now asking tentatively, 'This Carl guy. You say he's…'

'He's your fiancé.'

I feel him flinch. 'Don't take the piss.'

'I'm not. You've lived with him for two years. Now you're going to marry him.'

Another silence. 'What's he like?'

'He's great. He looks after you. He loves you.'

'Is he sexy?'

'Course he is. You can't keep your hands off each other.'

'Do we live in a nice house?'

Their flat is like a squat with good hi-fi, but I say, 'It's perfect. A work of art.'

'How did I meet him? Carl.'

'At Bowie's. On a Saturday night.' I'm whispering again. 'He was sitting with a bunch of guys in the quiet zone. I knew him from work and you asked to meet him. So I introduced you. And that was it. An hour later you went home with him, and you never really left.'

He's whispering too. 'Did I live with someone before him?'

'God no. You were never with anyone more than a month.'

'But Carl's different.'

'He's too good to let go. That's what you said. Too good to let go.'

'I want that.' It sounds like he's crying. 'I want to find someone like that.'

'You will. It's difficult now, I know it is. But you'll be happier than you thought you ever could be.'

He squeezes my hand, very hard. 'You're a great sister, Suzey.'

'It's okay.'

'Don't leave me again, Suzey. Don't leave me alone.'

'I won't. I promise.'

Finally, his breath is slowing and deepening. I wait a long moment, murmuring 'It's okay, you're okay' into his hair. He starts to snore quietly. I let out a long breath, and finally let myself drift towards sleep, even though I know I could easily be breaking my promise, just a moment after it was made.

Chapter 16

I open my eyes onto weak daylight. It's early. The wall before me is pale, marked with dark spots and stains. My nose is freezing. Experimentally, I pull the duvet below my chin and breathe out. The air mists.

I'm still here.

Jamie is lying against my back, his arm around my stomach, snoring gently. I wonder if that's what has woken me, until I realise there is, unmistakeably, an early-morning erection pressed against the base of my spine. I try to shift away and find I'm on the edge of the mattress as it is. It's no big deal, I tell myself, he's fast asleep and, what's more, it's freezing out there.

Shit. I'm muttering about 'bloody single beds' as I slide out into the icy air.

Jamie mumbles and pulls the covers around him. Thanks a lot, I think. But then it's probably just as well I'm up. Mum'll get freaked out about the bed-sharing thing, better if she doesn't notice. Chittering, I run downstairs.

Mum is sitting beside the fire, also modelling a tracksuit-and-bathrobe ensemble. 'Kettle's just boiled,' she says, without looking up. I go into the kitchen and find she's left the old teabag in a mug for me, with a splash of watery milk. I make the tea, sneaking in a spoon-tip of sugar, then hurry back through. The living room is warm and pleasantly musty. I'm reminded of my gran's house, the flowery wallpaper and the china Whimsies gleaming in the yellow light. I pull the footstool up to the fire and perch there, hands cupped around the hot mug. Mum and I sit without speaking.

Finally she says, still staring down at the hearthrug: 'Is your brother still asleep?'

So she *has* noticed. 'Aye, he's out of it,' I say. I'm waiting for a sharp comment, but she just nods. 'What did the polis say he's to do?'

'He'll get a summons.'

'They'll probably just drop the charges then.' She looks at me, not at all convinced. 'They cannae lock up everyone, just for that.'

Mum hands something to me, a picture done in bright jewel colours: a postcard of an impossibly white beach and green jungle and blue sea and sky. It says *Greetings From Melbourne* in curly script. 'It's from your Uncle Jim,' Mum says, not before I've turned it over and read the whole message: *Hope to see you soon.* Mum's brother is not one for small talk. 'Is he coming out to see us?' I ask.

She laughs sharply. 'Why would he want to come here?'

'Because we're here.'

'No. He wants me to go out there.'

'Are you going to go?' She nods. I have a horrible feeling I can see where this is going, but I still ask. 'How long for?'

'For good.' Before I can speak she hurries on. 'It's much better out there. You can get a chance. There's jobs, they need people—'

'You're just going to swan off and leave us?'

'Of course I'm not. You and Jamie can come too. Make a fresh start—'

'What about Claire? What're we going to do, abduct her?'

'We'll never get to see Claire again.' Her voice is flat and harsh. 'They'll never let him near her.'

'But they'll let you. You're her gran, you've not—'

'Aye, they'll maybe bring her here once a fortnight. With a social worker to watch us.'

'No, they—'

'Yes, they *will*, Suzey.'

I'm shaking my head. 'Jamie'll not go off and leave her like that.'

'He'll need to. He'll get over it. He's young.'

'For God's sake, Mum!'

'He's made this bloody mess! Why couldn't he just stay at home, with his wife and his child! If he wanted them that much!'

She's started to cry. Her hands are trembling as they rake through her white hair. This is not right. She's supposed to be brown-haired, active, plotting yet another sunshine holiday with her glamour-granny mates. Not sitting here, an old woman, fretting over her fucked-up kids, hunched over a one-bar fire that can't hope to keep her warm. I go and perch on the arm of her chair, and take one of her icy hands and start rubbing it. 'Mum, it's okay. We'll sort something out.'

'He'll have to come out there with me. They don't care about stuff like that out there.' But, I think, they might care about a criminal record. I say nothing, though, and she carries on. 'It'll be warm. We can go out in the country.' I have an image of the three of us on horseback, wearing Stetsons and galloping across a rolling plain, and I smile in spite of myself. 'Your Uncle Jim'll put us up till we find our feet.'

'It sounds lovely.'

She looks at me fiercely. She knows when I'm humouring her. 'It'll give you a chance, Suzey. You're young. There's nothing for young folk here.'

'I know. But…'

'Aye, well, just think about it.' We hear shuffling upstairs, the flush of the toilet making the pipes clang. We're sitting innocently in opposite chairs, looking composed, by the time Jamie makes his appearance.

He's dressed and combing his hair, although he looks tired and ill and won't meet Mum's eye. 'I'm going in to work,' he says.

'You sure?' I say.

'May as well.'

Mum nods. 'Best to get on with it.' She looks pointedly at me. 'You've got stuff to get on with as well, haven't you?'

'I'm going to the library today.'

Mum makes a tutting 'all right for some' noise, but gets up to go to the kitchen. We can hear the kettle boiling – she'll be making a tea for us all – but Jamie gets his coat, gives me a wan smile and goes out without another word.

I'm not at the library long. I actually don't need to be there at all – I've just managed to persuade Mum I have to, so I can get out of the house for a sanity break once in a while. Also, the library has a phone that's almost permanently working. I get in the queue.

I've got to call Raj's number three times until I catch his phone working too. It's just his answer message. I'd expected that, he was going to be in Edinburgh for one night at least. But hearing his voice, clipped and impersonal, I realise how much I was hoping he'd still be around. At the beep I mumble incoherently, then spend ages figuring out how to erase the message and start again, while the queue coughs and shuffles impatiently behind me. In the end I just say, 'Call me when you get in.'

I spend a few more minutes at the library's leaflet table. I've tried to go online: hopeless. Have to do this the low-tech way. I rifle through stacks of colourful A5 sheets with catchy headlines: *Depression, the Facts*;

Hypothermia, the Silent Killer, Ibrox Mother and Toddler Group. I finally find one that looks promising: *The Harline Centre – Gay & Lesbian Support Centre.* They're in one of the Infirmary buildings, I know the place; surely they can put us in touch with someone. I pocket the leaflet, feeling slightly better; then I choose some clever-looking grammar and spelling textbooks (Mum doesn't know my laptop checks these things) and set off home.

I work till just after lunchtime – books and papers spread out on the coffee table, Mum reading in her chair by the fire, domestic peace for once – when Jamie reappears. The sky is starting to look inky, so at first I think his office has closed early, but one look at him tells me that's not what it is. His face is grey, the way it looked when he broke his arm ten years ago. He's clutching a rolled-up newspaper, which he passes to me without a word. It's the *Standard,*

MIRACLE GIRL'S BROTHER CAUGHT WITH BOY. It's the second headline, but it's big enough. There's a picture of Jamie – it's a Jamie-but-not-Jamie, looking older, furtive, sweaty. Under the picture it says *Indecent behaviour.*

'Sweet Jesus,' I say.

Jamie slumps onto the couch. 'The age is halfway down,' he says. 'You can hardly even see it.'

I look halfway down the column, where the text is a lot smaller. It says *aged 19,* in letters small enough to miss it completely. 'Jesus *Christ,*' I say.

'Mum?' Jamie's voice is sharp. Mum must have stood up, because he's caught hold of her arm and is lowering her gently back into her chair. 'Oh, God,' she's saying. 'Oh, God…'

I fetch water, then whisky – which she doesn't touch. Jamie sits on the arm of the chair, holding her hand and talking firmly. 'It's okay. You're fine. Don't worry. I'll sort it. It's all right…'

His voice is calm, the determined man-of-the-house. She looks up at him beseechingly. 'What will you do?'

'I'll get a lawyer.'

'Oh…'

'Mum,' I say softly, 'do you want go and lie down for a while?'

She doesn't move; overwrought or not, she knows fine we'll start laying plans in her absence, and she wants to be in on it. 'A lawyer. That'll cost you, won't it?'

'We can get one through this centre,' I say, as confidently as possible. I pull out the Harline Centre leaflet. She takes it, looking slightly reassured: it's got a leaflet, so it must be a proper organization, with people who know what they're doing. 'Oh, okay.'

We hear footsteps on the path outside, and voices: men, at least two or three of them. Mum's hands start fluttering again. 'I'll get it,' I say, and head for the door.

As I reach for the front door handle, it has already started to turn. The door swings inwards; I grab it and yank it towards me, making the man outside stumble forward. He looks at me and smiles, completely unabashed. 'Suzey,' he says.

I've never seen this guy before. I step forward to block the doorway; I'm already blinking in the snow-light when a lightning-flash goes off in my face. A camera. An anoraked man is taking pictures of me. Beside him are two more guys in parkas; one has a black box balanced on his shoulder, the other is shoving something metal and alarmingly phallic-looking into my face. I blink a couple more times. It's a microphone, of course, and the black box is a camcorder. But I'm no less confused. The first man is still chatting like I'm an old pal: 'Suzey, how do you feel?'

'What?'

'How are you feeling? How are your family holding up? What do you say to the charges?' He's serious now, grave but sympathetic. I'm beginning to think I do recognise him after all. 'Are you with the *Standard*?'

'That's right. Is Jamie admitting the charges, Suzey?'

'You should be bloody ashamed of yourselves.'

'I see it's very distressing for you, Suzey. Can you tell us how you feel?'

'The guy was *nineteen*. He wasn't a boy. He was a man, for God's sake—'

'So Jamie *was* with him then?'

'Well…' I take a step back, although he hasn't pushed forward. 'I mean— no.' I take a deep breath. 'My brother's done nothing wrong. Nothing.'

'So you're saying he's innocent?'

'I'm saying he's done nothing – yes, he's innocent. Now go away, would you? My Mum's not well.'

'What's wrong—' he begins, but I slam the door in his face. While I'm turning the deadbolt and attaching the chain, he's knocking on the door, still shouting, 'What's wrong with your Mum, Suzey? Does she not keep well?

Has the doctor been—'

I escape into the living room and shut the door. It's a lot darker in here now – Jamie has been putting the blackout in place. Now he and Mum are staring at me. I don't want to meet their eyes, so I start crashing about, looking for the phone. 'Where's the damn thing gone now?'

'Who do you want to call?' says Mum, faintly.

'Anita Black. She's high up in that place. She'll get this stupid story put right—'

'Look at the article, Suzey,' Jamie says.

I've still got the *Standard* clutched in my hand. I look again at the front page, although I know from Jamie's tone what I'm going to see. *Story by Anita Black.*

Beyond the blackout curtains, the reporter starts to tap on the window. I throw the paper at the curtain. It doesn't help much.

We spend hours like that, sitting in the gloom behind the curtains. Footsteps go up and down the path, the doorbell rings, hands rap on the door or the window. Voices travel round the side of the house; we lock the back door. We don't say much to each other. The house seems very small, the air very close.

I get out the ancient laptop and get on with the typing. I make a lot of mistakes. The doorbell rings, and keeps on ringing – someone's leaning on the button. Jamie slams into the hallway; there's a wrenching sound as he pulls the doorbell unit out of the wall. Mum makes a soft protesting sound, but smothers it before Jamie comes back in.

There's a brisk, peremptory knocking at the door. It sounds official, might be the police. I ease back the curtains and peer out. Another flash in my face – it's just another one of those shutter-happy morons, getting impatient and (I hope) very cold. Before I close the curtains I notice a group of people on the pavement; the pushy reporter is holding the microphone towards them, and one woman is talking earnestly into it. They're neighbours; the woman lives just across the street. A man, I think he lives four doors down, is staring at the house. I meet his disgusted gaze for a moment before I retreat behind the curtains. 'They'll get cold and go away, surely,' says Mum. 'Before too much longer.'

We agree that they will. At least I do. Jamie just gets up and goes quietly upstairs. After a moment we hear his feet overhead; he's making sure the blackout curtains are in place. 'Well,' I say again, for want of anything else. 'I'll start making the dinner.'

There's a dull sliver of daylight around the kitchen window; I fix the curtain and snap on the lights. It gives the room a clinical look, but at least it's bright. I put the mince on to brown, and throw in the onion powder. I'll cook it in lots of gravy, almost a mince soup, that way we can swallow it straight down without having to bite on the gristle. I drain, add water, a corner of precious stock cube… No, fuck it, I'll put in the whole cube. I bang pots and pans and cupboard doors, it's almost soothing. Then I dust in a little paprika, and the room starts to smell warm and spicy.

I'm just about to open the cans of spuds when Jamie comes in. He checks the back door is locked, then pushes a chair against it for good measure. 'I'm going to go away for a while,' he says.

I didn't expect that. 'Where?'

He shrugs.

I start thinking through a list of his options. Are any of his friends likely to take him in? But they're mostly Katie's friends too, and all his gay contacts are casual. Could he get a flat of his own? That'll take ages, if it happens at all. What about a job outside the city? Where? Doing what? Won't he have to stay put anyway, for the police and everything?

'Jamie,' I say, 'I can't think where you'd go.'

'It doesn't matter.'

'Of course it *matters*.'

'You and Mum don't need all this crap—'

'Jamie, don't be daft.' Shit, I've burnt the mince now. 'Open the spuds, would you? If you're going to be running away from home you can have your dinner first.'

He opens the tins of boiled spuds and lets them thunk onto the bottom of the pan, brine splashing over them. 'See,' I say, 'where else are you going to get such fancy cooking?'

'I'm serious, Suzey—'

There's a loud thud from the front of the house, and a little shriek from Mum. We both run for the living room. Mum is staring at the curtain, one hand over her heart as if she's pledging allegiance; it would be comical if it weren't for the shock on her face. 'I think they threw something,' she says.

There's another loud bang on the window – no sound of breaking glass, thank God – and a much fainter thud as something hits the outside wall. They're chucking things, the bastards. 'Right, that's it.' I start towards the front door. 'This is—'

'*Don't.*' Jamie grabs my arm, hard. 'Don't open it.'

Mum takes my hand. The three of us stand for a moment, very close together, in the gloomy room. We can hear loud voices outside, singing, chanting. 'Mum,' I say. 'Call the polis.'

I disentangle myself from them and head for the stairs. The window in the front bedroom, that'll be best. I rip off the masking tape that's been holding the floral drapes in place. Daylight hits my face; an hour ago it would have dazzled me, but now it's grey. Small flecks of snow whirl past as I wrench the window open – it sticks, hasn't been opened for months – and stick my head out into the icy air.

In our front garden, and the pavement and road beyond, is a mass of people. Flashguns pop occasionally, and the microphone is being waved over someone's head; but most of the crowd aren't carrying, or talking into, any cameras. They're carrying placards, white banners on sticks, which they're jabbing at the sky to the rhythm of their chanting. My gaze falls on two women who are nodding to one another and almost smiling, but not quite. They look around my age. One of them is carrying a placard reading *PERVERTS OUT*.

And this is what they're all chanting. 'PER-VERTS OUT! PER-VERTS OUT!' A few of the men, the ones without placards, are punching the air. I read all the other painted slogans: *NO BEASTS HERE*, and *SAVE OUR SONS*, and *SHAME! SHAME! SHAME!* One of the signs stands above the rest like a holy icon, with a picture of a blonde haloed saint. It's Peter Balfour, with his golden curls and angel smile. Around his image are the words *GIVE ME JUSTICE*.

'Holy fucking *Christ*.' Jamie is beside me, looking out. His voice is barely a whisper, but dozens of white faces turn towards us. Jamie pulls me back, away from the great roar of voices. He slams the window shut as missiles bang against it, cracking the glass. Jamie is dragging me towards the door. 'Move, Suzey!'

'They broke our window,' I say, stupidly. Jamie takes no notice and pulls me down the stairs, so fast I'm scared we'll fall. Mum is waiting for us at the bottom, clinging to the banister. Behind the thin front door the crowd bellows; what sounds like a giant's fist hits the door, again and again.

'I couldn't get the polis,' Mum says, gesturing towards the living room and the useless phone. Her face is white, but her voice is bizarrely calm. 'Somebody out there will, though—'

The letterbox rattles – the insulation is yanked out. There is a stink of petrol as a piece of cloth, already wrapped in flames, is rammed through and tumbles onto the doormat. Mum and I shriek in unison – outside another woman echoes us. The doormat ignites like thatch but Jamie has already grabbed the nearest jacket, a wool greatcoat, from the wall, and thrown it over the mat. He starts stamping down the coat; there's more rattling from the letterbox. 'Jamie!' I scream. 'Get back!'

Something else pokes through: the blunt end of a garden broom or rake. It jabs ineffectively at Jamie, looking so stupid I laugh, my voice shrill and unrecognisable. The stick starts poking towards me and with it, through the letterbox, comes a man's voice, echoed by the crowd's voice, a stream of grunts and guttural threats: 'fuckin' pervert, fuckin' kill ye!' Jamie gets hold of the broom handle and yanks it in, hard. There's a satisfying grunt from outside and Jamie stumbles away from the door, still gripping the handle. He starts to yell too: 'Fuckin' CUNTS! Ma MOTHER'S in here! Ma SISTER'S in here! Fuckin' BASTARDS!'

'Get your coat on and get out,' says Mum, still calm. 'Quick. Round the back. Go on!' We're both clinging to her hands as if we were five years old again.

There's another thunderous boom from the door. I think I can hear them round the side now. Mum is propelling me firmly into the kitchen, towards the back door. I badly want to just open the door and run, but I have to wait for Jamie, who comes in carrying great slippery armfuls of outdoor clothing. Mum won't let us go any further until we're in our boots and our parkas.

Then she opens the door. She's not wearing her outdoor clothes. 'Go on then,' she says.

Jamie's staring at her. 'Mum?'

'I'm going to stay and have a word. I'm not running.'

'Mum, for God's sake!'

'They're not after me.'

She goes back inside. By the time I've tied my bootlaces we can hear her voice upstairs, high-pitched and querulous: 'Here! What d'ye think you're doing! Go away and leave us alone—'

There's movement in the corner of my eye. Someone is climbing over our back fence. It's the man from four doors down. He pauses, one leg on either side of the fence, when he sees me. He's lived here about three years, and always acknowledges me with a nod and a smile, which I always return. So that, surreally, is what we do now. Someone – Jamie – barrels past me towards him. The man, smile gone, shouts out a warning, but a moment later Jamie has grabbed hold of his ankle and hauled him so far onto our side that he topples sidelong into our snow-covered garden. Jamie is still holding the broomstick; the man's face shows, for a moment, the amazement of a bigot discovering that poofs are not soft. I don't look at what happens next, although in the corner of my eye I see red, and I hear a crack followed by a bellow of pain and rage. I'm already scrambling up the lumpy snowdrift that covers the compost heap; from there I can haul myself up onto the fence. There's no one in the back lane beyond. But I can still hear them, somewhere. 'Jamie!'

He's beside me. 'Mum—'

I look back; the door is closed, Mum's nowhere in sight. 'Jamie, come *on!*'

We both tumble into the lane. I land awkwardly, banging my knee and shoulder. We see them appear at the other end of the lane, indistinct shapes, some in vivid colours. There's nothing human in them now. We get up and run. Snowflakes are falling thick around us. Jamie holds me by the wrist, pulling me along, faster than I could go alone. Our feet should slip but they don't. I lose track of where we are. I can't hear anything behind us or ahead of us. We just run and run.

At last Jamie slows down; I slow too, realising all my momentum for God knows how long has come from him. I look back. There's no sign of anyone but us. My hood is down, and that's bad, because my face and hair are damp with sweat, but I don't pull it up until I've had a good look around to make sure they're gone.

The sun is trying to push through the clouds above us, but the sky ahead is a deep charcoal grey. We're standing on Bell's Bridge, the footbridge connecting the South Side with the North. Jamie is looking back the way we came. There's nothing to be seen, but we can hear sirens. 'Mum,' he says.

I look back too. 'There's no smoke.' He looks at me, stricken. I turn him back around. 'There's no smoke. They didn't put the place on fire.'

'The siren—'

'It's the polis, Jamie, not the fire brigade.' It might be an ambulance, I think, but I don't say so.

'But – oh, God, Suzey, Mum—'

'She'll be fine.'

'Do you think we should—'

'We need get going. We can go to that Harline place, remember? It's at the Infirmary.'

'Aye. Okay.'

The snow is falling heavier now. A northwest wind sweeps down the river, pushing us sideways into the barrier. I spare a quick look back over my shoulder towards my mother's house, and smile a little, remembering her standing firm in her hallway against the howling barbarians. She'll be fine, of course; how could she not be?

The Western is not far from here, but it's a long walk in a blizzard. I hold Jamie's hand to pull him along. Now that the momentum of our escape has burned out he has just stopped, like run-down clockwork. Before long we have scarcely ten yards' visibility, though it hurts too much to raise our faces to the stinging snow in any case. I follow pavements, huddling into doorways to scan the world for anything like a landmark. I end up gripping Jamie's arm by the wrist instead of the hand; I make him do the same. It's all too easy to imagine him slipping away, back the way we came, into the screaming white throat of the storm.

Chapter 17

We fall in through the glass doors. After spending far too many hours in hospitals, with Dad, I never thought I could be so glad to be in one. The blizzard, still making that deranged screaming sound, is trying to push the door open again. A woman's voice bawls at us to shut it but I don't need telling – I put my shoulder into it and bang the door to. The shrieking is muffled slightly. Against the darkness the snow whirls so fast it's a blur.

I pause to stomp the worst of the snow from my boots. There are plenty of melting footprints on the lino, but I have never seen an A&E on a Saturday night with so few casualties in it. People must have decided to bleed to death in the comfort of their own homes. Or perhaps the ambulances just couldn't get through… No, we're not going to think about that. There's a payphone near the door, unbroken as it turns out. I put in the last of my change and call Raj, to leave another message. But I can't get through, not even to the answer machine.

Jamie's standing exactly where I left him. If these people don't help us, we won't have anywhere to go. I take his arm and haul him over to the desk.

A nurse in a thick blue fleece looks at us impatiently. I can't remember what this fucking place is called. I start digging about in my pockets. I'm scared I dropped the leaflet in the snow, when I was too scared to think of anything but staying on the path and hanging on to Jamie. But in my last pocket I find it, squashed and pink. The nurse sees it and nods, her face softening a little. 'First floor, pet. Come out the lift and go right round to the left.'

I thank her, pathetically grateful for this scrap of kindness. The lift is broken so we plod up the stairs. The yellowing corridors are windowless and harshly lit, but warm. We pass signs for urology and genitourinary medicine, but nothing for the Harline Centre. We keep bearing left, though, and come eventually to a blank door with a copy of the pink leaflet sellotaped to it. I try the door, half expecting to have to knock and give a password, but it's unlocked.

We shuffle into a small waiting room, windowless and smelling slightly of feet. Alternate posters of smiling couples – two men, then two women, then men again – line the walls. There's a coffee table scattered with torn magazines, surrounded by banks of scruffy airport-lounge seating. Two young men are seated in the corner, talking intensely in low voices. Another guy sits nearby, older, with red-rimmed eyes, although he doesn't seem to be crying. All three look up, glancing for a moment at me, a moment longer at Jamie, then away again.

Opposite the door is a reception counter, behind which a large, short-haired woman is watching us closely. When we've closed the door behind us, she goes straight back to studying her paperwork; I just know she and I are not going to get along.

'Yes?' she says loudly before we're halfway to the desk, presumably wanting us to shout out our problems to the whole room. I wait until we're at the counter and have unwrapped my scarf before I go to answer. And then I realise I haven't a clue what I'm going to say. 'We need to speak to someone,' I eventually manage, looking at the door behind the woman and hoping there's someone else behind it.

She produces a clipboard with a tied-on pen and a badly photocopied form, which she pushes towards us. 'The counsellors are with people just now. You can wait, but you might need to come back tomorrow.'

I'm starting to feel sick. 'We can't do that. We've no place to stay.'

'We don't arrange accommodation.' She sounds like she's saying there's no sugar for our tea. When we don't answer she looks up at me. Her wide, flat face is expressionless. She really doesn't give a shit. She's going to put us out in the blizzard and her ugly face is still going to look like that. I don't know what to do. I don't—

'We nearly got burned out of our house.' Jamie's voice is quiet but carrying. 'They only didn't burn it cause my mum was in it. We're gonnae sit here till somebody sees us.'

I expect her to call security, but she looks hard at Jamie. Silence has fallen behind us. I glance back; the two young guys are watching us wide-eyed. The older guy just shakes his head a little. 'You go in ahead of us, son,' he says. He looks at the other two for assent and they nod vigorously.

I'm suddenly in tears. 'Thanks,' I say.

'You're all right, hen.'

Before we've taken our coats off, an older man in a duffel comes through the door behind reception, nods goodbye to the woman and leaves. With no sign of rancour, she shows us in.

We find ourselves in a tiny office, surrounded by posters and black-and-white prints of muscular men. The counsellor has his back to us, closing and locking a small filing cabinet. 'Come in and sit down,' he says. I honestly do not recognise him until I hear his voice, because his short hair is iron grey.

His hair is supposed to be black, I remember him getting it dyed. I laugh out loud. 'Why didn't I think of this? Where else would you be?'

'Sorry?'

'Nothing.' I hold out a hand. 'Jamie, this is Carl.'

Carl looks at me, warily. 'Have we met?'

'In a manner of speaking.'

Carl's nodding, still looking at Jamie. 'You do look familiar.'

Not much of a chat-up line, but we've all got to start somewhere. 'I'm Suzey,' I say.

Carl turns his attention to me. His face is paler than I remember it, more lined. The eyes are just the same, though, dark and watchful. 'I know you as well, don't I?'

Does he really know? How can he… 'Yes. Yes, you do, Carl.'

He nods to himself suddenly, reaches into a drawer of his desk and pulls out a newspaper. It's the *Standard*. 'I thought so. Jamie… Pherson?'

Jamie nods. Carl skims through the article, frowning, although he manages a smile when he glances up at me. 'And you must be Miracle Girl.'

'That's me. My superpowers aren't up to much, but.'

'So I see.'

Carl keeps on scanning down the page. It seems to take ages. When he turns to page two, Jamie says, 'We had to run out the house. There was a whole fuckin' mob of them. Mum's still there. Are you going to fuckin' do something?'

Carl just watches him till he finishes speaking. 'Finished?' He turns the phone on his desk towards us. 'Call your mother.'

Jamie grabs the phone and dials. He holds the receiver against his ear. For a long time. 'It's ringing out,' he says at last.

'She'll be okay,' I say.

Jamie nods, still clutching the phone to his ear. Eventually I have to take it from him and hand it back to Carl. Carl breaks the connection, making Jamie wince, and starts dialling. 'I'm calling the local polis,' he says. For a paranoid moment I wonder if we should run for it. But he means the South Side polis, Mum's local station. 'Hello, Carl Trainor at the Harline Centre… Yes, at the Infirmary… Could I speak to DS Thompson, please… Aye, I'll hold.'

He waits, and I whisper to Jamie. 'She really will be okay. They won't… do anything. You know. To her. It really will be—'

Jamie waves me into silence, as Carl wraps up his call. 'Ask him to call back as soon as he can, please. Appreciate it. Aye. Okay, bye.' He hangs up. 'They're calling back. Once they've got someone who knows about the situation.'

Jamie's knuckles are white on the arms of the chair. 'You mean they hadn't noticed the lynch mob till you pointed it out?'

Carl doesn't respond to this. 'So what's your situation now?'

I decide to get in first. 'We had to get out of the house. There was a big crowd of people, with banners and stuff. They were banging on the door. You know, trying to break it down.'

He's nodding, and taking notes. 'Then what?'

'Mum said she'd stay behind and talk to them. Then we ran away, we had to. They came after us.'

'Did you get hurt at all?'

'*We* didn't. That bastard coming over the fence did though.' I look at Jamie. 'I hope you broke his fucking teeth—'

Jamie's hissing at me to be quiet, but Carl's got the idea. 'You hit one of them?' he says sharply.

'He had to. No, Jamie, I won't *shush*. He was shouting for the rest of them—'

'And he attacked you,' Carl is saying firmly, still writing. He looks at Jamie. 'He was going for your sister. You were protecting her. That how it was?'

'Aye,' says Jamie, 'that was it.'

Carl nods. 'Okay. Now. Do you have any friends you could—'

Jamie and I both jump as the phone rings. Carl picks it up. 'Harline Centre for… Yes. Yes, just a minute.' He holds the receiver out to Jamie. 'It's for you.'

Jamie's hand closes tightly over mine, the other reaching for the receiver. 'Hello? *Mum*? Mum, is that you? Aye, I'm fine… Aye, she's here, she's fine. Are you okay?'

I wedge my head next to his, so my ear's right by the receiver. I can't make out the words, but it's Mum's voice all right. 'Are you all right?' I yell.

Jamie's crying now. 'Aye, that was her. We're both fine, Mum. I'm so sorry… I don't know what to…'

I prise the phone away from him. 'Mum, are you okay? Where are you?'

'I'm okay.' Her voice is high and quavering, more like my grandmother's than my mother's. 'I'm at Betty Campbell's.' One of her cronies a few streets over. 'The police brought me here. I told them about the Centre thing you were talking about, and they got the number for me. They've been very good.'

'But you're all right? You didn't… get hurt?'

'No, no. And the house is fine. They said I've not to go back there just now, but I don't think that's right. All my things are there.'

'Don't go back to the house, Mum. Stay at Betty's.'

'Oh, Suzey, I don't know about that. Those people are all away now.'

'Don't go back tonight, Mum. Don't.' I look up at Carl and say loudly into the receiver, 'The counsellor here's saying not to go back, Mum.'

'Oh… Really?'

'That's what he says. Here, ask him.' I hold out the phone to Carl. After a moment's bemusement, he takes the receiver and puts on an impressively official voice. 'Hello, Mrs Pherson… No, I think your daughter's quite right. You should stay put for just now. At least until it's light. Yes, that's right… Yes, we're looking after them here, they'll be fine. Mrs Pherson, could you put the police on for a minute? Yes, I'll tell them… You're welcome… Bye now.' When he speaks again his voice sounds back to normal. 'Carl Trainor at the Harline Centre. Who am I speaking to, please?'

He gets passed around a lot. Suddenly finding I can breathe again, I sit up straight and look around the room at the arty postcards of topless men, the slightly tatty posters for Pride Week, for GlasGay, even one for Gay Christian Scotland. Pinned to that one is a sheet of thick parchment paper, which looks somehow familiar. There are rainbows everywhere, a bit faded in the dull light. Photos of Carl with friends, mostly male, all grinning into the camera are stuck to the wall beside his desk. I don't know any of them.

'Right. Bye. Thanks.' He clearly means 'thanks for nothing', but his tone is polite. When he puts the phone down I say, 'Thanks for speaking to our Mum.'

'No problem. Right.' He looks over the pad he's been scribbling in. 'I asked those guys to contact your local polis, to let them know you've not done a bunk. They didn't give a shit, however, so I'll call myself in the morning, then we'll see what's what. Have you got a lawyer?' Jamie shakes his head. They're detached, formal; strangers to one another. 'There's one attached to the Centre. I'll call him tomorrow too.'

'Do you think they'll drop the charges?' I ask.

'Probably.' He pauses. 'But you'll need to speak to the lawyer. First things first, though, where are you going to be staying?'

We both stare blankly at him, and he repeats carefully, 'Where can you stay? Are there any friends or family who can put you up for a couple of days?'

'Well… No,' I say. 'That's why we're here.'

He doesn't believe us. 'No one at all?'

'Well, there's Raj…'

'Who's Raj?'

'He's my boyfriend.' Is that what he is? It's all happened so fast. But now isn't the time to think about that. 'After tonight,' I say. 'He's away tonight. But after that, for a wee while maybe…'

'No one else?'

I'm getting annoyed. 'Listen, he's just out the closet and I've been dead for a fortnight. How many mates do you think we've got?'

'Then I don't know what to—'

'Suze,' says Jamie, 'did you pick up any money before we went out?'

'No. Did you?'

'No.'

I turn back to Carl. 'We'll sit in the waiting room all night.'

'You can't—'

'We'll have to. There's nowhere else. I'll leave a message with my boyfriend – he'll be back in the morning. We'll be gone first thing, okay?'

He looks at us for a long time, then sighs. 'Call your boyfriend, then. It's nine for an outside line.'

I grab the phone before he can change his mind. For a moment of panic I can't remember Raj's number. I type it out slowly, and it goes straight to voicemail. I take a couple of deep breaths, then say as calmly as I can, 'Raj, we've had a bit of bother. We're at this place now, in the Infirmary. It's called the Harline Centre. Hang on, the number's—'

'Suzey?'

'Raj! You're there? I mean – you're at home?'

'The conference is off. The roads are too bad. Suzey, what's happened? Where are you?'

Suddenly I'm crying. Big, hiccupping sobs like a child. 'Oh, Raj... Oh God, I can't tell you...'

We have to walk. Carl gave us bus fare but the buses aren't running. It takes nearly an hour. I don't care.

The flat is cosy. There's a big pile of pillows and quilts on the couch for Jamie. I fall into Raj's arms and do a lot more sobbing, and he doesn't let go. Jamie sits on the couch, staring at the floor.

Chapter 18

Three days later and we're out of clean clothes. The polis retrieved the house's 'valuables' for us; unfortunately that meant the telly, the laptop, and nothing else.

So I'm determined: I'm going back in.

The sun is bright but heatless. I'm floundering through a night's heavy snowfall; it pours in over the top of my boots. Finally I reach the narrow pavement, which has thankfully been swept and gritted. They take care of things like that on this street – never know when a lynch mob might have to get through in a hurry.

I plod along, following the crescent, keeping my head down. In the corner of my eye, I see movement in the ground-floor windows I pass: my presence has been noted. I'd hoped that at least some of these arseholes would have jobs to go to during the day, but apparently not. When I look up, the figure at the window is always turning away.

Across the road from our house, three men are standing casually beside the break in the snow bank that leads out into the road. They might have been there for a while, or they might just have strolled out onto the pavement. One of them lives across the street from us. As I draw level with them, he says, in a cheerful voice, 'Where's the woofter then?'

'Piss off.'

They all go *Oooo-ooo!* My parka brushes briefly against the nearest man as I step out into the road. One of them says something I don't catch, and they all laugh. I don't look round, I won't give them the satisfaction.

Our garden is white and smooth. All those trampling feet must have left a slushy mess last night, but the blizzard has covered it completely. Pushing through the deep, powdery snow takes some effort, so I don't register immediately that there's something different about the house. Across the outside wall are some daubs of blue paint – presumably they once spelled out words, but now they've smeared and run. These fucking stupid neds, they can't even do graffiti properly. But that's not the main difference: the windows and doors now seem to be made of brown wood, with stripes of alternating yellow and black.

I blink a couple of times and realise what I'm seeing. The doors and windows are boarded up, and striped with police tape. I try to peer under the boards, but they're securely fixed, so I can't see if the windows are actually broken or if the cops have just sealed them up.

There's a metal bar across the front door, with a large padlock attached. I rattle at it a couple of times, but it's heavy duty. From across the road comes a falsetto squeak, probably meant to represent a female voice: 'Oh, let me in! Let me in!' More laughter.

I wonder about the back door. Presumably that'll be boarded up too, but perhaps not so securely. The garden's fenced off after all – the polis might have just left it locked.

But if I go round the back, those three might follow me. At the moment the whole street can see us, but round there is the high fence and the quiet lane beyond. I might be able to get into the house. But I might not.

I don't dare try it. My eyes sting with tears. Those bastards. I just don't dare.

I turn abruptly and walk back up the path. I think one of them says something, but I'm already wrapping my scarf around my head so my ears are muffled. I look out at the world through a tunnel of dark wool. I hear the footsteps and the whisk of waterproof material a second later than I might have otherwise. It's the neighbour, crossing into my path, still grinning cheerfully. He holds out a hand as if he's hailing a taxi. 'Whoa, whoa, wait till I talk to ye—'

I jump clumsily away from him, floundering sideways through the bank of snow. I stumble and feel my boots fill with ice, but I keep moving, parallel to the path, even though I'm walking across other folk's gardens. The neighbour keeps pace, laughing: I'm being silly and unreasonable. 'Aww, come on, hen.'

I keep going, still crossing other people's front gardens – the dividing line between pavement and lawn might be buried under two feet of snow, but it still matters. It'll be getting noticed. After a few more paces the man stops and falls behind out of sight. He shouts something after me, something with no laughter in it, and I try not to hear what it is. No one else comes outside, although I hear a front window being rapped indignantly as I cross in front of it.

I don't venture back onto the pavement until I'm round the corner, and into the main street. It's comparatively crowded, and no one seems to know who I am. Traffic is crawling along, but at least it's moving. A grimy bus chugs past; I realise it goes near Raj's place and run for it.

I spend half an hour in the crowded steamy warmth of the bus, staring at the filthy window and straining to make out landmarks beyond it, trying not to cry. I'm not entirely successful at either. The woman opposite stares at me mutely all the way. In the end, I'm glad to escape into the cold; at least the air's fresh.

In another minute I'm letting myself into Raj's flat – he's had keys cut for both of us – and the air's not quite so fresh again. Jamie's been in permanent residence on the couch for three days, and the living room is starting to smell a bit lived-in. He's in his daytime position now: sitting up, dressed, with the quilts shoved behind the couch for later. He looks up at me with the unconvincing half smile he uses as a greeting these days; his attention sharpens as he sees my face. 'What's wrong?'

'Nothing.'

'Have you been crying?'

'No, no.' I wave away this ridiculous suggestion. 'Just the cold nipping my eyes. Want a cup of tea?' This last is called over my shoulder as I go back into the hall towards the kitchen. I'm just taking off my coat and putting the kettle on, that's all. Not hiding till I can wash my face, not at all.

I can hear Raj moving about in the tiny kitchen – there's no hiding in a one-bedroom flat – and I squeeze in next to him, pushing the door almost closed behind me. He looks up and smiles, automatically lifting another mug from the cupboard. 'Tea?'

He's wearing his academic cardigan, a huge dark red woolly creation that no one outside a university could possibly find stylish. I wrap my arms around him and sink my face into the warm scratchy wool. 'In a minute,' I mumble.

He puts his arms around me and squeezes until my ribs creak. Then he lifts my face up towards him. 'What's up?'

'Nothing. Idiots. Back at Mum's house.'

'You went round there?'

'I needed my clothes.'

'Don't go round there alone, Suzey. If you must go I'll come with you.'

I imagine those three men watching us walking up that street – a white girl hand-in-hand with a half-Indian guy with an English accent. A few days ago I wouldn't have thought twice about it. Not now. Those utter, utter *cunts*. 'Maybe if I leave it a day or two—'

'No. Don't go on your own, ever.'

'I know. Stupid. I won't do it again. Okay?'

'Okay.' He hugs me again, mumbling into the top of my head. 'Just be careful. I don't know what I'd do without you.'

I start to tear up again. What *he*'d do without *me*? 'You'd get your house back,' I whisper.

'I don't want my house back.' The kettle starts whistling, so he has to turn away. 'Anyhow, the situation has to improve now.' When he gets no response, he looks up and clocks my blank expression. 'The charges?' He points through to the living room. 'Didn't he tell you?'

'No, he… Just a minute.' I go through to the living room. Jamie doesn't look at me, but I know he must have heard at least some of that. 'Got anything to tell me?' I ask.

He nods. 'They've dropped the charges.'

'Oh, thank God.' I sit down hard. 'Have you told Mum?'

'No, not yet. I've just found out myself,' he adds, slightly defensively.

He still makes no move for the phone. I take a deep breath, then reach over and take his hand. 'Jamie,' I say, 'this is good. This means things are going to be better. Doesn't it?'

He's nodding vigorously. 'Aye. Aye. It does.' There's that half smile again: still not convincing. 'Course it does.'

'I'll call Mum then, shall I?' It comes out sharper than I meant it to.

Jamie just shrugs. 'If you want,' he says.

So I do. Mum cries with relief, then wants to speak to Jamie. His voice is calm and upbeat, reassuring; if you couldn't see his blank face it would be utterly convincing. Then Mum wants me again. 'Do you think we can go home now?' she says.

'No, Mum. Not just yet.'

'But I need some of my things—'

'*No*, Mum.'

The three of us, Jamie, Raj and I, spend the night in front of the telly. I'm behind on the typing, so I have to work through the evening. I keep getting distracted by the telly and making typos, but there's no other room warm enough to work in. No matter, I'd rather keep an eye on Jamie, although there's no sensible point to it – he just sits and stares, motionless. He doesn't even react when McLean appears on the news, yapping on about immorality; eventually it's Raj who changes the channel.

Raj and I go to bed early, leaving Jamie the living room to himself. You'd think my sex life would be more active since I'm now shacked up with my boyfriend but it hasn't turned out that way. We're too aware that every cough and creak is fully audible throughout the flat. And I'm tired. I just want to get some sleep.

I'm suddenly wide awake. Raj mutters and turns over in his sleep. I prop myself up to see over him to the clock; it's half two in the morning.

I'm freezing. I must have had my arms outside the covers. As I burrow under the cosy and slightly whiffy duvet, I notice a seam of light under the bedroom door. It's coming from the living room; Jamie's still awake.

I wonder if I ought to go through. I find myself remembering when we were kids, and he'd wake up crying; I'd get him out of his cot and take him into bed with me. I only remember it happening when Mum and Dad were yelling at each other downstairs, although according to Mum I did it all the time. 'Leave your brother alone,' she'd say. 'You're disturbing him. Let him be.' Dad never said that, though. 'That's your wee brother.' That's what he'd say, towards the end. 'It's just the two of you.' In a bizarre way, I've always thought the illness made him wiser. 'That's your wee brother. You look after him.' And I did. We were a team, the two of us. That's how it was, whatever anyone said. I listen for Jamie now, but I can't hear anything. Maybe he's reading, or he's just fallen asleep with the light on. I'll leave him be.

Besides, it's freezing. I squeeze up next to Raj, as close as I can get. Still, it takes me ages to heat up. I must be coming down with something. I just can't seem to get warm these days.

Chapter 19

'Ah,' says Carl. 'If it isn't Miracle Girl.'

He closes the office door, and flicks on the kettle on the way back to his desk. 'How are you?'

'I'm fine.' I slide into a chair. 'It's the Boy Wonder I'm worried about.'

'Your brother?'

'Yes.'

'How's he bearing up?'

'He's…' I don't know how to answer. 'He's just not right.'

Without having to ask, Carl pushes a mug of tea across the desk. It's unbelievable how much of the stuff everyone drinks here, but I suppose it keeps you warm. 'Big shock for him,' he says. 'It's normal to be withdrawn.'

I wrap my hands thankfully around the cup. 'I just don't know what to do for him.'

'What you're already doing. Just be there.'

'I don't know if that's going to be enough.' It's dark in here, the afternoon sky grey against the window. 'Could you stick the light on?' I ask.

Carl looks surprised, but he does it. 'Are *you* all right, Suzey?'

'Yeah, fine. Might be coming down with a cold or something.'

He doesn't look convinced, but he doesn't press it. 'Are you still all right living where you are?'

No, I think. I've been with Raj less than a month. I can still count the number of times we've had sex. But he's already stuck with me and my problem family. It's not good…

'Yes, I suppose so,' I say. 'But my Mum phones me every day asking if she can go home. What do you think? Should we just go back and tough it out?'

'No.' He doesn't hesitate. 'Stay where you are.'

I knew he was going to say that. It's Carl, after all: I know him so well. But he doesn't know me at all. I'm just that weirdo from the papers, and Jamie's just my messed-up brother. Not Carl's fiancé. My brother. 'Have you heard anything from the lawyer?' I ask.

'Nothing new. But he thinks the chance of gaining access is much higher now that the charges have been dropped.'

'But shouldn't that mean he automatically gains access? Since there's no criminal record or anything?'

'Yes, it should.' He looks me in the eye for a moment. 'But it doesn't.'

We sit in silence for a while. I look out at the charcoal-grey sky. 'It's so dark.'

'Heavy snowfall coming.'

'It's not just that. It's like…' The words are out of my mouth before I know I'm thinking them 'It's like spring's not coming.'

'It's just a heavy cloud covering.'

'The days feel like they're not getting longer—'

'They are getting longer. Don't be melodramatic. It's just thick cloud.'

His voice is firm, but there's something else. I look at him closely. 'Sorry.'

'It's all right. Times are tough. We've got to keep a grip.'

He keeps his face expressionless. But I know him, even if he doesn't know me, and that was a prepared speech. 'Have you heard other folk talking like this?'

'Folk always talk like this.' He waves his hand towards the waiting room and the shell-shocked people in it.

'What are they saying?'

'You know. They're saying it's the end of…' He's looking out at the black sky, his hand wandering absently to a small badge on his collar. Then he realises what he's doing, and puts his hand firmly back on the desk. 'It's rubbish. Superstition.'

He's speaking emphatically, but my eyes are on the badge now. It's a small white enamel dove, with an olive branch in its beak. The olive branch is rainbow striped.

I look up at Carl, and my attention is caught by the Gay Christian Scotland poster behind him, and then by the attached sheet of parchment paper, which I've finally recognised.

Several pennies have just dropped loudly in my head. I'm so taken aback I don't know which one to deal with first. 'Carl,' I say, 'are you… religious?'

'Yes,' he says, somewhat defensively. 'I'm a gay Christian. Do you have a problem with that?'

'No. But after all the Church has… you know. The persecutions. How can you be a Christian?'

He looks angry for a moment, then shrugs. 'I don't know. I just am.'

'But you've always said religion was nonsense, delusions and…' But was that him? Or was it someone else? I feel light for a moment, as if my blood sugar's dropping. I can't remember. 'Was it you?'

'Are you all right?'

His voice is sharp. The moment passes. 'Yes, I'm fine. It wasn't you who said that, was it?'

'No.'

'Okay. But what about that?' I point to the sheet of parchment stuck to the poster. 'That's from McLean. You can't be going to that thing of his.'

'How do you know what that is?'

He sounds a bit indignant; he thinks I've been spying, reading over his shoulder. Luckily I've got the perfect reply. 'Because I've got one too.'

Now it's his turn to look astonished. 'You're going as well?'

'I've been invited. I'm not *going*. Are you?'

'Yes, I am.'

'Why? I mean… why did they ask you? You're gay. You did tell them, didn't you?'

'I told them.' He smiles grimly. 'As far as they're concerned I'm "struggling with my broken sexuality". I have to attend meetings with the Intercessors. They're going to pray for me to have purely "natural" urges. I've to be "willing to change".'

'And are you?'

'Of course I'm not.'

'Then why the hell are you going?'

'Because there'll be a lot of people there who think they can't be gay and a Christian. And I can tell them otherwise.'

'You're going to try to *convert* them?'

'Yes. I suppose so.'

'Carl, they'll crucify you.'

'Then I'll be in good company, won't I?'

'They'll crucify you upside down just for saying that. And *don't* tell me if some saint or other got crucified upside down, I don't want to know. They will *hurt you*, Carl. Don't you have any idea what these people are like?'

He looks at me sadly. He's going to do a speech, I just know it; he's going to talk about standing up to be counted. But in the end he just says, 'Well, I'm going anyway.'

And there's nothing more to say, except, 'Be careful.'

'I will.'

The clouds outside are growing thicker, I swear it. There's no sign of the sun. And once again words are coming out of my mouth. 'You were going to say the End of Days, weren't you? That's what people are saying. That the Last Days are coming?'

'People always say that. It's human nature.' His voice is firm, but he glances at the waiting room again. A lot of Carl and Jamie's friends I know are big on New Age stuff: tarot cards and palmistry and horoscopes and all that. I wonder what the cards and the planets have been saying lately.

'You've heard that one before as well, haven't you?'

He looks at me levelly. 'What are you, a mind reader?'

'I'm Miracle Girl, remember?' I stand up. 'I'll head off now. Good luck in Glencoe. Try not to get massacred, won't you?'

'I don't think that's very wise of him.'

Raj is the master of the understatement. I settle down on the couch between him and Jamie. 'That's putting it very mildly.'

'They must think he's going to repent. When they find out he's not…'

'That's what I said.'

'He's aff his fucking heid,' says Jamie. We look at him in faint surprise. He doesn't speak much at the moment, and we've grown used to talking over his head as if he were a child.

'He's brave, though,' I say.

'He's fuckin' nuts.' Jamie sounds thoroughly disgusted. 'A Christian. Jesus Christ.'

He hasn't noticed the irony, and I decide not to point it out to him. 'Well, there *are* gay Christians.'

'They'll nail him up.'

I've been waiting to hear some kind of concern or interest in his voice, but there's nothing. No more than Carl had for him. 'Well. I hope he'll be all right.'

The laptop screen keeps going dim on me, so by now I've got a permanent headache. And I'm cold. 'It's bloody freezing,' I mumble.

Raj's hand presses against my forehead. 'Actually, you're warm.'

Oh, great. I am coming down with something. Fuck it, the world can turn without me for a while. 'Think I'll go and lie down for a bit.'

Jamie does look up now, surprised. 'Are you okay?'

That's all we ever seem to say to each other these days: are you okay, are you all right?

'Think I'm getting a cold, that's all. Night night.' I get up and kiss them each on the forehead, one after the other. 'If Mum calls, I'm asleep. And no, she still can't go home.'

I escape before they can make a fuss about it. The bedroom really is freezing, I can almost see my breath in front of me. I put on the tracksuit I sleep in, followed by another layer of clothes, with gloves, and extra socks, and a scarf around my head. I crawl under the covers and shut my eyes.

I don't know if I've been asleep or not. If I have, it wasn't for long – Raj isn't here yet. But I'm hot now. I peel off gloves, scarf, extra tracksuit trousers. Extra socks.

Now the original socks too. I'm warm. It's a good warmth, like being in a tepid shower, pleasantly rinsing my worries away.

And it's light. I haven't opened my eyes yet, but I can tell I'm in a room of glorious sunlight, and the air is warm. I can move freely; my clothes aren't thick and constricting, but light and loose.

There's a lovely smell. Raj and Jamie must be cleaning the house, though it seems a strange thing to do at this time of night. And they must have done the bedroom too, the smell's that strong. Can't they leave it till I'm awake, for God's sake? 'Do it in the morning,' I mumble.

No reply. But I cam hear muffled voices, too. They must have the telly on…

No, it's not that.

I know what I'm going to find when I open my eyes.

Chapter 20

It seems that I'm walking.

I know this only because I can feel my feet on the floor. My eyes are still closed; the light pressing on my eyelids is bright. Something is gripping my elbow on either side. I can hear echoing voices, and a hissing sound, like heavy rain on a roof.

I ease open my eyes. Daylight: bright but with a rippling quality, pearly-grey. I must be underwater, bobbing along the bottom of the sea. Perhaps, if I tried, I could take big floaty steps like an astronaut on the moon. The thought makes me smile.

'Suzey?' The voice is at my right elbow – a young female voice, pleasant. 'Suzey, are you with us?'

White spots slide down my vision for a second, but I blink a few times and they soon clear, to reveal a woman with a white paper cap thing on her head… A nurse's hat. I think I know her, but I can't remember her name. Why's she so close? Are we marching in formation? No – she's holding onto my elbow. She smiles at me. 'Morning.'

I mumble acknowledgement and look to my left. I can feel another hand on my elbow but for the moment all I can see is the aqueous light. It's brighter on this side. We must be open to the elements… No, it's glass. Windows from floor to ceiling. The light's pouring down it in waves.

No, it's rain.

I stop dead. 'I'm back in the hospital,' I say.

The woman says something but I ignore her because I'm looking at the rain. 'Water,' I say. 'Spring rain.'

Someone blots out the light: the person on my left has stepped forward. I look up into a big smiling face. 'Hiya, Suzey,' it says.

I'm wearing light clothes – pyjamas and a bathrobe – and I'm not cold. 'It's getting warmer here,' I say.

The man squeezes my elbow gently in reply. A name comes to me.

'You're Charlie.'

The smile broadens. 'You're with us today.' He exchanges a pleased look with the girl on my left. 'How are you feeling, Suzey?' she asks.

I blink at her. 'Kirsty?'

'No, Suzey. I'm Rachel.'

I shake my head, still trying to figure out why there's so much light, so much glass… Ah, a corridor. A walkway between two buildings. A whiff of carbolic: the overboiled scent of bulk catering. Hospital smells.

We've reached double doors. Charlie shoves one open, still holding my elbow, while Kirsty – no, Rachel – hands me through. 'There we go,' she says, as if I were either very old or very young. 'Not far now.'

'Where are we going?'

Charlie answers. 'You've got a visitor, hen.'

I whisper, 'Is it Raj?'

But he looks blank. 'Don't know anyone called Raj, Suzey.'

'It's a woman to see you,' says Rachel.

A big room opens up in front of me, full of tables, one wall top-to-toe windows. It's the dining hall. Some of the tables are occupied; people are peeling off wet raincoats, talking across tabletops to people in indoor clothes or dressing gowns. I know some of the indoor people, but I can't quite think of their names. Charlie and Rachel are steering me towards the windows; a small but spiteful gust of wind spatters the glass with raindrops. 'Nasty out there,' Rachel says. 'They say we're to have snow.'

I laugh about this till I realise the hands on my arms have tightened slightly. I relax, follow them meekly, and let them install me at a small table across from a woman in a grey wool coat. I've no idea who she is. I say to Charlie, childishly, 'Can I have a drink of water?'

'Course, hen.' He smiles at the woman as he departs. She smiles back, shrugging off the coat and revealing an emerald shirt that brings out the green in her eyes.

It's Katie. Her hair is shorter, just past her jawline; she's running her fingers through it to dry it, although it's only a little damp. Similarly the coat has just a sprinkling of raindrops across the shoulders. She must have come in a car, on her way to work. Yes, I think I remember now – Katie with smart clothes and a car. She's smiling at me, nervously. 'Hi,' she says. 'How do you feel?'

She clears her throat and clasps her hands on the table. 'Everyone's been asking for you,' she says. Her eyes keep darting from my face to her hands, to the window, to the floor. 'Did you get our card?'

The light is blotted out again: Charlie the human eclipse is at my shoulder, setting down two paper cups full of water. 'Everything okay?' he says.

'Fine.' I take a drink, but my voice still comes out as a croak. 'She's just come to fire me.'

'No.' Katie looks shocked. 'No, of course I haven't.'

'What did you come for, then?'

'I've come to tell you your job's *safe*, Suzey. It's been to the review. They've extended your sick leave.' Failing to get a smile out of me, she looks at Charlie. 'They've given clearance for another six months.'

'There you go, Suzey, eh?' Charlie's voice is hearty, but he makes no move to go away. He's heard my tone of voice, and he's no fool.

I force myself to smile. 'Well, that's good,' I say.

Katie is encouraged. 'You can come back as soon as you're feeling better.'

'It's a load off my mind, right enough.' I must sound suitably humble, because Charlie pats my hand and walks away. Katie has to look at me again.

'So… How's the food in here?'

I can't look up at her yet. I know what you're capable of, I'm thinking. I know what you are. I'm almost pleased to get this opportunity. 'Have you seen my brother lately, Katie?'

'No.' She sits back, startled. 'No, I haven't. How's he getting on?'

'Fine. He's getting married, did you hear?'

'Oh. Married. To a… I mean, is he—'

'To a man, yes. And yes, he's still a poof. Disgusting, isn't it?'

'I hope he's very happy,' she says stiffly.

'Oh do you?'

'Of course I do.'

'Oh, right. That's why you slapped him about the face, then? When he told you he was gay. That's why you called him a, what was it now, a 'stinking pervert'?'

'That was ages ago.'

'And that makes all the difference, does it?'

'I haven't come to talk about this—'

'So it was just fine for your bitch of a mother to stand around screaming abuse at him, was it?'

Her lips pursed at 'bitch of a mother' and now she's pulling her handbag strap onto her shoulder. 'I don't need to listen to this.'

'Oh, poor you. You'd let those fuckers tear him apart, wouldn't you? You'd have sat there looking all holy and you'd have let them tear him apart.'

She's getting to her feet. 'Suzey, I've no idea what you're on about.'

I'm on my feet too. I can see people looking, but I'm not letting her go. 'Don't talk shit to me. I know you, I know what you're capable of.'

'I'll see you again, Suzey.' Her voice is calm and clipped. 'I hope you feel better soon.'

She doesn't get to be calm about this. 'Christ, I'm glad he's gay,' I spit. 'Least it got him the fuck away from you.'

Her face is suddenly inches from mine. Her cheeks are flaming red. 'You're pathetic, you know that? You're obsessed with your own brother. You make me *sick*.'

I'm grabbing for her, trying to get her face, but a band of steel clamps around my waist, lifting me off my feet, and Charlie's voice in my ear says, 'No you don't.' My chair goes flying, there are shrieks all around me. I'm kicking Charlie's shins, punching at his arms, but he still hauls me off easily, and I am being pulled away from her. So I just scream at her. 'You bitch! You BITCH! Fucking CUNT!'

Now there are hands grabbing my arms. Nurses, male and female, whisk me towards the door. One nurse has stayed behind, her hand on Katie's arm. *She* has lost all her colour, but is calm. As they drag me out, she very slowly and deliberately turns her back.

Then I'm out in the corridor, and these damn people are still hanging onto me. 'Get the hell off me,' I snarl.

'Don't think so, Suzey.' Charlie's voice is kind but exasperated, like a father with a fractious two year old. 'Just going to get you calmed down, eh?'

'No. I am calm, I am. I'm sorry I hit you, Charlie. Please let me go.'

We're at the door to my dormitory now. Rachel is pulling back the curtains around my bed. 'We can't let you go for people like that, Suzey,' she says, sadly.

'I'm not going to go for her. I'm not, but did you hear her?' I'm crying, sobbing, I sound like Clairey. 'Did you hear what she said?'

'I know, Suzey, I know…'

This time the needle goes in my arm. I scream, because it's so cold, they're injecting me with ice, it's freezing.

And I'm in darkness again.

Chapter 21

There is aching pressure on my hands and knees. Within seconds it goes from an ache to a stinging pain. I'm kneeling down. The ground is stone, freezing stone.

The wind is squealing and roaring around me. My ears hurt; I put my hands over them, but my fingers hurt so badly I have to tuck them inside my clothes. The cold stabs. Black and grey shapes: an abstract pattern, meaningless. I'm in semi-darkness, like the last minutes of twilight. There's a wall beside me. I cower up against it.

I'm wearing my scarf and I pull it up over my head and wrap it around my ears, mouth and nose. In the seconds it takes to do this, my fingers are numb – I'm wearing gloves, woollen ones, but they're thin and useless. My feet are stinging too, despite my boots. The cold soaks through my thick coat like icy water.

I might as well be naked. The killing cold.

The blacks and greys have settled into something recognizable: steps, leading upwards. Railings line either side of a short pathway leading to the steps. A bridge, I think. The railings lean over drunkenly on one side, like candlewax melted then hardened again. The scene is familiar somehow, but I don't hang around to think about it. I uncurl from my foetal crouch, wincing as the cold finds my back and stomach, and scuttle to the staircase. My boot skites straight off the first step; I catch at the metal banister, crying out as my chilled knee hits the step and my hand grabs the frozen metal. The surface of the step is knobbly ice, an inch or two thick.

The whole staircase is the same, a flash-frozen flood of dirty water. I get a firm grip on the banister – it freezes my hands, but it won't be for long – and start hauling myself up the stairs. But my feet slip as if the surface were oiled. After four steps I sit down, and start bum-shuffling backwards up the staircase. My hands hurt so much. I stop whimpering and start crying out; I still can't hear myself over the bellowing wind.

I finally crawl over the top step and into the path of the wind. If I'd been standing, it would have thrown me back down the stairs. As it is, I scramble sideways until I'm off the slick of ice and onto something firmer. The light is a little brighter now; I can see the ground a few inches from my face. It's black earth, hard as stone. Set into its surface, like metal in a rock face, are strands of pallid green: blades of grass, a lot of them. This used to be a lawn. I lift my head.

It's the University. Even in the dull gloaming, the clock tower is unmistakable. Something about the outline is different though. I stare at it stupidly for a moment before I realise the western wing is missing. Or rather, judging by the rubble strewn around the empty space, it has been knocked down like a sandcastle. I look back at the clock tower. Half past ten. The minute hand is still moving.

The wind is scouring my face. I get up, and pull my scarf up over as much of my face as possible. At the base of the eastern wing, still intact, is the archway leading to the quads. That should be reasonably sheltered. I lean headlong into the gale and struggle forward.

Something dull red is in the middle of the University driveway, blocking my path. I have to peer at it for a moment before I realise it's an upside-down car, sitting neatly on its roof. All the windows have been blasted out. A few feet away the slick of ice runs past the lawn and down the steps. Beyond the car I can see what looks like a small frozen pond – a crater, I decide, filled to the brim with ice. There is a fluttering movement at the edge, something blue. Fabric.

A sleeve.

I let out a small whimper of relief. There's someone here. I struggle over to the crater, calling out a greeting. It's a dark-haired man; he's in the crater, his head and shoulders above the edge, as if he's reclining in a Jacuzzi. I get closer, and slow down, stopping ten feet away from him. I remember seeing my grandfather in his coffin, and my father after that; I know what I'm looking at. This man, lacking an undertaker's care, is gaping at the sky. His eyes are still open. From the chest downwards, he is encased in grubby and uneven ice. There are glints of ice on his cheeks, frozen tears, or raindrops, or condensation.

It feels unkind to leave him there. But the cold hurts too much. I hurry towards the archway.

The gloom of the quads is disorientating; black walls, white snow. The wind does get in, although it can't sweep the snow away completely as it does outside; there is a ski-slope of white against the south wall, piled up to the second-floor windows. I manage to find a sheltered doorway and huddle there for a moment, looking back through the archway. From here I should be able to see the lights of the city, covering the Clyde valley.

There's just a dark, empty space.

The sky is a uniform dark grey – no black of the night. The wind, which should have driven off the heaviest clouds, has no effect. It seems to howl and scream in protest; I can almost hear voices in it, shrieking across the sky.

This is daytime. The clock showed half ten in the morning.

This is not my world.

My stomach is starting to cramp. My lungs are tightening, and my muscles ache. It's the cold, passing through skin and flesh like fog. Chilled, I think, idiotically, to the bone. I imagine bones, polished blue-white and laid bare beneath the grey sky.

Sobbing, I run around the quad, tugging on the heavy wooden doors. All locked. I try the windows, one after the other – all shut tight. I shove at the thick lead glass, then thump it; it doesn't even crack. 'Hello!' I wail. 'Is there anyone here? Please help!'

There's a scraping noise overhead. Snow is shoved off a window ledge, and lands powdery around me. A head leans out and a voice whispers, 'Hello?'

It can't be… '*Raj?*'

'Who's there?'

It is. 'Raj! Oh, love, it's me! Raj, let me in, please!'

'Suzey?'

'Yes, it's me! Come down and open the door, Raj, please, I'm freezing!'

He mutters something, then tells me, 'Window. Right under here. Look.'

I tug at the handle of the window. It doesn't budge, but this time I don't move onto the next one. After three more tries, it judders in its frame, then creaks open.

I'm climbing inside when I catch a movement in the corner of my eye – something grey against the white banks of snow. A wolf, shaggy coat and skinny legs, head turning from side to side. It sees me teetering on the window ledge and an instant later it's sprinting towards me. I scramble in, shrieking, and slam and lock the window behind me.

Then I run for the stairs, and I don't stop until I reach the top floor.

Mournful howls follow me all the way. There is flickering light under the door of Raj's office. Gratefully, I push open the door.

The room is smoky, and stinks of sweat and piss and vomit. But there is a fire, in the middle of the floor, and nothing else matters. I fall to my knees in front of it, the cramps already subsiding. 'Raj,' I say. 'Oh, thank God, thank—'

Raj comes out from behind the screen. His voice is cracked. 'Suzey…'

His face and head are red, bloody. There are sores like burns all over his skin. Oh, his *hair*… His hair is missing at the front. His scalp is bare and red-raw right back to his ears. As he comes slowly towards me I can smell him: dried puke, unwashed crotch, and a coppery smell like blood. I stand up and take a couple of steps back, but he staggers and almost falls, so I catch hold of him.

'So it's true,' he mutters. He's heavy, so I ease us both down to the floor. He's roasting; for a moment that feels wonderful, but then I realise he's burning up. 'You're not well, Raj,' I say stupidly.

'You've come back,' he says. He rests in my arms for a moment, and then sits bolt upright again. 'It's true, then. They're coming back.'

'Lie down, pet,' I say. 'You're not well.'

I don't think he heard me. 'The dead come back. The world ends. It's Ragnarok.'

'Stay there.' I go to the window and push it open, bracing myself against the blast of the cold. There's still a little snow on the windowsill; I scoop it up. Far below me, I can see movement, grey on white. Wolves are milling about the quad, too many to count. One of them looks up, sees me, and raises its muzzle in a high-pitched howl. The others join in, high and low voices harmonizing. I slam the window and hurry back to the fire.

Raj sits calmly for a moment, letting me dab his fiery skin with the melting snow. But then he reaches past me to grab a stack of papers. I think he's going to throw them on the fire but instead he stacks them neatly, and slots them carefully into a metal box beside him. I peer at it in the smoky firelight; it's a small safe. 'What are you *doing?*' I say.

'Recording it.' He seems surprised by the question. 'For the people who come after.'

'What people?'

'The people of the new world. The dead rise, and the world ends. Then the new world comes about.'

'With the dead in it?'

'No.' He looks at me sadly. 'No, you and I stay dead, Suzey.'

I've started to cry, helpless shivery sobs. 'We're not dead, Raj.'

'Yes,' he says, 'we are. I saw you die, Suzey. You died in the second blast. In the firestorm. The firestorm. Don't you remember?'

'Stop it, please…'

'I'm sorry, Suzey.' He puts his arms around me. He stinks, and I can't bear to look at his ruined face, but his voice is soft, and for a moment the mania is gone. Then he pulls away abruptly, and picks up more papers. He waves them under my nose. 'This is how it happened,' he says. 'See?'

I look. On top of the bundle is an old newspaper cutting: a picture of a beautiful 12-year-old boy, with a halo of golden curls. The headline shrieks *KILL THE MURDERING BEASTS*. 'That's Peter Balfour,' I say.

'No.' Raj is shaking his head. 'No, it's Balder. *Balder*. The beautiful one, beloved of the gods. He is murdered. The gods will have their revenge. That's how it begins. Then. *This*.'

He produces another paper cutting. His voice has become quite mild, as if he's back in the lecture hall, but his eyes are rabid. 'Him. Loki. The mad god. The Destroyer.'

I look. Dozens of cuttings. Articles, all written by Matthew McLean. I scan them. *CRUSH THESE BEASTS… MURDERING SCUM… WIPE OUT THE PERVERTS*.

I turn over paper after paper. McLean's face in monochrome, over and over again. *FAITH OF OUR FATHERS… Return to DECENCY and COMMON SENSE… ZERO TOLERANCE*.

Then *GOD'S COUNTRY… BOMB THREATS… held to ransom by violent fanatics? We say teach them a lesson… STRIKE NOW*.

Then nothing.

I let the cuttings fall. McLean's pallid eyes stare up at me from the floor: wolf eyes. 'He started a war,' I whisper.

Raj's eyes are losing focus. 'The great sword blazes like the sun,' he says. 'The serpent spews poison over all the earth. The sky cracks open, and the earth burns. Then ashes, only ashes.'

'Raj—'

'Fenrir.' His voice is hoarse now, and weak. 'The Great Wolf. The one who swallows up the sun. The end of the world. Ragnarok.' He chokes, spits out thin watery vomit.

'Raj, please.' The fire is dying down. The cold and the dark are pressing all around me. 'Raj, stay with me, please!'

'It's all right, Suzey.'

'Raj, don't—'

He lets out a great sigh, all the air rushing out of him.

'Raj! *Raj!*'

He's not moving, not moving, he can't be…

'Raj! Oh, Christ, no. Don't leave me! No!'

The howling of the wolves rises outside.

'Raj! *No!*'

'Suzey!'

'Raj! Come back, please!'

'Suzey, wake up!'

It's his voice. 'Raj? Raj?'

'Wake up, Suzey!'

My arms are around him. He's warm.

'Open your eyes, Suzey.'

Raj is leaning over me, his hair against my face. I reach up to him – I won't believe it till I touch him. But it's true. I hold his healthy, sore-less face in both hands, and I start to cry.

'Christ, Suzey, what's wrong?' Jamie is speaking now. 'What's wrong with her?'

'Just a nightmare. Hush, Suzey, calm down.'

We're in our bedroom, Raj's bedroom – warm and safe, and not even smelly. Raj is in bed beside me. The single-bulb light is on, and there are slivers of dull daylight around the blackout curtains. Raj is holding onto me as if I'm about to have a seizure. Jamie is standing in the doorway, wearing pyjamas and suffering from serious bed-head. 'Suze, are you okay?'

'No,' I whisper.

Raj looks at Jamie. 'She's freezing. She needs a hot drink.' Jamie, looking relieved to have something to do, disappears towards the kitchen.

Half an hour later I'm sitting up in bed, trying to drink hot sweet tea with whisky in it. My teeth keep hitting the side of the mug; Raj has his hand under mine to stop the drink slopping onto the covers. I can't stop shaking, or stammering. 'I saw it. Rag – Ragnarok. It was so, so *real*.'

'Shh. It's okay now.'

'No, it's not.'

It takes a while, but I manage to tell them everything about it. Especially McLean. The Destroyer.

Jamie's face has gone white. 'Jesus Christ. He's going to *do* that?'

'No.' Raj's voice is sharp. 'Not here. If it happened at all, it happened somewhere else. Not here.'

'But if it could happen there…'

'It would already have happened here, if it was going to.'

I remember his red-raw face, his cracked voice whispering "Balder". 'But you said it was inevitable.'

'*I* didn't say that. *He* said it.' He waves his hand, looking faintly exasperated. 'Everything happens somewhere. Parallel worlds. We've been over this, Suzey…'

'You didn't see it.' I pull away from him, and scramble over to the window. I yank the blackouts aside, so hard they come adrift from two of the curtain rings. Early morning daylight appears, dull and grey; it's not enough. 'You can't imagine it, you didn't *see* it, you don't *know*.'

'No, I don't. I'm sorry.'

He takes me in his arms again. I look over his shoulder at Jamie. His face has gone grey. He looks like *he* could imagine it.

I won't let Raj put the blackout curtains back up so he gets dressed in the bathroom. He comes back into the bedroom combing his hair; I watch him search for his watch, tie, wallet, then he bends over me and puts a hand on my forehead. 'Your temperature's down,' he says. 'Are you tired?'

'A bit. Are you going out?'

'I have to go into the office. Get some sleep while I'm out.'

'No,' I say immediately.

'Try. The fever's gone now. You need to rest.'

He smiles down at me, but he looks exhausted. I realise I've spent much of this morning telling him what he looked like when he died. No wonder he wants to get out. 'All right, I'll try.'

He bends down and kisses my forehead. 'Jamie will be here.'

'I know.'

I wait until I hear the front door close and then I lie back and shut my eyes, just to rest them. No chance of falling asleep, I tell myself, not with the room full of daylight. I'll just rest.

Jamie shuffles in and stands in the doorway, but he doesn't speak. I should probably say something, reassure him. And I will, in a minute, if he doesn't say anything first.

I let out a long, long breath. I think he says something, but I'm probably wrong.

I really am very, very tired.

Chapter 22

The noise of the front door and footsteps in the hallway wakes me.

It's still daylight, but it's different. Without checking, I can tell it's afternoon. I've been asleep for hours.

Keys jingle in the hall; the footsteps go into the living room, accompanied by the unzipping and unfastening of a coat. Then I hear a cough. It's Raj. 'In here,' I call.

The bedroom door creaks, and Raj looks in and smiles. 'Hi,' he says. 'Did you sleep?'

'I must've done. What time is it?'

'Just after two.' He sits on the bed beside me, and puts a hand on my forehead. 'Your temperature's still down. How do you feel?'

'Okay.' I do feel much better. I swing my legs out of bed. 'I'm getting up.'

He's watching me carefully. 'Did you have a dream, or…'

'No, nothing.'

'All right.' He gets up to go. As he's on the way out I think of something: there is no background noise. In this flat you can hear everyone breathing, and I can only hear myself and Raj. 'Where's Jamie?'

'Gone out,' Raj calls back.

'Where?'

'For a walk, apparently.'

That sounds hopeful. He's scarcely been out of the flat since he got here. I pull on some clothes and follow Raj into the living room. 'Do him good to get out,' I say. 'Some fresh air.'

'Absolutely.'

I flop down onto the sofa. 'And it gives us a bit of time to ourselves.'

Raj sits beside me, squeezing up close. 'That never crossed my mind.'

'Like hell it didn't.' I haven't washed, and I feel pretty disgusting, but Raj doesn't seem to mind. 'You probably gave him a tenner to go to the pictures.'

'I didn't.' He starts nuzzling into my neck. 'But I'll keep it in mind.'

I pull him up close. 'How long've we got?'

'Mm?'

'How long did Jamie say he'd be?'

'He didn't. He left a note.'

The moment goes cold. 'A note?'

'Yeah. What's wrong?'

'Where is it?'

'What?'

'The note. Where's the note?'

He points to the mantelpiece.

'I'm sorry. Just a minute.' There's a piece of lined paper propped up on the mantelpiece: I grab it. 'I know it's nuts, I've just got to…'

Dear Suzey (and Raj),

    I've just gone out for a walk. I've been thinking about things. I think I know a way to put all this right. Don't worry.

    Love, Jamie.

'Oh, God,' I say.

'What?' Raj sounds almost irritated. 'What is it?'

'Didn't you *read* this?'

'Yes. Of course I did. You don't think he…'

'I don't know.' I grab my boots from underneath the sofa and start shoving my feet into them. 'I'm sure it's nothing.'

He's looking at the paper again. 'It's just an ordinary note.'

He's right, of course. I pause… But it's no use. 'I know. I'll just feel better if I find him.'

I finish lacing the boots up, and make a dive for the hallway. Raj makes no move to follow, he's fed up indulging me. Can't blame him, I suppose. I start struggling into my coat – and then Raj is there, putting his coat on too. 'If it'll set your mind at rest,' he says.

'Thanks.'

'That's the only reason. There's no danger.'

'I know.' I'm already out of the flat, taking the stairs two at a time. I burst out of the close door and into the street.

The sky is a swirl of greys, bright and dark. I squint through my watering eyes: the street is empty, piles of mucky snow line the roadside, the cleared pathways show no footprints. A bundled-up figure is walking away. I shout, 'Jamie!'

Raj emerges from the close, almost bumping into me. The bundled figure around – it's not Jamie. 'Do you have any idea when he went out?' I ask Raj. 'Any at all?'

'No. How could I? Suzey, you need to put warmer clothes on.'

I've forgotten to put on my waterproof trousers – I'm wearing leggings and tracksuit bottoms and that's all. I already feel like my legs are bare, but I say, 'I'm fine. We won't be long. Come on.'

I make my way up the street, looking out for someone to ask. There's no one about, though – these days people stay inside and keep warm. Which is what we should be doing. Nevertheless I shuffle across the road, with Raj behind me. It takes ages, but no cars come along. People don't just drive about any more.

They don't just go for walks, either. I look up towards the canopy at the far end of the street. 'Maybe he went to the corner shop,' I say.

'He doesn't have any money.'

Not there, then. Where could he go without money? I look towards the other end of the street, where the snow cover is pristine and the black trees are laden with bundles of white. 'The park,' I say. 'He might be there.'

Raj frowns. 'Why would he go to the park?'

'Not for the reason you're thinking.' I've already set off for the park, but I manage a smile over my shoulder. 'Sex mad, you are. It's freezing out here.'

'I'm a man. I can't help it.' He makes a grab for my underdressed and chilly rear end. But I keep walking. 'We'll just have a quick look,' I say, 'then we'll go back.'

There's an exasperated sigh behind me; I ignore it and keep going. It's not a big park, it won't take long. He might be sliding down the hill, or under the trees by the…

By the pond.

I start to run, although with my heavy boots and the slippery path I can't get above a jog. But if he is in the park, and he probably won't be, he's probably just walking or throwing snowballs or something. Though it's more likely he's gone to see Carl, or even Mum. There's no need to worry.

Raj shouts something – I'm leaving him behind. 'Come on,' I yell over my shoulder. I pause on the kerb while a big 4x4 dawdles past. Raj catches up with me. 'What's the hurry?'

'No hurry. I'm just cold.' It's started to snow again, tiny flakes blasted in a spitefully cold wind. 'Come on.'

We shuffle across the road and through the park gates. The paths haven't been cleared, and immediately we're wading. To the left, the clean snow has been churned underfoot; a wandering line of footprints, large and small, human and canine, leads up the slope, although there's no sign of life there now. To the right, a single set of footprints has tracked toward the trees around the pond. They're human, adult, big enough to be male.

Raj says, 'Are those his?' but I've already begun to run. By the third step my momentum has gone, the deep snow holds me down like treacle. My thin trousers and leggings are already soaked; I may as well be wading through icy water. I try to step into the footprints, but you can't lift your feet that high when you're running.

Raj is calling something behind me but I ignore him. I'm panting for breath, and my muscles are aching with fatigue and cold.

I collapse against the first tree I come to. This is silly, so silly. Raj is struggling behind in my tracks. He'll say I'm daft. When Jamie comes home, he'll say I'm daft too. 'You're off your chump, Suzey,' he'll say.

I'll just walk through the trees, have a look at the ice – the empty and unbroken ice – and then I'll go home and get warm. That's all there is to it.

I make my way through the trees, clambering through drifts, pulling up my hood when an overladen branch dumps its snow load on me. Too late – it's down the back of my neck. It'll take me ages to warm up now.

A few poles stand around the perimeter of the pond, holding up gaudy orange lifebelts under their little wooden snow-capped roofs. The pond itself has been cleared of snow, perhaps for safety. The footprints stop there.

The pond is a smooth unbroken sheet of ice. Someone is standing on it, towards the far side but still close to the centre. They're wearing a parka, but the hood's down. Light brown hair is blowing about in the freezing wind.

'Jamie!' I scream. '*Jamie!*'

He takes no notice; maybe he can't hear me above the wind. He just stands still, looking down at the ice. I stumble over to the nearest lifebelt, wrenching it off its wooden board. There's a rope attached to the pole; I tug at it, and it holds. Clutching the lifebelt, I take a step onto the ice.

I think I hear it creak; but above the wind I can't be sure. I fill my aching lungs and scream, '*JAMIE!*'

His head lifts, turns towards me. I can't see his expression from this distance. He takes a step towards me, across the centre of the pond. 'No!' I shriek, waving him away, backwards. 'Not that way, Jamie, no! No!'

But he keeps going. The world is full of shrieking – mine and the wind's. I can't hear the ice. Jamie's feet rise and fall. The snow whirls and I can't see.

Then Raj is behind me. 'What's the matter with—'

This breaks my paralysis. I thrust the lifebelt into his hands. 'Throw it! Throw it to him!'

'What—'

'For Christ's sake, throw it!'

So he does. But it's just a doughnut of light plastic, it can't compete with the wind. It skims and lands halfway between us and Jamie. He walks forward, bemused, and stops to look at the lifebelt. Then he bends to pick it up. Swinging it from one hand, he starts towards us again.

I pick up the rope, wrapping it a couple of times around my arm, then step out onto the ice again. I take a few careful steps, my feet skidding. Another one. Jamie is now only yards away from me. He looks at me, confused. I stretch out my free hand. 'Here! Take it!'

He does. I propel myself backward, feet hitting the ice sharply. Raj is behind me – I reach back and he grabs my hand. I shout at him to pull, and he does.

I'm off the ice. I've got Jamie's hand. I pull him onto the path.

Jamie still looks bemused. Checking that I'm completely off the ice, I put myself between him and the pond. I take a couple of deep, shuddering breaths. And then I'm yelling again. 'Oh *Christ*, Jamie, don't you dare! *Don't you dare!* Jesus *Christ!*'

All the time he's just gaping at me. 'Suzey? What's—'

'Oh, you little sod, how could you! What about Mum, it's—'

'Suzey.' Raj's voice cuts in. 'What's wrong?'

'What's *wrong?* Didn't you see him out there?'

'Yes, of course I saw him. What's wrong?'

He looks stern, but otherwise as confused as Jamie. 'He was on the ice,' I say.

'Yes. And?'

'It could have broken. It's the Drowning Pond. People have gone under the ice, you know. I remember it. They drowned.'

'Suzey,' Jamie says. 'The ice is a foot thick.'

I just gape at him. He steps back onto the pond; when I reach towards him, he stamps his foot. Not a sound or a movement. The ice is like a sheet of marble. 'See? Solid.'

'Oh. But… I remember people falling through it. It's…'

Jamie's starting to smile. 'You're a daft besom, Suzey,' he says.

I rally a bit. 'But what was I meant to think? That note. What were we meant to think it was about?'

Raj gallantly doesn't point out that I was the only one who thought that. Jamie looks serious. 'Christ, I'm sorry. I didn't mean it like that.'

'Then what the hell did you mean?'

'I've made up my mind.' He's very serious now. 'I know what I'm going to do. If you'll help me.'

'Of course I will.'

'I'm going to go to McLean's Glencoe thing. I'll take your place, Suzey. I'm going to tell them I'm repenting of my wicked ways. Penitent sinner equals good publicity. Hey, presto.' He makes a conjuring gesture. 'I get Claire back. Maybe Katie as well.'

There is a long silence. Raj eventually says, 'You two are just as mad as each other.'

'Jamie, that's the stupidest thing I've ever heard,' I say.

'But Suze—'

'No! Now I'm cold and I'm bloody soaked, and I'm going home! And so are you. And put your hood up.'

He doesn't move. 'I need this, Suzey.'

'You'll *both* catch hypothermia if you don't get indoors soon,' Raj tells us.

Jamie still doesn't move. 'We'll talk about it inside, all right?' I say.

'All right,' he nods. Raj steers me towards home, and Jamie follows.

Chapter 23

I manage to hold out for half an hour before I have to agree. I tried saying I don't know the number, but he found it in the phone book. Then I told him I threw out the invitation letter, but he said he'd ask for another one. Then he makes me look at a picture of Claire, and that's the end of it. 'Fine then,' I say. 'Phone them. Have my place and good luck to you.'

Jamie makes a dive for the phone. I catch Raj's eye and we both shake our heads, like parents. They'll probably tell him no, in any case. Perhaps, I hope, he won't even be able to get through. But no. 'Hello, my name's James Pherson, it's about the *Spirit Fire* event.'

I listen while he gets passed around, repeating the same story over and over. They're obviously trying to put him off, but he's not giving up. Eventually he puts his hand over the mouthpiece and whispers, 'They're putting me on to Kerry.'

'Kerry?'

'McLean's daughter,' Raj murmurs, as Jamie turns back to the phone. 'Hi, Miss McLean? Hello, Jamie Pherson here, Susan Pherson's brother... I need to ask you something...'

And so on, with maximum little-boy-lost charm. Women usually soften pretty quickly when he does that, but judging by his responses, Kerry McLean is made of harder stuff.

'No, but... You see, she can't... Aye, I see...Look, I'll tell you what it really is...'

And then he launches into the penitent sinner story. 'Madness... My wife and daughter... So sorry...' I listen, wondering if she can possibly be buying this. Sounds unconvincing as hell to me. And right enough, Jamie's face is soon tripping him, and it's not part of the act. He's looking up at me now. 'Yes, I understand. Look, could she... Yes, she's here. Would you like a word?'

He holds out the phone, hand muffling the mouthpiece again. 'She won't let me go without you.'

'You know what the answer is, then, don't you?'

'Just speak to her, Suzey. Please.'

I sigh, and take the phone. 'Hello, Miss McLean?'

'Susan Pherson?' Her voice is deep for a woman's, and not at all warm. 'Miss Pherson, I explained the situation to your brother. He can attend as your guest, but not in his own right.'

'But if I'm not going, there'll be an empty place, won't there?'

'It's not that simple. Mr McLean himself compiled the list. I can't approve anyone who isn't on it.'

'But that doesn't make any sense.'

'I'm sorry.'

She's not about to budge. Okay, I think, I'll say I'm going, then pull a sickie in the morning. 'All right. I'll come.'

'That's good. Then you can sign your guest in.' She's way ahead of me. 'All guests have to be signed in by invited delegates.'

I spend long moment looking at Jamie's pleading face. 'Then I really will be there.'

'We'll look forward to seeing you. I'll pass you on to our travel coordinator, to arrange your journey.' She puts me on hold but I hang up – travel is the least of my worries just now. 'Well,' I say to my two astonished menfolk, 'I'm off to see the God-botherers.'

'This is a bad idea, Suzey,' Raj says.

'Probably.'

Jamie is trying to hide his delight. 'If you really feel bad about this, Suze, we'll forget it.'

'It'll be fine.'

He flings his arms around me. 'Thank you, Suzey.'

'It's okay. Just start swotting up on your Bible, you're going to need it.'

He lets me go, and we both notice the heavy silence coming from the other side of the room. So he makes himself scarce, ostentatiously putting a magazine under his arm and disappearing towards the bathroom. When the door closes Raj says, 'It's a bad idea.'

'I don't have much choice, do I? It'll give him a chance.'

'I don't want you to do this.'

'Don't tell me what to…' I stop, and take a deep breath. 'Look, it's just a few days in the country, all right? Nice hotel, good food—'

'Fanatical people. Whose beliefs you're going to mock.'

'We're not mocking anybody. And if it gets too bad we'll just take off and get a B&B, okay?'

He frowns. 'It's not that easy getting about, these days. Especially in the Highlands.'

'It's not the North Pole, Raj.'

He goes to say something – but in the end just sighs. 'Yes, you're right.' He smiles. 'I suppose I just don't like letting you out of my sight.'

'Would it make you feel any better if you came too?' I suddenly realise this would make me feel a lot better. 'If we could manage it?'

He looks up in surprise. 'Actually, yes, it would. But you're restricted to one guest.'

'I know someone I can ask about that,' I say.

Carl looks at me steadily across the desk. He must've heard some unlikely things in this office, because he looks only mildly taken aback. 'You want me to go away for the weekend with your boyfriend?'

'With me *and* my boyfriend, actually. And my brother.'

'That's the best offer I've had in a while, Suzey, but the answer's still no.'

'Are you already taking someone?'

A snort of laughter answers that one. 'No one I know is masochistic enough.'

'Except us. At least you wouldn't be on your own.'

'I'd rather be alone than with your brother.'

Wow. I can't believe I'm listening to these words coming out of Carl's mouth. 'That's not fair,' I tell him.

'Do you really think I can condone what he's going to do?'

'He's got to do it, it's for his kid. Wouldn't you?'

He pauses. 'I still can't condone it.'

'It's not Jamie you'd be condoning anyway. It's Raj. And he thinks this is a terrible idea as well.'

'So why is he going?'

Raj's voice, the Raj of my fever dream, comes back to me: The Great Wolf, The Destroyer. 'He's scared for me,' I say.

'What's he scared of?' Carl looks composed, but there's still that something…

'Do you think McLean is dangerous?' I ask.

'Yes.' His answer is immediate. 'Unquestionably.'

'Does he scare you?'

'Yes.'

'Why?'

'It's obvious, surely. He wants to set up a reactionary state, a climate of sexual repression—'

'No. I mean why does *he* scare you? McLean himself?'

'I don't know what you mean.'

But I think he does. 'He scares me, Carl. And I'll tell you why.'

So I tell him: different worlds; Fimbulwinter; Raj dying, and whispering about the *Destroyer*; Ragnarok. Carl watches me levelly, his face still and unreadable. At last he says slowly, 'Do you truly believe that?'

I don't really know if I believe it. It was a fever-dream; it happened yesterday, but already it seems like a long time ago. 'I'm not sure…'

'Because if it *is* true…'

'It's all right, Carl. You don't have to humour me. Just forget it.'

But he carries on as if he hasn't heard. 'If that were true, then we *have* to go.'

'What? Why?'

'He must be up to something. We could catch him at something, saying something. Something he'd only say to the faithful.'

'Carl—'

'There must be a weakness. Drugs. Women. One or two of the papers have it in for him, they'd print it—'

'Carl!'

'What?'

'Do you mean we should spy on him?'

He frowns. 'Someone's got to stop him, Suzey.'

'But us?'

'Well, yes… Why not?'

'So let me get this straight. We go up there. We spy on him. We catch him selling government secrets or something.' I don't think I can actually say this. 'We put a stop to him. And we… save the world?'

'Well…'

We stare at each other for a moment. And then we collapse laughing. I have to hang on to the edge of the desk so I don't fall off my chair. 'Do you reckon he's got a doomsday device in the basement?' I say when I can speak again. 'Guarded by killer robots?'

'I thought giant sharks, actually,' he says, and we both laugh till we cry. Eventually we have to pull ourselves together. 'Okay, seriously,' Carl says. 'We'll go. And we'll try. Can't hurt to try, can it?'

He looks rather plaintive. 'No, it can't hurt,' I say. 'But Raj is coming too, yes?'

'Why not. I don't have to share a room with him, do I?'

'No. He'll be sharing with me.'

He raises his eyebrows. 'Will he? You're not married.'

'Tough. He's sharing with me. You might have to share with Jamie, though.'

'That won't be happening.'

'Oh, don't get on your high horse. It'll be a twin room.' And the two of you are engaged, I think. At least, somewhere you are. But this isn't the time. 'You'll not have to share a bed or anything.'

'It's not that. He's a repentant sinner, if you remember. And I'm a *moral danger*, aren't I?'

'Bollocks to that. I'll phone them.' Laughter has made me bold. 'If they can't manage the sleeping arrangements we won't go. Read out the number, would you?'

I'd expected some holy space cadet to pick up the phone, but it's a proper receptionist, briskly pleasant. 'McLean Associates, how may I help you?'

'Hello,' I say, slightly taken aback. 'My name's Suzey Pherson, I was on earlier.'

'Oh, Miss Pherson.' Pleasant turns straight into warm and respectful. 'Just a moment, I'll put you through to Mr McLean.'

That can't be right. She must mean his secretary, or assistant or something.

'Hello? Susan?'

The male voice is rugged and affable. My God, it's him. 'Yes. Is that… Is that Mr McLean?'

'Aye, that's me. You were speaking to Kerry earlier?'

'Well, yes. It's about my brother, you see. He's…'

'He wants to come to us.'

'Well, yes. He's lost his family. Because of something he—'

'Aye, I read about it. And he wants to come and repent. That's marvellous, Susan, that's truly marvellous.'

'Oh. So he can come?'

'Of course.'

'Even if I can't make it?'

'You have to be there too, Susan.'

The statement is absolutely final. 'All right,' I say. 'We'll both be there.'

'I look forward to meeting you.' He sounds utterly sincere. 'Both of you. Goodbye till then, Susan.'

'Er, wait. Please.' I'm stuttering like an idiot here. 'I mean… Can I bring another guest as well?'

'Who is it?'

'It's…' I look away so I don't have to meet Carl's eyes. 'It's my fiancé.'

'Aye? Congratulations. Aye, he can come as well.'

'And we've to share a room,' I blurt out. I feel like a defiant teenager. 'I mean… we'll have a double room.'

There's a silence, then a deep, warm laugh. 'Aye, we can arrange that. Just tell him to make an honest woman of you soon, eh?'

'Er, yes.'

'And I want an invitation to the wedding, okay?'

'Sure. Okay.'

And then he's gone. 'Well,' I say to Carl. 'I think we're in.'

'I heard.' He's looking at me shrewdly. 'He's keen on you and your brother being there, then?'

'Seems to be. Doesn't seem too fussed about me and Raj and the premarital nooky either.'

Carl snorts. 'I wonder what he'd do if they put that in the *Standard*?'

'He'd probably say "I would have gotten away with it too, if it wasn't for you meddling kids."'

That sets us off again. After a while, though, we get a grip. Carl has a waiting room full of people. And I've got to go home and tell Raj we're getting married.

If Raj's eyebrows were raised any higher they'd be on top of his head. 'This is all so sudden, Suzey,' he says.

'He wouldn't let us in if we weren't engaged at least. '

'Did you ask him?'

'No.' I'm avoiding Raj's eyes. I'm afraid he'll look horrified at the very mention of the e-word. I'm also afraid he won't. 'Of course I didn't ask. Be a bit obvious, wouldn't it?'

'I suppose it would.'

'I'll go to the Barras at the weekend. Get a cheap ring.'

'Fine.'

'And I asked Carl about the travel arrangements. We get the bus to Crianlarich, then the hotel will send transport for us.'

'They'll have to send a team of huskies. The roads will be blocked this time of year.'

'I think they'll send a snowcat.'

'Yes, that makes sense.'

I hover over him. We'll have to make the conversation quick – Jamie's tactfully hiding in the bathroom again, but he can't stay there all night. 'Are you really okay about doing this?'

'I'm fine.' He smiles, and pats the sofa beside him. 'I overreacted. I'm sorry.'

I curl up beside him. 'We'll stay in a posh hotel for three days, and keep our mouths shut. Can't be that difficult, even for me.'

The toilet flushes and Jamie starts coughing loudly to indicate he's on the way back so we'd better put on anything we might have taken off while he was gone. Raj says quickly, 'Do you think he can act well enough to pull this off?'

'Why not? He's been doing it half his life.'

And there's not much left to do but wait. We buy bus tickets and arrange time off work. Mum goes back to the house (with a police escort) to get clothes and suitcases so we can pack. She's happy we're going – she thinks getting Churched will put us both right – but she sounds dazed, acts confused, looks older than ever.

We read the Bible, as much as we can. It makes me dizzy: all that beauty, all that cruelty. Jamie memorises a few relevant passages about mercy and repentance. Raj, bookworm that he is, has already read the whole thing; we agree he'll do the talking, if it comes to it.

And we dream, or at least I do.

I'm standing at the Pass of Glencoe on a sunlit day, watching as a darkness opens up from the valley floor to the sky. It fills the width of the glen exactly, like the great glacier that carved it out in the first place. Near the shadow's crest, above the tallest peaks of the valley, two red lights move, and fire dances and spits.

The shadow begins to move down the Glen. I can't see them, but I understand there are people in its path; they're trying to scramble to safety, but the slopes are much too steep. They fall back and are consumed. The darkness roars, and a wet stinking gale blasts up the glen, ripping up trees and demolishing cottages. I can see more detail now: a line of bone-white where the shadow touches the ground, and another just below the red flames. Above that the darkness has an outline, with two pointed ears.

I am looking into the mouth of a great wolf. Its jaws gape wide, the lower scraping along the ground, the upper touching the sky. Drool runs from the white teeth and falls in floods to the ground. The creature snorts like a bull, and flames shoot from its nostrils. The red lights are its blank feral eyes. They fix onto me; they've seen me. The darkness grows and grows as the wolf leaps –

And then I wake up. Raj, a sound sleeper, doesn't stir. I coory up against him and go back to sleep.

I have the same dream twice, but on the third night it ends differently.

The wolf leaps as before…

And then I'm somewhere else, somewhere warm and stuffy. There's a smell of disinfectant. I'm lying down, with a quilt over me.

I'm in my room at the hospital. The windows are dark: it must be late at night. It's very quiet.

Beside me is a pool of light: a bedside lamp, angled downwards to soften the glare. Someone is sitting beside the bed, someone with dark clothes and white hair and eyes like emeralds. 'Hello, Suzey.'

It's Mister Lisbon. 'Help me,' I say.

'Help you how?'

'Stop this. Stop all this that's happening.'

'I can't.'

'Then tell me how *I* can stop it.'

He shakes his head sadly. 'You can't stop it either.'

'He's going to make the world end,' I whisper.

'Yes.' He bends closer to me. The light makes his hair a bright corona. 'Yes.'

'Help me stop it.'

'It has to happen.' A draught has caught his hair. It moves, sways, brightens and turns into silvery flame. His green eyes are glowing. 'Everything happens somewhere.'

'But not here,' I say.

As he melts into cold white light his voice is clearer than ever. 'It has to happen somewhere.'

'Not here,' I say. 'Not to us.'

And then I wake up.

Raj stirs beside me in his double bed, makes a questioning noise. 'Just a dream,' I mumble. He grunts and puts an arm round me, asleep again a moment later.

I won't mention any of this to Raj or Jamie. It's just a dream, it doesn't bother me.

And if they dream, they don't tell me about it.

And so the day comes.

The four of us are standing outside Crianlarich station, or what we assume is Crianlarich station – the whole village is covered in snow, landmarks are blurred. The bus has long since returned to the comparative shelter of the city. A north wind is ignoring our huge parkas, blasting us with ice as if they're not there…

We shuffle closer together. The emptiness is freakish; I assume Crianlarich is still inhabited, although our only clues are a few thin wisps of chimney smoke. The warm smell of wood smoke makes us lonelier than ever, and we shuffle even closer.

'It's supposed to be here by now,' says Jamie.

No one bothers to answer. I'm entertaining the fantasy of staying here. Burrowing under the snow until we find someone who'll let us stay with them in one of these snug little hobbit-holes until the spring comes, or at least the next bus back to the city. Raj seems to be reading my mind: 'If nothing happens soon, we'll have to get rooms for the night.'

But a few minutes later, something does happen. A high-pitched nasal buzzing, and it's getting louder. By the time it deepens into a noisy, droning engine, we can see something acid-yellow heading down the north road towards us. It soon resolves itself into a kind of minibus on tank tracks: a snowcat. It coasts easily down the icy road and into the village.

The driver sees us and lifts his hand, bringing the vehicle to a smooth and expert halt. The others gather up their small battered suitcases and hurry towards it, their apprehension overpowered by the urge to get into the warm. I find myself hanging back, dazzled by the fluorescent yellow. Carl looks over and catches my eye. 'Off to Castle Dracula, then, Suzey?'

'Ready when you are, Van Helsing,' I reply, following him towards the snowcat. And so we set off: off to Glencoe, off to save the world.

Part Four
The White Palace

....

This, all this beauty blooming,
This, all this freshness fuming,
Give God while worth consuming.

...

From *Morning Midday And Evening Sacrifice*
Gerard Manley Hopkins

Chapter 24

The sun comes out as we approach Rannoch Moor. There's a leaden sky ahead, but the moor is white and sparkling. The snowcat's windows are tinted, very discreetly, so we can enjoy the view without being painfully dazzled. Snow is very pretty when you're not actually out in it. It's hard to believe I'm looking at a landscape that could kill you in twenty minutes flat.

The cabin is insulated to luxury standards, the air still and just a little too warm. The engine is nothing but a peaceful hum, the sense of movement negligible. The tundra outside is like something out of a fairytale, harmless and sweet.

We are unused to such sensory deprivation. Opposite me, Carl is yawning hugely. I rest my head against Raj's shoulder and close my eyes. The snowcat rocks me, very gently.

A change. It's been there a while, I just haven't noticed. I'm still warm, the air a little stuffy, and my bum's gone numb, as if the upholstery's been taken from the seat. There's a slight smell of bleach, or something like it, not unpleasant. But no more hum, no more rocking. We've stopped. Voices echo around me… Echo, in the cabin? I blink open my eyes.

The light is golden, and still bright. I close my eyes again. I hear Jamie murmur, 'Look at her eyes,' then he says, louder, 'Suzey?'

Another voice repeats this: 'Suzey? Suzey?' It's my mother.

When I open my eyes again I can see three faces, close up: Jamie, with short hair, and Carl with black hair, and my mother with brown hair. Did we double back to Glasgow to get her?

Ah, no. It's a dream. A figure in white is coming up behind them. It's that nurse – Kirsty. Or is it Rachel? 'Suzey, love,' she says. 'Can you hear me?'

My mother is crying, just a bit. But she looks well. Jamie's arm is around her shoulders, and Carl is pressed close to him. They are all holding one another up. They look well. Tired, maybe, but well.

Now they are smiling, in response to my smile. They are as they ought to be. They'll be all right. The nurse is speaking, but I ignore her. I am sitting in a hard chair but I am rocking, just a little. I have so much to say to these three, but something is pressing into my cheek and I have no time. 'Goodbye now,' I whisper, and the light blazes up and I hear my mother's voice rising sharply…

…and then the golden light is gone. The pressure on my cheek shifts slightly. Someone close by is snoring.

I lift my cheek from Raj's shoulder. He smiles down at me. 'Hello, sleepyhead,' he says.

Carl is snoring opposite me; his grey hair is steely in the wintry light. Jamie is sitting with his eyes closed, long hair curling against his neck. I sit up, a little queasy from the movement of the snowcat. 'What did I miss?'

'Scenery.' Raj nods to the forward window.

Mountains rise from the flat moor ahead of us, steel-grey dusted with white, painfully bright in the sunshine. They do not sparkle, and they are not pretty. We are coming up to Glen Coe.

The road curves and we see down the approach to the glen. I know it because I can see the Great Shepherd on our left. The ground-level landmarks are gone, blanketed in white. I'm confused: shouldn't the King's House be on the right? Is it further on, or is it that large white bump in the wilderness? And shouldn't the ski centre be there on the Lesser Shepherd? But there's nothing but snow.

Two scraps of colour stand out against the snow – one blue and one red. They're moving, fluttering. I'm looking at a building – long and low and white, resting comfortably at the top of the slope where the ski centre used to be. There are glints of azure – windows. Flags rise above it.

There is a change in the tone of the motor: we're slowing down. The sledge tracks we've been following turn off through an impressive gate – only a few lighter impressions carry on into Glencoe proper. The gateway is flanked by two eight-foot Celtic crosses, probably poured concrete, but still impressive. To one side is a shorter stone monolith, inscribed in curly calligraphic script: *Wayfinder Ski and Leisure Centre*. The monolith is capped with snow and I realise suddenly that the crosses are not. 'Is this it?' I say, my voice shakier than I'd like.

'This is it.' The driver is steering us between the crosses into a broad driveway that curves up into a forest of evergreens. Jamie makes a derisive sound in his throat and I turn to follow his gaze. He's looking back at the crosses. I just have time to see the discreet wires running up the back of each one.

'Do they heat those crosses to keep the snow off?' Jamie asks.

'It's for the floodlights.' The driver sounds slightly offended. 'They're lit up at night.'

Jamie snorts but doesn't reply. We are plunged into dark green, pleasant after the glare. The pines are iced with white. The Christmas-card view is marred only slightly by the steel poles that line the driveway on either side, each crowned like a lighthouse with dull red glass. The driver flicks on the headlights and the glass tops flash scarlet, like glaring eyes. I'm quite glad when the road rises out of the woods and back into the white.

The route has been carefully planned for effect: we take a slow curve out of the pines until we're looking up at the Centre. I don't know what I'd been expecting – a fake St Paul's Cathedral, maybe, or a ten-foot neon Jesus – but it wasn't this. It looks like a Rennie Mackintosh: curved and elegant, white against the winter-blue sky, for all the world like the Hill House. The main part of the building is oblong, with simple deco designs on either side of the entrance. To each side of the building, and seemingly behind it too, are round white structures like castle turrets. It ought to look absurd, but it doesn't. It fits snugly, almost humbly, into the lie of the land, but it draws the eye as the land never could. Flags are flying from the turrets: a saltire, and a red banner marked with a golden cross. 'Holy shit,' I say. 'It's Camelot.'

The driver laughs about this as we follow the gentle rise of the driveway up to the main entrance. At one point the road loops around the other side of the hill, and we catch a glimpse of cable-car towers and machinery, with some fluorescent-clad figures shuffling towards them. Then we're back at the front again, pulling up beside the gold-and-glass doors. Two men in matching red-and-gold parkas emerge; while we're still struggling to our feet and massaging our numb backsides, the driver has already opened the boot and the parka men are loading our luggage onto a trolley.

I climb out, catching the driver's chivalrous hand as I stagger slightly. The air is sharp but I inhale it gratefully. I've gotten used to the tinted glass, so for a moment Glencoe is just a big bright blur. When my eyes clear I can see peaks outlined sharply against the blue sky. The slopes, and the valley floor, are muffled with snow. There's no way of telling what's under there.

The only movement is a tiny hornet-striped snowcat, inching its way along what is presumably the road. When it disappears behind a bank of white, there is nothing. I could be looking at a landscape on Pluto. Even from our elevated position, there's only rock and ice as far as I can see.

'It's this way, Miss.' The parka-men are looking at me in concern; they're not going to be happy until everyone is inside. I follow the baggage trolley towards the doors, leaving the others to sort out the driver's tip. Judging by the revving of engines I hear a minute later, the man was not impressed.

The automatic doors clunk shut behind us, cutting off any outdoor sounds. We're in a broad corridor that leads up to a slowly revolving door. The corridor is fairly plain – obviously part of an air-lock system to keep out the cold. Above the doors, a sign in gold lettering reads: *Welcome to Wayfinder. 'Come unto Him, all ye that labour, and He shall give you rest.'*

'Here goes nothing,' I murmur to Raj, and we step through the door and into the lobby of McLean's hotel.

It's more Rennie Mackintosh – sky-blue carpets and warm polished wood. Straight ahead is a long, curved reception desk, where people in navy suit jackets smile out at the world. They murmur to a mass of people in bright anoraks thronging around the desk. It's crowded, but still quiet; we can hear breathy Enya music in the background. To one side, sheets of water ripple down a marble slope into a raised pond. Raj and I, unable to get any closer to the desk, perch on the low wall, peering past the water lilies to the large golden fish. I dabble my fingers in the water, watching one of the fish rising lazily towards me. 'It's not much of a supervillain's lair, this, is it?'

Raj follows my gaze. 'Apart from the piranhas, you mean?' He chortles to himself as I leap about a foot in the air. The fish breaks the surface with its round toothless mouth.

'Bastard,' I say, flicking the water on my hands at Raj. 'You'd better behave. I only brought you here to have someone to fornicate with.'

'Your sister can't take a joke,' Raj says over my shoulder. Jamie's there, looking like he can't take one either. But this isn't a pleasure holiday, after all. 'Let's get checked in,' he says.

Soon I'm leaning over the polished reception desk, feeling like a scruff compared to the staff on the other side. Their dark blue jackets look like Armani, although surely they can't be. One of the girls, badged as *Shona*, smiles up at us; a pretty face with a light dusting of make-up, red hair partially cloaking the discreet head-set running from ear to mouth. 'Sorry to keep you,' she says, sounding genuinely sorry. 'How can I help you?'

'Pherson? Four people?' She nods pleasantly and, without making any adjustments I can see, starts murmuring into the mike. I crane over the desk, half expecting to see her rambling inanely at nothing but her shoes, but a screen flashes into life, letters scrolling across it. After a few more seconds I add, 'One might be under Trainor?'

Another pleasant nod and moments later she hits a key: found it. Extra respect comes into her voice. 'That's four single rooms for three nights?'

'Two singles and one double,' I say defiantly, edging towards Raj. Again, Shona doesn't turn a hair. 'Two singles and one double,' she says, in a voice that means she's talking to the mike – and apparently the mike can tell, because more letters flow across the screen. There's a low beep, and paper begins to roll out of a slot on the desk. Shona detaches it, tucks it into a white folder she's just produced from under the desk, and hands it to us. 'Welcome to Wayfinder. Please come with me, and I'll show you around.'

She comes out from behind the counter. Other guests at the desk look at us with mild envy – seems this five-star treatment is not for everyone. Too surprised to resist, we allow our bags and coats to be spirited away, and follow Shona for the grand tour. There's the lounge – Scots baronial, with leather sofas and the smell of wood smoke, and 'high tea to be served from four to six o'clock' – and then the dining room, where waiters in white linen aprons are laying out gleaming silverware on white linen tablecloths. There's the gym, full of intimidatingly athletic people pounding away on scary-looking equipment, goggling at TV screens to stave off the boredom. We're shown the sauna and steam rooms, and an outsize Jacuzzi that can seat about twelve. 'And this,' says Shona, with the air of someone showing off the Mona Lisa, 'is the swim centre.'

We follow her towards sounds of splashing and shouting, out into dazzling light. We are on a balcony, in a huge room of glass. Through the steamed-up panes comes the glare of the snow. Around us, weary-looking adults are sipping cappuccinos; below lies a vast network of pools, fountains, rapids and waterfalls, seething with children. Flumes coil around the walls – a particularly hair-raising one loops outside the building before dropping its shrieking occupants into a plunge pool. One pool laps right up against the glass; through the condensation I can see heads bobbing about outside.

At that moment a klaxon sounds; the shrieking gets louder, and half the main pool's occupants start splashing towards the deep end, while the other half make for the shallows. The pool humps up in the middle as if a whale is breaching, and within a minute there are five-foot waves dashing against the deep end.

The squealing reaches an ear-popping crescendo. I watch a young man and woman, probably the only adults not there to stop kids drowning themselves, clamber out of the main pool looking pissed off. The man speaks to a pool attendant, pointing to a pair of glass doors. Beyond the doors is a smooth floor of glass. No: it's another pool. A rectangular pool with lane lines on the bottom; unlit, calm and empty. The pool attendant is smiling at the young couple, but still shaking his head: no entry.

I look at Shona. 'Why don't they open up that pool?'

'That's the baptismal pool,' she says. 'It has to be prepared a few days in advance. Purified, you know.'

'Purified?'

'That's right.' She's already moving us on, perhaps sensing awkward questions in the air. 'I'll just show you the ski slopes, then I'll leave you to yourselves.'

We don't need to go outside to see the slopes. She takes us to an observation deck on the top floor, its north wall one huge pane of glass. We watch the skiers clinging to the ski tows, sliding away at the top, then off down the slope, and stamping off to the lift again. The peak of the Shepherd towers over them, but they don't seem worried. Shona has launched into her spiel. I tune in to hear her say, 'The slopes are regularly maintained, and pre-avalanched every night. Instructors are always on hand to help you. Do you have any questions?'

Three of us are muttering polite no's – but Jamie speaks up. 'When does all the *Spirit Fire* stuff get going?'

'This evening, after dinner.' Her smile broadens considerably. 'You must be looking forward to it.'

Raj says, 'Do the staff get to go?'

'Oh, yes. It'll be great.' She looks younger now, excited. The professional voice is gone. 'I just think it's so great. The faith that made our country is coming back. It's like we're coming home. It's just so hopeful, you know?'

Although it was Raj who asked, she's still looking at Jamie. No doubt she's thinking about how he's here with just his sister and his pals, free and single. 'I'll see you there then?' she says.

'I should think so,' Jamie replies. 'I'm the chief penitent.'

'Oh, right.' She lets out a small nervous laugh and sways slightly, as if she wants to back away from him. 'That's good, that's really good…' A deep breath and she's hearty and professional once more. 'Well, if you've no more questions…'

We don't. Shona flees. We go to find our rooms.

Our room is large and tasteful and warm. The carpet is cream, and soft as cotton wool. I run out of the bathroom in my scanties, and turn around with arms outstretched. 'Look!'

Raj, sprawled on the orgy-sized bed, is already looking. I do another twirl. 'No goosebumps!'

'I can see a couple of big ones.'

'You're getting a big bump yourself, you dirty bugger.' But I'm conscious suddenly of my flabby midriff and off-white knickers. Winter sunlight fills the room, stark and unforgiving. I scurry over to the bed and sit astride him, pulling the top sheet over my legs, although I'm far from cold. The warmth makes me feel summer-ish, languid. 'Have you seen the size of that bath?'

He runs his hands lazily up and down my bare thighs. 'Lots of incentives to sin here, don't you think?'

'You're telling me.' I start to unbutton his shirt, peeling back the fabric and kissing the bare skin inside. 'A shame Jamie and Carl aren't together, they'd love a bath like that.'

The hands pause. 'That's not an image I want in my head right now, Suzey.'

I giggle into his chest. 'Aw. Did I make your goosebump go away?' I do some exploratory groping. 'No, still there… And getting bigger now. Shame on you, thinking those thoughts in a house of God.'

I thought this teasing foreplay would go on for hours, but abruptly he pulls my face up to his and rolls half on top of me. I loosen my bra, and pull his shirt off over his head. There's a fair bit of escapologist fumbling on both sides, but he doesn't smile about it. He's already raising my hips to pull off my pants. I murmur something about closing the blinds, although I know the glass is tinted and there's only the mountain outside.

'I want to see you.'

We've never been together like this before, with nothing to cover us. We've seen each other piecemeal, in faint light and under blankets. It's almost frightening. We're both too pale, too flabby and wrinkly – a long way from movie sex, and it doesn't matter.

Afterwards we trace our fingertips along slippery skin. I sink my fingers into his damp hair and kiss his sweaty forehead. He kisses my neck and says, 'I love you, Suzey.'

'I love you too.' We lie wrapped around each other, in the humid warmth, for a long time.

While he's in the loo, I turn my back on the window and pull the sheet up to my shoulders. It makes a little tent; I feel bizarrely reassured by it. I drag over the Spirit Fire brochure. I haven't seen such quality paper in a while – a white eggshell finish, with a gold embossed cross. I'm looking for the timetable as the bathroom door opens, and Raj climbs smiling into the sheet house. 'Can I come in?'

'If you don't want to rush off to…' I check the sheet. '*The Scottish Family – Endangered Species.*'

'I'll pass.'

'How about…' The next item is in a Crayola-type font, indicating that Family Fun is to be perpetuated. Which should clear all those kids out of the swim centre. 'Come on, let's go downstairs for a bit.'

He glances at the sheet and raises his eyebrows. 'You want to go to *Puppet Theatre's 'Daniel in the Lion's Den'*?'

'Only if they're holding it in the Jacuzzi.' I find my bra squashed up under a pillow and start to untangle it. Raj whisks it away from me, holding it at arm's length so I have to climb over him to get it. 'We haven't tried the bath yet,' he says.

'It's not a Jacuzzi. Not even we can fart that much.'

'We can try something else…'

'Just give me it.' My voice is sharper than I meant it to be. He gives me the bra. There's a silence as I struggle into it. Eventually I say, 'We should go and find Jamie.'

'Why?' There's an edge to his voice now, too. 'Why do you want to find him?'

'To see if he's okay.'

'Why wouldn't he be?'

'I don't know. I'm just worried. That's all.'

'We'll keep an eye on him.' He pulls me into a hug and kisses my face, working round to my neck. He's pressed up against me – I should be annoyed, him only thinking about one thing. But I start kissing his shoulder, then touching my teeth onto his skin, working downwards.

Clearly we're not going downstairs. This time I'll close the blinds.

I squeeze into my Red Dress for dinner. It's flapper style, all sequins and fringing. I got it for my eighteenth birthday and it's been lurking at the back of Mum's wardrobe since my nineteenth, waiting in the feeble hope I'd get back into it some day. God knows why Mum picked it up when she went back to the house. But I'm glad she did, because now I can actually do up the zip, which represents such a triumph I hardly care about my bulgy bum and stomach. Might be a bit much for God-fearing company, mind. I consider toning it down but then think to hell with it and slap on red lip-gloss to match. I pull my hair severely back from my face, frowning at myself in the mirror. 'Is this too much?'

Raj comes up behind me in the mirror, and slides his hands across the silky fabric pulled tight over my hips. '*Very* scarlet woman,' he breathes into my ear, and starts kissing round to the back of my neck. I disengage, giggling, before he can find *that* spot just above my spine, in which case we'll end up missing dinner altogether. 'Come on. I need to refuel first.'

He tuts. 'Weak and feeble woman.'

We find Carl and Jamie in the lounge outside the dining room. They're looking glum, although Jamie smiles a bit when he sees me. 'Hey, it's the Red Dress!'

Carl surrenders his chair for me, which I've never known him to do – perhaps he's afraid the dress will split if I have to climb over him to a free seat. 'You look very nice, Suzey.'

Jamie's in nostalgia mode. 'All my pals used to fancy you something rotten in that dress. Derek Dale spent my whole fourteenth birthday trying to get a look down your cleavage.'

'How nice.' I lower myself into the chair. 'What about a drink for the Whore of Babylon, then?'

Two glum faces look back at me. 'The place is dry. Apart from wine with dinner.'

'Now aren't you glad we didn't miss dinner?' I say to Raj. He smiles at me sidelong and casually rests a hand on my knee; his thumb just touches my dress's sparkly hem, which has ridden up considerably since I sat down. I look around to see if I'm in danger of being stoned to death. Most of the other women are in regulation Scotswoman-on-a-night-out uniform (the suit you wear to the office, but with a colourful blouse and more makeup), but there are a few other slinky dresses about, although I'm the only one to have plumped for hoory-red. The people at the next table are getting to their feet and for a moment I think they're protesting the sight of Raj's creeping fingers on my nylon thigh. But then I hear the double-doors creaking back – the dining room is open. 'Shall we?' I say.

'Oh aye.' Jamie is already on his feet. He adds in a murmur, 'Thank God you get wine at least. This is not a place you want to do sober.'

But so far everything seems, well, normal. I take Raj's arm, using this as an excuse to press up against him; he reaches across with his other hand, ostensibly to squeeze my fingers, actually to cop an extremely unsubtle feel of my boob. We couldn't look less like a respectable husband and wife if we tried but no one's turning a hair.

We end up seated with a pleasant couple with soft American accents. They are Mark and Sandra. They are obviously very much married, and Sandra is wearing a demure floral dress, but they don't seem horrified by us. The four men bond by arguing over the wine list (my three know bugger all about wine, but that doesn't stop them) and Sandra and I bond by rolling our eyes heavenwards about it. The males don't even notice when the wine waiter returns, so I say, 'What's the cheapest wine on the menu?'

My menfolk look exasperated, but the waiter laughs. 'The three house wines are complimentary.'

'I'll have the sparkling,' I say immediately.

'How many glasses for the sparkling?'

'Just give her a straw,' says Jamie, rather sourly. But he cheers up when the red arrives. Meanwhile, we've been eavesdropping on a monologue coming from the next table, which bears out one of my expectations: a honking American voice declaring its Christian right to bear arms, apparently to use on the IRS. Mark and Sandra are squirming. 'We're not all like that,' they mouth across the table to us.

Then the double doors are flung open and in strides McLean. He looks orange under the lights, but his suit is dark and well cut, and he moves well. He is followed by a procession of more men in nice suits, women in elegant dresses, and, a step behind the great man himself, daughter Kerry. She is heavy built; she would be an inch or two taller than her father if she stood up straight, rather than walking with slumped shoulders and bowed head, as if she wanted to disappear behind him. But she doesn't have to worry here – all eyes are well and truly on McLean.

Applause breaks out. People reach out to him as he passes by, and he pauses at each table to greet his guests. At our table, he grasps Carl's hand, but doesn't look at him: his gaze fixes onto me, then switches to Jamie. Then he's gone, moving briskly to the top table.

The suits and dresses settle around him, like a bridal party. The man himself remains standing until they're all seated. Misunderstanding, a few people around us clasp their hands and go to bow their heads. McLean smiles, motioning them to stop. 'Just sit for now,' he says. He is using his accent, the Glaswegian tones warm and earthy (but slowed down so the Americans can understand). 'My dad always said, "Don't thank the Lord for your food till it's sitting in front of ye."'

The room loves this. The top table people laugh, too, if not quite so heartily. One of the women, a beautifully slim brunette in a black sheath dress, flicks back her hair a little as she laughs. She looks almost like…

'Shit,' I hear Carl say. I'm already on my feet. There's a glug as my glass topples, a flurry of napkins around the table. She glances towards the disturbance, half smiles, and looks away. She hasn't even fucking recognised us.

Raj has caught hold of my wrist, and I can hear Carl muttering something to himself.

She looks like a natural brunette; but then she looked like a natural blonde when I saw her last. She's smoothing out her immaculate designer dress, her head angled towards the man whispering into her shoulder; she smiles gracefully at whatever he says, but her vision slides sideways to inspect me again. I'm no one she recognises – just a woman in a cheap red dress, probably drunk. I take a step backwards, just to regain my balance, but Raj's hand tightens on my arm. I'm about to shove it away when Jamie catches my elbow. 'It's all right,' he says.

It's not all right, but I can't balance with both of them tugging at me so I sit down hard. Her gaze leaves me and settles on Jamie, her interest suddenly sharp. Jamie turns deliberately away. Carl, ever the diplomat, is smiling at Mark and Sandra, who are trying to fade into the wallpaper. 'Not one of our best friends,' he says.

'Who is she?' says Sandra.

'That's Anita Black,' I say. 'She's a lying fucking bitch.' My voice comes out hoarse and slurred.

'A journalist,' translates Raj. This gets a laugh. He tries to squeeze my hand under the table, but I yank my arm away. I don't want to look at him. Carl is saying something calm and reasonable, involving 'lies' and 'defamation', to Mark and Sandra; under cover of this Raj mutters, 'It's a press thing. She was bound to be here.'

'I'm going to say something to her.'

'That's not going to do any good.'

I nod. I'll forgive him, even for that patronising tone, because once I'd have said the same thing. But of course, it *would* do some good. It would stop the woman who destroyed my brother's life from sitting there laughing without a care in the world. Just for a moment, it would wipe the smile off her fucking face. Jamie, who has kept his gaze on his plate, now lifts his eyes to mine, and I know he's thinking the same thing. But he shakes his head slightly: I've to back off.

So I look at Raj's concerned face and I smile. A waiter is beside me, covering the spilled wine with a white cloth, setting another glass in front of me and pouring out the bubbly. Delicious smells waft across the room. The food has arrived.

And oh my God, what food. A delicate broth seasoned to perfection, accompanied by warm bread slathered in soft, melting butter. Then there's a tangy sorbet. And the main course: beef so tender it falls apart under the fork; spicy chicken made entirely from breast meat; and fish, white and boneless. The four of us swap around a lot. Other than that we scarcely raise our heads. Mark and Sandra watch us with amused sympathy. 'Can't talk,' says Carl in his best Homer Simpson voice, 'eating.'

They laugh again. I'm now full enough to feel slightly mortified by our starving European routine; but then the dessert arrives. Orange bread-and-butter pudding, or profiteroles. When I've finished mopping up the decorative cocoa powder with my last bite of choux pastry, the embarrassment creeps back in again. Only one thing to do about that: I pull the empty bottle out of the water at the bottom of the ice bucket, and wave it at a passing wine waiter. Two minutes later he's back with more ice and a new bottle. 'More fizz, anyone?'

They all say yes – looks like I don't have to crash the dignity barrier all on my own. I look around the room: a few diners are drinking Coke and looking tight-lipped at those who aren't, but most of the tables have alcohol on them. McLean himself is on the red wine. We could be at any social gathering, anywhere.

Eventually the coffee comes around, dark and nutty and strong. I have two cups, and the warm, fluffy feeling in my head subsides a little. There are chocolate mints in gold foil. I watch Jamie absently put a few in his pocket, for Claire, then slowly take them back out again. I put a hand on his arm, but before I can speak there's the musical ting of a knife tapped against glass. McLean is getting to his feet.

The conversation starts to subside; chairs are scraped around so everyone can see the top table. McLean starts to speak before we're all settled, confidently, knowing his voice will hush us. 'Brothers and sisters,' he says, 'let us pray.'

We bow our heads. McLean waits a beat before he begins. 'We thank you, God, for bringing us together this evening. We thank you, God, for this good fellowship.' His voice seems to be everywhere at once, although I don't see a microphone in front of him. 'We thank you, God, for this good food. And we thank you, God, for the freedom to meet here in your name.'

A few muted cries of 'Amen' fill the silence. McLean carries on smoothly, 'We thank you, God, for the liberty to speak this prayer: Our Father, which art in Heaven, hallowed be thy Name…'

The audience joins in. I can hear Raj and Carl – they're word-perfect. I mumble along, waiting for their prompt for the bits I've forgotten. Jamie stays silent. I'm still peeking through my eyelashes. The light is trembling, and seems to be fading out. But the light beside the top table is bright, and getting brighter. 'For thine is the Kingdom, and the power and the glory…'

There's stirring round about me – seems I'm not the only one peeking. 'For ever and ever… Amen.'

At last we get to look. There is a cross of light against the far wall. It must be on a screen, but I can't see any controls. The main lights are now all but out. McLean begins to speak again. 'The Lord says to us, people of Scotland, why have you turned away from the Cross? Why have you abandoned the faith that built your country? Why have you turned away from the truth that sets you free?'

There are a few more cries of 'Amen', but McLean carries on like a recording. The light from the cross is almost blinding now. 'People of Scotland – how long will you listen to the counsels of despair? How long will you hear the doctrines of political correctness, which are empty at their heart?' More muttered agreement. Someone nearby says 'Yes!' McLean's voice has become sorrowful. 'People of Scotland – why do you despise your own folk? For two thousand years the men and women of Scotland have come to the Cross. For two thousand years!'

Something is passing through the table beside me. An arm, insubstantial as mist. A figure in a long skirt. She is *passing right through me*. I cry out, and hear myself echoed by other cries around the room. People are shrinking back in alarm. Around them, and through them, wraithlike figures are walking slowly towards the welcoming light of the cross.

'Since the days of Columba they have come to the Cross. They have forsworn pagan darkness and turned their faces to the light...'

Raj nudges me and points upwards. Tiny projector lights are tracking across the ceiling, converging on the illuminated cross. From each projector the beam of a spotlight, invisible until you know it's there, reaches down to a ghostly figure. I'm perched on the edge of my seat, and I make myself sit back, although I still flinch when a phantom in a monk's robe flits in front of me. There are more monks, and men carrying spears, and women in rough plaid shawls. They walk into the light and disappear.

'At the time of the Bruce they came to the Cross. When our nation was born they gave thanks to the Cross...'

An armoured knight walks calmly through Carl, who laughs nervously in the gloom. Knights, ladies, peasants... The clothes keep changing, but the people keep coming. Now it's Renaissance: men in tights, women in Gloriana gowns. Puritan women, then men in frock coats and wigs. It's speeding up now: top hats and bustles, soldiers, flappers, soldiers again, and civilians carrying gasmasks. 'In peace they gave thanks to the Cross. In war the Cross was their shield. In good times and bad they turned their hearts to the Cross…'

I catch a brief glimpse of long hippy hair, women in pinstripe, then they are rushing into the light, and the light is so bright I have to turn away.

A whirring sound, which I wasn't aware of before, ceases. And we are in darkness. A negative-image cross swims before me.

Then low light begins to fill the room, growing gradually brighter. The cross is gone. People are turning in their seats, exclaiming. Mark and Sandra are smiling at us indulgently – presumably such technology is everyday stuff where they come from. I look at the top table, where Anita Black seems to be making notes. But my attention is caught on McLean, who leans forwards slightly, resting his elbows on the table as if he were weary. The hubbub is dying down. Everyone waits for McLean to speak.

He smiles, a little sadly. 'Brothers and sisters, walk always to the light. The final days are at hand. Where will you turn, when the darkness comes forever?'

No one speaks. McLean smiles again, and raises his hands in blessing. 'Go forth in peace. May the blessing of the Lord go with you.'

He steps down from the table as applause erupts. His entourage hurry to follow. The audience is cheering; some are on their feet, weeping. McLean passes between them, holding out his hands so they can touch him. He takes a detour between the tables. He is soon in front of the four of us.

Again, he ignores Carl and Raj. His gaze lingers on me, then on Jamie. His pale eyes are blank, like a doll's. I see nothing in them.

Late in the night I wake with a jump. The room is dark except for the luminous alarm clock – it's 2.15. I'm wide awake.

My heart is thumping. I'm boiling. I've thrashed out of the covers in my sleep, but it doesn't help. Raj's arms are wrapped around me; we're both soaked with sweat. It's like cuddling in a sauna. We've always fallen asleep in each other's arms, rolled together in the centre of Raj's beaten-up bed. Seems this romantic stuff only works in a cold climate. When I struggle out of his grip he makes a startled sound, but I murmur 'Going to the loo,' and he grunts and turns his back.

Out of bed the warmth is pleasant. I'm naked, but I can stroll unhurriedly into the bathroom and linger as long as I like. I mustn't get used to this – in two more nights we'll have to leave, and everything will be back to normal. It's a depressing thought.

My heart's still hammering, making me feel almost nervous. Of course – the coffee. I'm not used to the real stuff any more. Now it'll be ages before I can get back to sleep. I switch on the mirror light, and leave the bathroom door open a crack, so I can ferret around the bedroom looking for my jeans and sweatshirt. When I'm decent I kiss Raj's sweaty forehead. 'Going for a walk,' I whisper.

The corridors are deserted. Seems all the good Christian folk are abed. But no, I hear laughter coming from the reception area – the night staff, no doubt getting a bit stir crazy as night staff generally do. I could go down there, but I can't face all the concern and offers of milk and polite conversation I'd get. Insomnia is a solitary business.

I set off for the observation lounge. From somewhere comes a muted crash, like thunder, although the night is clear. Someone must have dropped something.

None of the lamps are on in the observation room. Beyond the barely-there picture glass, a near-full moon hovers above the mountains, turning them lunar white. The longer I look, the more stars appear, bright and sharp. After a few moments, to the amazement of my city-dweller's heart, I can see quite well.

There's a slight movement from the black leather seats. I'm startled, but not surprised to see who it is. Caffeine intolerance runs in our family. 'Can't sleep either?' I ask.

Jamie shakes his head, moving up so I can plonk myself on the couch beside him. 'Dynamite woke me.'

'Eh?'

'Dynamite. They're bringing down the avalanches.'

I look out at the Great Shepherd. It seems very close. 'They're *what?*'

'Controlled avalanching. They divert them away from the hotel.' He's watching me in amusement. 'How did you think they did it?'

'I didn't think about it.' And I'm not too happy to be thinking about it now. 'So somebody goes out there at night and does it?'

'Aye, that's right.'

'That's their job? Official avalancher?'

'I suppose.'

He seems very muted. Generally, his boyish love of big explosions would have his nose pressed up to the glass like a five year old. 'You okay?' I say.

'Fine.' He studies me. 'You?'

'Yeah, okay.'

'You really like him, don't you?' He nods in the general direction of my room and the sleeping Raj.

'Yeah.' The guilt is back. My brother's going through a life crisis and all I can think about is shagging my boyfriend. It's not right. 'Picked the wrong time to get all loved up, though, didn't we?' I say.

'You get it while you can.'

'D'you like him?'

'Yes. He's a good guy.' And there's no *but* coming after. My family like him. I'm torn between joy and terror. I want to ask what he thinks of Carl, but resist the temptation. Instead I say, 'Do you still want to be here?'

'Not much choice.'

'We could go home.'

'No.'

'You're going to do it then? Get baptised, and all that?'

'Not much choice,' he repeats.

'And then what?'

He shrugs. He was like this as a kid, the exasperating little sod – when it really matters, he won't tell me a damn thing. 'Then we'll see what's what,' he says.

'Aye. Things'll be better.' He's playing their holy-holy game, it's got to make a difference.

A boom makes me jump out of my skin. It echoes and echoes, all around the mountains. A white chunk of the Great Shepherd detaches itself, and slithers down the western slope, crumbling to powder as it goes. It slides out of sight and clouds of white puff into the air like smoke. The boom is still reverberating.

Jamie gets up. 'I'm off to bed,' he says.

Chapter 25

The next day dawns too bright and too early. By the time the four of us meet, bleary-eyed, at the breakfast table, we can hear loud, cheerful music from the main hall. The simple beat is thumping through the floor, reinforced by clapping, singing and the occasional shout of joy. Even the waiters are looking alarmed.

We meet up with Mark and Sandra – or, rather, we meet up with their son: a small dark-haired boy who sees his parents smile at us, and takes this as an invitation to come hurtling over. 'Whatcha doin?'

I'm currently trying to mainline some caffeine. I lower the coffee cup and say shortly, 'Having our breakfast.'

'Neddy.' Sandra has come to apprehend him. She and Mark look slightly the worse too. 'Don't disturb these people.'

'We're going to the swimming pool,' Neddy informs us.

Sandra sighs and Mark says sternly, 'No, we're not. We're going on the snowcat, remember? We're going to see Glencoe.'

Neddy pouts. 'But I don't *wanna*.'

Jamie says casually, 'You don't want to see where all those people stuck swords in each other?'

Neddy's eyes go big. 'Swords?'

'And knives. And guns.' Jamie nods sagely over his coffee. 'They all jumped out of bed and tried to kill each other.'

'And they were like, *urgh, urgh*!' Neddy starts miming wild sword thrusts, nearly knocking over the milk jug. 'And they went, *Aaah, don't stab me, aaah...*'

'That's right, that's what they did.' Sandra is tugging him away. 'Come on now.'

Neddy points at Jamie. 'Can he come?'

'No. I expect he wants to go to the big prayer meeting,' says Sandra, wistfully. 'He doesn't have wild little boys to look after.'

Jamie's already on his feet. 'We'll come to Glencoe,' he says, and the rest of us nod vigorously.

Ten minutes later, we're suited up and heading outside. Ahead of me, Neddy is swinging between his father's hand and Jamie's, tugging to make them go faster.

A young woman is waiting for us beside the snowcat. She is slight and blonde, no older than Shona but more serious-looking. The badge on her red-and-gold parka says *Emma*. She smiles at the boy. 'Hiya, Neddy.' A slight Aberdeen accent. 'Coming for a trip with me?'

'I wanna see the swords!'

'It's a long story,' his father sighs as we pile into the snowmobile.

At the bottom of the drive, after we're past the two Celtic crosses, we turn left, into the very faint tracks that run towards Glencoe. But after a few yards we turn again, to the right, towards the big white bump I thought I recognised. 'Is that the King's House?'

Emma, peering over the wheel, nods. 'It's shut just now.'

'You mean *shut* shut, or just…'

'No, it opens in the summer. For folk doing the West Highland Way.'

'It's a hotel,' I explain to Mark and Sandra. 'It used to be a cattle-drover's inn.'

'It sold cheap alcohol to foolish men,' Emma says, tartly. 'They got drunk, and then they were put out in the snow to die. It was a dreadful place.'

She's going to be a laugh a minute. I watch the hotel go past; there's snow halfway up the walls, and heavy on the roof. You'd hardly know there was a building there. We cross the small bridge – the river too is nearly hidden, frozen solid then smothered in snow. We turn to the northwest, and start trundling uphill.

For a while Emma keeps up a commentary, all mountain names and geological data, which I ignore. Neddy is climbing over us, particularly Jamie, who is making up lurid tales of past bloodshed for him ('…and they found the head right over *there*, where that big rock is…').

Then I hear Emma say, 'And over there is Jacob's Ladder.' I look in the direction she is pointing, searching for some new building or structure, but see nothing. 'What's Jacob's Ladder?' I ask.

'It's a steep mountain pass into the glen. The West Highland Way goes over it.'

'That's the Devil's Staircase,' says Raj.

Emma frowns, glances at Neddy. Seems we can't use the D-word. 'Mr McLean's renamed it,' she says.

There's a pause. 'How can he *rename* it?' Raj says at last.

'It's a bad name. It's not a good name to use.'

'That's hardly up to him.'

'It's a wicked name,' she insists. 'The men who drank at the inn called it that. They were wicked and foolish.'

'It's the Devil's Staircase.' Raj is getting angry, his voice taking on that Alan Rickman drawl. Ooh, sexy. I wriggle a bit closer to him, but he doesn't notice. Carl says soothingly, 'He can call it what he wants, surely. Doesn't make it official.'

'It is official,' Emma retorts. 'Or it will be soon. Mr McLean's filed the new name with the council. They agree with him. Why should it be called… *that*… just because a few drunks fell down it?'

'That's not the only reason. Invaders used the Staircase to enter the glen. Reinforcements for the Massacre came down it. The name is a warning.'

'Well,' says Emma, and shrugs. The conversation is over, as far as she's concerned. But Raj has other ideas. 'Do you know what it was called before?'

'No.'

'Nor do I. Nor does anyone.'

Awkward silence. Then Neddy, who is climbing up Jamie to see through the window, demands, 'Are we going to see the swords now?'

'Give those two another minute,' says Jamie. We laugh, and Raj smiles a little. Emma doesn't, although she might just be distracted by the road ahead. We trundle down an incline and turn right. We're now on the valley floor.

Sleigh tracks stretch ahead of us; looking through the windshield I can see another snowcat, a blob of bright yellow, some miles in front. Beyond and above is blue sky but from the side windows I see only sunlit white. I press my nose against the glass, squinting upwards; a peak is just visible. Glencoe is narrow and very deep. I'll be glad when we get there.

Sandra and Carl, with every semblance of enthusiasm, are studying crumpled copies of the *Spirit Fire* programme. 'I'm going to *What Difference Does Prayer Make?*' Sandra is saying. 'Then the Zionist thing. Where is it… *God's Country*. That one.'

There's a faint note of distaste in her voice. Carl is emboldened to ask,

'Are you a Zionist yourself?'

'Not the way Israel is going about it. I don't think it can be right to wage war in the Holy Land.'

'How can we *not* wage war?' This is from Emma. 'How can we call ourselves Christians and just let the Holy Land be defiled?'

'Doesn't war defile it?' There's an edge to Sandra's voice now. 'Do you want to see guns in the streets of Bethlehem?'

'I don't want to see godless men destroying Bethlehem.'

I'm recalling news footage, of bearded men calling on Allah and waving machineguns. 'I'd hardly call the Palestinians godless,' I say.

Emma's shaking her head, probably speechless at my blasphemy. 'Mr McLean can explain it a lot better than I can,' she says.

'And with better special effects,' adds Carl. We laugh again but Emma turns away, looking huffy. Sandra smiles at Carl. 'So what events are you going to?'

Carl doesn't have to look at the paper. '*Loving the Sinner, Hating the Sin*; *The Pretend Family*; and the *Intercessors for Britain* thing.'

The common theme could scarcely be more obvious. 'Oh,' says Sandra. 'Do you have pastoral care of someone who's homosexual? I mean, has homosexual inclinations?'

'No,' says Carl. 'I'm a gay Christian.'

'Oh,' says Sandra. 'Oh.' She looks to her husband for help, but Mark is buttoning up Neddy's jacket with intense concentration. Sandra says helplessly, 'I didn't know…'

'Does that bother you?' Carl asks, quite gently.

'Well. It's not for me to judge.' Sandra tries on a smile that's a little too small. Emma has gone quiet, facing forwards – her shoulders and neck look stiff. 'I don't know much about it,' Sandra finally volunteers. 'Is that why you're going to the Intercessors? You want to…'

'Change?' Carl shakes his head. 'No. We believe that God made us this way, and that's good enough for us.'

Sandra gives another tiny smile, then Carl, who's the type that can't leave a sore spot alone, says, 'We're hoping other Christians can find it in their hearts to support us.'

Emma makes a small incredulous sound. If she says anything I'm going to lamp her one with my backpack, driver or not. But she doesn't, and it's

Mark who breaks the silence. 'There's no one without sin,' he says stolidly.

'But he doesn't think it *is* a sin,' Jamie says. He looks at Carl. 'Do you?'

'Perhaps it is. No one can live without sin. We just hope God understands this is the best we can be.'

'Oh, Carl,' I say. Jamie is looking at him with utter contempt.

Sandra has spotted Jamie's disdain but misinterpreted the reason for it. 'We are all sinners,' she tells him reproachfully. 'We shouldn't judge.' She adds to Carl, 'We'll pray for you.'

'Thank you,' says Carl, apparently quite sincerely.

This is getting much too strange for me. The cabin suddenly seems to have gotten a lot smaller, and we travel on in awkward silence. Even Neddy has gone quiet, looking warily from one adult to another. I decide that staring out of the window is by far my smartest option. The landscape to the south is bare as can be; there's something missing. 'Where's the Visitors' Centre?'

'In the village,' says Emma.

'No, it's way before the village. Over there.'

'Oh, the old centre. Avalanche got it.' We all stare at her, aghast. Hastily she adds, 'That was before they put the new system in. It's all pre-avalanched now.'

'Pre-avalanched?' I echo.

'Aye. Computerised.'

'Computerised avalanches?'

'Same software they use for air-traffic control,' she says, firmly. 'It's failsafe. There's a thing about it in the new Centre.'

We are not much reassured. But by now the end is in sight. We swing around a corner and a flat expanse opens up before us: Loch Leven, frozen over and gunmetal grey. The islands, too, are clear of snow; I can see dark rock, and even a dab of green.

'Look,' I say. 'That's the Island of Kings. That's the graveyard of the clan chieftains. Look, Neddy, that's where they used to bury the kings when they died.'

'Did they get killed in a battle?'

'Mostly. Or they got murdered.'

'Or they fell off a mountain,' Jamie chips in, 'and got squished. Or they got the plague, and they had big runny sores all over, and they all burst all at once, like BANG!'

This pleasant history lesson tides us over into Glencoe village. At least,

I assume it's the village. All the cottages and hotels seem to have been replaced by giant cuckoo clocks – alpine chalets, all dark wood, gingerbread trimmings and high, pointed roofs. Some of them are about five stories high. 'You took a wrong turn,' I say to Emma. 'We're in Switzerland.'

'They're holiday cottages. Popular in the summer.'

'Doesn't anyone actually live here?'

'A few. Folk who work in the shops and the Centre.' She is now steering us towards one of the biggest buildings, a long and over-decorated structure like the Burgomaster's house in a fairytale. Half a dozen snowmobiles, of various sizes and bright colours, are parked outside. A well-padded figure on skis zips past, stopping expertly right outside the building's wooden double doors. Our snowmobile shudders to a halt. 'This is us,' says Emma. 'Visitors' Centre.'

We wrap ourselves to the minimum level; we are no more than ten yards from the door. Emma pulls down the snowcat's step and waits to hand us all down to the ground. Neddy, wriggling and protesting, is swept up in his father's arms and carried at a run into the centre, his mother close behind. Emma smiles for the three of them, but her expression becomes fixed as the four of us clamber out. As we hurry towards the Centre, I turn back to look at her. She is staring after Carl with an expression of furious distaste. I step into her line of vision and catch her eye. She shrugs slightly, and turns away to close the doors.

A gust of wind hits, cold but endurable, just. There is wood smoke in it, and pine trees. I don't particularly want to go into the Visitors' Centre, but I'm not properly dressed to stay outdoors.

The skier is now in the doorway, stripping off outer clothing with practised ease. The profile is now recognisably female. She is looping her arms through the straps of a rucksack, and shouldering the skis. The face peeping from the fur-lined parka is young and nut brown, with a sparkling nose stud and a flyaway strand of bright pink hair. I hold the door open so she can manoeuvre the skis inside; she smiles, and thanks me in a Cockney accent.

Inside there's the usual air-lock system of a short corridor followed by more doors to keep the heat in. We stamp the snow off our boots and pass into the inner sanctum, to find ourselves faced with a huge, red mountain. The lobby is not large, and the picture takes up most of the wall. It's the Great Shepherd, lit by a red summer sunset. I watch for a moment – but it's a photograph, it's not going to change. There is background music, something electronic, with a soaring treble and a tolling bell. I hear words over the syrupy backing track: 'My restless soul will never sleep, I am MacIain…' I feel the hairs rise on the back of my neck.

Then a vision in tartan comes clomping into sight. A large red-haired man in a full plaid, a white lacy cravat and an enormous badger-skin sporran has emerged to greet us. 'Welcome to Glencoe,' he booms.

Mark, Sandra and Neddy are staring at him in delight. Clearly the rest of us Scots, in our jeans and T-shirts, have been a big disappointment to them. Plaid Man beams at them; his only overtly modern feature is a plastic badge reading *Rory*. 'Would you like me to show you around the Centre?' he asks, in a pleasant east-coast accent. His smile gets even wider when he looks at Sandra, who has gone a bit pink and giggly – your first sight of a good-looking man in a kilt can get you that way. Neddy speaks up for her: 'We wanna see the swords. And the battles. Guys getting killed.'

'Aye, well, you're in the right place for that.' He points up a side corridor to a sign reading *The Massacre of Glencoe*. We can hear tinny recorded voices, and the background rumble of fairground carriages. Clearly this is not just an exhibit, but also a ride.

'Think we'll have a coffee just now,' I say, as Neddy rushes whooping towards the noises. Rory turns to the four of us; he meets our stony gaze and has the grace to look embarrassed. 'Café's that way,' he says.

The café boasts a spectacular view of the loch and the mountains beyond. We commandeer the table furthest from the sunshine and buy coffee and packets of shortbread from the gloomy woman behind the counter. I ask how business is. 'Quiet,' she says. 'Since the ski centre opened at Ballachulish.'

I've seen pictures of the centre at Ballachulish: nice big bars and no religion required. This little place just won't be able to compete. Soon the only winter population of Glencoe will be McLean and his people. Almost pleadingly I say, 'Does no one actually live here any more?'

'Oh aye.' She gives me a look of offended pride. 'Some of us are still here. In the old part, round the back of these…' She waves a hand distastefully at the gingerbread roofs we can see from the window. 'And there's other folk sometimes. But they come and go.'

I wonder briefly where they come and go from – there are no other homes to be seen for miles around. But coffee calls. I was last in the queue, and only a minute behind the others, so I'm startled to see Carl get to his feet, pouring the last of his coffee down his throat. 'See you later,' he says to me, and makes for the door.

I'm still in the huff with him. But it doesn't seem entirely right, him just walking away like that. I hiss to Jamie and Raj, 'Where's he off to?'

Raj looks surprised by the question. 'Toilet, I assume.'

There are toilets at the other end of the café, but Carl's heading out the main doors. I dither, watching him leave. 'Do you think he's okay?'

They shrug. I sit down, still watching the door. 'Maybe someone should go after him?'

'He'll be fine.' Raj is smiling at me. 'Stop trying to save the whole world, Suzey.'

This is annoying, especially when Jamie smiles in agreement. Patronising gits. 'But he might be upset,' I protest. 'You should've seen the look that poisonous bitch gave him outside.'

Jamie shrugs again. 'Should've kept his mouth shut.'

This is not like Jamie. Not like *my* Jamie.

But this *is* my Jamie, look at him – he's there, stirring his coffee the way Jamie does. He's just… not himself.

I can't cope with all this today – my mind is too fuzzy, the light is too bright. A headache is starting behind my eyes. 'Better lay off the booze tonight,' I say.

We all agree that we should (which of course doesn't mean that we will). Eventually, with two mugs of coffee slopping about in my belly, I propose making a move, and we set off to see what other wonders the centre has in store.

Next to the café is the shop. I go to work with a will, searching for something buyable. It's pretty much what you'd expect: woolly jumpers, racks of postcards, tins of tablet, fridge magnets shaped like haggis. Behind the counter, a tweedy woman is bending over a CD player – an operatic tenor starts warbling that his 'heart's in the Highlands'.

I poke about amongst the 'novelties' – dollies in kilts, stuffed Nessies, tea towels with the Selkirk Grace printed on them, Saltire T-shirts, and posters telling outrageous lies about 'The Unique Tartans of the Clans'. Nothing I'd buy even in my most deranged shopping frenzy. But the back of the shop opens out into a larger hall, marked *Local Artists and Craftsmen*.

Perhaps in the right season it's a busy marketplace, but at the moment there are only half a dozen stalls, with just a handful of shoppers inspecting them. One of the stalls is hung about with paintings, mostly winter landscapes, all in white and azure; Carl is there, pointing to a small picture that the stallholder is lifting down for him. Raj goes over for a look and Jamie and I wander on, past fleeces, walking boots, pewter quaichs, novelty stone chess sets and silver jewellery. Jamie spots a second-hand bookstand and makes for that; I'm about to follow him when I spot Emma strolling towards the stall at the end. At the last moment she steps back, scowling, and turns deliberately away. That's good enough for me. I walk past her expression of outraged virtue to check out the end stall.

It's rather shabby, and I wonder vaguely if the centre knows it's here. It's festooned with Indian cotton clothing, wide muslin skirts and tie-dyed tops. There are colourful posters, exotic-looking jewellery, candles and joss sticks. Also – and this is probably what put Emma in such a snit – little statues of Buddha and Ganesha, sitting neatly on top of books with titles like *The Wheel of Karma* and *The Goddess Within*. The stallholder is setting out some small wooden carvings; she is now wearing a long muslin shirt, with no trace of her skiing gear, but her pink hair is unmistakable. With Emma's glare burning into my back, I give the girl a big happy smile and point to the carvings. 'What are those?'

She pushes some of them forward. They are crudely done, but now I can see them more clearly I can hazard a fair guess what they are. The girl says, 'They're fertility symbols. This is the Phallus of Odin, and this is the Yoni of the Great Goddess Freya. See?'

I can see all right. Resisting the evil urge to call Emma back over, I point gingerly to one that's sort of T-shaped; if this is also the Phallus of Odin, Odin needs to get to a doctor quick. 'Is that one a fertility symbol too?'

'No, that's Thor's Hammer.' I bite back a smutty joke; the girl is speaking very earnestly. 'It's a symbol of power and strength. Power against evil.'

'I could use some of that.' Behind the carvings are airbrushed pictures of large blonde warriors in tiny fur loincloths; at the front are pendants, polished stones on long black cords. Each stone is marked with a different symbol. 'Runes?' I say. She nods. I ask, 'What do they mean?'

'You just pick one. And that one's yours.'

I study them. The symbols are all straight lines and corners – no circles, no curves at all. They were not made to be written on paper, but scratched into wood and stone. I choose one that looks like an elongated S:

'What's this one?'

'Yggdrasil.' She's smiling: evidently this is a good one. 'The World Tree. It goes up into the heavens and down into the underworld. It's the Life of the World.'

'What're you up to?' Raj has come up behind me.

'Choosing my own rune.' I add to the stallholder, 'Don't let him do it, he'll cheat. He knows all about this stuff.'

She considers this quite seriously. 'You choose for him, then.'

I pick the closest thing to an R:

'That means the Road,' she says. Unexpectedly, she reaches up and places it round his neck like a medal. 'You're a traveller. This will bring you luck.'

It's a good sales technique – Raj thanks her solemnly and leaves the pendant on. Moreover, her gesture has attracted attention: Carl is coming over now, and Jamie is following at a distance.

There isn't a rune that looks like a C, so Carl plumps for something completely different:

'Humanity,' she tells him. 'Company, friendship.'

So far so good. I turn to Jamie. 'Your go.'

'No,' he says, already turning away. 'You're fine.'

'Come on.' I've already checked the price, they're dirt cheap. 'I'll treat you.'

'You can buy me a book then.'

'Sorry,' I say to the stallholder. 'I'll pick him one.' I study the spiky little symbols, but my inspiration seems to have deserted me. 'Can't you just tell me what they mean?'

She's watching Jamie, a thoughtful frown on her face. 'What does he *need?*'

Now it's getting silly. 'Lots of things,' I say. 'Things he can't have, mostly.'

She nods, and picks up a pendant marked with a slanting F:

'The ash tree,' she says. 'Endurance.'

'Endurance it is.' I'm getting out my purse. 'How much do I owe you?'

But she's picking up a roll of manuscript paper, and unfurling it in front of me. 'Would you like one of these as well?'

The short answer is no. No one in their right mind would want one. The girl adds, with the ruthlessness of the small shopkeeper, 'It's by a local artist.'

Politely, we bend down for a closer look. The top half of the page is a drawing, obviously done by hand and then inexpertly photocopied. It shows a large-breasted woman kneeling and holding up her hands in supplication. She has huge goggle eyes, the kind you see in really disturbing animation. Beside her kneels what looks like a midget – probably meant to be a child – also goggle eyed and pleading. They are in a doorway, beside them lies the corpse of a man, in a puddle of bright red. Over the woman and child stands a Redcoat soldier, leering down the woman's cleavage as he prepares to run her through with a bayonet.

Under the picture is some shaky calligraphy: *The Unclean Sacrifice*. The stallholder unrolls the paper all the way, and we are treated to the rest of the words:

> *Unclean blood is spilled on the Hearth*
> *Blood of Host, blood of Guest!*
> *Blood of sacrifice, blood of life*
> *Turns to poison, soaks into the Earth.*
> *The Earth is cursed!*
> *The Earth turns against us!*
> *Gods of our Fathers, tell us*
> *What sacrifice can cleanse this Earth again?*

Some folk shouldn't be allowed to watch *The Wicker Man*. The poet's name is scrawled along the bottom: *Seamus MacIain*.

'MacIain?' I ask, 'Isn't that…'

'The old chieftains of the glen.' The girl is smiling proudly. 'Seamus is their direct descendant.' She has blushed slightly – she likes saying his name. 'This is his homeland. He's going to reclaim his heritage.'

'So he lives in the village, does he?'

'No.' She's deadly serious again. 'Not yet, anyway. It's unlucky to live in the glen. Since the Massacre, you know? The soldiers were guests, and they murdered their hosts. It was a terrible breach of Highland law.'

This is going to turn into a history lesson. 'So why won't he live there now? Does he think it's haunted or something?'

'Seamus says it's cursed.' Her voice is firm. 'He says it'll have to be purified before anyone can live there. No one wants to live there, except *him*, of course.' She practically spits this last part. 'You know. The false chieftain.'

I know I'm going to regret asking, but I have to. 'The false chieftain?'

'Him. *McLean*.' Her face is getting redder, and she's not smiling any more. 'Preaching hate. Demonising the old ways, the worship of Odin and the Great Mother. He thinks McLean can be the new MacIain, but that'll never happen. He's the enemy.' She leans towards us conspiratorially. 'And he's descended from the Campbells, you know.'

Behind me, Jamie says loudly, 'I think that's our lift now.' Sure enough, Emma is making for the door. Gratefully, I settle up, adding one of Seamus's manuscripts to the bag. Then I smile nicely and flee, the others close behind me. When we're out of earshot I say, 'Is everyone we meet here going to be fucking nuts?'

'The weekend's young,' says Raj. We follow Emma out into another corridor, keeping our distance; she's pretending she hasn't seen us anyway. She heads through the lobby and into the café, where we hear Neddy's overenthusiastic yells of greeting. Clearly we're not leaving just yet.

As soon as the café door swings shut behind her, Jamie says in a low voice, 'Could you please not offer to buy me Odinist symbols while the holy folk are listening?'

'Eh?'

He points to the pendant around my neck. 'Those things.'

'Are they Odinist symbols?'

'Of course they are.'

'Folkloric symbols,' says Raj.

'Well *they're* not going to say that, are they?'

He's really annoyed. 'Fine.' I hold up my hands. 'No more shopping for Satanic artefacts. So d'you want to get another cup of tea?'

But Raj is already halfway down a side corridor. 'Let's have a look at this,' he calls back, in a casual voice that means he's really interested. 'Just for a minute.'

We follow him. The short corridor ends in a door, and on the door is a plaque: a square piece of artificial ice, so convincing I have to poke at it before I believe it's only crystalline plastic. Scratched on the surface are blue-black letters: *SCACS – Taming the White Dragon.*

'Have they got a crack problem round here?' I mutter. No one dignifies this with an answer, so I follow the others inside. The room is dimly lit; in the centre is a long table covered with something pale.

All of a sudden a booming voice announces, 'Avalanches!'

'Shit!' I barge backwards into Jamie. He steadies me and pats me on the shoulder. 'You should cut down on the caffeine, Suze.'

I ignore him – like *he* didn't jump – and watch blue-white light flicker into life on every wall. Four huge screens are flashing up identical shots of a snowy mountain. The camera is flying, looking down, the helicopter's shadow rippling across the peak below.

Suddenly, there's a change: some of the white is moving. Sparkling vapour rises as a chunk of mountainside heads for the valley floor, spilling all over the black line of the road.

'Responsible for over two hundred deaths a year in the US alone…' It's that voice again: female, American, slightly smug. It flows smoothly from discreet wall-mounted speakers in each corner of the room. 'Avalanches are as deadly as earthquakes, and just as destructive. To those who live in their paths, they are the White Dragon – lethal, unstoppable, and above all, unpredictable.'

There's a *but* coming…

'Unpredictable, that is, until now.' The shot changes: techy men leaning over a computer. 'The Safety-Critical Avalanche Control System, or SCACS for short, has brought the White Dragon under human control. A network of sensors, spanning all hazard areas, measure snowpack conditions and stop potential avalanches before they start.' Next we are shown a long metal post on a laboratory table, surrounded by a spaghetti of wires, crowned with a blue light. 'Each sensor can use a small charge to trigger fluffing of light unstable snow…'

Did I hear that right? 'Fluffing?'

'Sluffing,' corrects Raj. On the screen, one of the metal posts is now half buried in snow; it emits a sharp *crack* and snow obediently tumbles away down a slope. The slide breaks harmlessly around the ankles of a ski-suited man, who turns to the camera and grins.

I've suddenly realised I'm the only one watching this. Jamie and Carl are examining the flat screens, talking admiringly about pixel flow and SCART ports and God knows what else. Raj is looking at the table, so I wander over there. Atop it is a range of tiny winter mountains. It's a miniature Glencoe, cute as a dollhouse, but highly detailed. Its peaks and flanks are covered with a network of little blue lights. They are particularly concentrated in the places I'd always assumed to be frozen riverbeds – long straight pathways slicing through the forests, all the way down to the valley floor. I poke at one of the blue lights. 'This'll be SCACS, then?'

'This is it,' he agrees. A rumbling sound begins to fill the room, as if an earthquake is about to shake the tiny glen. I look up at the screen to see a boiling white cloud flowing downhill like a river. Tiny dark-green splinters shiver before it: pine trees. There is just time to see them snap before they are engulfed. The screens cut abruptly to another shot: a moving wall of grey ice, darkening quickly, falling on the camera like a tidal wave.

'This system's safe, isn't it?' I say to Raj.

'It's safe enough.'

'How safe's *that*?'

He smiles. 'McLean wouldn't let his American guests go through it otherwise. Their lawyers are too good.'

Good point. 'We'd best stick with Mark and Sandra then. I don't fancy our chances with Emma if—'

The door opens and Emma herself appears. 'We ought to be going now,' she says. 'The weather's changing.'

Emma was right. The sun is still bright, but the landscape has dulled. Clouds are coming in from the north, grey and bloated. Neddy complains loudly as he is marched smartly across the car park by his mother. 'I wanna toy. You *said*. You *said*…'

Sandra takes no notice and bundles him into the snowcat. Mark, who's following just behind us, says with a fatherly grimace, 'We didn't have time to visit the gift shop.' Jamie winces in sympathy.

As soon as we're all aboard, Emma starts reversing the snowcat. 'Put your seatbelts on, please,' she says over her shoulder. She didn't tell us to do this on the way here. Naturally, it goes down like a lead balloon with Neddy. We look tactfully away as Sandra fights to get the strap around him. The clouds seem even lower over the Visitors' Centre, and tinged with sepia.

The centre door opens; there's a flare of bright pink as the stallholder sticks her head out. She's still there, studying the sky, as we leave the village.

We trundle along in silence, tracing the road around the Pap of Glencoe (wonder what McLean's going to re-christen *that*). Well, not quite silence: one of us is still making enough noise for everyone. 'It's too tight. You're hurting me! You're *mean*!' Sandra is starting to look grim, and it's a relief to everyone when she manages to click the belt into place and finally sits back. 'Wow,' she says, in that loud hearty voice that means whining children are being ignored. 'Got a real storm coming.'

I follow her gaze, through the windscreen ahead. Not that I have to. I don't know if it's the clouds, or the mountainside cutting off the sun, but all of a sudden it's like a lid has come down. The white slopes have lost their sparkle. We're in the Glen now. 'Yeah,' says Mark over the grizzling from the far corner, 'gonna be a blizzard.'

'No, just a wee squall.' Emma is actually smiling; she obviously takes a Scot's perverse pride in our crappy weather. 'We'll be back long before it starts. Don't worry.'

I wasn't worrying. Should I be? Raj smiles and puts his arm around my shoulders. Is he trying to reassure me? Oh, get a grip, woman. I smile at Neddy, who is drumming his heels angrily against his seat. 'Did you see the swords then, Neddy?'

'No!'

'Yes, you did,' says Mark. 'You liked them.'

'I hate them.'

'Neddy,' say both parents in unison.

'Did you not see them cutting that guy's head off?' says Jamie.

He pauses slightly, and then shouts, 'No! Go away!'

'Neddy!'

He sits back, still mumbling, and starts kicking the chair again. My eyes are starting to ache; I listen to Neddy's drumming feet, wishing the little turd a hundred miles away. You wouldn't catch our Clairey behaving like this.

The dull light should make the white mountainsides easier on my sore eyes, but there's a nasty glow where the grey snowfields clash against the iodine tint of the clouds above.

My stomach curls queasily, and pain sinks into my right temple. Oh, great, I think, a headache *and* travel-sickness. That's all I need…

'Ned,' says Sandra. 'Leave that alone.'

Neddy is fiddling with his seat belt fastening. He's meeting Sandra's gaze, apprehensive but defiant. Mark says sternly, 'You heard your mother. Leave it.'

Neddy's fingers keep working. 'Don't want to…'

'Edward Gray, you leave that alone and you SIT! RIGHT! *NOW!*' Sandra's using the mother-voice, the one that can't be disobeyed; us adults sit up straight before we know what we're doing. Neddy drops the seatbelt and bursts into tears. Sandra sighs and looks at Mark – a mother's place is in the wrong. I would sympathise, if I wasn't starting to feel like absolute shit.

There's an air-con nozzle set into the roof. The irony of having to use air con in a heated snowmobile is not lost on me, but right now I don't give a damn. I twist it on and start breathing in great gasps. 'Are you okay?' asks Raj.

'Just a bit queasy…' I direct the wonderful cold air onto my throbbing eyes. Bliss.

I hear Mark say, 'Be quiet now, Neddy. The lady's sick,' and the sobs stop. 'Is she gonna barf?' asks Neddy.

'Yes.' My stomach has settled a little, so I'm able to add, 'I'll barf all over you.'

'And you'll be all *bluuurgh! Uuurgh!*' He starts making explosion noises, for no obvious reason, and giggling happily.

Then there's a change in the sound – for a confused instant I think it's Neddy, but in fact it's the snowmobile's engine, slowing down. 'It's okay,' I say to Emma, 'I'm not really going to be sick.'

'Aye, I ken.' Her Aberdeen accent comes through more strongly now she's distracted; she's hunched over the wheel, staring dead ahead as if she's driving through a pea souper. On the road ahead, as far as we can see, the tracks we've been following are gone. Wiped away. The snow looks fresh and untidy. The drone of the engine changes key as we start to cross it.

'Has it been snowing here?' says Sandra.

Our driver mumbles into the wheel. 'Naw, it's just a bit sluffin'.'

Carl translates, 'It's just a bit of sluffing. Some loose snow come down from the mountains.'

'Oh. Oh, okay.' We all look at one another. No one's going to use the A-word. Eventually Raj says, 'The SCACS system does it three or four times a day. It's a computerised system, used for clearing the slopes. It's routine.'

The confident professor voice works (as does that wonderful euphemism 'clearing the slopes') and Sandra looks reassured. But she didn't see Raj back in the Visitors' Centre, bending over the SCACS lights on the miniature Glencoe, checking and checking as if he suspected something wrong. I watch him now. It's never occurred to me before, how poker-faced he is. Nothing would show if he didn't want it to. He sees me watching, smiles, and tries to pull me close, but I disentangle myself, mumbling about not feeling well; I want to keep my hands free, my feet on the floor. I want to be ready.

There's a change in the note of the engine as we pass the sluffing, and find this morning's tracks again. We're speeding up, and the engine is loud. Surely it wasn't that loud before? No one else seems to have noticed. They're all smiling. 'Home soon,' I hear someone say.

I've got to get a grip here. There will be no boiling cloud. No tidal wave. Two hundred, the voiceover said, but that's out of hundreds of thousands of people. The likelihood is a million to one – more!

But of course, that's exactly what they would have thought. Every one of the two hundred. All sitting here like me, watching the roulette wheel spin. Someone has to be double zero. Why not me?

There's the thud of an impact. I hear myself cry out as we are surrounded by dark grey. 'Everyone okay?' asks Emma.

We've just entered the pass of Glencoe. The road runs through a massive formation of rock; the passage is cut as neat and smooth as a slice of birthday cake. We're slowing, slowing… stopped. 'Had a wee bump there,' says Emma. 'Just going to check everything's okay.'

The rock towers over us. I can see white icing the top edge, leaning, ready to topple over onto us. And then I know. 'Keep going,' I say.

'I'll not be a minute—'

'It's going to come down.'

She's shaking her head, she thinks I've misunderstood. 'No, it's okay—'

'For Christ's sake get moving.' This voice, hoarse and ugly, is not mine. But somewhere beyond I can hear it coming: the cloud, the tidal wave. The White Dragon. 'It's going to come down! Move! Fucking *move!*'

'Get going,' says Raj. That seems to decide it. She starts the engine. It revs, once, twice, and we lurch forward. Sandra shrieks as the rock jumps at us. Then we're going, but not fast enough. I can hear roaring. Flecks of white are whirling before my eyes.

Then we burst through into daylight and the roaring subsides, slightly. The echo must have been trapped in the pass. The snowmobile charges on, flinging us around as we take corners much too fast. And at last we're out in the air.

When the Celtic crosses come into view, I scream at Emma to stop. She slams on the brakes at once and I'm out of my seatbelt and opening the door before we've come to a complete halt. I'm out into the glorious cold fresh from the moor. Specks of white whirl before me, but I can still see the glen.

I will see it when it comes. I can hear it now, the roaring. Here it comes!

The white specks whirl into a blur, more like TV interference than falling snow, and the roar is replaced by a squealing whine. I'm on my knees in the snow. I start to retch.

The vomiting goes on for a while.

It stops quite suddenly. A hand is wiping my face gently. Another is holding my arms so I don't fall.

The pale specks are still squirming in front of my eyes. There is a strong smell, like fruit, sweet but wholesome. I feel stronger. I look up.

Their faces are a blur. I can't see what they're wearing, but there's a suggestion of leather, sheepskin, fur. But they are veiled and swathed in gold. As they bend towards me I reach for the shining fabric, and feel hair.

'Suzey? Feel better now?' It's Raj's voice, at my ear. He's beside me, holding me up. The squirming spots clear a little. Holding my elbow is Mark, splashes of vomit down his coat. In front of my face is Emma.

She's looking very annoyed. My puke-stained fingers are holding onto her hair.

'Oh,' I say, weakly. I pull my hand away. 'Sorry.'

Everyone is staring at me in varying degrees of concern, shock and disgust. I look beyond them into the valley. No rumbling, no rising vapour… In short, no avalanche.

'Oh,' I say again.

'D'you think you're bloody funny?' demands Emma. 'Was that your idea of a bloody joke?'

'Leave her alone,' says Jamie. 'She's not well.'

I protest feebly, 'It wasn't like that…'

'We could've all been killed!' shouts Emma.

'Then we'd go straight to heaven, wouldn't we,' says Jamie, taking my hand. 'Up you get, Suzey.'

Emma looks like she's going to explode. She's drawing breath to speak, but Raj cuts her off. 'The storm's coming. Let's get indoors.' He hoists me to my feet, and I lean into him gratefully. Jamie takes my other elbow. 'All right, sis?'

'I saw it. I really saw it…' But no one's listening.

Mark opens the snowcat door, giving me that big hearty smile you give to the deranged or mentally challenged. 'Feeling better?'

Actually I am – the nausea's gone and the headache has dulled. I flop into a seat, feeling weak and empty. When Emma bangs the door I hardly flinch. When we're all aboard she drives off, muttering something, but it's under her breath. Good – all the easier to ignore her. I look around the awkwardly smiling faces. I'm getting a bit indignant here. 'I'm sorry,' I say. 'But I thought I was saving our lives.'

Carl is frowning slightly. 'Did you have a headache before you were sick?'

'Yes. Why?'

'What did you see? Little white dots?'

'Yes.'

'Did you hear anything? A roaring noise?'

'Yes.'

'Have you ever had a migraine before?'

'I think so, but…'

Now Sandra is nodding. 'Oh, yeah, my sister gets those. Her vision's shot to heck for hours. And you had one once, didn't you, babe?'

Mark's nodding. 'I saw spots in front of my eyes.' He gives me a kindly smile. 'It was very frightening.'

This is getting annoying. 'That's not what it was.'

'You can get all kinds of symptoms with them.' Carl is nodding sagely. What is he, a migraine counsellor? 'Really weird stuff. Tinnitus. Losing half your vision. Smelling oranges.'

'Oranges?' The protest dies in my throat. I remember the figures, the golden hair, and the sweet, wholesome smell of fruit. 'I did think I smelled some,' I admit. 'But that was after the…'

Carl's still nodding. 'It can be very real.'

I put my hands over my face, ostensibly to rub my sore eyes, but really because I don't want to look at anyone. I can feel my face flushing. Oh, kill me now. 'Sorry,' I mumble. 'I'm really sorry.'

Lots of murmured reassurances fill the small space. 'You thought you were saving us all,' says Sandra sympathetically. After a pause she adds, 'Thank you.'

They all echo, 'Thank you.' Now I *really* want the ground to swallow me up. I look out of the window, feigning a deep interest in the Celtic crosses as we drive between them. I finally notice what's odd about this situation: I can't hear Neddy. I look around, but he's still there, holding his father's hand and staring at me wide eyed. 'Okay, Neddy?' I ask weakly.

He nods dumbly. Mark says, 'We thought for a coupla minutes you had the Second Sight, Suzey. The gift of prophecy. Aren't people from around here supposed to have it?'

'My Gran's from the Highlands.' I'm trying to salvage my dignity here. 'Maybe I've inherited a bit of it.'

Jamie bursts out laughing. 'You've inherited the ability to look at Glencoe in winter and see snow? You're a regular Highland Seer, Suzey.'

'Fuck off.'

Carl chips in, 'It must be the Sixth Sense. "*I see avalanches…*"'

'Fuck off.'

Everyone's laughing now (except Emma, naturally) in spite of my bad language. Bastards. I try to look ill, and pray for death to come quickly. Or at least to get out of this bloody snowmobile.

The last one, anyhow, comes quickly. No one helps me out, the unsympathetic bastards (I can walk well enough on my own, but that's hardly the point). The other passengers are still grinning, but it takes a lot more than that to put a smile on Emma's face. 'I'll need to report this,' she snaps.

'Who to? Jesus?'

'You've no business here with decent folk.' She looks from me to Carl and then to Jamie. 'None of you.' She slams back into the snowmobile; we step back quickly as it revs away.

Once we're back inside the warmth of the hotel, the smell starts to rise, and I'm conscious of the puke stains on Mark's jacket. 'I'm really sorry,' I say.

At this point Neddy comes back to life. 'That was cool. Can we go back again?'

Now even I'm laughing. We draw close to one another; we have Been Through Something together. 'Say bye now,' says Sandra, taking hold of Neddy's hand.

As a delaying tactic, he insists on throwing an arm round each of us in turn. Sandra keeps hold of his other hand.

Carl is last in line for the one-armed hug. Sandra's smile remains in place. She doesn't pull Neddy away. But she rocks back onto one foot, the one farthest from Neddy, as you'd do with a child looking out of a window, or over a drop. Ready to pull him back. I don't think she even knows she's doing it. Then the little family are leaving; Carl sighs, smiles goodbye to us and sets off in the opposite direction. Jamie watches them all go, nodding as if something has just been confirmed to him. 'See you later on,' he says, and then he's gone too.

I look up pleadingly at Raj. 'Please put me in a nice hot bath.'

'Excellent idea.'

I don't think there's anything in the world as wonderful as hot water. I'm floating in a mass of Vanilla-and-Ginger scented bubbles: movie bubbles, the type that don't melt away in seconds. There's even a waterproof pillow supporting my neck. I lie back, fragrant steam rising into my face, and try to turn the tap on with my toes. Can't quite do it. 'Slave!' I bellow.

'Did you say something?' Raj sticks his head around the door. 'Are you okay?'

'No, I'm too weak to sit up. Turn the hot tap on, would you?'

He bends down, reaching towards the tap, but grabs instead at my toes. 'Time to get out,' he says, as I squeal and wriggle away. 'You're going all pink and wrinkly.'

'So?'

'You'll look like a hippo.'

'Wouldn't mind being a hippo. Spend your whole life floating in warm water.' I wallow about a bit to illustrate the point. 'There's loads of food, and you're too big for anything else to fuck with.'

He makes another grab for my foot, like a fisherman tickling trout. 'You'd be very ugly.'

'Not to other hippos. Ow, stop it. You're getting your sleeve all wet. Take your clothes off if you're going to do that.'

He raises his eyebrows at me. 'You are feeling better, aren't you?'

'Better enough for some things.'

'Good.' He gets up briskly. 'Then you're well enough to come down to dinner. It starts in fifteen minutes.'

'Can't we get room service?'

'No.'

I pout. 'I want room service.'

'It's not included in the bill.'

'Oh, all right.' I haul myself upright, staggering as I have to support my own weight again. 'I'm not getting poshed up, though.'

Ten minutes later, in baggy jeans and not a shred of makeup, I'm following Raj into the lobby. A smell of roast potatoes wafts from the dining room. My stomach starts to growl. I spot Jamie on the other side of the lobby, looking at the noticeboard with his back to us. I call his name but he doesn't turn: cloth-ears. Steering around a large group of guests, who are all looking affronted about something or other, I make my way across to him.

I recognise the cutting on the board before I'm close enough to read the headline. Even the layout is imprinted on my mind. This is a good-quality copy, probably downloaded rather than photocopied. You can see Jamie's face very clearly. And the headline is sharp: *MIRACLE GIRL'S BROTHER CAUGHT WITH BOY*.

Jamie turns to me, looking as if he's going to throw up. He's clutching a fistful of crumpled papers; he unfolds them, and they all have the picture and the headline. 'They were in all the lifts,' he says.

I look around the lobby but there's no sign of any others. 'Do you think there's more?'

'I don't know.'

I rip the paper from the noticeboard. 'We'll go and look.'

Jamie's shaking his head, looking over his shoulder. Another group of people are heading for the dining room. They're murmuring to each other, and glancing at Jamie. One of the men steps towards Jamie, but a woman grabs his arm and pulls him away. I can't hear her, but I can tell what she's saying: 'Not worth it.' They disappear into the dining room.

I jump as someone tugs at the paper in my hand, but it's Raj, and behind him is Carl. Raj exclaims softly when he sees the cutting, but Carl doesn't even look at it. 'Those things are all over the place,' he says. 'There's one in the dining room.' He looks at Jamie. 'You'd better stay out of sight.'

'No.'

I take Jamie's arm. 'Come on. Let's go back up to the room.'

He disentangles himself and heads for the dining room. 'No. I'm going for my dinner.'

'Jamie!'

But he's going inside. I run after him, Raj and Carl close behind. In the doorway, Raj stops and catches my arm. 'Go back up to the room, Suzey. We'll get him out.'

I shake him off. 'No you won't.' The dining room is brighter than I remember it, and bigger. Almost every table is occupied. Jamie is walking straight down the central aisle. As he passes each table, heads swivel; people lean together and whisper like conspirators. The chatter of conversation lowers to a hiss. Jamie keeps walking.

Raj swears quietly when Jamie selects a table close to the central aisle, right beside the top table. An elderly couple are already sitting there; when Jamie smiles at them and sits down, they get up and walk away. 'Jamie,' I whisper, 'what do you think you're doing?'

He pours himself some water, his hand shaking slightly. 'I'm being a penitent,' he says. 'Remember?'

'We shouldn't be here,' says Raj. 'Let's go.'

Jamie shrugs. 'Go if you want.' He glances sideways. Everyone is looking at him, their faces flat and ugly under the yellow light.

'You're putting your sister in danger,' Raj snarls. Jamie looks at me, shock dawning. 'Suzey, go on upstairs,' he says.

'Fuck off, Jamie.' I've just noticed another newspaper cutting, pinned to the edge of the top table, right by McLean's seat. I notice too that there are no doors at the back of this hall, not even a fire exit. Behind us, someone has really begun to hiss like a snake. The sound rises as more and more join in.

The doors open at the far end of the hall and the McLean processional enters: the guards, the rich suits, the posh frocks, the daughter, and finally the wondrous Presence himself. The hissing stops – God forbid McLean should think it's directed at him. People are turning to him, speaking emphatically, gesturing towards us. One woman even stands up and reaches out for him. His bodyguards are there in an instant, but McLean steps between them, catches the supplicant's hand and pats it, says a few soothing words before he passes by.

As he reaches his place at the centre of the table, one of the waitresses is unpinning the printout. Before she can spirit it away, however, McLean holds out his hand for it. The rest of the top table hover indecisively; those who haven't sat down remain standing, those who have perch on the edge of their seats ready to spring up again. McLean takes his time; once he looks up and scans the room, his eyes resting for a moment on Jamie, but then he goes back to studying the paper. Everyone is watching him.

Finally he puts the cutting down in front of Kerry, making a small sit-down gesture. Kerry sinks into her chair, the rest of the table following suit. McLean, however, is still standing. He steeples his hands in front of his face, apparently deep in thought, and closes his eyes as if what he sees hurts them. Into the absolute silence he says, 'There's a matter in this room that's abhorrent to me, brothers and sisters. I'll speak of it now, before we break our bread.'

There's a soft clink as a waiter emerges from the kitchen carrying a tray of prawn cocktails. Kerry waves him back furiously. Most of the audience doesn't notice; nor does McLean.

'I've been reading a book by a man called Dante. A man who lived over seven hundred years ago. He lived in violent times my friends. Wars. Murders. Dissent, grief, sorrow. Crooked politicians. A bloated and corrupt Roman church peddling false doctrine for profit.' There's some rumbling at the back. 'Oh yes. And I ask you, my friends, were Dante's times worse than ours? Has anything changed?'

There are shaking heads all round, and the rumbling gathers momentum. 'It's just the same,' someone cries.

McLean pauses like an auctioneer waiting for bids. 'You think nothing's changed? Well, I'll tell you. Times have changed, brothers and sisters. And they have changed for the *worse*.

'That's right, my friends, we are the worst off. Do you know why? Because Dante was allowed to speak of God's truth. Dante knew there was no God but Christ, and he said so. He knew there was no way to find God except through the holy Gospels of Jesus Christ – and he said so.

'He didn't have to look Muslims in the face and tell them their false prophet Muhammad would win them a place in God's house. He didn't have to listen to the rubbish of the chattering classes, and allow them to tell young people that their pick'n'mix approach to God's laws would win them his favour. And he knew about sin, my friends. Oh yes. He was no saint, he was a sinner like the rest of us. But he knew that's what he was.

'There was something he didn't know. He didn't know about *alternative families*. He didn't know about *valid lifestyle choices*. He didn't know that. But he knew one simple thing – that a life of sodomy, dress it up how you like, would lead you straight to the fires of hell.

'Dante set all this down for us. He wrote a book and he called it *Inferno*, to warn us where our *alternative lifestyles* lead us: straight to Hell. And he showed us those men in Hell, and he laid bare their sin for them. There was no more talk of *love*, or *gender-bending*, to cover over their unnatural sin. No more lies about their *right to sexuality* while they abuse young boys. They will walk through torrents of flame. They will no longer be able to mock the holy state of matrimony. Their heads will be twisted around, so they can spend the rest of eternity contemplating the male buttocks they loved so well in this life. They will scratch and claw at the foul diseases on their skin. And the shit they loved to sink into in this life – well, they'll be immersed in it for the rest of time.

'There's one among us this evening who has committed those sins, brothers and sisters. By his own admission, he has done all these things and more. You all know who he is. And shall I tell you what disgusts me, my friends? What's so abhorrent to me?

'That all of you think you can *pass judgement upon him*.' His bellow echoes across the room. 'You wish to cast out this young man. He has come to us hoping to change his ways, and you presume to think this can't be done? Oh, ye of little faith. I tell you, there is more rejoicing in Heaven over one lost sheep returned to the fold than in a hundred who have never strayed.' He steps out from behind the top table, and moves to stand behind Jamie's chair. Jamie flinches as McLean rests his hands on his shoulders, but he keeps still.

'This young man was dead, but by the grace of the Holy Spirit he will come back to life. Will you help him? Will your prayers raise him above the filth into the kingdom of the Lord? Or will you pass by on the other side?'

The crowd shout their support, and McLean stands back from Jamie's chair, holding out his arms to him. 'Come here, son.' Without hesitation, Jamie stands and throws himself into his arms. Clapping and cheering floods the room as they embrace, slapping each other's backs so it looks suitably manly. Eventually McLean stands back, and gently steers Jamie back into his seat. 'God bless you, son,' murmurs McLean, quietly. 'We'll get your family back.'

Now McLean turns to me. If he tries to hug me, I'm going to kick him. But he takes both my hands and smiles at me. 'You've stuck by him. God bless you.'

His eyes are flooded with tears. I can hardly believe this is the same man we saw last night.

Chapter 26

It's hard getting up the next morning. Not that we'd had a late night – we called it quits just after dinner. A few people – mostly women – came up to congratulate Jamie, making a big show of shaking his hand. But there were a lot more (mostly men, though not all) who spent all night growling in the background, watching us with incredulous rage. Even Jamie agreed we should disappear for a while. The four of us spent hours in me and Raj's room, flicking through all the TV channels and not talking much. At one point Carl piped up, out of the blue, 'He's talking crap anyway. It's not the sodomites who get thrown in the pool of shit. It's the flatterers.'

When we all turned to look at him he added, 'In Dante's *Inferno*. And it's the sorcerers with the twisted heads.'

'The man's a stupid bastard.' Raj was indignant. He's an academic, to whom textual inaccuracy constitutes the worst kind of fraud. 'He's got all those fools hanging on every word, and he hasn't even read the bloody book.'

'What about the itchy people?' I ask Carl.

'Liars, I think. Or it might be usurers. People who lend money for profit.'

'Like those investment banker types he was sitting with?'

'He's an irony-free zone all right.' We laughed. We were cleverer than McLean; we could go back to feeling superior. It was a comfort, but not a large one.

When Carl and Jamie were gone, Raj and I carried on staring at the TV. Sleep wasn't about to come any time soon.

The light in the dining room is pallid. Outside the snow is falling thickly, and the wind is building up. We are heading for a blizzard.

Jamie is sitting at a table in the middle of the room, about as conspicuous as he could possibly be. He's not about to skulk in corners; I don't know whether to be proud or exasperated. Sitting beside him is a youngish man with a strained and lined face. He is speaking earnestly to Jamie, his hands waving and fluttering on the tabletop. Sometimes his fingers brush Jamie's wrist, and then he jumps back as if he's had a shock of static. Jamie is listening to him gravely, nodding occasionally.

The young man sees us coming, and jumps up as if he expects us to tip him out of his chair. He says something to Jamie, then gives me a wan smile as he hurries past.

'Don't tell me,' I say, sitting down. 'He's here to Pray Out the Gay?'

'Aye. He's with the Intercessors.' Jamie lowers his voice. 'Poor bastard.' I need coffee. I look around for a waitress, and see them all standing in a huddle by the door, talking to a woman with a blonde ponytail. It takes me a moment to recognise our driver without the red parka and the sour expression, but it's Emma all right. She and the waitresses look up and stare right at me, as if I've just dropped through the ceiling. One of the waitresses hurries over to fill my cup. She asks if there's anything she can get me, anything at all? Bewildered, I tell her I'm fine.

'What's the matter with these people now?' I grumble to Raj. He's not listening; he's watching Emma, who is moving from table to table, speaking quietly to all the diners.

Eventually she gets to us. 'Are you feeling better?' she asks. She seems genuinely concerned. I am highly suspicious.

'Is there something we should know about?' I demand.

'We're just telling everyone,' she drops her voice a little bit, 'the road's blocked just now. There's been an avalanche.'

I set my cup down, carefully, although it still spills into the saucer. 'Where?'

'On the southbound road. Just the other side of the rise.'

'But not in Glencoe itself? Not where… I thought it would be?'

'No. But not far off.' She actually smiles, and then goes to speak to another table. All the diners listen intently; some of them turn to gawp at me.

I realise I've been holding my breath. I let it out with a gasp. 'She had me going for a minute there.'

'What's up?' Carl has just appeared; sensitive to atmospheres, he looks around warily.

'There's been an avalanche. No, don't look like that, it wasn't in the Glen. It was south of here.'

'But they still think you…'

'Yes, that's just what they think.' I glance around the room. 'I'm going to get burnt at the stake here.'

'Actually, I don't think you are.' Raj is looking around too. 'You're here as Miracle Girl, if you remember. I think your status has just been enhanced.'

I follow his eye. People look back and smile, gazing at me in something approaching awe. 'This is getting silly,' I say, feeling just a tiny bit creeped out. 'They must have millions of avalanches around here.'

'But what about the SCACS,' Jamie murmurs.

'It goes onto half function at night,' says Raj. 'And even on full it couldn't cope with the snow load it got yesterday. Even the sluffing would be big enough to cover the road.'

'So the road home's blocked?' says Carl.

'Effectively.'

There's a silence.

'Well, we're not going till tomorrow anyway,' I say.

The others agree. We listen to the howling outside.

Jamie pushes back his plate. 'I'm off to get ready,' he says.

The baptism is at noon. It is scheduled to take place in the glass-roofed Olympic pool, under 'God's good sunlight'. But by five to twelve the staff are flicking on the fluorescents. We are in near twilight: the blizzard has taken hold.

Raj and I are shown to our seats. The storm is roaring and pounding at the glass all around us. Carl, very sensibly, has decided to give the ceremony a miss. He said he was going to the cinema on the basement level; like every sane creature on a day like this, he has gone to ground.

I avoid looking out of the windows – the snowflakes are swarming too much like the migraine spots I saw yesterday.

If Jamie didn't feel obliged to go through with this farce, I wouldn't be within a hundred miles of it. He's sitting amongst the other penitents in the front row, smiling and chatting to the woman beside him. It looks like some bizarre graduation ceremony: all the penitents are wearing white gowns like choirboys' surplices. It says a great deal about my brother's natural appearance that he actually looks good in it. Mr Pray-Out-the-Gay is leaning over his shoulder, laughing uproariously at something Jamie's just said.

Indeed, everyone but Raj and I seems to be in a holiday mood. All around us are the people we've spent the past couple of days around, all wearing their best clothes and their biggest smiles. They keep glancing at the double doors beside the shallow end of the pool, as if they expect Elvis to walk out.

Raj leans over to me, pitching his voice below the level of excited chatter that fills the room. 'Can you smell that?'

I inhale. I had thought the woman beside me was wearing too much perfume, but he's right: the heavy floral scent is filling the room. 'Is that incense?'

He nods. 'Attar of roses, I believe.'

I look around. There's nothing obviously smoking or burning, but maybe it's being piped in with the air conditioning. 'Bit papist for our man, isn't it?'

Raj grins. 'Do you think he knows Dante was a Catholic?'

'I'll give you twenty quid if you tell him.' We giggle, but quietly. The storm screams, thumping on the windows. I shut up, feeling chastened. Jamie turns around and smiles up at me.

The double doors slam back and in enter two men in suits, pushing down the floor-level bolts so the doors stay open. The audience breaks into applause. Out comes Kerry, all alone: no money men today. Music blasts suddenly from the speakers, the rhythm surprisingly fast and heavy. And finally, Elvis himself: McLean, wearing a blue Gandalf robe over his suit. It ought to look silly, but he knows how to carry it. Then everyone around us is on their feet, clapping and cheering. McLean takes a microphone from Kerry, and says to us, 'Sing.'

So we do. Raj and I mumble along – everyone else seems to know the words. But the tune is annoyingly catchy, and by the second chorus we're joining in. 'Immortal love, eternal love, let us sing of his immortal love…' Actually, this is quite fun.

The song finishes and we sit down, although half the crowd are ready to leap up again at a moment's notice. McLean gives us just enough time to settle before he clasps his hands around a microphone and says, 'Let us pray.' He then proceeds to shout the Lord's Prayer at us. I bow my head, squinting sideways at the woman beside me. She keeps her face raised and her hands far apart, swaying slightly as she recites along with McLean.

As soon as McLean says 'Amen', the music starts again. It's slower this time, a sway-along. We all jump to our feet. Again, the words are easy: 'Shine, Jesus, shine. Be my sun in all my days…' People are lifting their faces and hands to the sky, smiling although the storm still howls around them. I feel a touch on my hand: the woman next to me has taken my hand, and raised it to the roof with her own. We sway together.

The music ends. We sit down, embarrassed, and I pull away my hand. The room is warm and humid, and the floral scent is getting heavier, mixing unpleasantly with the chlorine smell from the pool. It's making me feel queasy. I look around, trying to gauge what will happen next; if we're having another singsong, I'm nipping out to the bog.

But no. The crowd has gone quiet, focusing on McLean. He moves to the front of the pool, pausing before the broad steps that lead down into the water. Perhaps he gives some cue I haven't noticed, because a stir goes through the white-robed people in the front row. McLean's timing is immaculate: when the whole room is hanging on his words, he begins to speak.

'Let us welcome our brothers and sisters into the ranks of the saved. Rejoice for them. Their names will be written into the book of life, on this, the very eve of the world's destruction.'

Music begins to play in the background. It has a slow, pulsing beat. For a surreal moment, I think it's *We Will Rock You*. People around us start to clap and to murmur very quietly: 'Jesus, help us. Jesus, save us…' McLean's voice rises over them. 'Make no mistake about it. The end is coming. The day of God's anger is at hand.'

Amens and hallelujahs echo back from around the hall. A few people in the row in front of me are swaying. McLean's voice takes on a singsong rhythm. 'No use waiting till next year to repent. The Lord God is coming, my friends, and he is coming now. He is ready to put them in his wine press – the wicked, the faithless, the worshippers of false gods. The blood of millions shall be poured forth onto the Earth.

'And what will they do then? The fornicators, the adulterers, and the whoremongers. Where will they hide? Who will save them? No one. One third of the Earth will be destroyed, and they will be of that number!

'So come forward, and be saved.' He walks into the pool, ignoring the water that rises almost to his waist. 'Come forward. Cling to the Branch of David, Our Lord Jesus Christ. Come and accept his salvation.' He opens his arms wide. 'Come forward, and be spared the fire!'

Hotel staff are moving into position: one at the poolside, one halfway down the steps and one beside McLean. A middle-aged woman comes forward, tugging at her white surplice, and steps gingerly into the water. As McLean reaches out to receive her, someone behind me starts to speak rapidly in what sounds like German. McLean takes the woman in his arms like a dance partner, and dips her once under the water, murmuring to her. She comes up spluttering, but by the time the staff have handed her back on to dry land, she is smiling joyfully. As another woman is coming forward, two more voices behind me have begun to babble.

'Blessed are you.' McLean dips one after another with practised ease. 'Blessed are you who repent, for the wicked will not repent. The unbelievers will see one third of the Earth destroyed, but they will not believe. The liars and the blasphemers will see, but they will lie and blaspheme all the more. And the Lord will come, and the Lord will spew them out of his mouth.'

The heat is getting unbearable. I struggle out of my jumper. I must have bumped the woman beside me, because she says something. 'Sorry,' I mutter.

She's oblivious to me. Her eyes are half closed. She's saying something over and over, something like 'Ach an toka, ach an toka oh…' It's gibberish. The man beside her, and the one behind them, are doing the same. It's nonsense, but it's said as if it might save their lives. Their voices are loud and harsh. A headache starts to burrow its way into my temple.

'Tongues.' It's Raj. His head is haloed by whirling white: the blizzard outside. 'They're speaking in tongues,' he says. His voice seems to come from a long way off.

But McLean's voice is everywhere around me. 'And there are those who will see, and they will not repent. They are the molesters and the befoulers of the body. The murderers, the abortionists, the rapists, and the sodomites. All those who drink the wine of violence. All those who wallow in their own uncleanness. All those who befoul the Holy Land with their filthy steps. So I say to you, put on the white garments of innocence. Come forward and be saved.'

Jamie is rising from the front row. Unaccustomed to his robes, he shifts his arms a little as he steps forward; the sleeves lift like white wings. The babbling around me seems to grow louder as he steps into the pool. McLean reaches up to him, looking more like the penitent himself. 'Blessed are you,' he says quietly, as Jamie steps down to stand before him, his waterlogged sleeves trailing on the pool's surface. McLean takes Jamie in his arms, and ducks him under the water.

A needle-sharp pain sinks into my aching temple. I feel something happen in there, as if a blister has popped. Tears flood my eyes. I screw them shut, and then open them…

And they open *wide*, wider than ever before. And I can see…

A light so bright, unbearable. And utter silence.

And then the light is gone. Jamie and McLean are gone. Now more light is coming: red firelight. And then the wind, bellowing like the storm but so much louder…

There are screams all around and the windows shatter, obliterated. A plume of fire curls through the broken wall and over the pool. The mountains outside are all fire. The sky is fire, it's rushing down, it's coming it's coming for me OH GOD NO!

Then singing, clapping, smells of chlorine and roses. Raj's face is in front of mine. He's saying something but I can't hear. The needle is pushing into my head, something is coming loose. I close my eyes and open them again and…

Twilight. Cold. Snow gusting through the ruined wall, settling on the surface of the pool, dirty chlorinated ice. Things are caught in it, chairs and metal girders and other things I will not let myself see. Caught like amber in the ice.

I shut my eyes.

There are hands on me: gentle hands, lifting and laying me down, tucking something soft under my head. Voices of strangers, calm and soothing. Familiar voices too: Raj, and Jamie.

I open my eyes. They're both looking down at me, looking worried. Jamie is soaking wet. Behind him are a dozen more soggy penitents, gazing at me with open-mouthed awe. Raj is ordering them back, talking about 'letting her breathe'. Jamie leans in close to me. 'Suzey? Are you okay?' he says softly.

'I saw fire,' I whisper back. 'I saw ice.'

There's a disturbance in the ranks, and then McLean is looking down at me, his face uncomfortably close. 'You saw the flames of God's anger,' he says. 'Hallelujah.'

'You want it to happen,' I say.

He doesn't seem to hear. He has one hand on Jamie's shoulder, one hand on mine. 'You are blessed. The one who repents, and the one who sees. You'll eat with me tonight, both of you.'

Then he's gone. I hear his voice bellowing, filling the room. 'A vision has been given us today, brothers and sisters. Rejoice, for the time of the Lord is at hand!'

'Please get me away from here,' I say to Jamie and Raj. They hoist me to my feet and half carry me out of the room, as a hundred gabbling prayers rise to drown out the storm.

Part Five
Ragnarok

....

This life's five windows of the soul
Distorts the Heavens from pole to pole,
And leads you to believe a lie
When you see with, not through, the eye
That was born in a night, to perish in a night,
When the soul slept in the beams of light.

...

William Blake

Chapter 27

I wake with late-afternoon sunshine in my eyes.

I check the clock: I've been asleep for a couple of hours. I'm swaddled in a soft cover in the middle of our enormous bed. I'm on my own – Raj has obviously found the company of his comatose girlfriend less than thrilling, and gone walkabout. I unravel myself from the faux-fur coverlet, and pad over to the window.

The storm has exhausted itself, leaving behind a fresh blanket of sparkling white, and an innocent blue sky. The sun is westering, and will soon turn gold. Something gilded gleams on the window ledge: a wicker basket, covered in cellophane and tied with honey-coloured ribbons. Under the wrapping I can see jars and bottles nestling in shredded paper. They carry a logo, discreet but recognisable: *Aztec Gold*. Nice stuff, very expensive.

A card is taped to the basket's handle: *With Compliments. Please join us for dinner tonight*, followed by a pair of short, incomprehensible squiggles, the last of which is probably *McLean*. I'm assuming the first one is *Kerry* – wouldn't do for daddy to be sending toiletries to strange women. There's Gold for Hair, Coffee Gold and Goddess Bath Milk. In other words shampoo, body lotion and bubble bath. I pick up the basket and head for the bathroom.

The Goddess Bath Milk isn't bubbly; it leaves a golden sheen on the surface of the water, and smells deliciously of spice and roses. I lie back into it, massaging the Gold for Hair into my scalp. It's rich and creamy, and shot through with gold. I haven't blonded my hair in ages – this stuff isn't going to lighten it, but it does promise *deep sparkling highlights*, and at Aztec Gold prices you can expect it to deliver. It's been on a good few minutes now, so I scrunch up my knees and let my head sink into the warm water.

When I surface again I hear Raj's key in the door. 'I'm in here,' I shout, trying to sluice shampoo out of my ears.

The bathroom door opens. It's Jamie. I'm still sprawled in the bath with my arms and legs akimbo. 'Oh,' I say. 'I thought you were…'

'Sorry. He gave me the key. Just come to see if you're okay.'

'Oh, right.' I manoeuvre myself around so I'm lying on my belly, forearms resting on the end of the bath so I can face Jamie. My face is getting hot, but that's just the warm water. 'Yes, I'm fine.'

I expected him to retreat to the bedroom, but instead he comes right inside and perches on the side of the bath. And why shouldn't he – he's seen me in the scud loads of times. 'Where's Raj gone?' I say.

'He went to check on the weather. Wanted to see if the road was open.'

'Does he think it might be? Could we go home tonight?'

He frowns. 'Do you want to?'

I shrug, trying to look more casual than I feel. 'They're all fucking psychos here, Jamie.'

'I've still to see this through, Suzey.'

'You've seen it through.'

He's shaking his head. 'I've got to stay on.' He looks at me. 'Do you need to leave?'

'I'm not leaving you here on your own.'

'I'm being serious.'

'So am I!'

He smiles. 'Thanks, Suze.' He slides off the side of the bath and kneels down on the floor, his forearms resting next to mine. He still smells slightly of chlorine. 'I can't get by without you. Never could.'

'You'd manage.'

'No, I wouldn't. Even when we were kids. You used to come and get me out of my cot when I was crying, remember?'

'I used to take you into bed with me.' I can't believe he remembers this, he was so young. 'I think half the time it was me that woke you up.'

He shrugs. 'You didn't like it when Mum and Dad were fighting.'

'They never seemed to stop. Even when he got sick, she wouldn't cut him any slack.' I can hear the bitterness in my voice. 'She said he still knew what he was doing. That it made him cunning. Unbelievable.'

'It was hard for her.'

'Pretty bloody hard for us too.'

'I remember.' Jamie and I are face to face now. Even after all these years, I can't get over how alike our eyes are. It's like looking in a mirror. He lifts his hand and gently brushes a lock of wet hair away from my face. 'Soapy,' he says. 'Don't want it in your eyes.'

'Jamie, what is it? What's wrong?' The words come out in a rush. 'What are you going to do here?'

He holds my gaze for a long moment, moving closer until our faces are nearly touching. Then he rocks back on his heels, slaps his knees and gets to his feet. 'Getting cramp.'

'Aye, and I'm getting cold. Go and wait through there.' I motion to the bedroom. I don't want Raj to come and see him in here with me. Though Raj surely wouldn't get freaked out. He's not Lewis. But still, it seems better that he doesn't see us. I shoo Jamie away again, and he goes obediently.

By the time Raj gets back, I'm fully clothed and sitting on the couch towelling my hair. Jamie is lying on the bed reading a magazine. Raj, of course, doesn't turn a hair, unlike Lewis, who never seemed to think my brother should be around me without making a formal appointment. I shouldn't even be thinking this stuff; all that claptrap about sin and guilt must be getting to me.

'Did you check the road?' I ask Raj.

He nods. 'We're not going anywhere tonight.'

I glance at the window: blue skies and golden light. 'The weather looks clear enough.'

'The snowplough turned back at Crianlarich. There are avalanche warnings all along the south road.' He flops down beside me. 'How are you feeling?'

'Fine, thanks.'

'You should see a doctor when we get back. Get something for the headaches.'

I laugh, not very happily. 'How about the visions of the end of the world?'

'Is that what you saw?'

I hear paper rustling: Jamie has lowered his magazine to watch me. I shrug. 'McLean wants it to happen.'

'That doesn't mean he'll do it. It doesn't mean he *can* do it.'

'But it's possible.'

'Anything's possible. If there are an infinite number of worlds, everything happens somewhere.' He's looking at me seriously. 'It still makes the odds here minuscule. We talked about this, remember.'

I nod, humouring him, all the while remembering the blast that shattered the glass walls of the swimming pool, and the sound of roaring fire behind it.

Cold City

'Well,' I say, 'only one more night.'

'Thank God.' He lays his arm along the back of the couch and I nestle my head in the crook of his elbow. From behind us comes the thump of Jamie's feet as he slides off the bed and heads for the door. 'We're not chasing you out,' I say.

'You're fine. Just going for a kip before dinner.' He pauses in the doorway. 'Are we dressing up tonight?'

'Don't know. Do you want to?'

'Might as well.'

'I'll put my dress on, then.'

He smiles. 'See you down there.'

As Jamie closes the door, Raj is already sliding along the couch so he's pressed up against me. He starts twining a lock of my hair around his finger. It tugs a little. 'Your hair's all shiny,' he says.

'Aztec Gold.'

'Pardon?'

'It's Aztec Gold. You know, bath oil and stuff? It was in the basket Kerry sent.'

He buries his face in my hair. 'And why would Kerry McLean want to get you all shiny?'

'I'm sure I don't know.'

'I think I do.' He starts kissing down the side of my neck, sliding his hands under my T-shirt and up to my breasts. After a moment he looks up at me, frowning. 'No?'

'Sorry. Not in the mood.'

'It's all right.'

I know it is. But I keep quiet, resting my forehead against him. That feels nice. But he reaches for the TV Guide and starts flicking through the pages. I wish I could fall asleep again, but I've never felt more awake in my life. God, I wish it was this time tomorrow, and we were home. If the weather holds, that is.

'What will we do if the roads are closed tomorrow?'

'Stay here, I suppose.'

'I can't stay here another night.'

'What the hell d'you want me to do about it?' he snaps. 'Do you think I control the weather?'

'Oh, how nice. I wouldn't fuck you, and now you're in a bad mood.'

He looks startled. 'It's not like that. '

'Aye, whatever you say.'

Silence. I know he's warming up to something, and at last he says, 'I don't like how your brother's behaving.'

I don't like it either, but I'm not telling him that. 'Not much I can do about it.'

'I just don't want you getting caught up in it. '

His worry seems sincere, and I soften a little. 'It's just for the one more night.'

'Do you trust him, Suzey?'

Now it's my turn to be startled. Trust Jamie? It's like asking if I trust gravity. 'What's that meant to mean?'

'I don't know.' He sighs; he looks like I feel. 'I don't know.'

There are a hundred retorts to that but all of a sudden I just can't be bothered. 'One more night,' I say.

He looks like he's going to answer, so I pick up the remote and turn the TV on. I channel-hop until I find *The Simpsons*. We watch that for a while, laughing in all the right places. We don't speak much.

I spend ages on my makeup. I use a lot of blusher so my face looks sharper, and trace smoky grey around my eyes. I outline my lips before I fill them in, so my mouth looks painted on. Then I fasten my hair up, and step back a little from the mirror; it hardly looks like my face any more, which was exactly the effect I was going for. My neck looks bare, and I didn't bring any jewellery with me, so I put on the rune stone, doubling up the long black cord so it sits on my neck as a choker.

Raj has been lying on the bed watching the whole performance; I can see him in the big mirror, although I pretend to be too taken up with face painting to notice him. When I put on the rune pendant he says, 'It's not a good idea to wear that.'

He's probably right, but I just can't seem to care any more. 'I've not got any other necklaces.'

Raj doesn't answer. Clearly there's something wrong and he wants me to ask what it is, but I'm just not going to. I concentrate on struggling into my tights without laddering them, then on slithering into my red dress.

The bed creaks as Raj gets to his feet; he zips up the dress and starts fiddling with the clasp at the top. 'Would you like to stay in and get room service tonight?'

I start looking for my shoes. 'Could you not have said that before I got all dressed up?' I find my heels and perch on the bed to put them on.

'Are you feeling all right?' he says.

'Fine. Shall we go?'

Two youngish women are on either side of Jamie in the bar, smiling and laughing with him. Carl is sitting off to the side. The two girls get up to leave as we approach, blushing and looking rather coy. I half expect to see them ask for his autograph. Jamie smiles benevolently after them. He has made himself look good tonight; he's wearing a blue shirt to match his eyes, open at the neck to show the rune-stone pendant, though he's turned it round, so all you can see is polished stone. When I sit down beside him I catch a scent like wood smoke and spices, and see the sheen of gold in his hair. 'Aztec pour homme?'

He nods. 'Did he send you a basket too?'

'He?' Raj does not sound pleased.

'I thought it was from Kerry,' I say.

'Mine wasn't.'

I look at Carl. There is nothing golden about him, but I ask anyway. 'Did you get one?'

He shakes his head. 'Maybe you had to be at his mass dooking session. I hear you crashed out again, Suzey? Or did you just fake a seizure to escape the toxic levels of bullshit?'

Jamie hisses at him to shut up, although there's no one within earshot.

'No,' I say. 'I just crashed out. But I'm okay now.'

He's watching me with his counsellor's face on. 'Are you sure?'

God, not him as well. Jamie answers for me, 'She's doing fine, aren't you, sis?'

'Fine.' People are moving towards the dining room. 'Are we going in, then?'

There's a holiday atmosphere in the dining room, laughter and smiles all around; seems the baptism really hit the spot for these people. We autopilot to the table we were at last night. But before we can sit down, a smiling girl in hotel uniform appears at my elbow. 'Would you like to come with me, please?'

She's awful small for a bouncer. She sees my blank face and prompts me, 'You're going to be joining Mr McLean tonight?'

Jamie's nodding. 'That's right.' He's already moving towards the top table.

We start to follow him but the girl's voice cuts in, anxiously. 'No, it's just the two Phersons. Mr and Miss Pherson?'

'I think you'll find there are four in our party,' says Raj. He sounds incredibly pompous.

'It's just for tonight.' Jamie's hand is on my elbow. 'I'll bring her right back.'

Raj glares at him. I can't believe he's making a fuss about this. 'See you in a bit,' I say, and follow Jamie.

The top table is on a raised platform; my heels click on the low step. The light seems brighter and hotter up here – it's like walking out on stage. The waitress pulls out our chairs, on either side of the centre seat. A small sign, *Miss S. Pherson*, sits beside my dessert fork. I slide into my seat, trying to stop my skirt riding up; the waitress shakes out a napkin and drapes it across my lap.

I look out across the room, to find that everyone is looking at us. For one stomach-cramping moment I think I'm meant to be doing a speech. I look at Jamie, who is nodding gravely to various people in the audience, apparently unfazed by the limelight. Raj catches my eye and gives me a weak smile. This is ridiculous, I'm going to go and sit with my boyfriend... But before I can even lift the napkin from my knee, the doors are flung back and McLean makes his entrance.

The audience starts to clap and stamp as if the Beatles have just walked in. McLean lifts his arms in acknowledgement as he strides to the top table. His usual retinue trail after him: Kerry, the bodyguards, the suits and the cocktail dresses. Doesn't he go anywhere on his own? I have an image of him crammed into a toilet cubicle with his two bodyguards, while Kerry waits outside the door and the frocks hover beside the urinals. Hastily I turn a laugh into a cough.

I'm still grinning when McLean arrives at his seat. 'That's a lovely smile to be sitting next to,' he says. One of the suits tries playfully to sneak in beside me. 'No,' says McLean. 'That's my seat. Got to be some perks to being the boss.' He smiles as he says it, although he looks rather sad; I can't help returning the smile, even while reflecting that the man's mood swings are borderline schizophrenic. And sure enough, he looks at the hovering waitress and his expression turns to one of slight irritation. Kerry is standing at my elbow, glaring; this must be her usual seat. 'If there's been a mistake...' I say.

'No, no.' McLean pats my forearm to keep me where I am, and jerks his head towards the end of the table. Kerry moves away, slumped like a large, unhappy child.

A willowy figure in flowing white moves up the table, glancing at the place cards. Anita Black, perfect as ever. She fixes a professional smile on me; I look away. She flits on, and finally slips into the seat beside Jamie. I hold my breath… What's he going to do? But he just nods to her and looks away, and that seems to be that.

McLean, having just sat down, now gets to his feet again and the whole room stands with him. It's time to mumble the Lord's Prayer. When we're done McLean stays standing, eyes closed, lips moving inaudibly. After a minute he lifts his head, claps his hands together and sits down, rubbing his palms together as he nods to the waiter lurking at the back of the hall.

There's no wine list tonight, at least for the top table; bottles wrapped in black foil just arrive in front of us, and soon corks are popping like Hogmanay. I don't know if it's champagne or just sparkling white, and I'm not going to show my ignorance by asking. But it's very, very good, crisp and dry and cold. I've knocked back half a glass before I know what I'm doing; I try to catch Raj's eye and toast him with the rest, but he's talking to someone else and not looking my way. Beside me McLean says, 'Is it good?'

I nod vigorously and he laughs. 'Not a teetotaller, then, Susan.'

I look at his half empty glass. 'Neither are you.'

'Our Lord himself drank wine, after all.'

'Not in five-star hotels he didn't.'

'He visited inns and rich houses, Susan. Do you think he had no care for the wealthy?'

'I really don't know.'

'You should know, Susan. He came for all of us. He said to us, ask and you shall receive. He told us to shine like the City upon a Hill. Our deeds must be seen, and our words must be heard…'

I'm saved by a crash of dishes at the back of the hall. The waiters are bringing out the main course, and they've had a slight collision. McLean turns to end of the table to glare at Kerry. She jumps up, still chewing a mouthful of food, and hurries to the scene of the accident. 'You treat your daughter like shit, do you know that?' I say.

I didn't mean to blurt that out; I can feel my face reddening. McLean quietly watches Kerry harangue the waiters, and looks like he's about to cry. 'She's my one and only, you know. She's all I've got in this world.'

'You're not that bad,' I mumble. 'It's maybe just the way you come across…'

'I don't know what I'd do if anything happened to her.'

'I'm sure she knows that…'

He's actually dabbing at his eyes. Beside him, Jamie and Anita Black are both watching him intently. Jamie gives me an enquiring look; I shrug. Beyond them, I can see Kerry hurrying towards her father, her face drained of colour. But before she reaches him, he's giving a beaming smile to the people at the table in front of us, who have been watching him anxiously. 'Sometimes the Spirit just moves you that way, eh? Praise God for it.'

Now they're beaming too. McLean looks tenderly at Kerry. 'Come and get your dinner, pet. Don't let it get cold.'

Kerry does not look reassured.

All night, the bubbly keeps on coming. By the time the coffee and mints are going round, I should be absolutely shitfaced. But I just feel mildly relaxed. Though I've been talking to McLean for most of the evening, and I don't want to stab him with the fish knife, so the booze must be doing something. Everyone I can see is looking blissful; whether it's the wine or the Holy Spirit I've no idea. Everyone except for Raj and Carl, that is, who are like a pair of wallflowers. I lift my hand to wave, but then there's a tap on my arm.

'Susan.' It's McLean. 'Our next mission meeting will be in a fortnight, in Edinburgh. Can I count on you to be there?'

He says it as though asking is a mere formality. 'You can tell me something first,' I say, looking out over those good Christians who yesterday were ready to lynch my brother. 'What is it about your God of Love that makes you all such cunts?'

He looks at me for a long while. I try to hold his gaze, but my face starts to burn and I have to look away. 'You're a silly wee lassie,' he says at last.

'They were going to hurt my brother, and they call themselves Christians!'

'A silly wee lassie.' He sets down his coffee cup. 'But I'll save your soul yet.' He turns to Jamie. 'You'll join us for drinks upstairs, James?'

Jamie turns around quickly. He looks a bit guilty and I realise he's been whispering to Anita Black. If I didn't know better I'd say they were conspiring about something, but what could those two possibly have in common? 'Yes, great,' he says.

'Good.' McLean pushes back his chair. The Emperor has arisen and everyone in the room scrambles to their feet. I stay put, and only partly because the champagne has turned my legs to rubber. I meet McLean's gaze defiantly but to my annoyance he looks merely amused. 'Would you care to join us, Miss Pherson?'

I've got a hundred smart replies to that but before I can pick one, Jamie takes my elbow and hoists me to my feet. 'Come on, Suze, upsadaisy.'

'I'm not going.'

'Come and keep me company,' he says. 'Please?'

Well, I think, why miss out on good bubbly? I let him steer me after McLean. I glance back to catch Raj's eye; he's looking at me, angry and bewildered. What a fuss, I'm only going to a wee party. He shakes his head and starts to say something, but by this time McLean's entourage is in the way. Then we're out of the hall, crossing the lobby, and going through a door marked *Private*.

Beyond is a short corridor; at the end is a lift. McLean turns a key into a button on the wall, and we wait. There's only six of us; McLean, Jamie and I, and Kerry and the two bodyguards. Anita and the suits have vanished. 'Where's everybody else?' I say.

'Gone to the bar, probably.' Jamie doesn't seem at all bothered by any of this. He's now carrying a small cardboard box: a disposable camera, the kind you can buy in the shop. I don't remember him buying one; maybe he got it in the Visitors' Centre. He's now holding the camera up to his eye: 'Say cheese.'

One of the bodyguards reaches out for the camera, but McLean waves him away. He's the only one smiling when the shutter clicks.

The tiny lift arrives, and we pile in. I try to avoid contact with anyone but Jamie, but I still end up wedged against Kerry. We all seem to be sweating too much and wearing too much perfume. The control panel has only two buttons: *Ground* and *Apartment*. This building only has four floors, but this is taking ages. I pretend to study the back of my hand. No one speaks.

When the doors finally slide open, it's like walking into a different building. I have to blink a couple of times, after the whites and azures of the rest of the hotel, because the room is red. The high ceiling is pale cream, and the fittings are dark brown, but the walls are scarlet damask. My heels sink into the thick, wine-red carpet as I step gingerly across the threshold into McLean's apartment. I imagine Carl intoning, in his best Bela Lugosi voice, 'Enter freely and of your own vill…' It's not as funny as it should be.

'Sit down, James, Susan.' McLean is pointing us towards a brown leather sofa, draped with red throws, in front of an elaborate mahogany fireplace. The sofa is a four-seater, and the mantelpiece is over five feet tall, but they both look petite; this has to be the largest private room I've ever seen. The damask wallpaper has an expensive sheen; I think it's silk. There is a dining table away to the side, and an uncluttered writing desk, all of the same brown-black polished wood. After the bright Deco lines of the rest of the hotel, it all seems rather dark and hulking. And, just to tip the whole thing over into parody, sepia paintings adorn the walls, showing misty hillsides and stags at bay. 'Did you choose the décor yourself?' I ask McLean.

'Yes.' He looks at me with surprise. 'How did you know?'

'It's just so *you.*'

Jamie breaks up the potentially awkward moment by squeezing past us; I assume he's making for the colossal TV and sound system on the other side of the room, but he seems to have other needs at the moment: 'Which is the, er…'

Kerry points to a door and he goes through it, briefly revealing a bathroom fit for a Roman emperor. McLean is waving me towards the couch. 'Sit down, Susan.'

The couch is surprisingly comfortable, although I have to yank my hemline down firmly so my skirt doesn't ride all the way up. I'm still showing a fair bit of leg though; Kerry eyes me dubiously. 'Dad,' she says, but McLean is already speaking to the Men in Black. 'You can go now.' They leave quickly.

'Dad,' Kerry says again. McLean looks at her, apparently surprised that she's still here. 'You don't have to hang about,' he says, quite kindly.

'Dad, you promised you'd speak to Mr and Mrs Sinclair tonight. They'll be waiting for you.'

'I'll see them tomorrow. Tell them to come along after breakfast.'

Kerry stays put, twisting a bracelet round her wrist. She clearly wants me to piss off so she can talk to him, but short of hiding in the bedroom there's nowhere for me to go. 'But Dad, we promised them.'

'I said tell them to come after breakfast.'

At this point Jamie emerges from the bathroom; Kerry sees the camera swinging from his wrist and sits bolt upright. 'You put that away. You don't take any pictures in Mr McLean's private rooms, do you hear me?'

Jamie sets the camera down on the mantelpiece, and holds up his hands in a don't-shoot-me gesture. 'Kerry, go downstairs and see to our guests,' says McLean.

'Dad, I've told you before. You've to think how this looks, you can't just—'

'You silly wee bitch, will you get out!'

As soon as voices are raised, the door opens and one of the bodyguards looks in. Kerry is already hurrying for the door. She pushes past the man, sniffling and dabbing at her eyes. The guard, showing no surprise, pulls the door shut after her.

'So much for "she's your one and only",' I say. But my voice comes out weak and girly; the dark room seems to soak up sound. McLean smiles down at me indulgently, and says to Jamie, 'She's a fierce one, your sister.'

I glare at Jamie, daring him to smile back, but he's already saying, quite seriously, 'She's had to be.'

'Aye. We live in a wicked world.' McLean bends to the fireplace, which I'd assumed was real; there's a shiny brass poker stand beside it. But now there's a faint click, and flames leap up instantly. McLean straightens up like a magician after an easy trick. 'The end is coming and we must be ready. Thank the Lord you're here. What will you drink?'

It takes me a moment to realise the last question wasn't a metaphor. 'Do you have any more of that bubbly?' I ask.

'Bubbly for the lady. And for you, James? A single malt?'

'Don't you have anything harder?'

I elbow him in the ribs but he pays no attention. 'I'll have no drugs around me, James,' says McLean. 'Drugs are destroying the Scottish way of life. They are poisoning our people.'

'And alcohol isn't?'

'Alcohol is allowed to us. Christ showed us the way. It's the water of life.' He's pouring whisky into three thick crystal glasses, apparently forgetting I asked for champagne. 'It was given to us as the blood of his redemption. The blood of Christ. Drink.'

I take a tiny sip. I'm not keen on whisky, but this has a nice peaty smell, and it warms my mouth.

McLean lifts his glass to us. 'Drink, and make yourselves full of Christ. When the end comes you will be spared. But your task will not be easy. You must make ready.'

I mouth 'Task?' at Jamie, who shrugs. McLean doesn't seem to notice. 'You must cleanse yourselves. Only then can you throw off the Adamic curse and live as Man was meant to live, in wisdom and innocence.' His face is reddening, and a fleck of spittle flies from his mouth.

A ringtone sounds from his chest and he grabs a mobile phone from inside his jacket. His voice clicks back to calm and businesslike. 'Matthew McLean. Yes?'

We hear a rushed, female voice on the phone, and then a burst of static. McLean cranks his voice up a few decibels. 'Hello? Yes. Have you spoken to my daughter… Hello? Wait. It's the signal. The *signal*.' I'm awed by the fact that his mobile works at all, but McLean looks annoyed. Getting to his feet, he excuses himself and heads for his bedroom.

Before he's even closed the door, Jamie is saying, 'Come and see this bathroom,' and tugging at my arm. I follow him, curious. He's never been excited by interior design, so this lavvy must really be spectacular. And so it is: all white and terracotta, with blue-jewelled mosaics set into the walls and floor. Massive bath, separate shower and a bidet. And for that final touch of kitsch, gilded dolphin taps and handles. 'Wow,' I say, 'Bet he designed this too.'

'Listen.' Jamie grabs me by the shoulders and turns me to face him. 'There's a webcam inside the camera I put down. We're filming.'

'But it's just a disposable.'

'Anita Black gave it to me. No, *listen*. She knows he's not squeaky clean but they've nothing to go on. We've got to get him doing something, saying something. Anything.'

'But…' He must mistake my idiotic stammering for anger, because he says, 'I'm sorry I had to bring you, Suze, but he wouldn't see me without you. He wants to speak to us both together.'

'What for?'

'Fuck knows. You've seen him, he's aff his heid. He must be on something. He's got pills in the cabinet there. They're all prescription but there might be something there. But it'd be better if there was something else, like sherbet or Angel Dust. Something we can get him on. Maybe sex—'

'Jesus *Christ*, Jamie!'

'For fuck's sake, Suzey. I'm not going to let him touch you.'

'Well that's fucking good of you!' I'm out of here. But my heels skid on the shiny floor, and Jamie's still holding onto me. 'Please, Suzey. Just stay ten more minutes.'

We hear the bedroom door opening in the other room.

'I'll do the talking. Please, Suzey. Please.'

'We'll not get Claire back,' I whisper.

'Hello? James?'

Jamie's face is pinched and frozen. 'We'll not get her back anyway, Suzey.'

'Susan? James!'

My brother's face is like ice. Like the baptismal pool, after the firestorm. 'All right,' I say.

McLean bursts in, but by this time Jamie is on his knees beside the bidet, making a fountain leap three feet in the air. He looks like a kid who's got the top off a fire hydrant. His shirt is soaking; he looks up at McLean with an impish grin that could bring half of Bowie's to their knees. 'I always wanted one of these,' he says.

McLean smiles, looking him briefly up and down. 'Come back through now,' he says softly.

'I need the loo,' I tell them. I lock the door behind them and lean heavily on the sink, my heels skidding slightly on the wet floor. I look up and catch a glimpse of myself in the mirror – still red-lipped and kohl-eyed, but the rest of my face is pale. The right side of my hair's come adrift and is hanging over my ear, so I spend a good few minutes taking out the grips and tying it up into a neat ponytail, rather surprised that this makes me feel slightly better. I should be in an advert: *when I'm trying to incriminate a top Christian evangelist, I just don't have time for problem hair!* I shove my knuckles in my mouth to stop myself laughing out loud.

A giggle creeps out anyway. I turn the taps on full to mask the sound. That reminds me… I prise open the medicine cabinet, hoping the running water will drown out the click of the door. The cabinet's full of razors, shaving foam, shampoo, men's scent, the usual things, all expensive brands. There's a brown glass medicine bottle, too: *MEMANTINE*. That rings a bell, but the bottle is discreet and says nothing more. I ease the door shut.

Now I've got to go back out there. After a couple of deep calming breaths (which do fuck-all good) I go back into McLean's living room. I don't dare look at McLean. Fortunately he seems to be listening intently to Jamie, who's saying, 'If drugs were available to Jesus, how do we know he wouldn't have taken them? That's what they'll ask us.'

They've both made considerable inroads into their whisky. I sit beside Jamie, and without comment he passes me my glass, which now contains a triple measure. I try to look at nothing in particular. The brightly packaged camera is burning a hole in the corner of my eye. I almost wish he hadn't told me about it. I take a large gulp of whisky – the stuff's not so bad, actually – and try to tune back into the conversation.

'Because drugs are the Devil's tools,' says McLean. 'The wretched infidels use them in their false ceremonies to their false gods. The Devil comes to them and takes possession of them, and they are given over to lechery and the corruption of innocents. The Lord is not in these wicked substances, James. They are things of Satan.'

'I know all that, of course, but how are you going to convince them *you* know it? You've never touched anything harder than *this*.' He waves the glass of whisky. 'They'll laugh in your face.'

'*You* will convince them, James. Tell them that before you were born again, you were just as they were.'

'They'll still know you sent me. Holier-than-thou McLean, what's the worst thing you've ever done? Taken your library books back late?'

'I have sinned like every other man.'

Jamie laughs. 'With all due respect, I don't think you have. These men have sinned in ways you couldn't imagine. They think they can't come to you, that you'll be disgusted by them. How am I going to convince them you won't?'

'I welcome all lost souls into the fold of our Church, I was also a sinner—'

'What did you do?'

I'm carefully studying the toe of my shoe, not meeting anyone's eye. But I look up in surprise when McLean laughs aloud. 'When His forgiveness is granted to us, James, the darkness of the past is forgotten,' he says. 'I walked apart from the path of the Lord. That's all that need be said.'

He's not taking the bait. I wish I could kick Jamie on the shin, but we're both in full view of McLean.

'They're just going to say we're out of touch. Young people have all these pressures nowadays.' He looks to me for backup. 'They'll want to do sex and drugs just because their pals are.'

'Peer pressure,' I mumble. I couldn't sound less convincing if I tried. But McLean is nodding; apparently, like most middle-aged parents, he's prepared to swallow this crap wholesale.

'You'll show them the way,' he insists. 'Both of you. You're God's chosen.'

'But you don't understand the temptation these—'

'Enough now.' He holds up a hand for silence. 'This is for another day. I didn't ask you here just to talk about sin. Yes, Susan,' he says, and smiles at my open-mouthed expression, 'I do have other topics of conversation.'

'Like what?'

'A man can't have his mind on the Almighty all the time. I'm glad for your company.'

'So what do you do,' says Jamie, 'when you're not thinking about the Almighty?'

His voice sounds horribly fake to me.

'I haven't much time now. It's up to me to make things right.' I look up and find him gazing at me. 'You know how special your sister is, don't you, James? You're very lucky.'

'I know.'

'And you yourself. Just as special.' He is misty eyed. 'I'm lucky to see you both here.'

This is useless. The only headline we're going to get out of this is *Man Drinks Whisky and Talks Shite*. I shift forward in my seat, preparing to climb to my spiky-heeled feet. 'Well, I think I'll—'

But McLean jumps to his feet; he takes the camera off the mantelpiece and swings round to face the two of us. 'Say cheese!'

We grin obediently. The shutter clicks. McLean turns the camera over, flicks a speck of dust from the lens then tosses it back to Jamie.

'Now you,' Jamie says to McLean. 'Come on Suze, you get in as well.' I stand up, not very smoothly; whisky and heels are a bad combination. I'm half-expecting McLean to hug me, but he just stands beside me with a hand on my shoulder, like a Dad in a formal portrait. If Anita's hoping for a shot of him groping my arse, she's onto plums: he's a perfect gentleman. I take the camera and wave Jamie and McLean closer together. 'Now you two,' I say.

I watch through the lens as they shuffle together. McLean stands upright, with an avuncular hand on Jamie's shoulder. I push the button and the shutter clicks; there's a very faint whirring sound, but otherwise nothing to suggest this isn't an ordinary disposable.

I'm beginning to wonder if Anita Black's been having Jamie on. There's no sign of any hidden technology in this thing. I hand it back to Jamie, who places it oh so casually on the arm of the couch. Anita's got him convinced, that's for sure; but then Anita tells lies for a living.

A fresh glass appears in front of my face; McLean has made me another triple measure. Well, waste not want not. 'Cheers,' I say.

McLean raises his glass silently and we all drink. I'm beginning to feel rather warm and fuzzy. McLean is watching us with what looks for all the world like paternal affection. Strangely, in this dark red room, his eyes appear light blue. For some reason I'm remembering Dad. Dad, watching ten-year-old Suzey lugging five-year-old Jamie about; Dad saying seriously, 'That's your brother. You look after him.' I ask McLean, 'Is everything okay?'

He nods absently; I'm not sure if he heard me. Suddenly he sits up straight, sets his glass down on the hearth and looks at us earnestly. 'I'm glad the two of you came to see me,' he says. 'I'll give you all the help any man can. But you must be strong. Your life won't be easy.' He looks directly at Jamie. 'Your wife and daughter won't come back to you.'

'You said you'd get them back.' I sound like Neddy. 'You said you'd help!'

'They won't come back.'

'You promised to help me,' Jamie says. His voice shakes slightly and I take his hand. 'You promised me.'

'I will help you. But it will make no difference. Your wife and her family have hardened their hearts against you.'

'If you think that, why did you ask me here?'

'To baptise you into the faith. Is that not why you came?'

Jamie says nothing and McLean nods, as if something has been confirmed. 'A publicity stunt, then. To win over your wife.'

'It wasn't just…'

'But it hasn't worked. She knows about your baptism. But whenever you try to call her, she won't speak to you.'

I grip Jamie's hand; he looks like he's going to jump off the couch.

'Checking up on me, were you? Getting one of your wee slaves to listen in at the switchboard?'

'I don't need to listen. I've seen it before. She won't talk to you, she hangs up on you, she won't even let you speak to your child.'

Jamie sits forward, one hand raking through his hair. 'Jamie?' I say. 'Did you phone Katie?'

'I could hear Claire in the background,' he says. 'She wouldn't put her on.'

I put my arm around his shoulders. He feels thin and agitated, like a fretful child. 'She's a miserable torn-faced bitch,' I say.

'Crudely put, Susan,' says McLean, sounding amused, 'but basically true. I've seen the type too often. She has hardened her heart. No matter what the law tells her to do, she won't let you see your daughter again.' Jamie is rubbing at his eyes, and McLean's tone softens. 'I understand why you lied to get here. But it will do you no good.'

Jamie begins to sob. I've never seen him cry this way as an adult, not even when Dad died. He clings to me, burying his face in my shoulder. He's shaking as if he's having a seizure. I brace myself to try and hold him steady, but of course he's bigger than me now and we're both shaking. I pat his back, murmuring soothing nonsense. 'It's okay, you're all right, it's okay…'

'Now do you see the—'

'Shut up, will you,' I snap. McLean sits back, smiling as if I'd said something beautiful. I'm trying to be stolid and supportive, but I'm too warm and full of whisky, and I can't stop thinking about the candle and the snow lantern and the fearless child. So I cry too.

McLean waits until the sobbing is done, although we stay hugged together. I'm more muzzy-headed than I was before, and I have an oddly numb sensation, like pins and needles, so that I can scarcely tell where I end and Jamie begins.

'I'm sorry for your grief, James. And I'm sorry you felt you had to lie to come to me. But you're here now. As you were meant to be.'

'What the fuck are you on about now?' says Jamie.

'I'm telling you to close your foul mouth and listen to what God is telling you. Your wife has turned against you. The men you've been with have vanished away. Who has always been with you, and always will be?'

'Let me guess. Jesus?'

'You're a damn fool.' He speaks without anger. I look up and am surprised to see him smiling at me. 'You see?' he says, to Jamie.

'See what?'

'See who fights to defend you. Even when you don't deserve it.' Jamie goes to say something, but McLean has already turned to me. 'And you, Susan. No, it's Suzey, isn't it? You've not had much luck either, have you? No husband. Some boyfriends, but they never quite stay the distance, do they?'

'That's not right.' It takes a moment to get the words out. 'I'm with Raj now.'

'Yes, I saw him downstairs. Not happy, was he? He objected to you spending time with your brother and not with him, isn't that right?'

'Well—'

'Do you think he'll be any different from the others?'

'You shut your mouth,' Jamie says. Feeling tears coming, I turn away and bury my face in his shoulder. His arm tightens around me. He smells of clean sweat and cotton and Aztec Gold.

'Forgive me. But it's time to open your eyes.' McLean's voice is gentle. His own eyes are blue, like Dad's – how could I have thought they were any other colour? 'James, Susan, you may love others, but those loves will fail. Parents will die, children will leave you, lovers will come and go. Who will you depend upon? Who have you ever had to depend upon, but each other?'

I keep my face pressed into Jamie's shoulder. I feel like I never want to turn away again. I can feel his breath in my hair.

'Your path will not be easy. I wish I had more time to guide you. But the end will come soon. The Kingdom of Heaven is at hand. An Age of Gold awaits you, but first you must see everything you think you love destroyed.'

A little sob escapes out of me. Jamie holds me tighter, and begins very gently to stroke my hair.

There's something wrong with me, I don't feel right at all. It must be the whisky. He's put something in the whisky.

'I knew it when I saw your pictures. Your faces. The two who escape death and become one. A new Adam and Eve, needing no marriage because they are already one flesh.'

It's the whisky, the whisky. I'm afraid to open my eyes. But McLean must know this, for he says, 'Don't be afraid. James, look at your sister. She's yours, and you are hers. Look at her.'

Jamie's hand is under my chin, gently lifting my face, and at last I look at him. And I have to laugh, just a little, because my brother's face is beautiful, and it is also my own. Same eyes, same bone structure. A lock of gilded hair trails across his cheek; I smooth it back behind his ear, smiling because I can feel an identical lock brushing my own skin. 'We're the same,' I whisper. 'We're just the same…'

'That's right. There is no shame here. There is only what—'

'Shut up,' Jamie says, without looking at him. An obedient silence falls. I blink away a stray tear; Jamie kisses it away from my cheek, and follows the track upwards, kissing across my eyes, my forehead. His cheek grazes mine, very slightly.

I mesh my fingers through his. My hand is smaller, a bit slimmer, but the pale colour, the long fingers and square nails are the same. I lift up our twined hands to show him and he smiles. Is that my smile? Then I understand, suddenly, what Raj and Lewis and all the rest have seen, why they all tried to make me laugh, why they kept coming back again. And I understand, as well, what pushed them away. I know, finally, what it is that I want.

I mirror that smile, and lean forward to kiss it.

His hand is behind my neck, very gently, and I couldn't move away for all the world. I shut my eyes and sink both my hands into his hair; it feels and smells just like mine.

McLean says something. I don't know what it is and I don't care. I can't think of anything but his tongue touching my lips. I twine my arms around him and pull him close, licking and tasting him as we fall together. And it's all right, because he's mine, my own image. His hand slides down my flank. A whimper escapes from me. He leans back slightly, and his hand skims down my neck, across my breast, down to my belly, and then back to my face.

I gasp and open my eyes. He is so close, all I can see is one blue eye, and my own reflected in it, and his caught in that, and…

CRACK.

Piercing white light, and something breaks in my head. I try to open my eyes but pain corkscrews through my skull. Not right, none of this is right. I hear myself whimper.

'Suzey!' Jamie's voice is blaring in my ear; the pain flares up again, and I shove him away. His voice comes again, softer and more distant. 'Suzey, can you hear me? Suzey?'

'What's she doing?' It's McLean, he sounds irritated. 'What's the matter with her?'

'Suze, are you all right?'

I rub my hands over my temple, reassuring myself that it's still in one piece. Jamie is beside me, McLean in the background. I don't look at either one of them, but try to stand up. My silly heels skid on the carpet and I sit back down again.

'Stay where you are.' McLean sounds annoyed now. Jamie takes my arm; I claw at his hand, and he pulls away with a cry of surprise. I get up under my own steam and stand there, swaying. Jamie's trying to catch hold of my arm again. 'Suzey, I'm so sorry, please…'

'Get off me.' I pull away and make for the door; but then Jamie is in front of me again. 'Wait, please, Suzey.'

He's crying again. I am so fucking sick of watching him cry. I slap his tear-stained cheek as hard as I can. The sound seems to echo, and brings us all up short. Red marks bloom across Jamie's face. 'I'm going,' I tell him.

'Sit down,' says McLean, 'and listen to me.'

'Fuck off, you old pervert.'

McLean blocks my path as I try to leave. 'If you walk away now, your lives are forfeit. All human life is—'

'We're not being in your wee fairytale, all right? Get the fuck out of the—'

'You listen to me!' It's a high-pitched shriek, almost feminine. I'd expected him to shout and roar, but this stops me in my tracks. 'Don't you dare walk away from me, young lady!'

His face is red with his fury. He takes a step towards me, and I step back, bumping hard into Jamie. 'And you!' he says to Jamie. 'You'll not defy me in my own home! Sit down like I telt ye!'

'Go around him,' Jamie says, steering me towards the other end of the couch. As we start to back away he follows us. 'Did you hear me, boy?'

'We're going now,' Jamie says. 'Get out the way.'

McLean's face is nearly purple and his hands are clenched at his side; he looks like a giant toddler throwing a tantrum. 'Don't you speak to your father like that! You'll be sorry! You'll be punished!'

Your *father?* 'Please,' I say. 'If you just calm down—'

'Shut your mouth, you cheeky wee bitch! What did I do to get the pair of you! Ungrateful wee bastards. You'll be punished…'

He's winding down, like a clock. He sits down heavily in his chair and great fat tears begin to roll down his cheeks. 'Wicked, the pair o' ye. I gave ye everything ye've got.'

He's sobbing, his nose is running, and he does nothing about it. And I've finally remembered: memantine. The brown glass bottle, beside Dad's bed.

'Mr McLean?'

'Jesus Christ,' says Jamie. 'What's he on?'

'Hush.' Memantine. Dad in the bed. Mum crying, because Dad's asking who she is. 'Look at him. Remind you of anyone?'

'What? Who?'

Christ, he's slow. 'Dad.'

Jamie stares. Finally, the light's coming on. 'Alzheimer's?'

McLean lifts his snottery face. 'Kerry? You'll stay with me?'

'Hush, you're okay.' I find a hankie in his jacket pocket, and wipe up his face as best I can. 'You'll be okay.'

I put a hand on his forehead, to soothe rather than to check for a temperature. But he pulls away, suspicious. 'You're not my Kerry.'

'Shall we get Kerry for you? She's—'

'You bitch. You came to rob me. Where's my daughter?' The shriek is gone, he's bellowing again, the force of it driving me back. 'Where is she!'

The door opens and the bodyguards run in.

'WHERE IS SHE!'

'You'd best get Kerry,' I tell them. 'He's not very well.' I bolt past them into the corridor, Jamie behind me. McLean's indistinct bawling echoing after us.

I fall into the lift and hammer on the button; the doors are closing when Jamie steps inside. 'Suzey,' he says.

'Shut up.' I lean my aching head against the cool metal wall, and the lift's motion buzzes through my skull. The floor bounces as we reach the ground, and I stagger slightly. Out of the corner of my eye I see Jamie reaching for me, so I pound on the exit button until the doors open and I can make my escape.

I let my hair swing over my face as I plough through the crowd in the lobby. My feet are numb and clumsy, and I don't think it's just the shoes. I stumble into other bodies, ignoring their protests. The main lift is just going up; I push in, just in time, but I know he's still behind me. An American voice says, 'Honey, are you okay?' but I ignore it; Jamie is mumbling some answer when I reach my floor.

'Suze, are you all right?' He follows me along the corridor. I reach my door, and realise I don't have a key. I start pounding on it: 'Raj! Raj!'

Raj is a calm man, impassive, so his face just goes very still when he sees me. He gathers me into his arms and holds me tight, and when he asks what's wrong I shake my head.

'Good God, what happened to you?' asks Carl as Raj carries me into the room.

'It's my head,' I whisper. I'm shivering, so Raj sets me down on the bed and wraps the fur coverlet around me.

'Another migraine?' says Carl. 'What's—'

'Suzey, look at me,' says Raj. 'Is this like the time in the snowcat? Are you seeing things? Hearing things?'

'No,' I whisper. It hurts to shake my head.

'Can you tell me what happened?'

That's the last thing in the world I can tell him. When I don't respond Jamie says. 'I think McLean gave us something. In the whisky.'

'What did he do?'

'Nothing. I mean, he didn't lay a hand on her. It wasn't like that.' Jamie is pushing his hair back from his face; the back of his hand is bloody, gouged in four long scratches. I feel Raj gently turning over my right hand; there are specks of blood under my nails. Raj is staring at Jamie. 'So what happened?'

'The guy's aff his heid. You wouldn't believe it. He kept giving us this whisky—'

'I said *what happened*?'

I flinch. 'Christ, deafen her why don't you?' says Jamie.

Carl's voice cuts in, low and calm. 'Jamie, do you think you were doped? Did you lose consciousness at all?'

'No.'

'Was Suzey alone with him at any point?'

'No. No, she wasn't.'

'All right. Suzey, pet, how do you feel?'

'Okay,' I whisper. I do feel a little better, now everyone's stopped shouting. Raj tucks the fur cover around me more securely.

'Did you see McLean mixing your drink, Suzey?' says Carl.

'No, I didn't.' Of course. It was the whisky, something in the whisky. That's all it was. 'I didn't see any of it.'

'Jamie, did you see?'

'No, he had his back to me the whole time.'

'He didn't give me what I asked for,' I say. 'I asked for bubbly.' He drugged us. That's all it was. Oh, thank God, it was just the drugs. 'He made us both have the whisky.'

Raj is looking at Jamie's hand. 'So how did you…'

There is a tiny sound behind us, the creak of a floorboard perhaps, and we all turn. The movement makes me clutch at my head. We can't have closed the door properly behind us, and now Anita Black is inside the room, watching us eagerly. 'McLean put something in your drinks? Did he try to touch you?'

Raj is already on his feet. 'This is a private room.'

'Did he say anything to you?'

'Get out!'

Anita pushes the door closed and smiles up at Raj. 'I'm sorry, but I have an appointment with Mr Pherson. Jamie? Did it work?'

I look directly at Jamie. He looks sick and tired. The disposable camera is looped around his wrist; he must have picked it up when we made our escape. 'I don't know,' he says.

Anita frowns. 'You didn't get anything?'

'I'm not sure.'

'Jamie,' I whisper.

'No,' he says. 'I didn't get anything.'

'Nothing at all? He didn't do *anything*?'

'Just talked a lot of religious stuff. Nothing he wouldn't have said in public.'

'Well,' says Anita, sounding very ungracious. 'I'll have my camera back then.'

Jamie un-loops the camera from his wrist, and starts tearing off the bright cardboard covering. 'What are you doing?' says Anita.

'Taking the memory card out.' He pulls the last of the cardboard off the small black box. Carl, eyes widening with technophilia, leans closer for a better look. 'Unless you think the *Standard* wants an hour-long lecture on the Book of Deuteronomy?'

'Just give me the camera,' she says. Jamie pockets the memory card carefully, and gives Anita the webcam.

Carl frowns. 'You know that thing copies everything onto the hard drive?' he says to Jamie.

Anita breaks into a run. Jamie swears and goes after her. She is almost out of the door when he grabs her by the arm and hauls her back in.

'What the hell is going on?' says Raj.

Anita is furious. 'That's assault! Get out of my way!'

'It's the latest edition,' Carl is explaining to Raj, sounding impressed. 'Automatic backup on everything it records. Costs a packet.'

'Wipe the hard drive, Anita,' says Jamie.

'You can send the footage straight to web if you want.'

'It's a webcam?' Raj raises his voice above the quarrelling. 'You were recording McLean? Without his knowledge?'

Anita glares at him. 'I think you'll find it's perfectly legal.'

All I can think is *straight to web*. 'It didn't broadcast,' I say, 'did it? I mean, it wasn't going out live?'

I shut up as I realise how much my voice is shaking.

'What happened, Suzey?' asks Anita.

'Nothing.'

'It was the drugging, wasn't it? That's what you were talking about?'

'I don't know. I mean, it was nothing. It's not worth bothering about.'

'We'll see about that, won't we?' She clicks something on the camera and I hear McLean's voice, tinny and distant: '*those loves will fail. Parents will die, children will leave you, lovers will come and go.*'

Jamie lunges at Anita. She stumbles into Raj, who takes the camera from her.

'Switch it off,' I beg.

Jamie reaches for the camera, but Raj shoves him away. McLean's voice carries on: 'Who will you depend upon?' Jamie sits down on the bed and hides his face in his hands.

I run into the bathroom and lock the door. But I can still hear something, that voice murmuring, so I go to the sink and turn both taps on full, scattering the objects around them: toothbrushes, soap, Raj's razor. The gushing water masks all other sounds, but I press my hands over my ears as I kneel on the wet tiled floor and hang my head over the toilet. But nothing comes up. I kneel there gaping for a second, then I start to cry.

The sobs are high pitched and wailing. I've never heard myself make such noises before. They echo around the tiled walls. I sound like a room full of crying babies. It's quite impressive, really, that I can do that all on my own! I giggle a little. I should be on the stage!

There, that's better, I'm laughing now, although it doesn't sound much different from the crying. But you've got to laugh, haven't you? The gushing taps sound like a waterfall – no, a cataract. That's a better word! Even if everything else is fucked, I can still come up with the right word! And I'm okay in here. Kneeling on the hard floor, elbows on the toilet bowl, smelling whatever flowery-clean substance has turned the water blue. Things could be worse.

Could be worse. Would be better, in fact, if my skin wasn't getting so itchy. Everywhere Jamie put his hands is getting itchy. He must have had hand cream on or something. I'm scratching at myself, my arms and neck and the tops of my breasts; red welts are flaring across my skin. Christ, I must be getting eczema. What the hell did Jamie have on his hands? It can't be Aztec Gold, it must be some cheap stuff. Nasty, very nasty. I scratch and scratch; it's not getting any better.

I pull myself to my feet, grabbing at the sides of the sink. I switch off the hot tap and wait for the water to run cold. Then I start slapping water against my arms and neck and breasts. Nice. I start rinsing, letting the icy water run across my reddened skin. The front of my dress is getting soaked, but I've got to get the stuff off, can't let it get worse.

Now I need something to put on it. I look around the top of the sink. Aztec Gold moisturising lotion, no doubt loaded with perfumes and chemicals. No, thank you. Toothpaste, that's what I need. Full of menthol, very cooling, but doesn't it have salt in it? As an abrasive? I'm sure I heard that somewhere. So toothpaste is out. God, what does that leave me with?

There's the razor, of course.

But I mustn't be hasty. Raj's razor is closed up neatly inside its black casing. An old-fashioned barber's razor. I know how sharp he keeps it. I could just peel off the top layer of skin, just the irritated part… If I was careful it wouldn't even draw blood. No, that's silly. I'm not peeling potatoes; of course there'll be blood.

And blood might be good, now I think about it; it would wash out the irritants.

The whole business would hurt, of course. But as much as this rash? I don't think so.

So come on, Suzey, just get on with it. My eyes must be cloudy from all that crying, because I see only a haze of red. Clothes and face and skin, blazing and inflamed. And of course it will get worse. I put the razor's edge to my neck.

And then I'm cold. Cold all over. Oh wonderful, wonderful… I reach out to embrace it and I fall into it. There's a sharp pain in my knees, and then I am immersed in the cold…

Walking, walking. Every step through knee-high snow. Faint moonlight makes the ground blue-white. The others are round about me, I can hear them pushing through the snow. Someone is struggling badly. The air is sharp with wood smoke and pine needles and ice.

The inflammation is gone and now it's the frozen air that hurts. My clothes are too thin. The snow is inside my shoes. I look ahead and I see no lights, nothing, and my clothes are too thin. Oh no, no…

The pain in my temple throbs, once. I shut my eyes and I feel a change.

It comes in a single smooth movement, like the neat tick of a clock's second hand. The pain and the fear are gone. I open my eyes.

I am up above now, looking down. Now she is walking through the snow, not me. She is frightened and in pain. Jamie and Carl and Raj walk beside her. I know somehow that this Suzey has not felt her brother's hands on her. Things were different with her. I know what she remembers. She was lucky: her McLean burst into tears and wet himself a moment after Jamie told her about the camera.

She is me, but not me; she has gone on ahead. They got to her quicker, men came and…

I am on my knees. They hurt and they are wet. I pull myself up slowly. How long have I been kneeling there? I look into the mirror, at my soaked dress, hair dark with water, pale skin striped and blotched with red. Some of the scratches have drawn blood, but the burning has gone out of them.

I shut off the tap and hear raised voices in the next room. I wrap a huge, fleecy towel around myself, and open the bathroom door.

'You have to understand, it's not just…' Anita's voice trails off as she catches sight of me.

'Jesus fuck,' says Jamie.

There's no sign of Raj. I hobble over to the bed. After all that's happened I'm still wearing these stupid shoes. I sit down next to Carl, and tug the things off, not caring if the straps break. Of course I have to take one arm out of the towel to do it; an impeccably manicured hand, with a camera strap looped around the wrist, reaches down to touch the abraded skin. I slap the hand away. 'Piss off, Anita.'

'I understand. You don't want to be touched. Jamie, do you see this? Look what's happened to your sister because of that man.' Her voice quivers with righteous indignation. It might even be genuine. 'Are you just going to let him get away with it?'

Jamie kneels down in front of me. For a moment I think he's going to kiss my feet. 'I'm sorry, Suzey.'

'Where's Raj?'

'I don't know. He went out. I told him it was my fault. Suzey, I'm so sorry.'

'It's okay.'

'It's not okay. I don't know…'

Carl says loudly, 'Are you not staying, Anita?'

'Shit!' Jamie scrambles to his feet; the black disk falls out of his pocket and lands by my discarded shoes. He grabs Anita before she can run from the room, taking the camera roughly from her hands. 'Give me it.'

'I'll get security onto you!'

'Aye, you do that. How do you wipe this thing? '

'Don't you *dare!*'

Carl frowns. 'You want to wipe it?'

'Fucking right I do. Don't worry,' he says to me, 'I'll erase all of it.'

'But we wanted evidence on McLean,' says Carl. 'And now we've got it.'

'We're not using this. I'm not bringing Suzey into it.'

'Then why the hell did you bring her here?'

Anita cuts in, her voice smooth again. 'All right, Jamie, I hear what you're saying. You want Suzey kept out of this. That's fine. We can edit the film. We can edit her out. You too, if you like.'

There's a long pause. Jamie looks from me to Anita and back. 'Fine,' he says at last. 'Do the edit, then. Let's see it first.'

'I can't do it here.'

'So where can you?'

'I need to take it back to Glasgow. I know,' she says, as Jamie goes to interrupt, 'you don't trust me. But this is too important. You know it is.' She looks at each of us in turn, holding my gaze for a long time. 'You have to take a chance on me. All of you. You have to.'

Jamie shakes his head. 'You must think we were born fucking yesterday, Anita.'

'I give you my word. You can record it if you like. I *will* do the edits.'

Carl laughs. 'Of course you will. You'll make them just the way your proprietor wants them. And since your proprietor is in Mr McLean's golf club, I don't think he'll be in a hurry to lead with *him*. But these two, they'd be front-page material, wouldn't they?'

'How could I show them without showing McLean?'

'With your lovely editing software. You can lift out McLean and drop in anyone you want. Who were you thinking of, I wonder? Raj? Or me? Or just some anonymous old perv who likes watching sisters and brothers at it?'

'Shut it,' says Jamie. 'I'm wiping this now.'

'Listen. I don't have any interest in you or your sister. People won't care about that. They care about McLean. That's the only story worth running. Let me show you how I'll cut it. You don't have to agree to anything, just look.'

'Fine. Show me.'

She starts murmuring a commentary. 'We'll lose that, don't worry, but keep this part…' I stop listening.

Carl smiles at me. 'How're you doing, hen?'

'Did Raj say where he was going?'

'I think he just went for a walk. He'll be back.'

'I fucked up, Carl.'

'Everyone fucks up.'

Strangely, I feel slightly better. I watch Jamie and Anita for a while. They're whispering. Jamie now has his arms folded; he's shaking his head. 'He's going to wipe it, isn't he,' I say.

'Aye. Don't worry,' says Carl. 'It'll be all right.'

He seems sincere, but I know him better than he thinks I do. While he was watching Jamie make his big refusal, he looked sick to his stomach. 'It wouldn't make that much difference anyway, Carl.'

'Probably not.'

'I mean, if he's in that guy's golf club and everything. He knows too many people.'

'Aye.'

'And it's fakeable anyway.'

'Aye, I know.' He sighs, then bends down and picks up the disk. I watch him casually turn it over in his hand. From the doorway Jamie says, 'Take that off him, Suzey.'

'Christ, I wasn't going to…' He spreads his hands wide, all indignant innocence, but he doesn't give me the disk. I whisk it away from him, wondering if he really would do it. He can't look at me.

'Need to find something else for your website, Carl.'

'That's not the point.'

He has the nerve to sound annoyed with me. I clutch the disk tighter. 'Piss off. You've no right.'

He shrugs. He can look as self-righteous as he wants; it's not him on that fucking recording. I feel a tiny button click under my fingertip. A faint green light illuminates my fingers. There's a tiny line of text on the side of the disk: *Send straight to web? Y/N.*

Jamie and Anita are still arguing in the background. I tip my cupped hands sideways, so Carl can see the text on the disk. His eyes widen; a second later he remembers to look serious, but before that it's pure gadget-loving awe. Seems the webcam is even more advanced than he thought.

The disk itself can transmit straight to the web.

It makes no difference. I'm not sending it.

Christ, my life would be over if this came out. No one's got the right to ask it of me.

I'm remembering the frozen pool beneath the shattered windows. It's not going to happen. If it is, there's nothing I can do. *This* won't make any difference.

I remember Raj, in his devastated office with the wolves howling outside. White faced and stinking. Balder, not Balfour. Ragnarok.

Raj said it doesn't mean it's going to happen. That's what he'd tell me if he were here. I should destroy the disk.

But I saw it. I can't disbelieve it, however I try. I saw it.

I shut my eyes and take a deep breath. I'm hoping for another episode, something to take me away from this. But when I open my eyes, Carl is watching me.

I find the small black button on the disk, and press it.

Straight to web – are you sure? Y/N? This time it's defaulted to the *No* option. I fiddle around until *Yes* is highlighted.

The door slams open into Jamie and Anita. They fall back, protesting, as Raj snaps at them to move.

I push the button.

Raj slams the door behind him. He looks over at me, but doesn't meet my eyes. If he's shocked by my scratches he doesn't show it. He turns his attention instead to Jamie and Anita. 'What the fuck are you doing?'

'We're editing the film.' Anita's voice is calm and soothing. 'We're taking Suzey and Jamie out of it.'

'I've not agreed to anything,' says Jamie.

'I know, I'm just showing what—'

Raj pulls the webcam out of Jamie's hand and wrenches off the back panel. Plastic snaps and metal pieces fall to the floor. Anita grabs at him angrily; he shoves her, hard, and she slams against the wall.

Raj is crossing the room and picking up a heavy lamp, ready to smash it down onto what remains of the camera. Anita is hanging onto his arm, still shrieking.

Transmission complete. It sounds like something out of *Thunderbirds*. I start giggling in spite of myself, pushing my fingers into my mouth to try to stop.

Raj and Anita freeze. 'What did you do?' he says.

Carl gently takes the disk from my hands, and holds it up for them to see. 'It's gone to the web already. Direct to the public forums.'

'How much of it?' Anita snaps.

'All of it.'

'Why?' says Jamie. 'Why in God's name would you…'

'Because he's insane.' Carl's voice begins to rise. 'Because he's taking us back to the Stone Age. Because he wants to start a new Crusade in the Gulf. Because he's trying to start a fucking war. Why the fuck do you think?'

'You stupid prick,' says Anita. 'He's going to sue you.'

'I did it,' I say. My voice is high and shaking. 'It wasn't Carl. I sent it.'

Anita hardly pauses. 'Do you know how fakeable that material is? He'll take us all for every penny we've got.'

Raj drops the lamp and gets hold of Anita instead. While she shrieks and protests, he marches her to the door like a bouncer and shoves her out, throwing the remains of the camera after her. Then he swings round and heads for me.

I scramble sideways. But he's not going for me at all. The blow catches Carl on the jaw; Carl lashes out at his chest. After that it's just thumping and swearing and pounding. I have to crawl over the bed to get away from them, hearing my dress give somewhere at the seams as I land in an undignified heap on the other side. 'Stop it! Raj, *stop it!*'

And he stops, as suddenly as he started, but Carl, who has blood on his face, goes after him and keeps on hitting. Jamie puts his hands on his shoulders and after a moment Carl allows himself to be pulled back.

I go to Raj, kneeling down to look up at his face. He keeps his head in his hands. 'Raj, please.' I'm starting to cry. 'Please.'

He lowers his hands. 'Do you know what you've done?' he says hoarsely.

'I needed to,' I say.

We both jump as there's a pounding on the door, so hard it rattles the door on its hinges. This is definitely not Anita. Before any of us can open it, there's a scrabbling at the handle, and the lock clicks open. Men in red-and-gold uniform pour in. Four of them. I can see two more outside.

'It's okay,' says Jamie. 'They've stopped.' He nods at Raj and Carl. 'Sorry for the trouble.'

The men push past him. One of them opens my suitcase and flings it on the bed. Another opens the wardrobe and starts throwing clothes towards the suitcase, while number three – the driver who picked us up in Crianlarich – goes into the bathroom. The fourth stands guard at the doorway, eyes flicking from Raj and I to Carl and Jamie.

Raj finds his voice. 'What do you think you're doing?'

'You're leaving.' Number four looks down at me, checking out the cleavage and torn nylons with obvious contempt. 'All of you. Get your stuff. I'll give you five minutes.'

Carl shoves Jamie towards the door and they go.

'Where are we going?' I ask.

The man shrugs. Two of his colleagues are closing the case, clothes sticking out on either side. 'I've still got stuff in the drawer,' I say, but they ignore me.

Number four snaps his fingers at us. 'Up.'

We get to our feet. I'll give him fucking *up*. 'You're way out of line here—'

'Leave it,' says Raj.

'That's right, bitch.' The man jerks a thumb towards the door. 'Leave it.'

In much less than five minutes, they've marched us down to the lobby. Carl and Jamie are there already, carrying half-empty bags. Carl's nose is still bloody, but he's ignoring it. From the dining room we can hear a man's voice, high-pitched and railing: not McLean's. And a crowd growling agreement, getting louder and angrier with every moment.

Kerry is crossing the lobby, her face white and her eyes raw. She stops in front of me, towering over me. 'What did you do to him?'

She hasn't seen the recording yet. 'I didn't do anything to him. I'm sorry, Kerry, your Dad's just not well.'

There's a quick movement and something bashes into the side of my head. I clamp my hands over my temple just before the pain hits. I back away as Kerry comes for me, hand raised for another blow, bellowing in my face. 'You filthy wee hoor!'

'He's not right, Kerry. He's got Alzheimer's. He's fucking senile, and you know it.'

She hits on my cheek, and again on the top of my head. I keep my arms over my face and my throbbing temple. Something tightens painfully around my throat – she's got hold of my rune-pendant. 'You witch! Filthy wee witch!' Raj is trying to prise her fingers away, but she clutches the stone in her fist, trying to push it into my face while the cord throttles me. 'What did you do to him? Witch!'

At last the security guards intervene, and she has to let me go. As I stagger back she keeps on screaming, spit and snot flying as she curses and sobs. She goes quiet as she sees, at the same time I do, that people have emerged silently from the dining room. They're watching Kerry, and they're watching us, and I can tell they want to hurt us, very badly.

Then we are being marched towards the main door. One of the guards is gripping me tightly above the elbow. Behind us the mob is grumbling; I look back and see Sandra, her hand over her mouth. Then we're gone, through the doors and out into the cold.

'Where are you taking us?' says Carl.

'Out.'

He means outside. In the snow. 'I think you'll find this constitutes manslaughter,' says Raj.

'I think you'll find.' He puts on a la-di-da voice, and one of his men laughs. 'Keep walking. Move!'

Jamie twists away from them and turns back towards the hotel. Carl joins him. They're both terrified. Number four is reaching for something on his belt: a baton. They've all got them. I slide to the ground as my guard relaxes his grip on me.

'Please,' I whisper. I'm crying and shivering. My face is snottery and my red dress is torn. 'Please…'

They're all looking down at me now, at my legs and breasts. One of them says something I don't catch, and the rest laugh. I look from one face to another, and find what I'm looking for: troubled eyes that won't meet mine. The driver, the one who collected us from Crianlarich, looks upset. 'Please,' I say. 'Please help us.'

The driver shuffles his feet. 'They're right enough. Might be a manslaughter charge.'

The leader glares at him.

'I'm just saying. I mean, she's not going to last outside.'

'Fuck's sake.' The leader looks back towards the lobby, and heaves a sigh. 'Right yous. Move.'

He produces a card, and swipes it through a wall panel disguised as a decorative plaque. A door opens onto a grey service corridor. I am hauled to my feet, the guard's knuckles pressing against the side of my boob.

The concrete floor numbs my stocking feet; I push away from the man who's holding me, trying to keep his boots away from my toes. My temple aches where Kerry hit me, and there's a whining in my ear. We crash through the fire doors and emerge onto a concrete stairwell.

We descend, the small space filling with the clatter of boots on concrete. At the bottom there's a security door with a control panel. One of the guards punches in the code and we shove through into a cold room in complete darkness.

Fluorescents flicker into life and reveal the underground car park. There are two snowcats under tailored plastic covers, a couple of cars, and a Land Rover. The leader takes a key out of his pocket and throws it to one of his men. 'Get them the Rover.'

The man tries to catch the key but misses; while he's scrabbling around on the ground he asks, 'What d'you say?'

The leader glares at him. If I weren't so terrified I'd find it funny: the guy wants to be a movie soldier, but he clearly just can't get the help. 'Get the keys for the fucking Land Rover out of the office!'

Pain is pulsing in my temple. I squeeze my eyes shut and breathe deeply.

'Suzey,' says Carl. 'Are you okay?'

'Yeah,' I whisper. 'Headache.'

The guard hurries back from the office, keys jingling in his hand. The leader grabs them and shoves them at Raj. 'Get moving.' The Rover looks nearly new, and has snow tyres fitted, but beside the bulk of the snowcats it looks small and fragile.

Raj frowns. 'We'll need a snowcat.'

'Get in or you're walking!'

Carl is already opening the driver's door. I notice there are drops of sweat on his forehead, like tiny glass beads. 'I'll drive.'

'No,' says Raj, pushing Carl out of the way. I climb into the back seat, with Jamie following; the security men bundle the suitcases in after us. Raj is already revving the engine as Carl gets into the passenger seat beside him.

'Leave it where we can pick it up,' says the leader. 'Call me tomorrow. If you don't I'll get the polis on you.'

'Lock the doors,' says Carl. Raj fumbles across the control panel; the central locking clicks and Carl relaxes visibly. 'Thank God. Start moving.'

Raj ignores him, craning around to look at me. 'Suzey, are you all right?'

'It's just a headache. I'm okay. Let's go, *please*.'

The leader is looking through the window at Raj, yelling something we can't hear and gesticulating towards the far wall. A huge metal door has been cranked open; two security men are beside it, stamping their feet against the cold and waving us outside.

We move off, bumping and jerking around until Raj figures out the gears. The security men are sarcastically waving us off; I see one mouth 'Bon Voyage!' Then we're outside.

Chapter 28

Floodlit snowflakes whirl past the windows as we trundle past the hotel's main entrance onto the long curving driveway.

My breath is puffing out in front of me; the Land Rover is no more proof against the cold than a biscuit tin. 'Put the heating on,' I say. Raj flicks a switch, and air comes roaring in; it's still cold. 'Take a minute to heat up,' he says.

My suitcase is half on the seat, half on Jamie; I tug at the handle, although my hands are already chilled and aching. Jamie gets the idea and starts pulling out jumpers, socks, hiking trousers. I put them on as he gives them to me, one on top of the other. I'm stiff with cold, and it hurts to move my head; so Jamie helps me, tugging up my socks, pulling the jumper over my head as if I'm four years old.

Then he looks for his own suitcase; he has to put on the internal light because we've left the spotlights behind. Dark pine trees loom up at us in the headlights. Carl's suitcase won't go between the front seats, so Jamie starts passing him fleeces and thick socks. Raj is still in his suit and must be freezing, but he keeps driving. I find a rug behind the back seat. 'Put that over you,' I say, passing it forward. He doesn't take his hands off the wheel, but I see him studying me in the mirror.

Red eyes wink at us through the windows: the reflector poles. There are two more lights at the bottom of the hill – the Celtic crosses. They really are floodlit at night. Raj slows to a stop just before them, and leaves the engine running as he struggles into the clothes Jamie hands to him.

Carl lets out a long breath, scanning the road ahead. 'Any suggestions where we're going?'

'The South road's still blocked,' says Raj. He releases the handbrake, and we roll into the main road. 'We'll have to go to Glencoe village.'

'We'd have to go through the glen,' says Carl.

'I know. It's safe.' Raj is already turning left. 'The SCACS is on.'

'You said it went onto half function at night.'

'It does.' We bump over something and I clamp my hands over my aching head; when I look up Raj is watching me in the mirror. He looks worried, but he speaks calmly to Carl. 'Half function's still enough.'

'It was half function on the south road!'

'That was a much bigger snow load. It'll be fine.'

As we push forward into the glen, the ride gets smoother, thank God. But Carl's shaking his head. 'We should go to the King's House.'

'It's shut for the winter,' I say.

'We can get in through one of the windows. They'll have firewood. Tinned food maybe. We can last till tomorrow.'

Raj says something quietly. I don't catch all of it, just the word 'hospital'. Carl turns to stare at me. At last he says, 'You doing okay, Suzey?'

'I'm fine. I bumped my head. It was just a bump on the head!' I look to Jamie, but it's too dark, I can't see his face. 'Jamie, tell them I'm fine!'

'Aye, I know. You're fine. But we'll just get it checked, okay?'

Raj cuts in, calm and soothing. 'It's minor concussion at worst. But the sooner it's caught, the shorter the recuperation time.'

'I still say we should wait till morning,' says Carl.

The car starts to slow. There's just a faint sensation of brakes labouring. Raj reaches over Carl and opens his door as we come to a stop; the light goes on, and the cold comes howling in. 'Then get out. Go and wait till morning.'

Carl hesitates. Tiny freezing snowflakes speckle my face. 'For fuck's sake shut the door!' says Jamie.

Swearing under his breath, Carl shuts the door. Raj releases the brake and we're off again. There's a muffled rattling under our feet: the metal bridge, left behind as soon as it appears.

'Put your seatbelts on,' says Raj. Everyone obeys. Raj makes a few one-handed grabs at the buckle beside his ear; each time he has to put his hand back on the wheel before he can pull out the belt.

'Carl,' I say, 'help him.' Carl reaches over but pulls back, shrugging – he can't reach without getting between Raj and the windscreen.

'I'll get it in a minute,' Raj says; my concern is rewarded with a brief smile in the driver's mirror.

We're in the glen proper now. I take Jamie's hand. He flinches slightly; in the dim light I can see dark lines on the back of his hand, where I scratched him. I keep my fingertips away from them.

The cabin is warming up now. I loosen my top buttons and zips, although my feet are still cold. I peer ahead, hoping to spot a landmark. Instead, I see little green lights – two chains of them, exactly parallel – springing into life in front of me. I close my eyes and wonder if I dare take another look, but then Jamie says, 'Are any of yous seeing green fairy-lights?'

'It's the snow poles,' Raj says. 'They're motion sensitive.'

I take a good look at the next pair of lights as they rush towards us; the metal poles, which line the road like lampposts, are each topped with a gaudy emerald light. Up ahead, another pair light up; I turn my head gingerly to look through the back window and see the most distant lights wink out. 'The road's well marked,' I say. Everyone nods kindly as I state the blindingly obvious.

There's no wind, the soft flakes of snow drifting almost vertically to the ground. So why can I still hear it howling? Then another note joins in, and the sound is unmistakable.

'Good God,' says Carl, peering out of his window. 'I thought they only sounded like that in the films.'

'Can you see them?' Jamie is pressed up against his window, as if we're in a safari park. 'Is that them down there?'

I close my eyes, feeling sick. I'm remembering something, something to do with wolves – dark walls, fire, something awful happening to Raj. A nightmare, probably…

Jamie turns to me in surprise as my grip on his hand tightens. 'It's all right, Suze. They're not going to catch us up.'

'I know.'

'They're big fearties anyway,' says Carl. 'More scared of us than we are of them.'

'Are all the doors locked?'

Carl smiles. 'And they definitely can't work door handles - '

'Can we just lock the fucking doors!'

Shouting was a bad idea. I press my hands over my aching eyes.

'The doors are locked,' says Raj. 'It's all right. We're nearly there.'

We're nothing of the kind. I can still hear the howling. 'Put the radio on, would you?'

Carl pokes at a couple of buttons; static bursts out of six different speakers. Carl pushes a few more buttons to no effect, then reverts to the low-tech method and starts turning the dial. A deep voice becomes clearer, giving the shipping forecast. Carl dials on through further static.

He's just found some crackly Gaelic singing when I notice something weird about the green lights up ahead. They're going straight up into the air, as if we're supposed to take off like Chitty Chitty Bang Bang. But then the headlights pick out sheer rock; the lights are marking the entrance to the Pass. Raj slows down to steer us carefully between the vertical lights into the chasm.

It's darker in the Pass, but then green light flickers into life. The emerald lamps are set into the rock on either side of the road, casting a sickly tinge over everything. The Gaelic singing turns back into static.

The road has narrowed into a single track; snowdrifts, shouldered aside by the morning snowplough, stand four or five feet high on either side. I'm wishing Raj would go faster. The engine seems a lot louder.

The radio gives a burst of static, making me jump, and Carl turns it down. Now we can hear the squeal of the windscreen wipers, and the muffled creak of the tyres on the snow. The tracks we're following are filling up fast.

I am not going to grip Jamie's hand tighter. I'm not going to be worried. I had a migraine yesterday, when we came through here. I saw nothing. Nothing at all.

I shut my eyes.

'Suzey!'

'What?'

'Still with us?' It's Jamie. His face is losing its pallor. In fact, everything is, because the green light is fading. There is faintly moonlit snow beyond the windows again.

We're out of the pass. I pull my hand away. 'Jesus, Jamie.'

'I was just checking you were still…'

'I'm still here, still with you! For God's sake, you scared me half to death.'

'Sorry.'

I sigh, and take his hand again. After a moment Carl turns the Gaelic back up. The female voice, unaccompanied and solemn, is hypnotic. I watch the green lights ahead of us; one pair goes by and another comes on, one goes by and another comes on, one goes by…

'Switch that off,' says Raj. 'Try and find a weather channel.'

It's fairly obvious what the weather's going to do, but Carl starts dialling through the stations. Raj doesn't take his eyes off the tracks ahead of us, which are now nearly full. 'Find the roads report,' he says.

'Which road?'

'The one to Fort William.'

Static buzzes and pops. Carl homes in eagerly on an official-sounding voice, then curses when it turns out to be in Gaelic. The tracks are becoming just a shadowy hint in the headlights.

I tell myself it doesn't matter. The car's tyres are good, and we can't lose the road with the lights. Green flashes past, the radio buzzes. Carl tunes in to a Highland accent, in English. A male voice, level and pleasant, is saying 'And in other news today…'

'They'll do a report soon,' says Carl. Raj nods.

The soft voice is talking about roads around Aberdeen. I can feel myself nodding off. We can't be far now.

And suddenly there are a hundred green dots tracing the road far ahead, lighting us home.

The snow poles. They're all lit up.

Movement. They're sensing *movement*.

The engine roars as Raj floors the accelerator, and we're flung back into our seats. We're hurtling forwards, faster and faster; surely we're going to skid. I yell at Raj to slow down but he doesn't. Carl is shouting angrily, I can't hear him over the engine, and Raj is yelling something about *the lights, it's vibration, the lights, avalanche*.

A sound like thunder is coming from all directions at once. I'm screaming at Raj to turn around, don't go on toward the green lights, because they show where it's coming. But Carl is telling him to keep going, faster, faster. My hand is gripping Jamie's, locking tighter and tighter. We've got to hang on.

Raj is reaching back towards me. White is rushing up to the window beside me, and I'm trying to get away and Jamie's pulling my arm but the straps are holding me there. And there's a noise like a fist hitting the car and we're turning over, going much too fast, flipping like a fairground ride.

I can hear only screaming, mine, and there's a pain in my head and then black.

Chapter 29

Darkness; a smell of burnt rubber. I'm tilted over to one side and it feels like all my blood's draining that way.

I try to sit straight, but there are straps holding me. I tug at them and my fingers struggle to grip the slippery surface. What happened?

I'm in the car, which is tipped like a rollercoaster frozen just before the twist. I trace along my seatbelt and release the catch, holding onto the door. My head twinges in two places: where Kerry's blow landed, and exactly opposite, in my left temple. The pain throbs and then fades. It feels like the two spots are balancing each other out.

The sunroof is half open, and I push myself up towards it. It looks warped and buckled and as soon as my fingers touch it, it slides away, clattering off the roof of the car and landing with a strangely muted thump on the ground outside.

I hoist myself up through the hole, and swing myself outside. I find my footing on the roof, and straighten up.

Snowflakes feather my face. We are still facing forward, towards the end of the glen. Behind is a smooth new slope, which has almost buried the back of the car.

The glen is in darkness, the snow grey in the moonlight. I take in my surroundings, moving my head slowly, so I miss nothing.

And all the worlds turn with me.

I can see all the possibilities.

I laugh aloud as I flick through them, one after the other, like the turning of a slide carousel. *Click*, and the snow is falling more heavily; *click*, and there's no snow whatsoever. Here, the poles ahead of us are bent and broken; here, they're standing straight; here, a few are winking on and off.

I know there must be other worlds behind me, where the car is not jutting out of the avalanche, but inside it. But those are not my concern. The possibilities have narrowed down. I face into the ones ahead.

But I am not pulled into them. I don't have to live them. They wheel all around me like dancers in a reel. I lift my arms and laugh again, because I thought they could trap me, but they are free and possible, these futures, and each of them is mine.

'Suze, are you okay?' It's Jamie, peering up at me from inside the car.

'Fine.' I tear myself away from the patterns of the snow clouds overhead and kneel down gingerly. 'Are you all right?'

'Aye. Aye. Oh, Jesus Christ, Suze. Fuck.'

Raj. Did he put his seatbelt on?

I move Jamie's face to one side and lean into the car. I think I can hear someone crying. Raj is bent over the steering wheel but I can't see his face.

Oh God, is he moving?

But his hand suddenly grabs at the dashboard, twisting, and twisting again. He's turning the ignition. 'Fuck,' he's saying. 'Fuck fuck fuck.'

His seatbelt is on. Now I remember him reaching backwards, towards me, or so I thought. 'Raj?'

His face is ashen but unmarked. 'What are you doing up there?'

I laugh. All the other worlds, all the times he didn't reach the seatbelt in time, or didn't think to go for it at all, they slip away behind me, and I let them go. 'Looking at you down there,' I say.

Jamie says sharply, 'You okay?' but he's not talking to me or Raj. I crane further into the hole until I can see the passenger seat.

Carl's chest is heaving, as if he can't get enough oxygen. His face is wet with tears. His right hand is hovering over his left arm, which hangs straight at his side.

'Is it your arm?' says Jamie, reaching towards him. Carl howls and slaps his hand away. 'For fuck's sake! Oh Christ!'

Yellow light flashes on, a shock after the darkness. Raj has found the interior light, and the three men look slightly more assured. Carl is looking at his arm, which looks strangely twisted, and swallowing hard.

'It's broken,' Jamie says.

'Oh, d'you think so?' Carl glares at him. 'What else d'you think? Have we been in a car crash maybe? Have we been in a fucking *avalanche* maybe?'

'We should make a move,' says Raj. 'Come on.'

Jamie nods, and reaches up to me. 'Get back in, Suzey. We're leaving.'

But Raj is shaking his head. 'The engine's gone. We're walking.'

Everyone stares at the world beyond the car windows, or what little we can see of it in the dark. 'We can't walk it,' says Jamie.

'We've got the clothes,' I say. 'We can wrap up.'

'Aye, but…' He looks at Carl, who has started to tremble.

'It's not that far,' says Raj.

'We'll send someone back for you,' Jamie tells him, and Carl nods.

'You can't stay here.' Raj catches my eye; we both know what he's saying. 'The engine's knackered. There's no heat.'

'I can wrap up.'

'It won't be enough.'

'Aye, it will.' Carl is shrinking back from him. I know what he means. The car is enclosed. The light is on. It seems so *safe*. 'I'll keep the door shut.'

'It won't be enough. You know that.'

'Thought you said it wasn't far?' He's shaking even harder now. 'Thought you said you wouldn't be long?'

I shut my eyes. I watch the possibilities. 'Carl,' I say.

'You going to spend all your time arguing? Move. Go on. Leave me.'

I clamber across the roof and slide down the side doors like a chute. Carl's side of the car is tilted slightly upwards. I open his door and push it upwards.

'Carl,' I say, trying to get as close to him as I can. 'Carl, pet, you'll *die*. You will.' I wipe some of the tears off his face before they freeze. 'Carl. Please.'

After a moment he nods. Then his eyes widen. 'Suzey, you've nothing on your feet.'

I'm still in my socks; I'd hardly even noticed. 'We'd all best get our shoes on, then,' I say.

We struggle into the rest of our clothes. Carl sits stiff-legged like a child so I can put his boots on for him. When the cases are empty, we survey one another. Raj's boots are missing. So is Jamie's coat. Without a word we all strip off jerseys and socks. A minute later Jamie is happed up in fleeces, and Raj is shoving on his dress shoes over four layers of wool. The shoes go on easily, so the socks can't be thick enough, but we haven't got any more.

Jamie, already shivering, goes to help Carl out of the car; I follow him. With perfect comic timing our feet skite out from under us, and we slide in unison down the glass-hard snow to land in a heap at the bottom. In other circumstances it would have been fun.

'Watch out,' says Raj. 'The snow packs solid after an avalanche.'

'You don't fucking say,' says Jamie, pulling me to my feet. Somehow we haul ourselves back up to the car. We manage to ease Carl onto his bum in the doorway, and then out on the snow.

Raj is struggling to plant his thin-soled shoes on the ice and starts windmilling frantically. I grab his arms until he finds his balance in some softer snow.

'Thanks,' he says. ' I think I can…' He stops dead. His back is to the light from the car and I can't make out his expression. 'Suzey, let me see you.' He turns me slightly into the light. He's staring into my eyes, and he's not being romantic.

'What is it?'

'One of your pupils is dilated. But it's all right; it's just the light. Of course, your eyes would be dilated. It's all right.'

'We have to go, Raj.'

Jamie has managed to get Carl on his feet and on stable ground. Carl is holding his damaged arm as far away from his body as possible. We all look at it. 'We should put it in a splint,' Jamie says.

I nod, then realise I've got no idea how to do this. We all look hopefully at one another. 'Does anyone know how to?' I ask, and everyone shakes their heads.

The wind shrieks. 'Well, let's start walking,' I say.

We set off, four abreast across the road. The green lights spring into life on either side; at least we can't lose our way. There is no sound but the crunching of our feet in the powdery snow. It's deep, and we have to do that high-stepping walk. But still, it feels good to be moving again, getting somewhere.

We pass another set of green lights, then another. My calf muscles are starting to tug painfully. With each step my feet are lifting lower until I'm just pushing through with my knees. The others are doing the same, and an idea comes to me, but just before I can say anything, Raj stops. 'Wait. Go in single file, in my footprints.'

I look down at his indoor shoes. 'Not in those. I'll go first in my boots.'

'My feet aren't going to fit in your footprints, Suzey.'

Jamie steps forward. 'I'll go first.' He ploughs on ahead of us, waddling slightly in his quadruple layers of fleece. His breath steams out behind. We follow, Raj bringing up the rear; we can't leave Carl at the back.

And so we go on. Carl making a tiny noise whenever one foot goes down, but I don't think he knows he's doing it. I keep my eyes on Jamie's back, black against the green-tinted snow.

When a pair of new lights blinks on ahead, I give a little cheer, my breath pluming out in front of me. No one responds. I think back to the view just before the avalanche hit. How long was the road ahead? How many lights?

I look into the distance, trying to spot the dark grey of the loch. But there's nothing but black sky and green snow. The eye makes no sense of it. I'm seeing flaring grey shadows everywhere, around Jamie up ahead, on the slopes to either side.

I recall dozens of lights. No, hundreds. The village is not near at all.

The high-pitched howling I can hear behind us has been going for some time. My city-dweller's ears have been processing it as background noise, sirens maybe. No one else gives any sign of hearing it, but we're walking fast. Carl is whimpering now, but he doesn't complain.

Then over the howling comes a sharp yelp, much closer. Jamie turns and looks back. There's nothing to see, but our cosy state of denial has been broken. 'Where are they?' he says.

We all look back into the shifting darkness, but no one volunteers an answer. 'Ignore them,' says Raj. 'They don't prey on humans. Keep going.'

So we do, but we keep looking over our shoulders. At the next set of green lights I stop and turn around. The wolves' howling echoes all around; they could be anywhere, everywhere. I grab Jamie's arm so he can't carry on into the shadows ahead. 'Stop. Let me think a minute,' I say, and shut my eyes.

I watch the possibilities turn. This time there's a new sensation in my head, a tiny crack as if something has split, but I ignore it. I know that somewhere, we must have set out earlier. I find that somewhere, and watch the consequences run.

There is darkness and laboured breath. Our voices, high with fear. Once with screaming – I let that one go instantly. Worlds with blizzards, even worlds with rain. And then...

One with firelight.

The men are clustered round me, speaking urgently. But there's another pop in my head and I can't quite hear them. So I shout, 'This way. Come on.'

I head off the road, away from the lights, ignoring the cries of protest behind me. After clambering in a deep drift, I find the way: the old road. I reach out, and my hand closes around cold iron – a metal post by the roadside.

The others are floundering; their eyes aren't adjusting to the dark as well as mine are. By the time they've caught up, swearing and gasping with fright, I can make out the twisting line of the old road in the starlight. Raj grabs me by the arm like I'm under arrest. 'Jesus *Christ*, Suzey!'

'I know a place,' I say. 'It's not far.' The wolves howl and yip; it seems they're getting closer.

'Where the hell are you taking us?' asks Jamie.

'Just trust me.' I set off uphill, leaning forward and taking long steps: my right arm is stretched out behind me, holding Raj's hand, while my left hand clings to Carl. I squeeze Carl's good elbow. 'Doing all right there?'

'Fair to middling.'

It feels better to be going uphill, leaving the wolves below. I know it's irrational, but it still feels better.

I tug Raj's hand and he tugs back, in encouragement or annoyance, I'm not sure, and then lets go. We keep climbing. I grab onto an iron pole every time I pass one, hauling myself up a little further. My shins are pushing through the snow, as are Carl's beside me; the pain has been forgotten now.

We walk into the deeper shadow of a pine forest, lining the road on either side.

But there is a sheen of yellow light on the road ahead. I say nothing, in case it's my imagination, but a dozen steps later, Carl cries out. 'D'you see it?'

'Oh, thank Christ. Is it a house?'

'No,' says Carl. 'It's a fire.' We're almost running now. The orange glow is just over the next rise. I make a mammoth lunge and stagger to the top of the hill.

It's a bonfire, about a quarter of a mile away, a tiny bright patch in a field of darkness.

Firelight fills the world in front of me. I can still feel my hand holding Carl's arm, but then comes the *pop* in my head, and that's gone too. I see nothing but a haze of gold.

The world is framed by the dark green of the pines. The gold is shaping itself into two figures, a man and a woman. They step forward, haloed in tawny light.

They are made of everything golden. Bright blond hair, to his shoulders and to her waist. Full-length clothing edged with white fur. He is broad shouldered, she is slender; they have the same fine, delicately-tanned features, and the blue eyes of a Botticelli angel. They can't be more than eighteen years old.

Lif and Lifthrasir. The new Adam and Eve. Viking, Christian, whatever. When the rest of us are gone, they will inherit the earth; they will usher in the Age of Gold.

I look at them for a long time, this blonde breeding pair. We are meant to die and get out of their way. They are to have their golden world, but it will be without my niece, and my brother, and my lover, and all the rest of us who are too young or too old or too dark or too gay to qualify.

And they're gone, and it's dark again, and my hand is gripping Carl's elbow. He doesn't seem to have noticed a thing.

The fire gets bigger, but very slowly. The light is broken by dark shapes: people, standing around the fire. A voice comes to us, carrying in the clear air. A male voice, chanting some prayer, or recitation. I had been wondering whether to call out or not, but now it seems best not to interrupt. The others behind me are silent too.

When we're about ten yards away, Raj pulls us quietly to a stop. We can see the people in the firelight quite well from here but we're still in darkness, so they haven't seen us. In the firelight, a copper torque gleams around the neck of a young woman; her red hair streams over a long shawl, held in place with cloak pin. Under the shawl is a dark cagoule which reaches almost to her knees. Matching waterproof trousers are tucked securely into hiking boots. Beside the girl is a young man in a parka; a plaid crosses his chest and gathers around his waist in a bulky kilt. He too is wearing trousers and boots. His hair is long and knotted into a plait. A green beanie hat is jammed down over his ears. Like the girl beside him, he has silvery tears on his cheeks.

The others I can't see clearly, but all around the fire are gleams of fluorescent nylon, and silhouettes of thick wool and fur. Most of these people are Jamie's age or younger, although, after a while, I can make out a few lined faces and some greying hair. Most are wiping their eyes.

My view is blocked by a large sheepskin-clad man in front of me but I can see that the speaker is flanked by two women, each holding a flaming torch. One of the women holds her torch awkwardly; she has to steady her elbow with her other hand, and keeps jumping when the flame sways towards her hair. She looks as if she's noticed the absurdity of holding a torch over a large bonfire, but she's not saying anything about it.

The other girl, however, is different. Perfectly composed, she holds her torch aloft one-handed, her expression solemn. It's the pink-haired girl from the stall at the Visitors' Centre. Her hair, secured by a string of red beads across her forehead, has gone fuchsia-red in the firelight. She looks like a warrior queen. Her gaze becomes proud and fierce as it shifts to the man beside her.

I step sideways to get him into my sights. He is still reciting, in what I assume is Gaelic, declaiming over a long covered sledge at his feet. He is tall, and broad across the shoulders. His skin is very pale, but his beard and long hair are dark, with glints of silver. No wonder the pink-haired girl looks so possessive; he's very handsome. Over his deep red cloak is an elaborately draped plaid in a green tartan. Under it his legs are bare. He doesn't seem to mind the cold at all.

His chanting pauses, and I jump as the group murmur a response. It sounds like 'Hear us'. Then the man stops speaking Gaelic and switches to English.

'Hear us, great goddess! Mighty Freya, mighty Ceridwen! Hear our call, mother of Earth! Accept our brother into your embrace! We give him not to you, pale Galilean! We return him to the Tree of Life! Fenris, send your children! He gives himself to you!'

Two men detach themselves from the circle and approach the sledge at his feet. There are a few quiet sobs around the circle as they lift back the covers to reveal a man. He is utterly still. His face is tattooed with symbols, runes and spirals; he is so bloodless he looks grey even in the firelight.

The two men draw back all the coverings. The man on the sledge is naked: pale as a fish except for his dark pubic hair, and the network of tattoos all over his body. No, not tattoos, I realise, spotting a smudge in the complex design of interconnected runes and Celtic knots: ink, possibly henna. The dead man is a canvas of painstaking and temporary art.

Two more men now step forward and all four stoop to lift the plank and its burden onto their shoulders. They take slow measured steps away from the circle. More sobs and sniffles follow them, along with the ringing voice of the dark man.

'We give him to you, Freya, Mother of Earth! He is a clean offering! He is yours! He is yours!'

The pink-haired girl steps forward, ahead of the men, bends down to sweep powdery snow from something. Underneath is a dark grey surface: a rock, wide and almost flat.

When the rock is clear, she steps back and holds the torch high. The other woman is just behind her, crying, her torch swaying dangerously. The four men walk forward, and set the board down. One of them slips, and the naked man's head lolls to one side. The pink-haired girl speaks sharply and the clumsy bearer gently takes hold of the still face, and carefully turns it away from the firelight. The bearers bow to the dead man on the rock then they make their way back to the circle, hurrying as if retreating from a lit firework.

The girl bends low over the still figure, still holding the torch above her head. A curtain of her hair falls forward to touch the man's cheek; for a moment his bloodless face blushes fiery pink. Then she drops a kiss on his forehead, straightens up, and makes her way unhurriedly back to the bonfire. As the torchlight moves away, the rock and the man on it fade into darkness.

Behind me, Jamie exclaims quietly. Then something cannons into the back of my leg, making me stumble. There are shapes all around, brushing against us at hip height. There is a thick musky smell; my hand is brushed by stiff warm fur. Raj and I grab each other for balance, as if we are waist deep in a fast river. As the wolves rush past us there are a couple of muted gasps from the group at the bonfire; their circle contracts as they take a step closer to the fire.

The wolves ignore them as utterly as they did us; they are making for the rock where the naked man lies. The dark man's voice sounds out, excited and incomprehensible. The grey and brown of the wolves' pelts fade into shadow, but we can still see them moving. The rock and the dead man vanish under a snarling, writhing mass of furry bodies.

In a moment, we all hear the ripping, tearing noises. There are a couple of shrieks from the circle, followed by sharp admonitions. Behind me, either Jamie or Carl is being loudly sick. Over it all the dark man's voice goes triumphantly on and on. I catch the word 'Fenris' occasionally, but nothing else. I say to Raj, 'Fenris?'

'The wolf god.'

'Thought so.' We both sound bizarrely calm, but then I'm figuring something out. 'Those wolf deaths,' I say. 'The man and the woman.'

'Yes.'

'D'you think anyone ever did a post-mortem on them?'

'Not a very thorough one, it seems.'

'No.' You find a body torn to pieces by wolves. Who's going to check if the poor sod was dead to begin with?

Jamie clamps my arm and nearly pulls me over backwards. 'Suzey, come on.'

'It's all right.'

'No, let's go. *Now.*'

The chanting has stopped. They're all staring at us. For a moment no one moves. Then the pink-haired girl detaches herself from the group. She strides over to us, still carrying the torch, and raises it above our heads, narrowly missing Jamie's hair.

The speaker leaves the fireside and comes to stand beside her. The others begin to close in around us.

'You interrupted our ceremony,' he says.

'We didn't mean to,' says Jamie.

'You have no right.' His voice is quivering. *'No right.'*

'We're sorry.' Raj is keeping his voice calm. 'We're trying to get to the village. There was an avalanche.' There are tiny gasps from the circle around us. Encouraged, Raj keeps talking. 'It tipped our car over. We need to call an ambulance.' He indicates Carl's helplessly dangling arm. 'He's injured. Please. We need help.'

'I've seen them before,' says the pink-haired girl. 'They came to the Visitors' Centre. I saw them leaving with *his* people. They're with McLean.'

'No,' says Jamie. 'We're not with him. He's thrown us out. We're not like him.' He turns to the girl. 'We bought your stuff, remember?'

The leader – Seamus – turns away and paces back to the fire. The others watch him, waiting. I can hear Carl trying to hold back sobs.

At last Seamus says, over his shoulder, 'You people will never leave us in peace, will you?'

Raj tries to break in. 'We didn't intend to be here.'

'Spies, now? He's sending spies? To our brother's *funeral?*' He turns, backlit by the fire and points at us accusingly. It's a corny gesture, but no one's laughing. 'We will stop him. Brothers and sisters, he has silenced us too long. We will *stop him.*'

I pull the scarves from my head and neck, and let my coat fall open to show the rune pendant at my throat. I hold Seamus's gaze. I know how I must look to him: the golden lights in my hair, the deep red shimmer of the dress, the symbol of the Tree of Life around my neck. Like Lifthrasir; like a goddess. 'Seamus MacIain,' I say. 'Listen to us. We're not your enemies.'

'You're with McLean.'

'We've destroyed McLean.'

'How?'

'I can show you.'

'Don't listen to these people,' says the pink-haired girl. 'They've profaned our sacrifice!'

'The children of Fenris still feed,' he says, gesturing towards the rock.

'But the ceremony. It's for the glen. The land needs the sacrifice.'

I say, as confidently as I can, 'The land already had its sacrifice, when the avalanche took your brother.' I must be right. What else could have killed him around here? They're all looking at me. Surely I'm right…

The pink-haired girl says, 'It was to the east. Not in the Glen itself.' But she doesn't sound sure of herself.

'Show us,' says Seamus.

I turn to Carl. 'Show them the film.'

'I can't.'

'What?'

'It won't work.' Carl digs in his pocket and produces the disk. 'It doesn't have a screen, you can't see anything.'

The pink-haired girl makes a scornful noise, and begins muttering something to the man beside her. I do my best to talk over her. 'We need something with a screen. A camera. A mobile?'

Seamus reaches under his cloak and produces a mobile phone. It's small and silver. Carl takes it from him and snaps the memory card into place. The four of us stand back while they're watching, clustered around the tiny screen. We say nothing. We can hear McLean's voice: 'James, look at your sister. She's yours, and you are hers.' I can't meet anyone's eye.

When it's over, however, I force myself to look at Seamus. I know the others must be looking at me with disgust, but it's only the leader that matters. 'That's in the public domain by now,' I say. 'McLean's finished.'

Seamus is looking from me to Jamie and back; he looks awed, nearly afraid. Then he smiles, and to his group he says, 'These people are our friends. They will come with us.'

I feel Raj relax beside me. I breathe in deep with relief. But it seems only fear was keeping me upright, because down I go, as if someone has cut the strings, down into the cold.

Bump, and I'm awake. I'm lying down. A metallic scraping sound, like huge ice skates, is coming from somewhere beneath my head. I'm moving.

Against my right cheek there is something warm and textured. Fur, I think. Beyond that I can see the legs of someone walking beside me. The figure is bulky and dark and could be anyone. The ground is a smooth floor of dull silvery glass.

It's the loch, of course. I'm lying on the sledge, and they're pulling me across the loch. I am covered in a thick rug, warm but smelly. I feel strange, fragile. There's a sensation of warm liquid trickling inside my head, unpleasant but not painful. I turn my head carefully, and look up into a jeweller's shop window of black and sparkling white.

I've always seen the night sky as dark. And I've always thought of the stars in constellations, a join-the-dots puzzle with big spaces in between. But I laugh now, so far from the city and its garish lamps, to see how wrong I was. Every inch of the sky is shining. We are sliding along, dark figures on the dull ice, and above us is a ceiling of light.

Now I see a glowing band, powdered diamond wiped across the pole. It's the Milky Way, at last. I laugh and reach up, my fingers tracing the line above me. Faint silvery mist wafts over me. It's frozen breath. Raj is looking down at me. Jamie's beside him, eyes full of tears again. 'Suzey?'

'Look, Raj.' I close my fingers, catching the band of stars in my hand.

'Look, love. It's the Asgard bridge. Do you see it?'

'I see it.'

'I never knew.' All this time, in cities, in the dark. I never saw. 'I didn't know, Raj.'

'It's all right, Suzey. We're going back with these people. They have a radio… Suzey? Can you hear me?'

There's a bump, we've stopped. Raj is still leaning over me. 'Suzey, stay with me. Stay awake for me, okay?'

I try to nod, but I can't move my head. It's not painful, I just can't move it. Raj takes my hand then has to let go as dark figures surround me.

Then I'm airborne. It's not a smooth ride like the sledge, just four guys bumping along. I'm on a stretcher. There are trees and rocks all around us, so I can't see much.

'You're on our island now,' says Seamus.

'The island of chieftains,' I say.

'You have nothing to worry about.'

And of course he's right. The possibilities have narrowed down, and down, and down again. There are very few possible futures left for me now.

We move somewhere indoors now. It's warm and stuffy, and smells of wood smoke and urine and sweat. The walls are dark and curved; it's an earthen igloo, set among the tombs of the MacIain chiefs. I am lowered down onto some sort of camp bed.

There's a mechanical squawking. Raj is bent over a microphone, before dark green whisks in front of him. A curtain. Jamie has pulled it around me, that's what it is. He kneels over me. His hand grips mine. 'Suzey, you're going to be okay. They're sending the air ambulance, okay?' He's crying.

I can hear Raj's voice behind him: 'The right side of the head. The pupil's blown. Yes, several times. Yes.'

Jamie talks more loudly to mask it. 'Just stay awake, Suzey. Talk to me.'

More possibilities are slipping away. There are fewer of them left with every second that passes. I shouldn't look. Don't look.

'Raj,' I say. He runs over, and I try to raise my voice over the background chatter, but he still has to bend close to hear. 'Raj, I love you. I'm sorry.'

He takes my other hand. He's crying now. 'I love you, Suzey. I—'

There's no time. 'Jamie,' I say. 'I love you. Listen, Carl. You too.'

'Stay with us, Suzey,' says Raj. 'The helicopter's coming. Can you hear it?'

'I think I can: blades beating the air like wings. But there's no time. 'You look after each other, you three. Promise.'

'I promise,' says Raj.

'I promise,' says Jamie.

'I promise,' says Carl.

There's more to say but I don't have time. Jamie has to go with Mum to Australia. Raj… Raj has to do something, I can't remember. And there's Carl. Carl and Jamie together, that's good, that's okay. And Raj…

Is that Raj? Is he crying?

It's a siren. I can smell sweat and boiled food.

Jamie? They've let go my hands!

'Suzey! Suzey!'

Is there only one left now? *Suzey!*

Voices going, quiet now, volume turning down and down. Wolves and

Cold City

Suzey! and something water running
    sharp scent of snow, clean fresh
    haar-frost – like vinegar!
    who's this now Mum tell him he's got to Raj too
    warm dark Raj! Jamie where what about Claire help I can't I can't
    dark and warm and warm

The smell of mild disinfectant. The sound of liquid running. Pattering feet. A low mechanical hum, and the soft murmur of women's voices. A rustle of polythene.

The warm air is stuffy, but clean. Under me is a soft mattress. I twitch my toes. My head feels strange, as if an iron clamp has just been removed.

The light's bright, fluorescent.

No, it's daylight. The voices continue to murmur around me, fading away, coming back. I hear the squeak of rubber soles.

Finally I look. The ceiling is institutional off-white. A hospital ceiling, no question about it. I have to squint for a moment to make out the window. Beyond the glass is dull daylight.

Rain is pattering down the glass. Rain.

My view is blocked by green hospital scrubs. The young woman in them looks down at me and smiles. Then she walks away, saying something I don't catch.

Heavier shoes approach. A head looms over me; hair a grey bob, face flat and impassive. White doctor's coat.

Dr Martin scrutinises me for a moment, then nods to herself.

'Ah, Suzey,' she says. 'There you are.'

Epilogue

Now do I see   the earth anew
Rise all green   from the waves again;
The cataracts fall,   and the eagle flies,
And fish he catches   beneath the cliffs.

Then the fields unsowed   bear ripened fruit,
All ills grow better,   and Baldr comes back.

...

The Poetic Edda

It's official: Glasgow is the City of Love.

Park Circus shines. The curving terraces are blond sandstone and dove-grey granite, bright in the May sunshine; the central ring of garden is green within the black railings. Each lamppost holds a long, rose-red banner, printed with the white heart logo of the Wedding Capital of Scotland. Parked cars have been banished, although the Rolls-Royces and limos just don't stop coming, and there's still a trail of manure where a horse-drawn carriage has passed by. A grey Daimler with a V of white ribbon across the bonnet noses into place outside the black-and-gold railings of the freshly cleaned, newly reopened Ceremony Suites.

The Daimler is empty except for the driver, so it's picking up, not dropping off. Nevertheless, there is a stir among the group around the far exit; placards are stabbed into the air, and a few step forward before the two policemen move tactfully in front of them. They are shouting about *shame*, and *blasphemy*, and one male voice is roaring about the DESECRATION OF GOD'S WILL!

I make a mental note for next week: hire a piper. If that doesn't drown the fuckers out, nothing will.

If I can get a piper, of course. According to the harassed admin woman at 22 Park Circus, you can't get a hotel room, a restaurant table, a hired car, a hired kilt, or even a bunch of flowers in this city for neither love nor money. Glasgow has taken gay marriage to its large, tolerant and thoroughly venal heart. Thank God all our arrangements were done weeks ago; the prices must be going through the roof.

The gold and glass doors are flung back and two more policemen emerge to take their places at the bottom of the steps. One fixes me with a hard stare until I back off to a safe distance. People in suits and flowery dresses are spilling out onto the pavement. They gather round the foot of the steps like paparazzi, and are soon rewarded by the emergence of two women in ice cream-coloured suits. The smaller, in strawberry pink, is laughing and holding a bouquet of yellow roses; the other, larger and dressed in mint-green, looks pleased but slightly embarrassed. It's the woman I saw in the Harline Centre. She doesn't have a bouquet. A little girl in a bridesmaid's dress skips around them, clutching a second yellow-rose bouquet (mystery solved), and looking like she'd fight to the death to keep hold of it. Cameras start clicking, and the crowd cheers and flings confetti; a uniformed doorman shouts *no confetti, no confetti!!*, but the crowd keeps throwing it anyway.

I check my watch as the newlyweds descend the steps to the Daimler. It's half past two. In exactly seven days, Jamie and Carl, in kilts and heather buttonholes, will emerge from those gilded doors, married. My brother, and my new brother-in-law.

I finalised the arrangements today – I was the only one still calm enough. I've just been released from the nuthouse, but right now I'm the sanest member of the family. Mum's up to high doh about the threats; Jamie's up to high doh about everything. 'I don't know how to do this,' he told me. 'I don't know what to call him. Is he my husband? Am I his husband? What do I do?'

'You love him,' I told him, 'so you marry him. And you have a life together. Simple as that.'

He hesitated. 'What about you, Suze?'

'I'm working on it.'

Now the Daimler is leaving, and a black Rolls is taking its place. I can't stand around here forever. On the other side of the road, the placard bearers are grouped around a trestle table loaded with garish posters and leaflets. A banner identifies them as *Scottish Family Protection*. I feel like turning back to the other exit, but I'm nearly past now. I'm deliberately not catching anyone's eye, although I can feel them watching me.

'Excuse me, dear!'

One of the men is hailing me. He was the one roaring about DESECRATION, although his voice is at a normal level now. For an awful moment I think it's McLean, but it's just a short man with a red face and an expression of outraged decency. He's waving a clipboard at me. I must look suitably heterosexual in my plain jeans and shirt.

'Would you like to sign our petition, dear? Save the Scottish family!'

Scottish Family Protection, which ones are they now? Oh yes, they condemned the threats against gay wedding parties, especially the ones about throwing acid, but they understood the *frustration* such people must feel. I've got something for this guy, and it's not my signature. I dig around in my bag, producing a pen in one hand and making a tightly closed fist with the other.

'Sign here, please, dear. It's a disgrace. These people get to do what they like.'

He thrusts the clipboard at me. I raise my fist and reach up over his head. He steps back, probably expecting me to hit him. I open my hand and let pink and white confetti spill all over him. Most of it goes onto the clipboard. I smile at him, then turn and walk away. He starts bellowing behind me, something about WEE BITCH! But I keep going, waving toodle-oo over my shoulder, not looking back.

I pass one of the policemen. He winks at me. I keep walking.

I am happy to be back in my city.

When I reach Woodlands Road, I stop and wait. I've never seen this road so busy. The traffic is crawling, every tenth car decked out in ribbons or with flowers in the back window. The pavements throng with plaids, morning suits and silk dresses. The cafés, daringly continental on the first warm day of the year, have put tables outside; pedestrians have to tightrope walk along the kerb to get around them. but no one seems to mind.

There are so many accents and languages: English, Irish, French, Italian, some I can't identify. The gay people of Europe, accustomed to having their rights clawed back at a moment's notice, have seized the day with a vengeance. Whenever Mum gets too worked up about the threats, I tell her there's safety in numbers. So, when the school blazers start to go past, I have to retreat uphill a little to see the kids' faces.

I should stop doing this. At least I've stopped lurking around the school gates at four o'clock – that could have been very awkward to explain. But he must live around here, he walks up Woodlands Road every weekday. So whenever I'm in the West End at this time, I wait.

And there he is. Peter Balfour. Older and taller, a bit gangling and awkward. He slouches along, a bag over his shoulder, pushing and laughing with his friends. A few weeks ago, he had his hair cut short.

I look at him and feel, yet again, that there must be something I should do. But what? We're long past the appointed day of his murder. I've checked the archived news, and I scour the papers every day, but it seems no other boy has died in his place. Should I try to warn him? Or the police? What could I possibly say?

So I watch him going past. Without the curls, his short hair looks darker, his face longer and thinner. The angelic beauty is gone.

I am reassured by this. He is no god's beloved now: he is as plain and ordinary as the rest of us. I think he'll be all right.

I'm still a little uneasy, though. I climb up the grassy slope, and lean against a tree. But that's worse – I'm in the shadow, and it's cold. I don't like to feel the temperature drop. I step out into the sun again, and stand for a few minutes. I breathe very deeply, and I don't shut my eyes.

I've tried to make sense of what's happened to me. Before I left the hospital, I tried to pin down Dr Martin. No joy, of course. Three months after ordering the ECT and getting my brain fried, she just looked at me one day and said, 'You can go home now, if you like.'

Of course, I wasn't complaining. When the order of release comes through, you don't ask too many questions. But still, I dithered in the doorway. 'So,' I said. 'Is it likely to come back?'

'If it does, come and see me.'

'Is that *it*?' She looked up in faint surprise. I persisted: 'I mean, is that the best you can do? What if I just wander off like that again?'

'Then I'll bring you back,' she said. 'I did it before.'

'So, is that it? Is that *all*?'

She thought for a moment. 'That's all.' She stood up and extended her hand to me across the desk. After a firm handshake and a faint smile she said, 'Goodbye, Suzey. I hope I don't see you again.'

I stand for a moment more in the sunshine, watching another wedding party go past. Two young guys, arm-in-arm, lead a procession of whooping friends and slightly stunned-looking parents. One of the mothers has pursed-up lips like a cat's arse, although the man next to her looks happy enough. The young couple are wearing gorgeous buttonholes, white roses surrounded by dark green leaves. I think, maybe we should change the buttonholes? Heather's so ordinary. I could check the florists. I'd have to talk to Jamie, of course, and soon. I should go straight home now.

But there's no more putting this off. I have to do it *now*.

I set off before I can lose my nerve again. I push gently across the stream of people, through the quiet back streets, and over the little footbridge until I am finally at the crumbling old steps. I have a quick recollection of these steps thick with ice, but it's gone in a second.

I pause at the top, bracing myself for another flashback, but the university looks pleasantly grubby in the sunshine. A few students lounge around on the grass, the gargoyles leering at them from the guttering overhead.

I go around the back way, to keep as far from the Registry as possible. I'm still on sick leave, so I don't want to see any of them. I creep furtively to the back of the main building, to the ancient lift.

I've gotten this far a couple of times: once last week, once the week before, but both times I chickened out. Today, however, I get in, close the rattling gates, and push the button before I have time to think about it. The lift grinds into life, and up I go.

I feel hot and cold, as if I'm ill.

I don't *have* to see him. I can just turn around. But I can't. I miss him so much I ache for him, this man who scarcely knows I exist. We can make it work, can't we? We did before. The lift reaches the top floor. I still can't shake the doubts. What if he doesn't like stargazing? What if he doesn't have that poker face, that way of looking sidelong at things he doesn't like? What will it mean, if the man I know doesn't exist?

I reach his office. His name is on the door, and I hesitate. But I'm ready. I've died and I've come back to life again, so what can't I do?

Without knocking, I walk in.

I stop, bewildered, not recalling what I'm supposed to see. Charts, photos, printouts, paintings? I make myself look, and find the wall plastered with pictures of wolves. It's the Wild Wolf programme, in pride of place. There's the picture of the wolf peeping out from behind the war memorial.

If those pictures are there, then behind me is the painting of the wolf swallowing the sun. I turn. A painting is there, but it's not the wolf one. It's much bigger, and done in shades of orange and gold. At the centre is a white emptiness.

I wait for a moment, letting the colours and whiteness sink in. Then I see it. A human figure, standing with arms spread wide. Waves of fiery colour radiate from it. Traced around the figure is a thin aura of pale gold.

I hear the creak of a chair, and footsteps. He won't surprise me this time. 'Raj,' I call.

He emerges from behind the screen. His hair is collar-length, pushed back behind his ears. He's wearing a dark suit, properly tailored so he looks tall instead of gangly, graceful instead of awkward. He looks so good, he could have any woman he wanted. He's looking at me with a polite expression that could break my heart. 'Hello?'

'Hi, Raj.' I gesture at the painting, and notice how it makes the whole wall brighter. I can't help but smile. 'I love this.'

He starts to smile too. 'It's Suzey,' he says, 'isn't it?'

'Oh yes,' I say. 'It's me.'